About the Authors

athy Williams is a great believer in the power of erseverance as she had never written anything before er writing career, and from the starting point of zero as now fulfilled her ambition to pursue this most njoyable of careers. She would encourage any would-e writer to have faith and go for it! She derives nspiration from the tropical island of Trinidad and om the peaceful countryside of middle England. athy lives in Warwickshire her family.

ie West has devoted her life to an intensive study of charismatic heroes who cause the best kind of trouble in the lives of their heroines. As a sideline she researches locations for romance, from vibrant cities to desert encampments and fairytale castles. Annie lives in eastern Australia with her hero husband, between sandy beaches and gorgeous wine country. She finds writing the perfect excuse to postpone housework. To contact her or join her newsletter, visit annie-west.com

Maisey Yates is a *New York Times* bestselling author of over one hundred romance novels. Whether she's writing strong, hardworking cowboys, dissolute princes multigenerational family stories, she loves getting in fictional worlds. An avid knitter with a dangerous n addiction and an aversion to housework, Maisey es with her husband and three kids in rural Oregon. ck out her website, maiseyyates.com or find her on ebook.

D1589841

Passion in Paradise

BOUGHT TO WEAR THE BILLIONAIRE'S RING

CATHY WILLIAMS

DUDLEY LIBRARIES	
000003145604	
Askews & Holts	06-Oct-2022
AF ROM	£7.99
2GL	

CHAPTER ONE

'So…' Leo Morgan-White handed his father a glass of claret and sat down opposite him.

Harold had travelled all the way from Devon and had been delivered only half an hour previously by his chauffeur. It had been a surprise visit, which he had been told by his agitated father the evening before couldn't wait.

Despite this, they had yet to get down to business and, although Leo knew what it concerned, he was still puzzled as to why it couldn't have waited until the weekend when he would gladly have travelled to Devon.

But his father was emotional and impulsive and so it was nigh on impossible to gauge just how important his news actually was. Leo couldn't think that it would be important enough to have him rushing up to London, a city he tried to avoid at all costs.

'Too noisy,' he was fond of complaining. 'Too crowded. Too polluted. Too many expensive shops selling nonsense. A man can't hear himself think there! You know what I say, Leo—if you can't hear the grass growing, you're in the wrong place!'

'What's going on?' Leo now asked, reclining back and stretching out his long legs. He carefully placed his glass on the table next to him and linked his fingers loosely on his stomach.

His father's eyes were glistening and he looked on the verge of bursting into tears. His chin was wobbling and his breathing was suspiciously uneven. Leo knew from experience that it was always better to ignore these signs of an imminent breakdown and focus on what needed to be discussed. His father needed very little encouragement when it came to shedding tears.

It was a trait Leo had thankfully not inherited. Indeed, anyone would have been forgiven for thinking that the two were not related at all as, both temperamentally and physically, they couldn't have been more different.

Where Leo was long, lean and darkly handsome, a legacy from his Spanish-born mother, his father was of an average height and rotund.

And where Leo was cool, composed and cut-throat, his father was unapologetically emotional and fond of dramatic outbursts. Leo's mother had died a little over a decade ago, when Leo had been twenty-two, and he remembered her as a tall, ridiculously good-looking woman who, having inherited her family's business at the tender age of nineteen, had been very clever, very shrewd and who had a natural flair for running a company. On paper, she and his father should have had nothing in common and yet theirs had been a match made in heaven.

In an age where men went out to work and women kept the home fires burning, his home life had been the opposite. His mother had run the family business, which she had brought from Spain with her, while his father, a hugely successful author, had stayed at home and written.

In a weird and wonderful way, opposite poles had attracted.

Leo loved his father deeply and his eyes narrowed as Harold carefully took a sheet of paper from his pocket and pushed it across the table to his son.

He fluttered one hand and looked away, before saying in a shaky voice, '*That* woman has emailed me this…'

Leo eyed the sheet of paper but didn't reach for it. 'I've told you that you need to stop getting yourself worked up about this, Dad. I have my lawyers working on it. It's all going to be all right. You just have to be patient. The woman can fight all she likes but she won't be getting anywhere.'

'Just you read what she has to say, Leo. I…I can't bring myself to read it out loud.'

Leo sighed. 'How is the book coming along?'

'Don't try and distract me,' his father responded mournfully. 'I haven't been able to write a word. I've been too worried about this business to spare a thought for how DI Tracey is going to solve the case. In fact, I don't care! At this rate, I may never put pen to paper again. It's all very well for you business types…adding up numbers and sitting round conference tables…'

Leo stifled a smile. He was worth billions and did a lot more than just add up numbers and sit round conference tables.

'She's made threats,' Harold said, sucking in a shaky breath. 'You read the email, Leo. The woman says she's going to fight for custody and she's going to win. She says she's spoken to her lawyer and although Sean stated in his will that Adele was to come to you if anything happened to him, Louise never agreed and now they're both gone. All that matters is that Adele's well-being would be put in jeopardy if she stays with that woman.'

'Heard it all before.' Leo drained his claret and stood up, massaging the back of his neck as he strolled towards the expanse of glass that separated him from the busyness of London which never stopped, even in the most prestigious of postcodes.

His apartment occupied the top two floors of an impressive Georgian building. He had hired the most prestigious architect in the city who had cleverly used the vast space to create an elegant blend of old and new, leaving the coving and fireplaces and ceiling details intact while changing pretty much everything else. The result was an airy, four-bedroomed testament to what could be done when money was no object.

The walls were adorned with priceless modern art. The decor was muted—shades of grey and cream. People's mouths fell open the second they walked through the door but Leo was barely aware of his surroundings. They didn't intrude and that was the main thing.

'This is different, Leo.'

'Dad,' he said patiently, 'it's not. Gail Jamieson wants to hang on to her granddaughter for dear life because she thinks it's a conduit to my money but she's utterly ill-equipped to look after a five-year-old child. She'll be especially ill-equipped when my money stops and she has to fend for herself. The fact is…this is a case I will win. I don't want to throw money at the woman but if I have to, I will. She'll take it and head for the hills because, like her daughter before her, Gail is a money-grabbing gold-digger who's not above manipulating a situation for her own advantage. Need I remind you of the train of events that led Sean to Australia?'

His father grunted and Leo didn't push it. They both knew Sean for the man he had been.

Seven years younger than Leo, Sean had arrived on their doorstep at the age of sixteen, along with his mother, Georgia Ryder, with whom Leo's father had fallen head over heels in love less than a year after Leo's mother had died.

From the very beginning Sean, an incredibly pretty boy with overlong blond hair and light blue eyes, had been lazy and spoiled. Once his mother had a ring on her finger and free access to the Morgan-White millions, he had quickly become even more demanding and petulant. His studies had fallen by the wayside and, cosseted by his mother, he had spent his time hanging around with a gang of like-minded teenagers who had gravitated towards him like bees round a honeypot. It hadn't been long before drugs had crept into the scene.

Leo's father, with the ink on the marriage certificate barely dry, had woken up from his grief-induced daze and realised the size of the mistake he had made. He didn't want a blonde bombshell twenty years his junior pretending to love him when the only thing she loved was his money. He wanted to mourn the passing of the woman he had loved. He wanted uninterrupted misery.

Leo had taken Sean to one side and had given him the talking-to of his life, which had done no good at all. The opposite. Within two years Sean had dropped out of school. Within four, he had become heavily involved with Louise Jamieson, an enthusiastic member of the club for losers to which he belonged, and by the time his mother, after a series of unabashed flings with men her own age, had quit her marriage to Harold and begun her bid for as much alimony as she could get, Sean had moved to Australia with a heavily pregnant wife.

By this time Leo's father had all but given up. His writing had stopped completely and his editor's frantic communications had remained unanswered. He had become a virtual recluse and Leo had been left to pick up the pieces.

Unchecked, Georgia had spent vast sums of money on everything under the sun, from diamonds and tiaras to horses, cars and exotic holidays abroad, while she still had access to her soon-to-be ex-husband's bank accounts. She had lavished money on her son. Leo, building his own career, had not had his eye sufficiently on the ball to have stopped the momentum.

By the time the nuts and bolts of the messy divorce had been ironed out, his father had been left with a bank account that had been severely dented. The fact that he hadn't put pen to paper for years hadn't helped.

Then Georgia was catapulted to her death off a hairpin bend on a road while vacationing in Italy with the money she had squeezed out of Harold. Left to make the decision, Leo would have thrown Sean to the wolves but his father, much softer and with a conscience that could be pricked by almost anything, had continued to send money to his former stepson. He had dug deep to make sure Sean's daughter had all the things he would have given her, had she lived in the same country. He had begged for photos and had been thrilled with the handful of pictures Sean had emailed over.

He had tried to make plans to visit but Sean had always had an excuse.

Georgia had been a disaster and her son had been no less of a catastrophe and, unlike his sentimental father,

Leo wasn't going to allow emotions to hold sway over the outcome of this bizarre custody battle.

He would win because he always won. Louise's mother, whom he had met once when he went to Australia, had confirmed all his suspicions that the last thing she was concerned about was the welfare of her grandchild. She was an appalling woman and no appalling woman was going to get the better of him.

'She says that it doesn't matter how much money you have to fight this, Leo. She's going to win because you're not fit to be a father to Adele.'

Leo stilled. His father's eyes had welled up. Reluctantly, he retrieved the paper from where his father had earlier shoved it to him and carefully read the email that had been sent by Ms Jamieson.

'Now you see what I mean, Leo.' His father's voice shook. 'And the woman has a point. You have to see that.'

'I see nothing of the sort.'

'You don't lead a responsible life.' Harold's voice firmed. 'Not as far as bringing up a young child is concerned. You spend half your life out of the country…'

'How else am I supposed to run my companies?' Leo interjected, enraged that a woman who appeared to have the morals of a sewer rat should dare to criticise him. 'From an armchair at home?'

'That's not the point. The point is that you *do* spend a great part of the year out of the country. How is that supposed to be good for the well-being of a five-year-old child? Furthermore, she's not wrong when she says that you…' His hands fluttered in a gesture of resignation and disappointment.

Leo's mouth thinned. He knew that the choices he

made when it came to women did not fill his father's heart with glee. He knew that Harold would have done anything to have seen him happily settled down with a nice, respectable girl who would have those home fires burning for him when he returned home after a long day toiling in the fields.

It wasn't going to happen. Leo had too much first-hand experience of how life could be derailed when emotions got in the way of common sense and good judgement. No matter that his father had adored his wife—when Mariela Morgan-White had died, he had been left a broken man. Yes, some idiots might fall for that hoary old chestnut about it being better to have loved and lost than never to have loved at all, but Leo had never signed up to that.

His father might not have agreed with Leo's choices but he had stopped trying to take him to task about them, and this was the first time in years that he had voiced his disappointment.

'Your face is never out of the papers,' Harold admonished, dabbing his eyes and then looking sternly at his son. 'There's always some…some silly little thing hanging on to your arm, batting her eyelashes at you.'

Leo flushed with irritation. 'We've covered this ground already.'

'And we'll cover it again, son.' Harold sniffed and, just like that, Leo realised it was as though the energy and life force had been sucked out of him, leaving behind a shell. He was an aging man and it seemed as though he had suddenly lost the will to live.

'You choose to do what you like when it comes to… women,' his father said quietly. 'And I know better now than to try and point you in the right direction. But this is more than being *just about you*. The woman claims that you're morally unfit to take guardianship of the child.'

Leo pushed his hands through his hair and shook his head. 'I'll take care of it,' he said grimly.

Theoretically, he and his father could simply reach an agreement to pull the plug on the money. Sean, after all, hadn't been in any way related to either of them, but he knew and personally agreed that the child should not be allowed to suffer because of the mistakes of her parents. Like it or not, she was a moral responsibility.

'It's a worst-case scenario.' His father shook his head and pressed his fingers to his eyes.

'You're upsetting yourself, Dad.'

'Wouldn't you if you were in my shoes?' He looked up. 'Adele is important to me and I cannot lose.'

'If the law refuses to budge—' Leo spread his hands in a gesture of frustration '—then there's only so much I can do. I can't kidnap the child and then hide her until she turns eighteen.'

'No, but there *is* something you can do…'

'I'm struggling to think what.'

'You could get engaged. I'm not saying married, but engaged. You could present the court with the sort of responsible image that might persuade them into thinking that you're a good bet as a father figure for Adele.'

Leo stared at his father in silence. He wondered whether the events of the past few weeks had finally pushed the man over the edge. Either that or he had misheard every single word in that sweeping, unbelievable statement.

'*I could get engaged…?*' Leo shook his head with rampant incredulity. 'Do you suggest I purchase a suitable candidate online?'

'Don't be stupid, son!'

'Then I'm not following you.'

'If you need to present the image of a solid, dependable, *normal* human being with a *serious* and *suitable* woman by your side, then I don't know why you wouldn't do that. For me. For Adele.'

'*Serious and suitable woman?*' Leo spluttered. He didn't do either serious *or* suitable when it came to women. He did frivolous and highly unsuitable. He liked it that way. No involvement, easy to dispatch. If they enjoyed his money, then that was fine because he wasn't going to marry any of them. When it came to women, the revolving door that brought them in and took them out was efficient and worked for him.

'Samantha.' His father dropped the name with the flair of a magician pulling a rabbit out of a hat.

'Samantha…' Leo repeated slowly.

'Little Sammy Wilson,' Harold expanded. 'You know who I'm talking about. She would be perfect for the part!'

'You want me to involve *Samantha Wilson* in a far-fetched charade to win custody of Adele?'

'It makes perfect sense.'

'In whose world?'

'Don't be rude, son!' Harold reprimanded with an unusual amount of authority.

'Does she know about this? Have you two been plotting this crazy scheme behind my back?' Leo was aghast. His father had clearly taken leave of his senses.

'I haven't mentioned a word of this to her,' Harold admitted. 'Well, you know that she only manages to get to Salcombe on weekends…'

'No, I didn't. Why would I?'

'You will have to broach the subject with her. You can be very persuasive and I don't see why you wouldn't bring those considerable skills to bear on this. It's not as though I ask favours of you as a general rule. I think it's the very least you can do, son. I would so love to know Adele is safe and cared for and we both know that Gail would make as bad a grandparent as her daughter made a parent. I would spend the remainder of my days fearing for what might happen to the girl...'

'Gail might be many things,' Leo returned drily, 'but aren't you over-egging the pudding here?'

His father breezed over the interruption. 'And you would condemn a child to a future with a woman of that calibre? *We both know the rumours about her...*' His eyes, when they met Leo's, were filled with sadness. 'I can't force you but I'm very much afraid that I... Well, what would be the point of my living...?'

Samantha hadn't been in her tiny rented flat for more than half an hour before she heard the insistent buzz of her doorbell and she grimaced with annoyance.

She had too much to do to waste time on a cold-caller. Or, worse, her neighbour from the flat upstairs, who had a habit of randomly showing up around this hour, a little after six in the evening, for wine with someone too polite and too soft-hearted to turn her away.

Samantha had spent many hours listening to her neighbour discuss her latest boyfriend or weep over a broken heart that would never be mended.

Right now, she simply had too much to do.

Too much homework from her eight-year-old charges to mark. Too many lessons to prepare. Too much red tape with Ofsted to get through. Not to mention the bank, who had been politely reminding her mother for the past three months that the mortgage hadn't been paid.

But whoever was at the door wasn't about to go away, not if the insistent finger on the button was anything to go by.

Sweeping the stack of exercise books off her lap and onto the little coffee table by the side of her chair and plunging her feet into her cosy bedroom slippers, she was working out which negative response, depending on who was at the door, she would be delivering so that her evening remained uninterrupted.

She yanked open the door and her mouth fell open. Literally. She stood there like a stranded goldfish, eyes like saucers, because the last person she ever, in a million years, had expected to see was standing in front of her.

Or rather lounging, his long, muscular body indolently leaning against the door frame, his hands thrust into the pockets of his black cashmere coat.

It had been several weeks since she had seen Leo Morgan-White.

He had nodded to her from across the width of his father's massive drawing room, which had been crowded with at least three dozen locals, all friends from the village where his father and her mother lived. Harold was a popular member of the community and his annual Christmas party was something of an event on the local calendar.

She hadn't even spoken to Leo that night. He'd been there with a leggy brunette who, in the depths of winter, had been wearing something very bright and very short, garnering attention from every single male in the room.

'Have I come at a bad time?'

He'd taken the bait. Sly old fox that his father was, Leo had been persuaded into doing the unthinkable by the threat of ill health and a return of the depression that had dogged his father for years and from which he was only recently surfacing.

Of course, Harold genuinely and truly wanted Adele close to him and safe and, of course, he truly believed, and was probably spot on, that Gail would turn out to be a horrendous influence on her five-year-old grand-daughter, but when he had pulled the ill-health-so-what's-the-point-of-carrying-on? threat from the hat Leo had confessed himself to be beaten.

So here he was, two days later, with the soon-to-be object of his desire standing in front of him in some dull grey outfit and a pair of ridiculous, brightly coloured bedroom slippers.

'Leo?' Sammy blinked and wondered whether it was possible for stress to induce very realistic hallucina-tions. 'What do you want? How did you find out where I live? What on earth are you doing here?'

'Lots of questions, and I'll answer them just as soon as you invite me in.'

Struck by a sudden thought, Sammy paled and stared up at him. 'Has something happened? Is your dad all right?' She was finding it very difficult to think but then the wretched man had always had that effect on her. Something about his devastatingly good looks. He was just so…*so much larger than life*.

Taller, more striking, with the rakish, swarthy sexiness of a pirate. Next to him, the rest of the male population always seemed to pale in comparison and, considering the long, long line of women he had run through over the years, she wasn't the only one who thought so.

Unlike that long, long line of women, though, she knew better than to let all that drop-dead male sexiness get to her.

She still cringed in shame when she thought back to that awful incident years ago. She'd had gone along to a party at *the big house*, as everyone in the village called the Morgan-White mansion up on the hill.

The place had been teeming with people. It had been a birthday bash for Leo and half the world seemed to be there. Heaven only knew why she'd been invited but she imagined that it had been something of a pity invite and, whilst she had cringed at the thought of going, she had been encouraged by the fact that several of the locals had also been on the guest list so she wouldn't be a complete fish out of water. She'd spent ages choosing just the right dress. She'd only spotted him from a distance later, when she had been standing in the garden and, miracle of miracles, he had shown up right next to her and they had chatted for what had seemed like ages. He'd torn himself away from his gilded crowd and Sammy had been on cloud nine until, late in the evening, a very tall, very blonde girl had broken free from the group and confronted her just outside the marquee which had been erected in the garden.

'You're making a bloody fool of yourself,' she'd hissed, words slurring from too much free champagne. 'Can't you see that Leo is never, and I mean *never*, going to give you the time of day? You may have grown up next to him but you're poor, you're fat and you're boring. You're making a laughing stock of yourself.'

Her infatuation had died fast. Since then, watching off and on from the sidelines, she had come to see just how repulsive his approach to women was. He picked them up and then, when he'd got what he wanted and boredom began setting in, he dumped them without a backward glance and moved on.

Romantic at heart, with a core of firmly held family values, Sammy marvelled that she could ever have looked twice at someone like Leo. But, then again, she'd been young and he'd been crazily good-looking.

'He's been better. Are you going to invite me in or are we going to have this conversation here?'

'I suppose you can come in.'

Great start, Leo thought wryly. *A very auspicious beginning to what's intended to be the relationship of a lifetime.*

He hadn't thought about how she was going to react to his proposition but he didn't expect too much protesting. He was, after all, bringing a great deal of money to the table and, as everyone knew, money talked a lot louder than words.

Anne Wilson, Samantha's mother, was a close friend of his father's and had been since Leo's mother had fallen ill and Anne, a nurse at the local hospital, had gone beyond the call of duty to help out. Their bond had strengthened over the years as she had proved to be a solid rock upon whom his father had often leaned, particularly after his acrimonious divorce from Georgia.

It was no surprise then that Anne had confided in Harold about her ill health and the money problems she was having with the bank because she had been forced to quit her job. Though Harold had offered to give her the money, and, when that hadn't worked, to lend it to her, she had refused.

'So…' Sammy folded her arms and stared at him almost before he had shut the door behind him. 'What have you come here for?' He was so good-looking that she could barely look at him without blushing.

Leo's fabulous looks had to do with far more than just the arrangement of his features. Yes, he was indecently perfect, from the long, dark, thick lashes that shielded equally dark eyes and the straight, arrogant nose to the sensuous curve of his mouth. Yes, he had the toned, lean, six-foot-two-inch frame of an athlete and the lazy grace of some kind of predatory jungle animal, but he also generated an impression of power that was frankly mesmerising.

'Are you always so welcoming to visitors?' Leo drawled, ignoring her bristling hostility to shrug off his coat, which he proceeded to dump on the coat hook by the front door.

The house had clearly been made into flats, each with a separate entrance and, from the looks of it, on the cheap. Too much door-slamming and the whole structure would collapse like a house of cards.

'I happen to be very busy at the moment,' Sammy said shortly. She led the way into the sitting room and gestured to the mound of exercise books which she had been about to look at.

He sat himself in a chair. He had come to visit for reasons she couldn't begin to understand and she was furious with herself for the silly heat that was pouring through her.

* * *

She was as awkward as he recalled. He'd never spoken to her without getting the feeling that she would much rather have been somewhere else. He'd never really paid a huge amount of attention to her appearance in the past, simply absorbing the impression that she didn't dress to impress, but now that she was going to be the love of his life he couldn't help but notice that she *really* had mastered the art of not making an effort.

Accustomed to women who bent over backwards to show off flawless bodies, who devoted unreasonable amounts of time to their appearance, he was weirdly disconcerted by someone who didn't seem to give a hoot. He stared at her narrowly, recognising that, despite the appalling dress sense and the mop of blond hair that had been piled on top of her head and secured with a fluorescent elastic band, there was a certain pretty appeal to her heart-shaped face. Plus she had amazing eyes. Huge, cornflower blue with long lashes.

'I take it you're not interested in pleasantries, so shall I skip past the bit where I ask you how you are and what you've been up to recently?'

'Do you care how I am and what I've been up to recently?'

'You should sit down, Sammy. The reason I'm here is because I have something of a complicated favour to ask. If you insist on hearing me out on your feet, then you're going to have aching calves by the time I'm through.'

'A favour? What are you talking about? I don't see how I could possibly help you out with anything.'

'Sit down. No, better still…why don't you offer me a glass of wine? Or a cup of coffee?'

* * *

Sammy resisted scowling. By nature, she was a kind-hearted woman who would never have dreamed of being downright rude to anyone she knew, but something about Leo always got her back up. She'd long ago written him off as too rich, too good-looking and too arrogant, and the way he had settled into her flat and was proceeding to order her about was only hardening her attitude.

She would quite have liked to have asked him politely to clear off.

As though reading her mind, Leo raised his eyebrows and subjected her to a long, appraising look that made her go red.

'Okay,' he drawled, 'I'll cut to the chase, shall I?' He shifted slightly, reached inside his trouser pocket and withdrew a small box which he dumped on the table in front of him. 'I'm here to ask you to marry me.'

CHAPTER TWO

SAMMY BLINKED AND then folded her arms, body as rigid as a plank of wood. Anger was bubbling up inside her. After one glance at the navy blue box he had dumped on the table, she hadn't deigned to give it a second look.

'Is this some kind of joke?' she asked coldly.

'Do I look like the kind of man who would show up on a woman's doorstep and propose marriage as a joke?'

'I have no idea, Leo. I don't know what kind of person you are.' Aside, she thought furiously, from the obvious.

'Open the box.'

Sammy eyed it with a guarded expression and did nothing of the sort. But her fingers were twitching and, uttering a soft, impatient curse under her breath, she reached down and flipped open the lid.

An engagement ring nestled on a deep blue velvet cushion. The exquisite solitaire diamond blinked at her and she blinked back at it, utterly dumbfounded. Her hand was shaking as she placed the box, still open, back on the table and moved to sit down on the chair facing him.

'What the heck is going on here, Leo? You can't possibly be serious. You show up here with an engagement ring, asking me to marry you. Something's wrong. What is it? Is that ring even real?'

'Oh, it's a hundred per cent real. And guess what? You get to keep it when this is all over.'

Sammy's head was swimming. Less than an hour ago, she was a stressed out primary school teacher with a stack of exercise books to mark. Now, she was the main character in some weird parallel universe story with a sexy billionaire sitting on one of her chairs and an engagement ring in front of her.

Nothing about this scenario was making any sense.

'When *what's* all over?' she asked as she tried to make sense of the situation and came up blank.

Leo sighed. Maybe he should have forewarned her but what would have been the point? She would still have been utterly bewildered. Much better that he was sitting in front of her so that he could explain the situation face-to-face.

If she couldn't believe that this was happening then they were roughly on the same page.

Beyond the fact that the words *will you marry me* had never featured in any scenario he had ever envisaged for his future, he certainly would never have chosen Samantha Wilson as the recipient of his proposal.

He had met the woman over the years in countless different situations and he had been left with the impression of someone so background as to be practically invisible. She'd never been rude to him. She had always answered his questions politely, barely meeting his eyes before scuttling away as soon as she could. Aside from one conversation years ago. A conversation lodged at the back of his brain... But, after that, he had met her again—had tried to engage her attention—and nothing. He had no idea whether she had a boyfriend or not, whether she had a social life or not, whether she had hobbies or not.

In his world, where women strutted around like flamboyant peacocks, she was the equivalent of a sparrow. Perfect, of course, for the job at hand but hardly the sort of woman he would ever have looked at twice in *that* way.

'I suppose you know about Sean and his wife,' Leo began.

She nodded slowly. 'I'm sorry. You have my condolences. It was a horrible end for both of them. What on earth would have persuaded Sean to take *flying lessons,* of all things? And to have flown solo in bad weather with Louise, without his instructor… It beggars belief. But I'm so sorry.'

'No need for the sorrow or the condolences—' he waved aside '—I wasn't close to Sean so I can't say his absence is going to leave a big hole in my life.'

'That's very honest of you.'

She was looking at him with those huge, surprisingly riveting blue, blue eyes and, while her voice was perfectly serious, Leo couldn't help but suspect a thread of sarcasm underlying her remark. She'd never struck him as the sarcastic type.

'I suppose you're also aware that my father has been extremely upset that Sean's daughter, whom he considers his granddaughter, remains in Australia as a ward of her maternal grandmother.'

'It's a shame, but I'm sure she'll be allowed over to visit your dad in time, once she's a bit older. Look, Leo, I still don't see what this has to do with me or—' her eyes flicked down to the box burning a hole on the table in front of her '—or that engagement ring.'

'When Sean and Louise died, it was presumed that the child would be sent over here to live with me. Louise was an only child from a difficult background, without any extended family who could take Adele under their wing and Louise's mother also had a somewhat… colourful history.'

'I know there have been rumours…'

'My father receives monthly requests from her for handouts and that is in addition to the money he continued to send to Sean over the years, well after his divorce from Sean's mother was finalised.'

'Your dad has a soft heart,' Sammy said warmly.

'A soft heart is only a small step away from being a soft touch,' Leo muttered and she frowned disapprovingly at him.

'I'm sure the money he sent over was really useful…'

'I'm sure it was,' Leo responded drily. 'The question is, useful to whom? But no matter. That's history. What we're dealing with is the present, which brings me to the subject of the engagement ring…' Admittedly, he had sprung this on her and had expected nothing but shock. Horror, however, hadn't entered the equation because, whether the engagement was fake or not, he couldn't think of a single woman who wouldn't have been thrilled to see a diamond like that and to know that it was destined for *her* finger.

Right now, the woman sitting in front of him was glancing down at the box with a moue of distaste, as though looking at something that could prove infectious in a nasty way.

'My father has recently received an unpleasant email

suggesting that Adele, against all common sense and certainly not in her best interests, may end up remaining in Australia with Sean's mother-in-law. The woman has clearly decided that it makes sense financially for her to hang on to Adele because, as long as she has the child in her custody, she will continue to receive money from my father, which, incidentally, is actually money from me. You may or may not know that his writing has been off the boil for a long time. The family company is doing well but I would rather not be financially embroiled with this woman forever.'

'I'm just wondering what all of this has to do with me,' Sammy confessed.

This had to be the longest conversation in recent years that she had ever had with the man and she was mortified because the cool composure she was at pains to display was at vibrant odds with what she was feeling. She certainly wasn't cool and composed inside. In fact, she was all over the place.

Her senses were on full alert and she didn't fully understand *why*.

Surely she was mature enough not to turn into a dithering wreck simply because she happened to be in the company of a man who was too attractive for his own good? She was a working woman, a teacher, with heaps of responsibility, someone with enough life experience behind her to recognise Leo for the man he really was as opposed to the one-dimensional, gorgeous cardboard cut-out who had once turned her silly teenage head...

Except...

Maybe her life experience was sorely lacking in a certain vital area. Maybe that was why just looking at him was making her skin tingle.

She had plenty of experience in caring for her mother, as she had been doing for the past year and a half. She knew all about communicating with doctors and hospitals and nurses and making her voice heard because her mother, although she had been a nurse herself, had been swallowed up with fear and confusion. She had needed someone strong to lean on and that person had been her, Sammy. And she had plenty of experience under her belt of taking charge, of controlling unruly primary school children until they were as meek as little lambs.

She had argued with bank managers and spent hours trying to balance the books and had exhausted herself with pep talks to her mother, convincing her that the cottage was safe even though the mortgage payments had fallen behind.

And, through it all, she had done her best to hang on to her sense of humour and her sense of perspective.

But there was that whole other area where she had no experience at all.

A vast, blurry, opaque space where she was a stranger because, despite having had two serious boyfriends, she had yet to test the sexual waters.

They had both been attractive and she'd liked them very much. In fact, they'd ticked all the boxes in her head in terms of suitability and yet…she just hadn't *fancied* them enough to go the whole way.

She and Pete had broken up over a year and a half ago, and since then she had resigned herself to the fact that there was probably something wrong with her. Some faulty gene in her make-up. Maybe it was because there had been no father figure in her life since she had been a kid, yet, even to her, that argument made no sense.

So she'd long stopped analysing the whys and maybes.

She hadn't taken into account that her lack of experience in that small, stupid area, *insignificant in the big scheme of things*, might have left her vulnerable to a man like Leo, with his sexy, spectacular good looks and that lazy, assessing charm that oozed from every pore.

'Sean had the foresight, strangely, to leave something of a will,' he was saying now, 'a scrap of paper signed by a friend. In it, he indicated that, should anything happen to him, I should take guardianship of the child. I'm sure,' Leo elaborated with scrupulous honesty, 'that that particular light bulb idea had something to do with my financial worth.'

'That's very cynical of you.' Sammy was still smarting from the realisation that while two perfectly good boyfriends hadn't been able to get to her, this utterly inappropriate man seemingly could. At least if the crazy somersaulting in her stomach was anything to go by.

'So I'm cynical.' He shrugged and stared at her. 'It's a trait that's always stood me in good stead.'

'If Sean meant for you to have Adele, then what's the problem?'

'The problem is the harridan of a grandmother who's decided to hire a lawyer to argue the case that I'm unfit to be the child's guardian. A scrap of paper, she maintains, counts for nothing, especially considering my former stepbrother lived with a stash of alcohol and drugs within easy reach.'

Sammy didn't say anything and Leo frowned because he could read what she was thinking as clearly as if her thoughts had been transcribed in neon lettering across her forehead.

'The woman isn't equipped to raise Adele,' he grated. 'Even if she had been an angel in human form, it would still be a big ask for her to take over the role of looking after an energetic five-year-old child. Had I felt that she might conceivably be mentally fit for the job then I'd back off, but she isn't. At any rate, my father is distraught at this turn of events.'

'He's always mourned the fact that he never got to see her. He talked about that a lot to me and Mum.'

'Yes, well…' Somehow that simple statement of fact, which came as no shock at all to Leo, indicated a familiarity that was a little unsettling. 'Here's where we're nearing the crux of the matter. I've been accused of having too many women and spending too much time out of the country.' He raked his fingers through his hair and gestured in a manner that was redolent with frustration and impatience.

Sammy remained silent because, from all accounts, those were some pretty accurate accusations.

'Well…' she finally said. 'I suppose there might be some truth in that. From everything I've heard, I mean, that's to say…'

'Please—' Leo scowled darkly '—don't let good manners stand in the way of saying what's on your mind. I take it the rumours about me have come from my father?'

'No!'

'Do you three just sit around gossiping about my love life?'

'No! You've got the wrong end of the stick.'

'Have I? From the sounds of it, once my father has

finished lamenting the fact that he's been denied access to his "granddaughter," he brings out the tea and biscuits and gets down to the gritty business of discussing my personal life!'

'It's not like that at all!' Sammy was mortified at the picture he was painting. 'Your dad mentioned ages ago that he wished he saw more of you and that you worked too hard. He worries about your health, that's all.'

'I've never had a day's illness in my life.'

'Working too hard can bring on all sorts of problems,' Sammy said, fidgeting, her colour high. 'Stress can be a killer. That's what worries your dad.'

'That being the case,' Leo drawled, 'he must know that I'm in no danger of collapsing from working too hard or being too stressed because I have my safety valves in the form of my very diverting playmates.'

Sammy's breath caught in her throat, which was suddenly so dry that she could barely get her words out.

It struck Leo that those very diverting playmates were going to have to take a back seat, at least for the time being, and he was a little surprised that he didn't feel more gutted at the prospect. He was a highly sexual man with a very energetic libido, but recently, beautiful and obliging women who were always willing to go the extra mile for him had left him dissatisfied.

His palate was jaded.

Perhaps now was a very good time to indulge in a fake engagement with a woman he had precisely nothing in common with. A couple of months pretending to be in love with someone who didn't stand a chance of rousing his interest might be just the ticket. He would resume life with renewed vigour and things would be back to normal. And a bout of celibacy never killed anyone.

'Which—' he brought the conversation neatly back to the point at hand '—brings us back to the problem. I don't, according to my father, make a credible guardian with my reputation, and I will be under scrutiny because I will be travelling to Melbourne to sort this situation out. Eyes will be on me. I need credibility—and here is where you come in. I need a fiancée to show my stability to the Melbourne courts and he's suggested that you would be perfect for the part.'

Sammy stared at him. So that was what all of this was about. The ring. The proposal. It was so preposterous that she was torn between bursting into manic laughter and propelling him out of her flat.

She did neither. Instead, she said, 'You've got to be kidding, right?'

'As I've already told you, I have better things to do than show up here for a laugh. This is no joke, Samantha.' He leaned forward and looked at her with utter seriousness. 'My father refuses to accept that he may never see Adele. The fact that Sean was his stepson for a short period of time rather than his own flesh and blood and that any tenuous family connection they might have once had ended when he and Georgia divorced makes not a scrap of difference to him, but then he's that kind of man, as I expect you already know. He sees this as his last chance to do something about the situation and he can't understand any hesitancy on my part to leap aboard the plan.'

'I'm not going to go with you to the other side of the world so that I can pretend to be your fiancée, Leo!' Agitated, Sammy leapt to her feet and began pacing the room. Her thoughts were all over the place and her body was burning.

'Why would you want me to be your *fake fiancée*, anyway?' She spun round to look at him, hands on hips. 'Why don't you just pick one of those women from your little black book? You have enough to choose from! Every time I open a tabloid I seem to see you somewhere in the gossip columns with a glamour model hanging on to you for dear life.'

Leo's eyebrows shot up and he gave her a slow, curling smile. 'Follow me in the tabloids, do you?'

'Trust you to put that spin on it,' Sammy muttered under her breath, which seemed to amuse him further. 'I won't do it,' she said flatly. 'You can have your pick of any woman you want so go ahead and pick one of them.'

'But none of them will do,' Leo said smoothly and Sammy paused to frown.

'Why not?'

He looked at her for a long while in perfect silence and it didn't take her long to get the message.

'Too glamorous,' Sammy said slowly, while she pointlessly wished the ground would open and swallow her, disgorging her somewhere on the other side of the world. 'You need someone plain and average, someone who would give the right image of a responsible other half, able to take on a young child.'

Accustomed to telling it like it was, Leo had the grace to flush. 'The women I date would be inappropriate—' he smoothed over the unvarnished bluntness of her statement '—it has nothing to do with looks.'

'It has *everything* to do with looks,' Sammy retorted, her voice shaking. 'I want you to leave. Right now. I'd love to be able to help your father but I draw the line at being manipulated into playing the part of your dreary fiancée so that you can try and fool the authorities in Australia into believing that you're a halfway decent guy with a few responsible bones in his body!'

Leo was outraged at the barrage of insults contained in that outburst. *Halfway decent guy? A few responsible bones?*

He stayed right where he was, a solid mass of sheer physical strength. He wasn't going anywhere and she would be more than welcome to try and budge him if she wanted. She wouldn't get far.

'Leave!' she snapped.

'Sit,' he returned.

'How dare you come into my house and…and…?'

'I'm not done with this conversation.' Leo looked at her steadily and she gritted her teeth in impotent fury.

There was no way she could force him out. He was way too big and far too strong. *And he knew it.*

'There's nothing else to say,' she told him in a frozen voice. 'There's no way you could persuade me to go along with your scheme.' Those cruelly delivered words from when she was a teenager had rushed back towards her with the force of a freight train. As an awkward, self-conscious adolescent she hadn't been his type and as a twenty-six-year-old woman she *still* wasn't his type…

She didn't care because, as it happened, he was no more her type than she was his, but it still hurt to have it shoved down her throat.

'Sure about that?'

Sammy didn't bother to answer. Her arms were still folded, her face was still a mask of resentment, her legs were still squarely apart as she continued to stare down at him.

He couldn't have looked more relaxed.

She marvelled how someone who adored his father so much could actually be so odious, but then he was a high-flying businessman with no morals to speak of when it came to women so why was she surprised?

'One hundred per cent sure,' she threw at him.

'Because I haven't just popped along here to ask a favour without bringing something to the table...'

'I don't see what you could possibly *bring to the table* that could be of any interest to me.'

'I like the moral high ground,' he murmured in a voice that left her in no doubt that the moral high ground was the very last thing he liked. 'But, in my experience, moral high grounds usually have their foundations built on sand. Why don't you sit down and finish hearing me out? If, at the end of what I have to say, you're still adamant that you want no part of this arrangement, then so be it. My father will be bitterly disappointed, but that's life. He won't be able to accuse me of not trying.'

Sammy hesitated. He wasn't going anywhere. The wretched man was going to stay put until he had said what he had come to say—the whole speech and nothing but the whole speech.

Why waste time arguing?

She perched on the edge of the chair and waited for him to continue.

He was truly a beautiful human being, she thought. All raven-black hair and piercing black eyes and fantastically chiselled features. It was hardly the time to be thinking this, but she just couldn't help herself.

Was it any wonder that there weren't many women between the ages of twenty-one and ninety-one who wouldn't have crashed into a lamp post to grab a second look?

She tried to imagine one of those women he dated trying to pass herself off as a suitable bride-to-be and, whilst it certainly worked from the gorgeous couple aspect, the whole thing fell apart the second a little girl was put in the equation.

'Your mother hasn't been well,' Leo said quietly. 'I'm sorry that this is the first time I've…commiserated.'

'She's going to be fine.' Sammy tilted her chin at an angle but, as always when she thought about her mother, the tears were never very far away.

'Yes. I've been told the chemotherapy has been successful and that the tumour has shrunk considerably. You must be relieved.'

'I don't understand what my mother has to do with any of this.'

'Then I'll come straight to the point.' He hadn't felt a single qualm when he had considered using money as leverage in this bartering process. This was the world he occupied. It was always a quid pro quo system.

Now, however, he was assailed by a sudden attack of conscience. Something about the way her eyes were glistening and the slight wobble of her full pink lips.

No wonder she and his father got on like a house on fire, he thought. They were equally sentimental.

It was yet another reason why the arrangement would work for them because her emotionalism was guaranteed to get on his nerves. There would be no chance of any lines between them getting blurred.

'It would appear,' he said heavily, 'that there's a problem with the mortgage repayments on the house your mother's in.'

'How do you know that?'

'The same way you seem to have great insight into *my* personal life,' he returned coolly. 'Our respective parents seem to do an awful lot of confidence sharing. At any rate, the fact is that there is a real threat of the bank closing on the house if the late payments aren't made soon.'

'I've been to see the bank.' Sammy's skin burnt because she hated this sliver of her life being exposed. It was none of his business. 'Mum's had to give up her job, with all the treatment, and I've had to move to a different, more expensive place here because the landlord in my last place wanted to sell. Plus there've been all the additional costs of travelling back and forth every weekend, sometimes during the week, as well. I haven't been able to contribute as much as I would have liked to the finances but they said they understood at the bank.'

'Banks,' Leo informed her kindly, 'have never been noted for their understanding policies. They're not charitable organisations. The most sympathetic bank manager, under instruction, will foreclose on a house with very little prior warning. I also appreciate that it costs you dearly to be working so far from your mother at a time when she needs you to be on hand.'

'Your dad had no right to tell you all that stuff...'

'Was any of it confidential information?'

Sammy didn't reply. No, none of it was confidential, although sitting here right now and listening to him explain her life to her made her think that perhaps it ought to have been.

Naturally, he would never understand what it might be like to really have to count pennies and to struggle against all odds to meet the bills. He had been born into money and, even in the village, his name was legend as the guy who had built his own empire and turned it into a gold mine.

'Didn't think so. I know he offered to give your mother money to help her out of this little sticky patch but she refused.'

'And I don't blame her,' Sammy said, her cheeks dully flushed. 'There's such a thing as pride.'

'Yes. It usually comes before a fall. No matter. I get it. But the fact remains that you are both facing considerable financial challenges, so here is my proposal.' He allowed anticipation to settle before continuing. 'In return for your services, so to speak, I will settle all outstanding money owing on your mother's house.' He raised one hand as though she had interrupted although, in fact, she couldn't have uttered a word if she'd wanted to. She was mesmerised by him. By the movement of his mouth as he spoke, by the steady flex of muscle discernible under his clothing, by the elegance of his gestures and the commanding timbre of his voice.

'Furthermore,' he continued, 'I understand that your dream is to work freelance. Your degree was in graphic art and, whilst you do as much freelance work as you can get your hands on, it's impossible to make the jump because you need to have a steady income.'

Sammy paled. 'Now *that*,' she burst out, 'definitely *was* confidential!'

'Is that some of your work over there?' Leo nodded to a desk by the window and the layers of stiff board piled to one side. Without giving her time to answer, far less swoop to the rescue of the job she was currently trying to find the time to work on, he began rifling through the illustrations she had so far completed while she remained frozen to the spot, mouth open.

'They're good.' Leo turned to face her. He was genuinely impressed. 'Don't glare at me as though I've exposed state secrets,' he said drily. 'This is the second part of my proposition. Not only am I willing to settle the debt on your mother's house but I will also get builders in to construct a suitable extension at the back of the property.'

'A suitable extension?' Sammy said faintly.

'To accommodate this—' he gestured to the desk and the artwork he had just been rifling through '—you setting up your own business where your mother is. No more commuting. No more wasting money on rent you can barely afford. And not only that, Sammy, but I will immediately instigate a steady income that will cover the transition period between you giving up your teaching post here and establishing yourself in your field.'

Sammy was beginning to sympathise with anyone unfortunate enough to have been run over by a steamroller. 'It's a ridiculous suggestion…' she protested, but she could hear telltale signs of weakness in her voice. 'Go to Melbourne…? Pretend to be engaged to you…? It's crazy.'

'Perhaps if you just had yourself to consider,' Leo pointed out with inexorable, irrefutable logic, 'you could spend the next hour talking about your pride or maybe just chuck me out of here immediately, but this isn't just about you. Your mother's future is involved here, as well.'

'And it's not fair of you to drag her into this.'

'Who said that life was fair? If life was fair, that harridan wouldn't be trying to hang on to a granddaughter she probably doesn't even want for the sake of what she thinks she might be able to coerce out of me. Agree to my proposal and I could have builders at the house first thing in the morning to ascertain what needs to be done. All you would have to do is hand your notice in and look forward to a life of no stress, close to your mother.'

Sammy thought of the amount of time she had spent trying to get the books to balance and trying to work out how many more hours she could put into her illustrations so that more income could be generated.

'What happens if you get custody of the little girl?' she questioned eventually, forcibly tearing herself away from that stress-free vision he had been dangling in front of her.

'I'll cross that bridge when I get to it. I can afford the very best day care, the very best schools and during the holidays there will be the option of spending time by the sea with my father.'

Sammy's brow pleated and Leo felt he should jump in before she began testing the moral high ground once again.

'I'm going to give you forty-eight hours to think about my proposition. Time for you to work out the nitty-gritty details and break the glad tidings to your mother, although there's a fair to middling chance that she already knows that I'm here with you right now, thanks to my father. I'll leave the engagement ring here. Try not to misplace it.' He told her how much it had cost and her mouth fell open. 'No point getting something cheap and nasty. You'd be surprised what a nosy reporter can spot through a telephoto lens. If you agree to this, no one must think that it's anything but genuine.'

'I may not agree to anything.'

'Your call.' He shrugged. 'Just think about the trade-off.' He stood up and glanced at his watch to find that far more time had gone by than he'd expected. 'One more thing to consider…'

Sammy had scrambled to her feet but she was still keeping her distance. She wasn't going to touch this offer with a bargepole. Was she? It smacked of black-mail and surely any form of deceit, however well intended, was a bad thing…

'What's that?' She eyed him warily.

'You asked why you're perfect for this…arrangement.' He kept his eyes fixed on her face as he began putting on his coat. 'You understand the rules. I don't mean the rules that involve pretending—I mean the rules that dictate that this isn't for real. You're not one of my women who might get it into their heads that a fake engagement might turn into a real engagement.'

'No. I'm not.' *Because there was no way he would ever consider getting engaged for real to someone like her.* She'd never wanted to slap someone as much as she had spent the past couple of hours wanting to slap him.

'So we're on the same page,' Leo drawled, tilting his head at her. 'Always a good thing. I'll be in touch for your decision.'

'You're going to traipse all the way back here…?'

'Oh, no. I'll call you. And no need to give me your mobile number. I already have it.' He allowed himself a mocking half smile. 'I look forward to talking to you soon…my wife-to-be.'

CHAPTER THREE

HE WAS SO damned sure of himself!

Sammy had spent the next forty-eight hours fuming. Her ability for recall was obviously world-class because she could remember every detail of Leo's visit and every fleeting expression on his face as he had laid out his proposal.

The fact that he had waltzed in with an engagement ring said it all. He hadn't expected to leave her flat without a satisfactory conclusion to his offer.

He hadn't arrived on her doorstep to ask a favour of her. He had arrived on her doorstep to blackmail her into helping him out. He'd held all the trump cards and he'd known that she would have been unable to refuse him.

As he had cleverly pointed out, her agreement to go along with him would make a world of difference to her mother and would relieve her of the constant low-level stress of worrying about the house and the unpaid remainder of mortgage. The fact that she would also have her daughter around and at hand for as long as was necessary had been just another bonus factor.

The deal was done before he'd issued her a time limit in which to make her mind up. He'd even correctly predicted that her mother had been well aware of his prop-

osition so there had been no shock or surprise when
Sammy had called to discuss it with her.

And now here she was, waiting for him to show up
like a sixteen-year-old nervously counting the minutes
until her date showed up to take her to the prom.

Except Leo was no normal date and her nerves did
not stem from eager excitement.

She saw his car when it had almost come to a stop
outside the house and she hurriedly flew back from
the window and then waited until she heard the buzz
of the doorbell.

She had dressed in defiant combat mode—literally.
A pair of combat trousers, a green long-sleeved thermal
vest, over which she had on her warmest army-green
jumper, trainers and her waterproof coat with its very
sensible furry hood.

She pulled open the door and, for a second, the breath
caught in her throat as she stared up at him.

It was freezing. Sleet was falling, the skies the
colour of lead. Yet, for all the discomfort of the weather,
Leo still managed to look expensive, elegant and sexy
in black jeans, a black jumper and a tan trench coat.

'You're not wearing the engagement ring' was the
first thing he said.

'I didn't think there was any need to stick it on just
yet.'

'Every need. The loving couple wants to adver-
tise their love, not hide it away like a shameful secret.
Where is it?'

'It's in my bag.'

'Then I suggest you fetch it out and put it on. And
there's something else.' He eyed her outfit. 'I'm under
strict orders not to tell you this, but there's a little sur-

prise reception waiting for us when we get to my father's house.'

Sammy, in the act of rustling through her backpack to locate the box with the engagement ring, froze. *'Surprise reception?'*

'My father's idea. You know he's inclined towards sentimentality.'

'This is a *fake* engagement, Leo! It's going to last until Adele is over here and then there's going to be a *fake* break-up!'

'Believe me, I told him that, but he said the whole thing wouldn't sit right without some kind of celebration marking the big event. He's got a point. Over the years, he hasn't exactly been reticent when it's come to voicing his desire to see me married off. After our last conversation, he confessed that he's done a bit of complaining to his cronies at the bowling club and the gardening club and all those other clubs he's joined, that he'd like nothing more than to have a wonderful daughter-in-law. Apparently, it's what my mother would have wanted. It seems he had chatty conversations with her every so often and she told him that she was keen to see me settle down. I have no doubt that that little titbit has also been discussed over fertiliser tips for the roses. It would seem odd if his dearest wish were to come to pass and he kept it to himself,' Leo told her flatly. 'His friends would be mortally offended and, worse, some might suspect that he was making the whole thing up.' He glanced across at her. 'And, like I said, there can be no room for speculation about this.'

'It just doesn't seem right, Leo.'

Leo clicked his tongue impatiently. 'We wouldn't

be doing this if Gail weren't so patently unfit to be in charge of the child.'

'You should stop calling her *the child*. It makes you seem cold and unfeeling.'

'We're getting off-topic,' Leo drawled. He held up a bag, which she hadn't noticed him holding, and dangled it in front of her. 'Little present here for you.'

'Huh?'

'Outfit for the engagement party you don't know about. I thought a dress might suit the occasion a little more than jeans and a jumper, which I somehow knew you'd greet me in. Little did I know that you would go one step further and dress for all-out war. And don't argue with me on this one, Sammy. Put it on and let's get going.'

Sammy bristled but he wasn't going to budge and she snatched the bag from him. Pink, with fancy black lettering, clearly designer. Clearly the sort of thing he liked seeing women in, which would be just the sort of thing she wouldn't want to wear. 'Bossy,' she muttered, heading inside.

'And another small point.' He stayed her. 'We're supposed to be engaged. People who are engaged are generally happy and pleased to be in one another's company. Sniping and snarling is going to have to stop. Do I make myself clear?'

Sammy went beetroot-red. 'I feel as though I've been forced into doing this,' she admitted truthfully. 'And now I'm being ordered to get dolled up.'

'I'm no more a fan of deception than you are, believe it or not. I've had to rearrange vast swathes of my working life to accommodate the joy of being engaged and getting out to Australia to sort out a woman who has been a thorn in my side since Sean died. Throw into the mix that I find myself coping with someone who seems to have perfected the art of moaning, and you get the picture that I'm not exactly a willing participant in this situation! And, just for the record, you should try thinking about all the upsides of being *forced into doing this*. Life is going to be very sweet for you from here on in. If stress causes ill health then you should be fighting fit for a hundred years! And you might just like the dress I brought for you. I'll wait here while you put it on.' He glanced at his watch pointedly and lounged against the wall in we're-on-a-deadline-here mode.

She had expected small, tight and borderline tarty. It was what the women he went out with wore. That was his preferred style of dress for a woman. So she was startled to find herself stepping into the most beautiful soft, dusky pink woollen dress imaginable. Long-sleeved, knee-length, simple cowl neck, it was soft and demure and fitted her like a glove and she hated to admit it but she loved it.

She also hated to admit that it challenged her view of him as a womanising playboy who had got his own way on this, secured his deal with her and now wanted to dress her up like the sort of doll he imagined would pass muster on his arm in the role of fiancée. This dress was classy and it had been, she was forced to concede, a thoughtful purchase. He had actually considered how she would react in her scruffy clothes at a surprise gathering and had pre-empted her embarrassment by providing her with the perfect outfit.

She was much subdued when she joined him back in the hallway, where he was still lounging against the wall, scrolling through his cell phone.

Brilliant eyes shielded as he looked at her, Leo straightened and briskly congratulated her on the quick change of clothes.

Not a word about how she looked, she thought with a flare of disappointment, which she immediately quelled because *none of this was real.*

'Do I look a little more presentable?' Had she actually meant to ask that?

'Definite step up from the war zone look,' he murmured. He opened the car door for her and she stepped inside. 'Now all we need is a smile now and again and some lingering, tender glances and you'll be the complete package.'

'You're very cold, aren't you?' She absently thought that he was truly breathtakingly handsome. 'And your dad is such a warm person.'

'And look where it got him,' Leo responded without skipping a beat. 'After my mother died, he couldn't cope with solitude so he allowed his emotions to carry him away and he ended up with Georgia. Need I say more?'

'He was vulnerable,' Sammy admitted, startled out of her idle gazing at his profile.

'He was vulnerable because he allowed himself to get swept away by his emotions. If that doesn't convince you that emotions are best left at the front door, think about Sean. I admit he was never the most focused guy in the world but who knows. He might have achieved something if he hadn't been taken in by Louise.'

'So your answer is to just…lock your emotions in a box and throw away the key?'

'It's stood me in excellent stead over the years.'

Sammy could now understand why his father was so desperate to have contact with Adele. He would have wanted to anyway because that was simply the kind of man he was, gentle and effusive and warm, but, with no prospect of his own son rushing down the aisle in a hurry to start the next generation of little Morgan-Whites, he probably saw Adele as his one and only chance of having what amounted to a grandchild.

'Don't you plan on marrying…for real?'

'Depends what you call *for real*,' Leo replied drily. 'If by *for real* you're asking whether I'll ever throw caution to the winds and nurture unrealistic expectations about fairy-tale romances lasting a lifetime, then no. Not a chance. If, on the other hand, you're asking whether I may one day seal a union with a woman with whom I can enjoy some intellectual banter, a woman who is financially self-sufficient in her own right and who has enough of a life of her own to not need constant attention, then who knows? It's a possibility, although it has to be said that it's nowhere near being on the horizon at this moment in time.'

'That sounds like a lot of fun,' Sammy couldn't resist saying and he burst out laughing, a rich, sexy laugh that made her bloom with confusing, forbidden pleasure inside.

'Of course,' he murmured, 'there would also have to be certain things in place for the equation to work.'

'Like what?'

He briefly took his eyes off the road to look at her and Sammy felt bright colour crawl up from the tips of her toes to her hairline because she realised immediately what those *certain things* were.

Flustered, she looked away and stared straight out through the window, out into an unlit blackness, and heard him burst out laughing again.

'So you see,' he murmured when his laughter had trailed off, 'this little rescue package is as much of a hardship for me as it is for you. Not only will my working habits have to be constrained but so will my—'

'I get it,' she interrupted hastily.

He laughed again and then asked conversationally, 'Not the same for you?'

'I don't change boyfriends,' Sammy retorted coldly, 'the way I change outfits.'

'Now, now, are you implying that I do?'

'Don't you?'

'I'm not looking for love ever after,' he told her. 'But I enjoy having fun and I enjoy being in the company of women who like having fun with me.'

'It's just as well this is a fake engagement,' Sammy told him airily, while her mind toyed feverishly with images of him *having fun with his fun women*.

'Because you're looking for your soulmate?'

'That's right. There's nothing wrong with that.' She thought of her ex-boyfriends and marvelled that the theory of the perfect soulmate could be so different from the reality. It didn't mean that the guy for her wasn't out there. It just meant that she had to kiss one or two frogs before she got to him.

'Well, to each their own.' Leo shrugged indifferently. 'And that, as I said before, is just one of the reasons why this is such a good fake engagement. We're not even beginning to sing from the same song sheet when it comes to relationships. Now, let's talk about how we met and how long we've been seeing one another.'

The sleet had turned to snow by the time they made it to Happenden Court, which crested a hill and was reached via a long tree-bordered avenue. In summer, it was a glorious approach to the magnificent country estate but now, in the bitter, biting wind, it was no less impressive but rather a bleak and haunting view, especially with nightfall fast approaching.

The house ahead, however, was bathed in light.

Sammy absolutely loved the house. Admittedly, it was way too big for one man on his own, but Harold had lived in a small group of rooms in the massive property, only opening up the rest of the house on special occasions. In summer, people actually paid to visit the gardens and the part of the historic house which was largely unused.

He claimed he couldn't part with it even though it was huge and expensive to maintain. Too many memories, he had told Sammy once.

'He needs to downsize.' Leo read her mind as he swung the car into the courtyard. 'He might be emotional, but he's as stubborn as a mule. Remember to look surprised when you walk through the door.'

'The entire village won't be there, will they? Hiding in the living room with the lights off?'

'That could be a dangerous approach to take, considering most of the assembled crowd are in their seventies and eighties. And remember to look as though you've found true love with me.'

'Why? Do you think they've got a hotline to the paparazzi?'

She knew how she sounded. Petulant and sulky and childish. And yes, she'd signed up for a deal with the devil and she knew that she should be taking it on the chin instead of moaning and groaning. And yes, he was right. Whether she liked to admit it or not, the financial pressures that had been keeping her awake for over a year would be erased. Like a teacher sweeping into the classroom, he would wipe the whiteboard clean and she would be able to start afresh.

How many times had she fantasised about this very thing?

But every time she looked at him, it hit home just how steep the price she would be paying was. He did something to her. He unsettled her. Between that and her conscience, the next few weeks were not going to be a walk in the park.

How could she pretend to be in love with someone who unsettled her? When she fundamentally disliked what he stood for? When his approach to life was so different from hers? Surely one glance and anyone would see through the sham. Especially Gail Jamieson, who had a lot to lose if she didn't gain custody of her granddaughter. They would be going to Australia and she would be playing out this charade in front of people who wouldn't be as forgiving and thrilled to see him engaged as the people waiting inside the house. Plus, deceiving people she had known since childhood didn't sit right and that, in itself, filled her with anxiety.

Thrilled they might be, but wouldn't they be able to see through her phoney smiles in a second? She could only hope that they would take their cue from her mother, who, after a long phone call with Sammy, knew the lie of the land.

'That's exactly what I'm talking about,' Leo grated, grinding the powerful car to a stop and turning to look at her as he killed the engine.

Sammy's thoughts were on her mother. She had been surprisingly upbeat about the situation, given the fact that it had been relayed by her daughter in a tone of voice that had been thick with resignation, doom and gloom.

But then her mother, Sammy reasoned, would have spent many more long hours as witness to Harold's despondency at not having his granddaughter in the same country. She would have lived through the nightmare of Gail's interference and demands and the horrible prospect of those demands continuing while any supportive role to Adele was shoved aside.

Plus she would have never argued that Sammy had made the wrong decision. If she *had* disagreed with her daughter, she would have kept her opinions to herself because the habit of being supportive of the decisions Sammy made was just too ingrained.

They had operated as a unit for a very long time.

'Sammy!'

'Huh?' Sammy blinked and surfaced out of her thoughts to focus on the man frowning at her.

Leo raked frustrated fingers through his hair and continued to frown at her because she'd been a million miles away just then. He'd been talking to her and, instead of paying attention to what he'd been saying, she'd blanked him out.

'I was *talking to you*,' he said grittily.

The surly edge to his voice suddenly lightened her mood and snapped her out of her thoughts. She looked at him, amused, because he had sounded, just then, like a sulky child.

'Care to share the joke?' He scowled and she grinned.

'You're angry because I wasn't giving you one hundred per cent of my attention? I guess,' she said shrewdly, 'you're not accustomed to women who don't give you *one hundred per cent* of their attention.'

'Don't be ridiculous,' Leo growled.

'I'm not! But just because you're *my fiancé* doesn't mean that I have to agree with everything you say and snap to attention the second you give a command.'

'Rebelling and being argumentative isn't going to persuade anyone that we're an item. Now, out we go. They're waiting for us and don't forget to look shocked. There's nothing worse than someone who isn't suitably flabbergasted at a surprise party thrown for them.'

Almost at the door, she paused to rest her hand on his arm.

Leo looked down at her, expecting defiance and that mulish stubbornness he was fast becoming accustomed to. Instead, she looked suddenly vulnerable and defensive.

Her complexion was so satiny smooth that he found himself staring. She had carved a niche for herself in the background and she had done that by deliberately making sure to downplay every single asset she had.

But the more he looked at her, the more appealing her attraction seemed to be.

He shook himself out of this strange line of thought, inserted his key into the lock and turned it, pushing open the front door and stepping back to allow her past him.

It had been several weeks since Sammy had visited the house but, as always, she stood for a few minutes breathing in its spectacular, unique magnificence.

Despite the historic interest of the building, it still managed to look lived-in, probably because of the eclectic mix of period furniture and the scattering of beautiful objects which Leo's parents had gathered over the years.

Mariela, having come from some wealth herself, had brought with her paintings and art pieces that were wonderfully exotic and there were unique touches everywhere that gave the house a very special feel. On the highly polished circular table in the hallway there was a massive arrangement of fresh flowers and Sammy breathed in the wonderful floral scent, as powerful as incense, temporarily forgetting why she was here.

Blissful oblivion didn't last long. She heard the babble of voices from behind one of the doors and quailed.

'Chin up,' Leo commanded. 'We're in love. Don't look as though you have a hot date with the hangman.'

He was walking briskly towards the sitting room and she hustled in his wake, horribly self-conscious and frantically wondering how she was going to pull this all off whilst looking suitably surprised. And, of course, delighted. She hoped that she might discover award-winning talents she had hitherto never suspected.

Leo knocked on the sitting room door then pushed it open and stood aside and, as she took a deep breath and hesitated, he pulled her into him and swung her round to face him.

He was smiling.

For a second, everything flew out of her head. This was a smile meant for her and, as she looked at him, she felt the whole room in front of her disappear—the voices, the people, the clinking of glasses, the laughter.

Her breath caught. Could she have forgotten how to breathe? Was that possible?

Her body was burning, her breasts aching and a strange sensation pooling between her thighs.

'Darling—' Leo laughed '—a little surprise party for us. I wanted to tell you but I was sworn to secrecy…'

This in a voice just loud enough to generate a round of delighted applause from, as she'd feared, at least forty of the great and the good from the village, all people she had known since forever.

And now she was going to have to look rapturous.

She began to turn and then he caught her face in his hands and lowered his head…

And kissed her. The tip of his tongue teased her full lower lip and Sammy instinctively opened her mouth, her whole body leaning into him, wanting the feel of his hard masculine body against hers. The taste of his tongue against hers sent desire ripping through her with the force of a raging inferno.

She didn't understand her powerful, immediate response to his caress. She just knew that it owned her.

And then he drew back, leaving her trembling and dazed, mouth swollen from his kiss, eyes over-bright and glittering.

'Excellent,' he murmured into her ear. 'I think it's safe to say that you don't have to worry about stage fright any more. We couldn't have been more convincing.'

CHAPTER FOUR

THE WHOLE VILLAGE now knew that Harold Morgan-White's son was engaged to lovely little Sammy Wilson. And wasn't it just fantastic because hadn't Harold been complaining for *years* about his overworked, stressed out son who was never going to settle down?

'If we don't escape soon,' he had told her as the last of the guests was being shown to the door, 'the next surprise occasion will include the vicar, the organist and a marriage service.'

'Our parents would never allow that,' Sammy had been quick to refute. 'Not when they know that this isn't for real.' But you wouldn't have guessed it from the way his father and her mother had basked in the congratulatory attention.

And she knew that to outside eyes she would have appeared equally thrilled because she had spent the remainder of the evening with that kiss still burning her lips. He had caught her off guard and had done the one thing which he must have known would have brought hectic colour to her cheeks and left her speechless.

It turned out she had had award-winning skills of deception in spades.

Lest she forget that they were a couple in love, he

had made sure to stick close to her side for the duration of the party. His hand had lain possessively around her waist and she marvelled that no one sought to question this sudden, overwhelming love affair that had smothered the pair of them.

Whatever happened to common sense?

And, whilst she could acknowledge that Leo was a good-looking, sophisticated and very sexy man, how was it that she could have cast aside all her doubts and allowed herself to be so affected by a kiss that had been purely for the benefit of the assembled crowd?

Since then, she had not seen him. He had returned to London to work on deals he needed to close before they left for Australia and she had used the time to hand in her notice, much to the disappointment of the head teacher.

And now, as she stared at the suitcases on the floor in her bedroom in her mother's house, she felt as though she had stepped onto a roller coaster that was picking up speed. It had nudged slowly to the top and she was poised, looking down at the loops stretching ahead of her.

She couldn't stop gazing at the costly engagement ring on her finger and vaguely wondering how she had ended up where she had, all in the space of a week.

But then she knew, didn't she...?

Leo had appealed to the very powerful part of her that had wanted to see her mother's stress alleviated, the part of her that had been frantically worrying about money, about the bank, about how much debt had piled up over the months. The part of her that had been worrying about her future and where she wanted to go with it.

Into this Leo had charged, with heady solutions and

a price to pay…because there was no such thing as a free lunch.

Had she not, reluctantly, felt sympathy for his cause she would have turned her back on his offer, but she was deeply fond of his father and had easily been able to see how the end could justify the means, even though deception was something she found abhorrent. She had also heard enough about Gail Jamieson and about Sean and his constant leeching of his ex-stepfather's bank account to know that Adele would not have a glorious, warm and loving environment if she stayed with her grandmother, who was, from all accounts, even more grasping than her daughter and son-in-law had been.

But, in return, she had had a glimpse of how difficult it was going to be to play the part of loving fiancée because being with Leo was just so unsettling.

She wasn't cool enough to deal with his massive presence. She had never liked the way he treated women and she disapproved of his casual approach to relationships and while neither of these things should have mattered because she and he were only linked by virtue of the charade they were playing, they somehow did.

She heard her mother calling her, carolling that the driver had arrived, courtesy of Leo, who had firmly decreed that a train to the airport wasn't going to do.

She lugged the cases down and found her mother waiting at the bottom of the stairs.

'Are you sure you're going to be all right while I'm gone?' Sammy asked worriedly. 'It will only be for ten days, by which time Leo should have a clear idea of what the outcome of the custody battle is going to be.'

Her mother's thin face was as bright-eyed as Sammy had seen it in a very long time. Which, frankly, was also worrying. She hoped her mother wasn't going to start believing that the pretence was for real. However, this was hardly the time to angst over that when the chauffeur was waiting.

'I'll be absolutely fine, darling. Amy is going to pop over every morning and I don't have any hospital appointments until you're back anyway. You just go out there and, well, enjoy yourself. It's been such a long time since you've had a break.'

'Mum,' Sammy whispered sotto voce as the chauffeur entered and, after a brief cheery smile, headed to the car with her cases. 'This isn't going to be about *having a break*. Remember I told you when I… Well, when I told you what this is all about?'

Her mother's eyes rounded and she smiled reassuringly, 'Of course and you're doing the right thing, darling. Harold is so relieved that this whole business is going to be sorted out once and for all.'

'Well, no one knows what the outcome is going to be,' Sammy pointed out constrainedly.

'It'll be fine with Leo in charge.'

Sammy rolled her eyes, halfway out of the door. 'He's not a knight in shining armour—he can't conquer everything!'

'Harold has a lot of faith in him and, by the way, Sam, you look lovely.'

'Mum, I have to go.' Her face was red. So what if Leo had breezily insinuated that her wardrobe only needed minor tweaks and packages full of beautiful, understated pieces that fitted her perfectly had subsequently arrived at her front door. If he had complained and tried to force her into wearing anything she hadn't wanted to wear then she would have dug her heels in and stood her ground, but he hadn't.

As the car ate up the miles between Salcombe and London, she wondered what he would think when she removed her coat and cardigan to reveal her light-weight cream trousers and her tan tee shirt and when she stashed away her boots, essential against the snow which had been falling when she'd left Devon, and pulled out her cream loafers. She was all covered up in her thick waterproof coat and scarf and gloves, but underneath was evidence of the effort she was making to fit the part.

Of course there would be no male appreciation in his eyes; as he had made clear from the very start, she was the ideal candidate because there would be no temptation for him to come near her. Unless circumstances dictated and he had to for show.

Or, at any rate, something like that.

She was a paid employee and, if it weren't for this weird situation, he certainly wouldn't be seeking her out to spend time in her company.

They made excellent progress and her nerves fluttered as she was helped out of the car with her bags and then, by some prior arrangement only possible, she assumed, with very, very rich and influential people, the chauffeur was permitted to leave his car outside the airport so that she could be delivered to the check-in desk without the hassle of having to manage a trolley herself.

Sammy had never experienced anything like it and although she didn't want to be impressed, she really was.

The crowd parted. People stared and whispered. Someone took a picture. Sammy felt like royalty. She wished she had had the foresight to dump the untrendy coat and scarf before exiting the car.

Cheeks burning, she was relieved to find Leo waiting for her by the first-class check-in desk.

He watched her slow progress towards him. Her hair was loose and it curled and danced around her heart-shaped face, falling in unrestrained ringlets past her shoulders. It was every shade of blond—vanilla streaked with gold with hints of strawberry—and it was brilliantly eye-catching.

The turquoise clarity of her eyes, fringed with dark, dark lashes which were at odds with her blond, blond hair also made him want to stare, he thought distractedly as she abruptly came to a halt in front of him.

'You're here,' he said, lounging indolently against the counter while his driver dealt with the business of the bags on the belt.

'Did you think I wouldn't turn up?'

'Your attitude when we last parted company wasn't reassuring.'

Sammy blushed. She could breathe him in and it was like breathing in some kind of dangerous, mind-altering drug. She stepped back a little.

'I'm glad to see you're wearing the engagement ring.' He took her hand in his and inspected her finger, looking at it from several angles while she fought the temptation to snatch it away.

'I put it on in the car,' she confessed, once she had her burning hand back to herself. 'I didn't want to wear it in front of my mum.' They had checked in and were moving with purpose through the airport, away from the crowds and the duty-free shops and directly towards the first-class lounge. Sammy followed in a daze, eyes darting around her, feeling that sneaky, pleasurable important feeling again because she knew that people were staring sideways at them. He commanded so much attention without even realising it because he looked neither left nor right and was uninterested in everyone around them.

'Why not?'

'She knows that this is just a…a…*charade*, but…'

'But what?'

'I just don't want her to get it into her head that there's any part of this that might actually be for real.'

'No.' Leo looked sideways at her. 'I'm sure she won't.'

'Yes, well, you can never tell,' Sammy continued, pausing only to stare around her at the lounge into which he had led her. It was beyond luxurious, the sort of place where you just knew that nearly everyone was stupidly rich and probably famous. 'Wow,' she couldn't help whispering as they came to a clutch of sofas.

'Wow?' Leo raised his eyebrows, amused at her lack of artifice. She was feisty, outspoken, stubborn as the proverbial mule and would certainly prove to be a challenging assault on his well-ordered world over the next ten days, but no one could accuse her of being anything but glaringly honest in her responses.

'I've never travelled like this in my life before,' Sammy said truthfully. 'In fact, I've only been on a plane twice in my entire life and it was nothing like this.'

'You can take your coat off and sit down.' Leo never paid a scrap of attention to the luxury that surrounded him wherever he went. Now, he glanced around him at the subdued, well-bred, quiet lounge that screamed *exclusivity*. Right about now, any of the women he was accustomed to dating would have stripped off her coat and would have been indulging in the sport of twisting and twirling and making sure that all eyes in the room were focused on her. Sammy was still in her coat. It looked as though she might actually have pulled it more tightly around her.

'You were telling me about your mother getting the wrong idea…' He began removing his laptop from his leather case, absently glancing at the headlines of the newspaper neatly folded on the table in front of the chairs.

He looked up.

The coat was off, as was the scarf. She was bending slightly to unzip her boots.

When he looked at her he could clearly see the outline of her breasts as she leant down. Her tee shirt was figure-hugging, the lightweight trousers lovingly contoured every rounded inch of her bottom and the surprising length of her slim legs. She wasn't looking at him. She was busy shoving the unsightly boots into a bag she had brought with her, replacing them with some cream shoes that complemented the outfit.

Nothing was revealing. There was nothing at all remotely attention-grabbing about what she was wearing. Yet she still managed to grab his attention and hold on to it.

Shoes on and outer layers removed and neatly folded and shoved into her carry-on, aside from the boots, which she had crammed into a canvas bag brought specially for that purpose, Sammy straightened and met his eyes.

For a few seconds she held her breath and wondered whether he would say anything about her outfit. When he didn't, the disappointment felt disproportionate but she pinned a smile on her face anyway.

She brutally reminded herself that there was nothing between them so there was no reason for him to remark on anything she chose to wear. As long as she played her part and gave no one any reason to suspect that there was anything amiss between them, especially when they reached their destination, then conversation would remain perfunctory.

'Yes—' she sat down and tucked her hair behind her ears '—I think that Mum's a little vulnerable because she's been ill. She's always been a strong woman and to have to accept that she wasn't as strong as she thought she was hit her hard.' Sammy frowned. 'It's only recently occurred to me, from a couple of things that Mum's said, that she was worried sick about leaving me single.' She laughed a little self-consciously. 'She seemed to think that if anything happened to her, I might have needed the support of someone by my side.'

'And you think that that worry might lead her to pin her hopes on this becoming more than just a fake engagement?' Leo was trying hard to quell his surging libido, which had suddenly decided to put in an appearance. He wondered why she dressed to hide her body when she had the sort of body that most men would drool over. Unashamedly *feminine* and sexy in its femininity.

'She actually told me that I should enjoy myself in Melbourne because I hadn't had a break in a long time,' Sammy confided.

'And there's no chance of that happening?'

Sammy opened her mouth to ask him how on earth she could possibly relax when she was going to be spending her time there in his company, pretending to be his fiancée.

But she stopped.

Why wouldn't she be able to relax? He would. He would work and when he wasn't working he certainly wouldn't be stressing out because his nerves were all over the place when he was in her company. His stomach wouldn't be doing somersaults when he was in her radius.

'I've spent so long worrying over stuff that I've forgotten how to relax,' she said vaguely, thinking on her feet.

'Then I'll have to change that.'

'What do you mean?'

'Engaged people go places, explore, seek out exciting new adventures.'

'Are you joking?'

'Why would I be joking, Sammy? We have to be convincing and if we spend our free time on opposite sides of the city it won't be long before Jamieson smells a rat.'

'But she's not going to be following us everywhere, is she?'

'Quite frankly,' Leo said with genuine honesty, 'I wouldn't put it past the woman. Think about it. If she loses custody of Adele, she loses access to my money. I owe her nothing. She's not related to me or to my father in any way whatsoever. As long as she can hang on to the child, she is guaranteed an income because neither my father nor, frankly, myself, would want Adele to suffer financial hardship. The tie with my father may not be secured with blood but it's there. So, that being the case, she'll do anything in her power to discredit me and what's the fastest way of discrediting me? By convincing a judge that I'm not the reliable, happily soon-to-be married man I claim to be.'

'I suppose so.'

'So you'll get the break your mother wants you to have,' he told her with silky assurance. 'Now—' he indicated the long counter brimming with delicious snacks '—why don't you go and help yourself? If I'm to have to focus on the custody battle while maintaining our happily engaged façade by mixing in some fun in the sun for the next week and a half, I might as well do as much work as I can while I'm still here.'

Despite what Leo had said about making sure that they stuck to their brief as the loved-up engaged couple, Sammy privately didn't think that anyone in Melbourne would give a hoot whether they looked loved-up or not. And whilst she had heard all sorts of rumours about Gail and her horrendous ways, she honestly couldn't picture the woman creeping around behind them wherever they went, in disguise, with the specific aim of trying to prove them liars.

Exhausted after twenty-two hours of flying, she was dazed as she emerged from the plane. He'd bought every seat in the first-class cabin because sharing space wasn't his 'thing' and it was less hassle than organising his company Gulfstream—and, besides, arriving in full view on a chartered airline worked. It was jaw-dropping extravagance but she had soon discovered that being up in the air for hours and hours and hours on end took its toll, however luxurious the seating arrangements.

Accustomed to functioning wherever he happened to be, and adept at working in the confines of a plane, Leo had not been disconcerted at all. He had pulled out his computer and had spent the majority of the flight working.

At some point, with neither her book or the range of movies netting her attention, she had turned to him and said airily, 'Do you ever get bored?'

'When it comes to work—' he had turned the full wattage of his attention onto her and she had felt, suddenly and inexplicably, like a flower, wilting in the shadows, exposed to the full force of the sun's rays '—I have an inexhaustible supply of energy. I also have to wrap up some pretty important deals before we reach Melbourne. Like I said, fun in the sun is the equivalent of taking time out and taking time out isn't something I can afford to do.'

'When was the last time you had a holiday?'

'You're beginning to sound like my father,' Leo had said wryly. 'Please do me a favour and spare me the long lectures about high blood pressure, premature heart attacks and stress.'

'I wasn't going to start lecturing you about anything,' Sammy had informed him. 'I was just curious and you don't have to think that you have to spend all your spare time with me. In fact, does Ms Jamieson even know exactly when we're due over?'

'You can't imagine that I would make this trip on the off-chance of finding her, do you? I have meetings arranged in advance with her lawyer and I have a team of people at my end, waiting and ready to go. I've made very sure to cage her in. Wouldn't want her to consider bolting.'

For a brief moment, Sammy had almost felt sorry for the woman. She had certainly understood in that moment why his father had had such an unshakeable faith in him securing the outcome that was desired.

He exuded absolute mastery.

But she had still privately thought that, whilst it sometimes paid to be cautious, he was being overcautious when it came to maintaining their charade.

Blistering heat greeted them as they emerged into the soaring summer temperatures. The sky was flamboyantly blue and cloudless and the strength of the heat was formidable. In her tee shirt and slacks, which she had traded on the plane for a set of silk pyjamas, she still felt her skin begin to perspire almost immediately.

She knew that they would be met by a chauffeur. She hadn't known that, along with the chauffeur who was dutifully waiting for them, there would also be a little cluster of paparazzi.

Startled and blinking, she instinctively stepped closer to Leo and felt his arm curve around her as he led her directly to the car waiting for them.

Once inside the air-conditioned space, Sammy craned back, staring at the reporters, then turned to Leo and whispered urgently, 'What on earth were they doing at the airport? I don't get it. We didn't have any of this in England. In fact, other than the people at the party, no one even knows that we're engaged!'

'What gives you that idea?'

'Why would anyone know? There certainly wasn't anyone taking pictures…'

'I've made sure to keep it low-key,' Leo informed her and she looked at him in utter astonishment.

'What do you mean?'

He was sprawled in the seat, leaning against the door, his big body angled to face her. Dressed in grey trousers and a short-sleeved black polo shirt with a tiny discreet insignia embroidered on one side, he was the last word in sophistication. He had *that look*. The look of someone who should be photographed. Rich. Powerful. Influential.

She recalled the way his mouth had felt against hers and quivered.

'I have an excellent relationship with the press, particularly the tabloid press. They're like sharks. They'll cheerfully rip you apart if it takes their fancy. It's always a good idea to keep them onside. I'm wealthy, I'm powerful but I'm not a Hollywood star. The less they print about me, the better, but I accept that my movements are sometimes of interest.' He shrugged. Sammy found it fascinating that he could sit there and talk about a world that was so foreign to her. He really and truly moved in a completely different hemisphere. A world where people were photographed and simple day-to-day things became newsworthy events to be recorded for public consumption.

No wonder he had reasoned that her presence by his side would give his cause gravitas. She was the embodiment of everything that was contrary to all of that—the embodiment of *normality*—just the sort of reassuring thing the lawyers would make note of when it came to sorting out custody of an impressionable young child.

Guilt shook her because this *normality* was only going to last as long as it took for him to have Adele under his wing.

She consoled herself with the thought that whatever was brought to the table by Leo and his wonderful, kind-hearted father was sure to be better than what lay in store for the little girl at the hands of a grasping grandmother, but she still backed away from thinking too hard about the rights and wrongs.

At the end of the day, she thought uneasily, it wasn't her problem.

Besides, whilst the world of extreme wealth was not one she inhabited, she knew that there were very many children of wealthy parents who did very well on a diet of private schools and boarding schools and nannies.

'I know a couple of the reporters,' Leo said as though it were the most normal thing in the world. 'The trick is to see them as humans in their own right and not a collection of pests. Humanise them and they're more likely to humanise *you* in return. At any rate, I spread the word that I was engaged and made it known that a flashy announcement wasn't going to do. I felt that was appropriate, given the circumstances, but no point broadcasting it when it's going to come to an end in due course.'

'No, quite.' She was finding it hard to keep up.

'They listened and did as I asked.'

'People do that, don't they?' she murmured and he looked at her and nodded.

'Different story over here,' Leo informed her. 'Ignore anyone who asks for an interview. I may not be as well known as I am in London but I do have considerable financial interests in this part of the world and...' He flushed darkly and paused, and something about that pause roused her curiosity.

'And what?'

'I did achieve a certain amount of unwanted notoriety for dating a certain Australian actress about a year ago.'

'Really?' Sammy had been so wrapped up in concerns about her mother's health at that time that she doubted she would have been able to remember anything that had been going on around her, never mind what had been unravelling in the gossip pages of tabloid newspapers.

'Vivienne Madison.'

'*The* Vivienne Madison? Gosh. I had no idea. What happened?'

'I'm surprised you missed out that little slice of my life,' Leo inserted wryly, 'considering you seem to have spotted me in the centre pages of tabloids in the past.'

'I wasn't really with it a year ago,' Sammy admitted. 'Mum was undergoing treatment and I was…in a different place. A scary place. I was barely functioning. I mean, I was going to work but taking a lot of time off and I couldn't focus at all. I don't think I glanced at a newspaper once for months.'

'The long and short of it,' Leo said heavily, 'was that she was found with a bottle of pills in a hotel room and the baying Australian press decided to go for me.'

'You mean she tried to commit suicide because you left her?' Immediately, she could feel herself pull back from him, deeply appalled that his way of life, his cavalier attitude towards women, might have resulted in someone actually attempting to take her own life as a result of being ditched.

Leo read the distaste on her face. Normally, this would not have fazed him. He never saw the need to launch into explanations for his behaviour or to justify decisions he had taken. As long as he stuck to his impeccable moral code and recognised his own personal truths, who gave a damn what other people thought?

But, for some reason, he didn't like the thoughts he knew were churning around in her head.

'Vivienne Madison was a seriously unstable woman.' He was unfamiliar with the process of explaining himself and found that his words did not come as easily as usual. 'When I became involved with her, I discovered that she had a drinking problem. She was also, I later found out, hooked on painkillers. But she was an amazing actress and managed to hide both those dependencies.' He sighed, his lean, handsome face unusually empathetic, the cold lines temporarily erased. 'She became dependent on me very quickly, although I had told her from the very beginning that I was not interested in settling down. But she was a highly emotional person and her addictions made her even more irrational than she otherwise might have been. I knew that it had to end but I made sure to get her signed up with an excellent counsellor as well as a rehab centre noted for its success rate. I may not have wanted her in my life but I wasn't going to cast her aside like a pile of used rubbish. The truth is that I felt deeply sorry for her.'

Sammy was impressed. That this formidable and ruthlessly controlled man was capable of compassion for a woman he had no longer wanted in his life was an eye-opener.

It didn't *mean* anything, but it certainly afforded her a different take on him. It was peculiarly complimentary to him because she could tell that he was less than comfortable telling this story and was doubtless only doing so in case it came out and she knew nothing about it. As his fiancée, it would be surprising if she was ignorant of what had happened.

'The incident with the overdose was several weeks after we had parted company but that was something the press over here omitted to mention. Later, there was a nondescript apology to me when they discovered that the overdose was in response to a rejection from one of the psychiatrists at the rehab centre. At any rate, my name will be linked to hers forever over here.'

'And is she still in contact with you?'

'In no way, shape or form,' Leo asserted.

That was the end of the conversation. She could see that on his face but it left her thinking that she could almost understand his antipathy towards emotional situations. He had had a substantial amount of experience in dealing with the negative side of them.

'So we have a schedule here,' she said, changing the subject.

'Meetings lined up with lawyers. I expect some sort of compensation will have to be given to Ms Jamieson if custody is awarded to me. It will be a very busy ten days.'

'Not much time for fun in the sun.'

'Tut-tut,' Leo said lazily. 'Is that the right approach for a newly engaged woman to be taking? I'm sure we'll find the time to escape and see some of Melbourne's sights, especially if there are interested parties pursuing us who need to be placated. Like nosy journalists. If Jamieson is playing hardball, then there's every chance she's got in touch with a newspaper and filled them in on what I'm doing over here. It's certainly got the ingredients for a good story, especially with my past association with Vivienne. But don't worry—' he reached out and slid his long brown finger along her arm, sending splinters of awareness skittering through her like quicksilver '—it'll be over in no time at all and you can return to your life.'

CHAPTER FIVE

It DIDN'T TAKE long before the car was pulling up outside a grand hotel and they stepped back out into the searing heat. It felt strange to be in a busy, vibrant city and yet to know that the sea was just a hop and a skip away. Sammy imagined that she could almost smell the salt in the air.

And the people looked different. Relaxed, sunkissed, moving at a slower pace. She had to keep reminding herself that this wasn't the break her mother had told her she needed but she could still feel a holiday spirit pushing through until they were shown up to their massive suite and she gazed around in confusion because there was just the one bedroom.

'Is this it?' she asked, as soon as their bags were deposited and the bellboy had left, quietly closing the door behind him.

Leo, immune to his surroundings as always, was heading to the well-stocked kitchen where he proceeded to fetch them both a bottle of ice-cold water. 'You'll find yourself drinking this by the gallon,' he promised. 'I would recommend that you carry a bottle in your bag whenever you're out. The heat over here can be ferocious and we don't want you getting dehydrated, do we?'

Sammy took the bottle from him. 'Thank you very much for your health tips, Leo, but where is *my* bedroom?'

Leo carried on drinking, looking at her as he drank, then, dumping the empty bottle on the kitchen counter and strolling towards the sitting area, he nodded in the direction of the bedroom.

'What?' She tripped along and watched as he coolly pulled out his computer and flipped it open, attention focused on whatever he had called up to peruse.

'Leo, could you at least look at me when I'm trying to have a conversation?'

'You wanted to know where your bedroom is and I showed you. It's behind me and yes, there's only the one room.'

'But...'

'But what did you expect, Sammy?'

'Not just one bedroom with one bed in it!'

'No?' he drawled coolly. 'Did you think that I would book us into separate rooms? Maybe on different floors? Or why stop there? Different hotels?'

'You're deliberately misunderstanding me.'

'I'm not deliberately misunderstanding you. Frankly, I think you are the one deliberately misunderstanding the situation. Did you honestly imagine that as a newly engaged couple we wouldn't be sharing a bedroom?'

'I hadn't thought about it,' Sammy stuttered.

'Engaged couples tend to share bedrooms these days. There was no chance, after all of this, that I would risk anyone suspecting that all is not what it appears to be in the land of the soon-to-be wed lovebirds.'

He was right, of course. They weren't living in an

era of chaperoned walks in the park and a ban on all forms of physical contact bar holding hands.

She hadn't really thought about that angle at all, just as she hadn't really thought about how open to scrutiny they would be because she had had no idea of the world he occupied.

Sammy dropped into the chair facing him. She wondered how she hadn't really noticed the huge differences between them sooner and then thought that that was probably because she hadn't seen him on enough of a regular basis over the years and, when she *had* seen him, it had always been in the rural setting of his father's house. She had ceased to be awestruck at the mansion in which Harold lived and he was such a lovable and down-to-earth man that, in the setting of his rolling country estate, Leo had been a lot more of an ordinary guy.

But he *wasn't* an ordinary guy. This *wasn't* going to be a low-key two-week situation. He *hadn't* overplayed the amount of attention they might generate.

'We're in this together for the next week and a half, so you might as well get used to it.'

'Thank goodness it's just going to be for a week and a half,' Sammy breathed with sincerity. 'I don't think I could live in it for any longer than that.'

'Oh, really?'

Leo imbued those two simple words with such sarcastic disbelief that she flushed and glared at him.

'I wouldn't want to live in a goldfish bowl,' she asserted dismissively. 'I'd hate to think that there might be people with cameras wherever I went, waiting to get a picture of me.'

'And yet you seemed to be mightily impressed by

the first-class lounge and the first-class cabin and the chauffeur-driven car...'

Sammy blushed, hating him just at that moment because he was right; she really *had* enjoyed that feeling of being treated like royalty.

'That's because it's a novelty. I'd soon tire of it,' she insisted and he shrugged with an expression that indicated that he was suddenly bored with the whole conversation.

'Which is just as well,' Leo drawled, 'considering the novelty isn't going to last very long. It would be a nuisance if you started getting too accustomed to it.'

'Meaning?'

'Like I said to you before, you're ideal for this role because you wouldn't be interested in prolonging it. Indeed, the fact that you don't like this lifestyle could come in very handy when it comes to citing reasons for our break-up. Two people, opposites drawn together by a powerful attraction only, sadly, to discover that opposites, in the end, do not have what it takes to make lasting relationships. But, getting back to the matter of the bedroom... We're sharing it and I'm afraid you're just going to have to deal with that. Let's not forget here that you're not in this because you're an altruistic saint only concerned with my father's welfare. You're in this because the price was right.'

Sammy went bright red. He had sliced through the waffle and got straight to the point and she couldn't dispute the truth of what he was saying.

She also knew that, for what she was being paid, sharing a bedroom was not exactly too high a price to pay. And what, exactly, was her cause for concern, anyway? It wasn't as though he was attracted to her. In fact, she could tell that he was struggling not to let his attention wander back to whatever report she had interrupted. And as soon as they were away from public view, he made no attempt to come near her or to even look at her as though she belonged to the female sex.

She was only his type when she had to be, which was when they were being observed.

She stood up stiffly. 'Okay. Fair enough.'

Leo's dark-eyed gaze narrowed. So she had bought into a situation and was now discovering that it came with certain clauses she might not have taken into account. He felt a degree of sympathy for her, even though he had no intention of revealing that because, as far as he was concerned, when you put your signature on the dotted line you agreed to all the terms and conditions.

But she wasn't like the women he was accustomed to dating. Naturally, she would have had experience of sharing a bed with a man—she wasn't a teenager, after all—but he was a virtual stranger and she was weirdly disingenuous.

Yet, after her initial appalled reaction, she had accepted it without further ado.

'You're perfectly safe with me,' he told her roughly and Sammy paused, her heartbeat suddenly accelerating as their eyes met.

She didn't know what to say and even if there had been anything remotely resembling a coherent thought in her head she wouldn't have been able to vocalise it because her mouth was dry and her vocal cords had stopped working.

'You don't have to worry,' he explained into the deafening silence, 'that I'm going to lunge for you in the middle of the night. I would offer to sleep on the sofa but it seems a ridiculous amount of hassle to make a sofa up with whatever spare linen we can rustle up from a cupboard, only to *unmake* it first thing in the morning.'

'I'm not complaining.' Sammy finally found her voice and was pleased that it sounded relatively normal. 'I was just a little taken aback, that's all.' She told herself that this was a job, as he had made sure to remind her, and part of the job would be to sleep next to him. No big deal. She would be well and truly covered up. It wasn't as though her change of wardrobe had extended to a collection of French knickers and frilly negligees. It would be as unthreatening as if she were sleeping next to a potted plant.

'If you don't mind, I think I'll go have a bath now, freshen up. What are our plans for tomorrow?' She was still furiously trying to quieten her nerves at the prospect of sharing a bed with him and pretending that he was the equivalent of a potted plant.

Leo afforded her his sole undivided attention for a few seconds. 'I expect,' he said slowly, 'that it will involve you meeting the Jamieson woman at some point. My lawyers have emailed me over the proposal they've put to her lawyers and instinct tells me that she's not going to be over the moon. That's in the afternoon. Tomorrow morning, I suggest we visit a few shops.'

'Why?'

'Is that your response to the offer of going shopping?' Leo was amused.

'I don't like shopping,' Sammy admitted. She tilted her chin at a defiant angle. 'You can probably see for yourself why!'

'Come again?'

Sammy spread her hands down in a sweeping gesture and laughed. 'I'm not exactly built like a model. You, of all people, should be able to see that for yourself, considering you only date models. And actresses who have model bodies.'

'What does that have to do with anything?' Leo was genuinely bewildered and Sammy was already regretting her impulse to put herself down but, when it came to her appearance, it was something that had always come as second nature. If you laughed at yourself first, then it deflected other people from laughing at you.

'When you have a figure like mine, twirling in front of mirrors in changing rooms is a bit of an ordeal,' she said lightly, scuttling in small steps towards the bedroom door. 'You probably wouldn't understand,' she embellished, more embarrassed by the second.

'And that would be because…?'

'You must know that you're a good-looking guy!' She wondered how the conversation had strayed so quickly from her simple enquiry as to what the plans were for the following day. 'I don't suppose mirrors pose a problem for you. Anyway—' she brushed aside the conversation, uncomfortable under his perceptive gaze '—you were talking about shopping. Why are we going shopping? There are loads of other things I'd rather be doing.'

'I'm in complete agreement with you there. However, you're going out with me now, we're engaged and it would seem odd for you to be seen wearing cheap off-the-peg clothes.'

Sammy's mouth dropped open. 'You said you weren't interested in telling me what I could or couldn't wear.'

'And I'm not, although I confess that I'm relieved you

took the decision yourself to put the jeans and baggy tops on the back burner while we're out here.'

'So if you don't care what I wear, then what's the shopping expedition all about?' she bristled, fired up at an implied insult behind the suggestion. 'I'll bet you've never hinted to any of those women you've been out with in the past that you wanted to take them shopping because you didn't like their choice of clothing!'

'That's a thought,' Leo murmured, remembering what she had said about not liking shopping experiences. He didn't get why she would feel self-conscious of her body because there was an earthy voluptuousness about her that was powerfully attractive.

His eyes wandered.

She had slender legs, and a waist that was a hand-span slim, but her breasts were generous and her hips were downright sinful in their curves, fashioned to be contoured by a man's hands.

He looked away, frowning at his brief loss of self-control.

'Maybe—' he thought of his exes and their minimalist approach to clothing '—I should have steered some of my past girlfriends to items of dress that weren't the size of paper tissues. A diet of relentlessly non-existent clothing can get very boring for a guy after a while.'

'You don't mean that.' But she was foolishly touched that he had made an effort to counteract any offence she might have taken by indulging in a little white lie.

'It's not about *what* you choose to wear. It's about the *quality* of what you choose to wear.'

'I can't afford to blow my savings on clothes,' Sammy told him abruptly.

'You probably could,' Leo countered with cool, restrained honesty, 'when this little charade is over. But that's by the by. What I'm saying is that any woman of mine would be expected to be wearing the very best. The very best in twinsets and pearls, if that happened to be her choice.'

Sammy stared at him and then she burst out laughing. 'You have got to be kidding!'

Leo frowned. 'Why would I be kidding?'

'Leo, I'm not the kind of girl who expects any man to buy her clothes for her! That's incredibly old-fashioned.'

'And what sort of girl would you be describing?' he enquired with the sort of shuttered expression that would have signalled a warning to her across the bows had she not still been smirking at the concept of a man paying for what she wore.

'Oh, just an airhead who traipses along from shop to shop, happy for you to dip into your wallet to fund her wardrobe.'

'Have you ever,' he asked, 'been treated to a shopping spree by one of these chauvinistic dinosaur guys you don't approve of?'

'Well…'

'So that's a *no*. Maybe you should give it a try before you start passing judgement. The fact of the matter is this, as my fiancée, you would be treated like a queen. There's no way I would countenance you going out in cheap supermarket bulk-buy clothes. You would wear the very best, in whatever you chose to wear.'

'I didn't get my outfits in a supermarket.'

'You know where I'm going with this, Sammy. Were this real, I would want you to be wearing the very best. It would give me pleasure to indulge you.'

Sammy went bright red. The deep, sexy timbre of

his voice conjured up an image of this big, powerful man entranced enough with a woman to be possessive, generous and proud.

'But it isn't real.' She headed straight back down to earth before wayward images in her head could start giving her a thrill that would have been utterly inappropriate.

'No,' Leo agreed smoothly, 'it isn't. But, since that's not the image we're aiming to project, you're just going to have to subject yourself to the torture of the shopping trip.' He raised his eyebrows and looked at her speculatively. 'Who knows…maybe you'll enjoy it more than you expect. And if at the end of this you're too proud to keep the clothes you've bought you can always hand them back to me. A charity shop would be more than happy to take the discards.'

Sammy couldn't dwell on any of that for long because she was wandering back off to the appalling prospect of sharing a bed with him. Somehow she had convinced herself to forget about that while they had been sparring but her apprehension swamped her all over again as she locked herself in the bathroom and took her time having the longest bath in living memory, while listening out to hear whether he had entered the bedroom.

Her very-respectable pyjamas were neatly folded on the little circular table in the enormous bathroom. She only wished she weren't so nervous because her nerves prevented her from enjoying what had to be the most luxurious bathing experience of her life. The bathroom was a vision of pale marble, oversized fluffy towels, a walk-in wet room and a bath big enough to stage a concert.

Just like that, she thought back to him asking her whether she had ever been treated to a shopping spree by a guy. She was very quick to condemn the thought of it, and she knew that she wasn't going to *have fun* choosing clothes which someone she barely knew was going to feel obliged to pay for, but, that said, here she was, enjoying the splendour of a hotel he was paying for.

What did that say? She had always prided herself on her ability to stand on her own two feet. From an early age, she and her mother had presented a united front, soldiering on after her father's premature death. She had learned how to carry the weight of responsibility on her shoulders and that had been truly put to the test when her mother had fallen ill.

She had also learned not to depend on something as frivolous as her looks to get her through and, yes, she had privately nurtured some scorn for those women who relied on their appearance to provide the rungs on the ladder they could use to clamber upwards.

She wasn't going to turn to crafty feminine traits to see her through!

But something about Leo made her feel feminine. She found herself responding to his blatant masculinity in ways that were girlish and light-headed. She had wanted him to compliment her on her choice of dress and she could only blame the bizarre nature of the situation for fostering unwanted responses.

She listened carefully at the bathroom door before pushing it open into the adjoining bedroom. She was fully dressed, bathrobe on for good measure, but in fact she need not have worked herself up into a lather because he wasn't in the bedroom. The vast four-poster bed, bigger than a normal king-sized bed, was untouched.

She wasn't about to hazard a peek outside to see what he was doing or even whether he was still in the suite. She might be covered from head to toe but there was something about being dressed in pyjamas…

She dived into the bed, burrowed down so far to one side that she was inches away from tumbling off, hunkered down for the long haul and eventually fell asleep.

When she woke, daylight was doing its best to wriggle past the floor-to-ceiling curtains, which were still tightly drawn.

And Leo was nowhere to be seen, although his side of the bed had definitely been slept in.

She had no idea when he had got into bed and no idea when he had got out of it. It was after nine and she freshened up in a rush, changing into a summery dress, a cheap and cheerful addition to her wardrobe, and a pair of canvas espadrilles. She combed her hair loosely over one shoulder so it fell in soft waves and tentatively left the sanctuary of the empty bedroom.

Leo had been on the verge of waking her because time was moving on but, whilst he rarely suffered from jet lag, he accepted that she might need to sleep off the disruption to her body clock.

He was also strangely reluctant to venture into the bedroom.

By the time he had finally made it to bed, she had been fast asleep, her breathing soft and even. As his eyes had adjusted to the darkness, he could see that she had kicked off the duvet, just as he could see that her prim and proper top had ridden up and, from the angle in which she was lying, he could just about make out the soft swell of the underside of her breast.

He had felt like a voyeur.

Riveted to the spot, he had felt himself harden and, for the first time in his life, he had been unable to control his wayward libido as he had remained glued to the spot, staring at that sliver of pale skin, barely visible at all.

He had seen more of the naked female form than most men but he couldn't recall the last time he had been held captive by a glimpse of a breast.

Thinking about those few seconds, when he had barely been able to breathe, was enough to ensure he remain just where he was, at the desk by the window, waiting for her to emerge.

'You're up.' He pushed himself away from the desk and folded his hands behind his head.

She looked fresh and very, very young. Her pale hair flowed over one shoulder and caught the sun pouring through the huge windows, brightening the strands to a silvery white. She looked wholesome and sexy at the same time, although he was certain that she was utterly unaware of how appealing the combination was.

'I'm sorry I overslept. How long have you been up?'

'Three hours.'

'You should have woken me.' But she was relieved that he hadn't. She shied away from thinking about him shaking her until she opened drowsy eyes and looked at him, both in the same bed, warm from their shared body heat. 'I'm ready to go now, anyway.'

'Breakfast?'

'I'm not hungry.' She was starving but nobly decided to ignore her hunger rather than risk those cool, assessing eyes watching her as she tucked into a plate full of food.

'Sure?'

Sammy nodded, walking towards her handbag, which she had left in the sitting area on a chair. She stole a sideways glance at him as he rose elegantly to follow her to the door, casting a last look at the suite before opening the door for her.

She could see why he was taking her shopping. Next to him, her clothes shrieked *bargain basement* and whilst he really didn't seem to mind what kind of clothes she chose to wear, he certainly cared about the price of them.

Outside, she breathed in the heat, revelling in the sun as it poured down on her shoulders, and, as they were ferried to the most expensive shopping street in the city, she looked left and right at the enormous diversity of the architecture.

Old and new jostled side by side. Coffee shops spilled onto pavements. There were elements of the past in the gracious Victorian buildings and arcades and elements of the ultra-modern in spacious glass and chrome buildings that housed offices and shops.

The yellow taxis and glimpses of trams held her rapt attention because it was all so different in ways she couldn't quite put her finger on.

They entered an ornate arcade and he took her hand in his, linking his fingers with hers.

It didn't matter how many times she reminded herself that this was a business arrangement, she still couldn't stop herself from reacting to him and she was doing it now. Heat flooded her body and she knew that her face was red because all she could focus on was the feel of his cool fingers entwined with hers.

They hit the first shop, which, under normal circumstances, would have been way out of her price range. She didn't need to peruse the racks of clothes to establish that. She could tell at a glance from the lack of price tags and the elegant glacial beauty of the two shop assistants.

It was a large boutique, white and clinical, with a high-tech spiral staircase leading to an upper area.

Sammy hesitated by the door and felt him gently tug her in. 'Where's the excitement?' he murmured, leaning down, his breath warm against her ear.

'I'm not sure this is the sort of place that would stock anything I would like…'

'You haven't looked.'

'I can tell from the racks.' She smiled weakly at the saleswoman whose eyes briefly scanned her then moved on to Leo.

'Nonsense!' He firmly ushered her forward and Sammy watched, entranced, as he charmed the blonde beauty. Somewhere along the line, she got the impression that the other woman had recognised him, although, of course, it would have been totally out of order for her to have said anything. The actress he had dated was world famous. It wouldn't have surprised her if half of Melbourne recognised him.

'Now, darling…' he turned to her, dark eyes shielded '…take your pick.' He leaned down and gently cupped the side of her face in his hand, his fingers grazing her hair, which was as soft as silk and smelled of flowers. He lingered for a few seconds, startled by how much he was enjoying the feel of it, slippery under his fingers. 'If you feel the clothes here are a little too modern or revealing for you, then say the word.'

She was only twenty-six years old but he made her

feel like a granny. Who could blame him, though? There was no denying her outfits had an old-fashioned flavour about them. It was brought sharply home to her just how much she had grown accustomed to hiding her figure behind baggy and unrevealing clothes. Comfort dressing was obviously a habit that she had become used to.

The soothing, patronising tone of his voice got her back up and she pursed her lips before smiling tightly at the shop assistant.

'Why don't you go and have a wander?' She reached up on tiptoe to cup his face just as he had done hers, going one step further and pressing her lips against his cheek. 'You don't want to spend your time sitting here looking at your watch while I try on outfits, do you? That'll be really boring for you.'

The show of loving familiarity was all for the benefit of their attentive spectators but Sammy still wasn't prepared when he curved both arms around her and drew her closely against him, angling her so that their bodies were neatly pressed together, his legs squarely planted apart to accommodate her between them.

Breathless, Sammy's eyes widened. Her whole body tingled and she was aware of herself, of every tiny pore and every strand of fine hair on her skin, in a way she had never been in her life before.

She shivered, as helpless in his embrace as a leaf being whipped along in a force ten gale. Instinctively, she leaned into him, overwhelmed with a sudden craving that shook her to the very core. This was much more than a kiss—this was the feel of his hard masculinity against her and it sent flames of desire licking through every part of her body.

Panicked, she flattened her hands against his chest but she wasn't allowed to push him back.

With a deep-throated growl of masculine satisfaction, Leo kissed her.

He wasn't into public displays of any sort, least of all when there was an audience, and there was very much an audience in the shop. Indeed, he had heard the sound of the door opening as more people entered but even that was not sufficient incentive to tear himself away from her.

What had started out as a little lesson to teach her that if she wanted to touch him to make a point then he was going to touch her right back to make an even bigger point had turned into something altogether different.

Way too different.

He drew back, releasing her abruptly, and it took a few seconds for his sudden withdrawal to register and, when it did, Sammy stepped smartly back, shaken to the core.

How had that happened? How had she *let* it happen? For a few long, long moments it had felt as though that kiss were the real thing, as though he were a real boyfriend. She just hoped that he hadn't sensed it. She smiled brightly at him but her eyes were unfocused.

Leo was looking at her narrowly. Had she intended to draw him into that kiss? His instinct was to have said no, but the way she had responded, throwing herself into it…

He had felt the yielding softness of her body beneath the cheap cotton dress, had felt the fullness of her breasts pushing against him. She had known just how to get to him with that little teasing taunt, just how to up the ante so that, for a minute there, he had well and truly lost sight of the fact that she wasn't one of his lovers.

She made a big song and dance about not liking the world of money, paparazzi and untold luxury into which she had been thrown but he knew women and he had never met one whose head hadn't been turned by the glimmer of what his money could buy them. In fairness, most of them had needed no persuasion to kick back and enjoy what he could give them, but because she had started reluctant didn't mean that she would end up that way.

He hoped she wouldn't start getting ideas because that would be inconvenient.

And, just in case she *did*, even if the thought was just a shadow, a barely formulated shadow at the back of her brain, then he would have to cool the shows of ardour.

Certainly no more loss of self-control, which was what had regrettably happened just then.

'I like the way you're learning to play to the audience,' he murmured, low enough for her to hear and with an intimate smile that would convey to anyone who might be looking that sweet nothings were being whispered. Typical of a couple besotted with one another.

'Learning to play… Yes, well.'

'You're a quick study.' He dealt her a slashing smile and she smiled tightly back. 'No more cold war. No more protesting…I like it. It'll make this a whole lot easier.' He stood back and smiled at the saleswoman, who was managing to keep her distance without losing her quarry. 'Take care of her.' He gave her a little reassuring squeeze and waited until the blonde had approached them with an ingratiating smile.

'Darling—' Sammy looked up at him with a smile

that oozed sugary sweetness '—don't make me sound so helpless!' She patted his cheek and their eyes met—hers blue, pushing the boundaries, his dark, knowing just what she was up to.

'I can't think of anyone less helpless than you,' Leo murmured with heartfelt sincerity. 'I'll return for you in an hour. Think that will be long enough for you?'

'Oh,' Sammy said breezily, 'I might have bought the entire shop by then!'

Their eyes tangled and she could see exactly what he was thinking.

Bought the entire shop? Hardly. You don't like shopping, you don't care about clothes... You'll head for the least daring racks and you'll be done in under fifteen minutes.

Sammy smiled. 'I think,' she said slowly, batting her lashes and frowning in a faraway manner, finger tapping the side of her mouth, head tilted to one side, 'I might actually need a little longer. Why don't we meet at Giles King's offices at three?' Was this what being assertive with a man was like? It felt good, particularly when Leo frowned, caught on the back foot by a suggestion he hadn't anticipated.

It dawned on her that he was accustomed to calling the shots in every single area of his life. As far as he was concerned, he was paying her for her participation in this charade and he didn't expect her to do anything but follow his lead. She smiled brightly at him.

'You don't know where his offices are,' Leo pointed out.

'I think I'm smart enough to make my way there. I know the name of his firm.' She turned to the blonde, who was watching this exchange with fascinated interest. 'Men. They really *do* like to think of us as the weaker species, don't they?'

'I would never dream of being so cavalier where you are concerned, my sweet.' Leo wasn't sure whether to be amused by these antics, impressed by her ingenuity because she was putting on a show of loving familiarity that would have taken some beating, or uneasy because he wasn't on familiar ground and he had no idea where she was heading with this show of independence.

Then he relaxed.

Where could she possibly be going? As always, he had everything under control and, in the meantime, well, who ever said that life had to be predictable *all* of the time?

He thought that he might just start enjoying the next week and a half...

CHAPTER SIX

IT WAS A mad rush. Who knew that choosing some clothes and having bits and pieces done could actually take up so much of a person's time?

She'd whizzed through the shop, enjoying the heady feeling of having the snooty saleswoman bend over backwards to make sure she got exactly what she wanted.

Before they'd left the hotel, with Sammy still in protest mode at being told that her clothes were too cheap to be seen in when she was supposed to be engaged to him, he had urged her to buy whatever she wanted.

He already had details of her bank account and he had told her that if she didn't want him handing over his credit card to a salesperson because it went against her feminist instincts then she was free to use her own— he would ensure sufficient money was deposited into her account to cover all costs. He'd named a sum that had stunned her into silence and had shrugged when she had told him that she wouldn't know how to spend that amount of money because surely a few items of clothing couldn't cost very much.

Her plan had been to select the least outrageously expensive items of clothing and, likewise, the least flamboyant.

Plans, she discovered, could change in a heartbeat.

At the end of forty-five minutes in the boutique, and another forty-five minutes in two other boutiques farther along in the shady, exclusive arcade, she was weighed down by several bags, and two hours after that the hands holding those bags had been manicured and the feet shod in some rather delightful sandals, which were far more attractive than her canvas shoes and the hair... She felt like a million dollars.

But it had been an almighty rush. She hadn't been able to stop for food and, without breakfast, her stomach was intent on reminding her that sustenance was a lot more important than appearance.

And, for the first time in her life, Sammy didn't agree. She just had time to dash to the hotel, dump all the bags, change clothes and make sure she looked the part before she was back out to the car, which was on permanent standby just for her.

Now, with barely seconds to spare, she gazed at the graceful Victorian building that housed the law firm Leo was using to represent his interests.

Drawing in a deep breath, she purposefully strode towards the grey brick building, checked in at reception and was shown towards a conference room on the first floor.

Tension knotted her stomach. Nerves at the thought of the meeting that lay ahead and nerves at the new look she was sporting and how that new look would be received.

Did she look silly? she wondered.

She had felt so confident in the shop but then the saleswoman was in the business for a reason; she was adept at flogging very expensive clothes to women and part of her tactics would involve lavish praise and over-the-top compliments.

She told herself that instead of focusing on her silly clothes she should focus instead on what really mattered, which was the fate of a five-year-old girl whose life could be changed forever by what went on in that conference room.

This wasn't her. This person in shiny, expensive new clothes, seeking other people's approval and admiration. This wasn't her and it wasn't how she had been brought up!

Chin up, priorities firmly back in place, she took a deep breath and confidently entered the room, brushing past the young girl who had stepped back, holding the door open for her.

She only faltered for a second.

The room was absolutely enormous and there was nothing old-fashioned about the decor. A long, sleek table, so highly polished that it was as reflective as a mirror, dominated the central area, long enough to seat twenty people comfortably. To the back was a small circle of chairs and one wall was taken up with a white screen for presentations. There was a laptop in front of every chair. By the window, a sideboard, of the same highly polished wood as the conference table, housed coffee and tea-making facilities and plates of biscuits and tiny cakes, none of which appeared to have been touched.

Sammy took in all of this in a matter of seconds but, even as she was absorbing the surroundings, she remained entirely focused on the people sitting at that long conference table.

Leo easily dominated the group of eight. He was

sprawled back in his chair, which he had pushed away from the table, and his face was thoughtful and shuttered. He looked exactly like what he was—a lean, dangerous predator out to win.

But her eyes lingered on him for only a few moments because almost immediately she noticed the woman sitting directly opposite him and she knew, without having to be told, that this was Gail Jamieson.

She was small. Even sitting, Sammy could tell that she was no taller than five-two, maybe less, and she was the sort of woman who made jaws drop and caused heads to turn.

Her hair was a big bouffant and very blond, and her face tried desperately to belie her age, but the work she'd had done, rather than making her seem younger than her years, had somehow managed to age her.

Her eyes were wide and unblinking, her skin unnaturally line-free and her lips were pillowy and painted a bright fuchsia-pink, perfectly matching the colour of her formal suit which, likewise, matched her high stilettos.

She sought Leo, who had risen to greet her, and when he enfolded her in a brief embrace she wanted to stay there because she knew that the second she was released she would be in the firing line of Gail and her bank of representatives.

She had come out to play hardball and she wasn't going to pretend otherwise.

The conversation, the discussion of technicalities, voices being raised, Gail stridently talking over her lawyer and Leo responding coldly and with the sort of utter self-composure that should have been seen as a warning of armoury ready and poised for action passed in a blur and before she knew it the meeting was over.

As Sammy followed Leo—who was talking in a low, urgent voice to one of his lawyers—out of the room, Gail strode towards her.

'Funny,' Gail said, tugging Sammy to a stop, 'Sean never mentioned you when he spoke about his step-brother.'

'Er…'

'And he spoke about Leo *a lot*. But never mentioned you. Not once. Funny that, wouldn't you say?'

'Why is it funny?' Sammy finally found her voice. She darted a look at Leo, who had not noticed that she had been held back. He had his hands in his pockets and she could see from his body language that he was one hundred per cent focused on whatever was being said to him.

'Because…'

Bright pink nails dug into Sammy's arm. When Sammy looked down she was skewered by light blue, unblinking eyes.

'Because he followed everything Leo did, and I mean *everything*. Knew who Leo was going out with almost before he was going out with them! But he never mentioned you. Not once. So I'm just curious as to how it is that Leo's suddenly engaged to be married. To someone he didn't know from Adam two months ago.'

'Love.'

Leo's voice was deep and dark and held just the tiniest hint of menace.

Sammy felt his arm around her waist and she leant into him, relieved beyond belief that he had interrupted what showed promise of being a difficult exchange.

'Ever experienced that, Gail? Or has the love of a good deal always won out over the love of a good man?'

Gail's lips pursed. Her ample bosom heaved. Every strand of heavily dyed blond hair seemed to bristle with rage.

'Over my dead body,' she spat, 'are you going to get the kid. And don't think that you can fool me into thinking that you're suddenly Mr Respectable because you happen to show up here with some woman wearing an engagement ring.'

'I hope this isn't the sound of you spoiling for a fight,' Leo drawled. 'Because I don't like fighting but if I have to, I always emerge the winner.'

The pack of lawyers had disappeared, shooting off in separate directions.

'I've brought that kid up like she was my own!'

'Then I shudder to think what sort of upbringing your daughter was subjected to,' Leo informed her coldly. 'From what I've unearthed about you, a life of alcohol with a revolving door of unsuitable younger men hardly sounds like a woman who should have possession of a child.'

'Adele relies on me. I'm all she's known since she was born. Louise and Sean had their problems and I had the kid in my care more regularly than they did.'

'I have neither the inclination nor the time to get into an argument with you. If you want a fight, then fight through our lawyers. Don't ever let me find you trying to sideline my fiancée into any sort of conversation or, worse, trying to intimidate her in any way whatsoever. Do you read me loud and clear?'

He hadn't bothered to look in Gail's direction when he said this and his voice was calm and perfectly modulated but, even so, Sammy felt a shiver of apprehension on behalf of the other woman should she decide to ignore the warning.

And Gail must have felt the same. Her bravado evaporated as they stepped back outside into the sweltering heat and the pulsing throng of people in shorts and tee shirts.

'I don't want to fight either.' Her voice was plaintive. 'If it comes to it, I just want what's fair for me and all the time I've put in with the kid. If it weren't for me…'

'I've already heard that tale of self-sacrifice.' Leo's arm was still draped possessively over Sammy's shoulders and he was looking at Gail now, through narrowed eyes. 'It failed to impress me the first time and it fails to impress me now.'

Sammy found that she had been holding her breath and she expelled it in one long, shuddering sigh of relief as the older woman merged into the crowds, a dollop of bright pink that was visible as she weaved along the pavements, finally vanishing round a corner.

'Wow,' she said weakly. 'She's a force of nature.'

'She's an idiot for thinking she can win this.'

'She scared me,' Sammy confessed. 'I understand now why you felt you had to show up here with me in tow. I thought you had been exaggerating.'

His arm was still around her and she was suddenly self-conscious of how she looked. She had been talked into a long skirt that was light and fell beautifully to her ankles in various tie-dyed shades of apricot and grey. It was the height of modesty but the top twinned to go with it lovingly curved over her full breasts, dipping to expose just a hint of cleavage. The overall effect was one that made her look sexy and respectable at the same time. She had twirled in front of that mirror in the boutique and marvelled that she even had the ability to pull off a look like that.

She had thought that she would be excruciatingly self-conscious walking into that room in the lawyer's office but, in fact, she had barely been aware of what she was wearing.

'I hadn't expected her there.' There had been other things Leo hadn't been expecting, the way his *fiancée* looked in that outfit being one of them. She'd walked into that room and every head had turned in her direction and his stomach had clenched as he'd taken in those darting, quickly concealed looks of appreciation from the men in the room. Including his own top lawyer who was fifty if he was a day, short and balding. Hope, he had thought grimly, certainly sprang eternal. Which hadn't made him any the less annoyed.

'I think—' he found his eyes straying to the sway of her heavy breasts and had to force himself to look away '—she decided that if she caught everyone on the hop then she might have the element of surprise.'

As if by magic, their car was pulling to the kerb, slowing for them to hop in, which was a blessed relief because it was so hot and humid. The long skirt was far cooler than trousers or anything shorter or tighter, but Sammy had still started perspiring within moments of leaving the lawyer's air-conditioned office.

Resting against the seat with her eyes closed for a couple of seconds, Sammy then turned to look at Leo. 'I barely took in what was going on. I was very nervous.'

'Legal back and forth,' Leo said drily. 'I've sat through enough meetings with lawyers to know that it's a very delicate rally that gets played in any situation where two sides are trying to meet.'

'*Are* you trying to meet? I mean—in the middle with Gail?'

Leo dealt her a cool sideways smile. 'I'm prepared to make some concessions. Louise and Sean made lousy parents and there's some truth in what she says, that the care of Adele fell on her shoulders more than should have been necessary. I've done extensive background checks on the woman, however. And, whilst she was technically in charge of her granddaughter, everything she says has to be taken with a pinch of salt. She's been demanding and receiving vast sums of money from my father and, well, you can see for yourself where some of that money has gone. There have been some plastic surgeons rubbing their hands in glee every time she's phoned to make an appointment. I know down to the last penny where the money's gone.' He shrugged. 'But if she doesn't put up a fight, then I'm willing to leave her with some cash.'

'She doesn't believe that this is a real engagement,' Sammy mused cautiously.

Her body tensed then flamed as he ran his eyes very, very slowly over her. She hadn't thought he'd noticed what she was wearing and then she'd decided that it wasn't her place to feel disappointed if he hadn't commented because there was no reason for him to. He'd noticed. It was there in the heat of his brooding, fabulous eyes. By the time he had finished his leisurely inspection of her, her face was bright red and she would have told him in no uncertain terms that *looking at her like that* wasn't part of the arrangement except she had enjoyed every heat-filled second of that visual appraisal.

'Maybe she had her doubts when the news was first broken to her that I was no longer going to fit into the role of inveterate womaniser and unsuitable guardian which she had hoped for… Maybe she showed up here today with the express purpose of making sure her lawyers got on board with her way of thinking…but I think it's fair to say that after today…'

'I know what you're saying,' Sammy told him, breaking eye contact to find that the palms of her hands were slippery with perspiration and that had nothing to do with the temperature in the car. 'You were right. It would have looked peculiar if I had been wearing my department store clothes. Especially given that the woman looks as though she would be able to tell designer from fake without any trouble at all.'

'So good thinking. You chose just the right mix of daring and prudish. No one could doubt that you were a respectable teacher with just the right amount of sex appeal.'

'To attract a man of your high standards?' He'd noticed her but only insofar as she had chosen the right clothes for the job at hand. She gave a tinkling laugh that implied that she knew exactly what he meant.

'You're putting words into my mouth.' He wondered whether she was aware of just how incredibly erotic that alluring mix of daring and prudish actually was. He had given his lawyer some background details on her so they were all predisposed to think of her as highly respectable, moral, responsible—a shining example of just the sort of woman any man would bring home to his mother.

That said, had she looked too much like the moral, respectable teacher, they would all have been a bit bemused because how could a guy reasonably go from an actress whose face graced billboards to a teacher who was camera-shy and modestly dressed? Gail was astute. She would have sniffed out a phoney from a hundred paces and Sammy, resentful in borrowed clothing, would have been easily sniffed out. Better she be comfortable than bristling with transparent resentment.

But her choice of dress had been nothing short of inspired.

When they arrived back at the hotel he suggested dinner at one of the several excellent restaurants in the hotel. She could take her pick.

Sammy had forgotten all about her hunger pangs. Now, they resurfaced with a vengeance and no sooner had they sat down and bread was brought to them than she tucked in. To heck with pretending that she had the appetite of a sparrow, she thought.

'I'm ravenous,' she confessed, resisting the urge to help herself to more bread. 'What were you talking to your lawyer about? When we were leaving?'

'I don't think I've ever heard any woman admit to being ravenous.'

'I used to try dieting when I was younger but I gave up after a while. If you're hungry, I don't see the point of starving yourself.'

Sammy thought that since theirs was a phoney relationship based on necessity on both sides, there was no need to try and be someone she wasn't. She'd been out with guys in the past and she'd always been conscious of trying hard to be as ladylike as possible, which, in restaurants, had meant ordering healthy salads and dishes with weird ingredients that sounded good for you. But she wasn't out to impress Leo and he certainly wasn't open to being impressed by her. For him, she was a means to an end. She didn't have to edit her personality at all. She was the hired help. He touched her when he had to and when he looked at her, the way he had done just then, his dark eyes lazy and speculative, the only thing he was speculating about was how convincing she would be in her choice of clothing and whether there was anything else she could do to make sure he got what he had come to get.

'Watching their weight is part of some women's livelihoods.' He was fascinated by the enthusiasm with which she was working her way through her hearty starter of aubergine *parmigiana*.

'Of course it's important to be healthy. This is delicious. I don't do much eating out in expensive restaurants. On a teacher's salary, cheap and cheerful is usually all I can afford, and especially with the money problems Mum's been having.'

'As you know, my father offered her money countless times.'

'She's proud. She would never accept anything from your dad. I was surprised when she seemed to be all for this charade, though. I think it's a relief for her to know that I'll be getting something I've wanted for a really long time out of it and that it's not just about making sure that the mortgage is paid off.'

Plates were cleared. Wine was poured. She looked the most relaxed he had seen her since they had arrived in the country and he assumed that that was because the first steps had been taken towards resolving what they had come for.

The wine was also having its effect. She was on her second glass. He didn't think that she would be someone accustomed to drinking much alcohol.

Funny, he had known her for a long time and yet

he felt as though he was getting to know her for the *first* time.

She had ordered a pie for her main course. It arrived with much fanfare and he couldn't help grinning as she tucked into it, taking a few seconds first to appreciate the mouthwatering beauty of the golden pastry and the rich red wine gravy bubbling through the crusty lid.

Sammy could feel his eyes on her but when he spoke it was to say, pensively, 'I'm beginning to realise that a woman who doesn't enjoy her food is probably not a woman worth going out with.'

'What do you mean?' Sammy looked at him, her wide, bright blue eyes startled.

'There's something extremely sensual about food, wouldn't you agree? About someone who appreciates the pleasure of eating.'

Confused, Sammy, fork poised in mid-air and mouth half-open, was excruciatingly aware of Leo watching her as she ate a mouthful of the delicious beef and celeriac pie.

Leo watched her. It was an intoxicating sight. She was so unlike any woman he had ever been attracted to before. He could imagine that she was the sort of woman who came with all sorts of fairy-tale daydreams and unrealistic fantasies about happy-ever-after and soulmates. The sort who secretly collected bridal magazines and dreamed of having a dozen kids. A woman who came fully equipped with high moral values, which was why, he was forced to concede, she was so disapproving of him.

Disapproving but not immune.

With instincts that barely registered on any kind of conscious scale, Leo knew that.

It was there in the tide of colour that flooded her cheeks whenever he looked at her for a second longer than was strictly necessary.

Like now.

It was there in the way she lowered her eyes and half turned away when she was caught looking at him.

And it had been there in her reaction to him every single time he had touched her.

She'd quivered, as if her whole body had suddenly come alive with an undercurrent of electricity over which she had no control.

Sammy cleared her throat and frantically tried to find something innocuous to say to break the sudden electric tension stretching between them.

'You...you were going to tell me what you were chatting to your lawyer about. When Ms Jamieson got me to one side. Um...'

'Was I?'

'Stop...stop looking at me like that.'

'Like what?' Leo raised his eyebrows in amused query.

Squirming because she was so out of her comfort zone, Sammy licked her lips nervously and looked away. 'Is there something you want to say about, um, about the way I look?'

'Yes,' Leo said gravely and Sammy's eyes flew towards him in sudden consternation.

'You said that my choice of dress was...that you liked what I had selected to wear.'

'Do you want honesty from me?'

'I don't know. Maybe not.' Sammy was blushing furiously.

'Okay.' Leo shrugged.

The conversation resumed on less contentious matters. Leo had been to the country several times, although only to Melbourne twice, and over the rest of the meal he proved a witty companion, full of interesting anecdotes about the places he had been. She truly began to appreciate the extent of his vast wealth as he told her about the properties he owned, scattered across the globe. She listened, asked questions and kept thinking, *did she want his honesty?* What did he think he had to be *honest* about?

'You might as well tell me,' she said in a rush, putting down her fork next to the chocolate brownie dessert she was halfway through.

Leo had known that sooner or later she would ask him to explain what he had meant, although if she hadn't he had resolved not to push the issue. He was attracted to her and there was a danger in that situation. He had agreed to this charade, and to his father's choosing her as a candidate to help pull it off, because he had known that she would be a safe proposition. Sex complicated things and he had not wanted complications. Eventually persuaded by his father to undertake this mission, he had come to the conclusion that in and out as fast as possible would be his approach. Complications of any sort were to be avoided at all costs.

He signalled for the tab to sign but didn't take his eyes off her face. 'There is a small bar area farther along from the restaurant. They serve very good coffee.'

Sammy nodded. 'Just say what you have to say,' she half pleaded, tripping along beside him as he led the way to the cosy sitting area which, presumably, he had used before when he hadn't been in the suite with her. It was a perfect place to work in peace. Secluded, quiet, tucked away in a spot that was far from noise and crowds.

The fact that he was shying away from telling her what he had to tell her said something. It said that he knew she wouldn't be happy with whatever it was he had to say. Maybe his lawyer had said something to him during that little chat they had had when the meeting had come to a close.

She felt like a trainee about to be told that she hadn't, unfortunately, passed her probation because her work had not been up to scratch.

'When I agreed to do this—' he waited until she was sitting and then sat opposite her, adjusting his chair to accommodate the length of his body '—I decided that you were as ideal as it got for the job.'

'I know.' Defensiveness had crept into her voice. 'You knew how to get to me because of Mum. You knew that the money would be invaluable and you knew that my dream was to start my own freelance business so you had a good idea of what you could put down on the table to ensure I was left without much of a choice.'

'Spare me the victim speech, Sammy. You could have said no. We all have choices.'

'You thought I was convincingly *ordinary*,' she elaborated with grudging honesty. 'Have you decided that I'm just *too* ordinary? Because I don't know how I can overcome that. I can't turn into someone I'm not.'

Leo looked at her for so long that she began to fidget. 'You're not what I'd expected,' he said silkily. 'I'm seeing things I never saw before when we happened to bump into one another in the past.'

Sammy's mouth ran dry. She opened her mouth to

say something but nothing emerged. She had no idea where he was going with this. She felt as though she had deliberately jumped into the path of an unstoppable train and would have to live with the consequences. If she could break eye contact she might be able to do something sensible like stand up and leave, but she couldn't seem to do anything but stare.

'There's something about you,' he murmured roughly, his sharp eyes taking in every small reaction in her expressive face. He'd never made a pass at any woman without knowing the outcome in advance. In fact, he'd seldom had to make passes at all. But this was different and he felt a swift adrenaline rush as he contemplated laying his cards on the table without fully knowing how she would react.

He wanted her. It made no sense and it was a nuisance, but she appealed to him in ways that were visceral and primitive and beyond his control.

He knew that he could keep trying to impose common sense but wouldn't it just be easier to scratch that itch? They were both adults and he suspected that she was as interested in exploring the chemistry between them that had blown up as he was. The fact that he wasn't *entirely* sure, instead of being a turn-off, had fired up his libido even more.

'Something about me?' Sammy squeaked.

'You're sexy,' Leo admitted in a roughened undertone. 'I can't seem to look at you without wondering what it would be like to take your clothes off.'

Sammy was having severe trouble breathing. Was he joking? Was this some kind of sadistic lead up to something really offensive he wanted to say?

'Of course I'm not,' she breathed shakily and he

reached out and played with her fingers, toying with them and sending her scattered nerves every which way.

'And not just when you decide to make the most of your fantastic figure,' Leo assured her. 'So this has created a situation I hadn't banked on having to deal with.' He shot her a crooked smile that sent her blood pressure doing all sorts of irregular things. 'We're sharing a bed,' he told her bluntly, 'and I'm not going to beat around the bush. I want you. And I sense you want me, too.'

'Do you?' Sammy's voice was barely audible. 'I… I don't…'

'No?' He leaned forward suddenly, catching her by surprise. He reached out, hand curving at the nape of her neck, and drew her towards him. It was as if she had been hovering like a satellite circling a magnetic force which was warm and bright and irresistible and now that magnetic force was pulling her in and she wanted to go.

She could barely gasp before his mouth covered hers and his kiss was long and gentle and she fell into it with the ease of a hapless swimmer getting caught in a whirlpool. It just sucked her in. She closed her eyes, shifted closer, knew that she should push him back but couldn't find the strength.

He thought that she was sexy.

Her fingers trembled as they came into contact with his dark hair. This was the riskiest thing she had ever done in her entire life. Nothing else came close. He was so out of her league that they barely inhabited the same planet and yet here she was, kissing him and never wanting that kiss to stop.

She moaned softly.

This was her fantasy guy, the guy who had played a starring role in her adolescent daydreams.

A guy any woman would give her right arm to find herself in a clinch with—just like this one.

A guy who wasn't hers.

Cold, brutal reality asserted itself and she tore herself away from the embrace. She was shaking like a leaf. Her lips felt swollen and bruised from where he had kissed her and she had to resist wiping the back of her hand across them.

This wasn't about love or even affection. She was in a make-believe situation with a make-believe fiancé who would never have looked at her twice under normal circumstances.

Suddenly he found her sexy?

Hilarious. She had met him countless times over the years and he had never found her sexy on any of those occasions. Maybe his eyes had changed over time, maybe he needed specs.

Overcome with mortification at how easily she had leapt to that kiss, she was brutal with herself as she wrapped her arms around her body and looked at him.

'I don't want to…I'm not interested…'

'Sure about that?'

'And I think it's best we just put that behind us and remember that we're…remember that this isn't *real*.'

'The engagement isn't real,' Leo affirmed in a low, husky voice. 'My wanting to get you into bed, on the other hand, couldn't be more real.' He abruptly sat back and relaxed into his chair. 'But if you want to kid yourself that it's a one-way street, then that's fine by me. Moving on to what you asked me, I was talking to my lawyer about Adele. We meet her tomorrow.'

Head spinning from the change of subject, Sammy could only stare at him. He'd drawn her in only to suddenly drop her from a great height and he couldn't have been clearer in telling her that he might fancy her, and she still found that impossible to imagine, but he could take her or leave her at the end of the day. It was up to her.

Her brain struggled to focus on what really mattered.

'Tomorrow.'

'She will be delivered here to the hotel at lunchtime. It's been quite an achievement and Gail fought tooth and nail against it but she lost. She only found out when she spoke to her lawyer after the meeting today.'

He stood, waiting for her to follow suit. They were about to head for the bedroom, for the king-sized bed that would suddenly feel as big as a matchbox after what he had said. Her skin tingled at the prospect of getting into it with him.

'Don't worry,' he murmured, reading her mind or maybe her expression of full-blown panicked apprehension, as they headed for the bank of lifts to take them to their suite. 'I've never forced myself on a woman and I don't intend to start now. I have work to do when we get back and by the time I get into that bed you will already be sound asleep. Unless, of course, you decide that sex between two consenting adults who are attracted to one another is worth exploring...' He laughed when she pointedly ignored him and grazed his finger along her cheek, keen eyes watching the heat of her reaction.

'Sweet dreams,' he called as she disappeared into the bedroom but before she could shut the door on him. 'And don't forget—we're engaged... It's only natural to take things to their final conclusion!'

CHAPTER SEVEN

LEO HAD THROWN down his gauntlet. He'd been nothing but truthful when he had told her that being attracted to her had been an unforeseen curveball. She had skittered away like a Victorian maiden, shrieking with pious moral outrage, but then he'd kissed her and she had melted into his arms. He had needed no further evidence that she would be his.

Naturally, he wasn't going to pursue her.

He had been taken aback when they reached the suite to discover that she seemed to be sticking to her *hands off* moral high ground. She had stood in front of the bedroom door, like a bouncer on a mission to deter unwanted riff-raff, and informed him that she would be having a bath and perhaps he could make good on his promise to work until she had fallen asleep.

She had actually used the term *make good*, while he had stared at her as it had slowly dawned on him that she might just be sticking to her guns.

Leo had been genuinely confused. He'd taken the rash decision to bypass common sense and lay his cards on the table and, having done so, he had been gratified to find that the attraction worked both ways.

So where was the problem?

He had hit the bedroom an hour and a half after she had disappeared and had found her barricaded on her side of the bed, with two of the sausage-shaped cushions separating them.

He had woken at five-thirty, as he always did, wherever in the world he happened to be, and she had given no indication that she was awake. Her back had resolutely been turned to him and she hadn't moved a muscle as he'd made for the bathroom, showered, dressed and then exited the bedroom.

For the first time in living memory, Leo was finding it impossible to concentrate on work.

He kept looking at the closed bedroom door as the time ticked by. What was she doing? Was she up? Getting dressed? Abseiling down the side of the building in an attempt to get away from him?

He was distracted and he didn't like it. He was making himself a cup of coffee when the bedroom door finally opened so he remained where he was, lounging against the kitchen wall, cup in hand, watching her over the rim of it as he sipped his coffee.

'Get you some?' He raised the mug towards her and Sammy nodded politely.

Whilst she felt as though the bags under her eyes were as big as suitcases and just as obvious, he looked as fresh as a daisy.

And as drop-dead gorgeous as she'd hoped he wouldn't.

She'd heard him the second he had slipped out of the bed and every nerve in her body had tensed. Then he'd run his shower, not even bothering to shut the bathroom door fully behind him, and she'd sneaked a surreptitious glance at him, peeking out from where she was safely cocooned under the sheets and blanket. Her heart had almost stopped beating. He had taken his jeans into the bathroom with him and he was as indecently clad as any human could be whilst wearing trousers.

The top button was undone, the zip slightly down and, in the back light from the bathroom, she could make out every detail of his sinewy and completely bare upper half. The jeans rode low down lean hips and as he padded to the chest of drawers, quietly retrieving a tee shirt, she was treated to perfection in motion. He'd slipped the tee shirt over his head and she had squeezed her eyes tightly shut and drawn her breath in sharply because watching the ripple of muscle was just too much.

She had felt light-headed. How on earth was she going to be able to keep him at arm's length? No, more to the point, how on earth was she going to keep *herself* away from him at arm's length?

She'd never been so tempted by anyone in her entire life and she couldn't understand how it was that someone like him, who had absolutely *none* of the qualities she looked for in a man, would be the person to tempt her.

She had waited until he had shut the bedroom door behind him, then she had nodded off briefly before waking up and listening to make sure that he was well and truly absorbed in his work outside.

She'd felt like a thief, hiding out in a closet, forced to keep perfectly silent or else risk being caught red-handed with the family heirlooms.

Except what did she have to be sneaky about?

She'd kissed him back but then she'd pulled away and let him know in no uncertain terms that she was not up for a romp in the hay. She had stood her ground and she had retired to bed rather proud of herself.

The trouble was that her body refused to play along. She'd never found herself in the position of having to exercise denial when it came to a guy and denial physically *hurt*. Between her legs had throbbed and her breasts had ached. Her whole body had felt as though it needed to be touched and, lying in the darkness, her mind had been filled with images of him caressing her, taking her...

But Sammy knew that she couldn't allow herself to forget that this was a game. It would be dangerous to start blurring the edges between fiction and reality.

Consequently, she had dressed for the day ahead in the most sensible of the outfits she had bought.

It was going to be baking hot outside. She wasn't sure what the plans for the day were but she assumed that he would spend the morning working. At any rate, she would encourage him to do so, which would leave her free to explore the city until Adele was dropped off at midday.

She was wearing pale blue flip-flops, loose-fitting cotton trousers, also pale blue in colour, and a loose-fitting sleeveless top, patterned with a riot of tiny flowers that stopped at the waist so that when she moved a little sliver of tummy was visible. She had tied her hair in a high ponytail and escaped tendrils framed her heart-shaped face.

Leo took his time looking at her and when she blushed, he grinned and shrugged.

'I won't touch. At least not unless the occasion demands it.' He held his hands up in a gesture of mock surrender. 'But,' he drawled, 'I never promised that I wouldn't look.'

He turned around, fixed her a mug of coffee and sauntered towards her. Her blue eyes were wary but stubborn and he liked that.

'You shouldn't look at me like that,' Sammy said shakily.

'I can't help it.' He handed her the mug but he didn't move back. Instead, he remained towering over her, crowding her.

'I'm not going to sleep with you.'

'Did you hear me ask?'

'No, but...'

'I'm not going to pretend that I don't want to, though,' he said pensively, sipping the excellent coffee, amused when she shimmied away from him. He wondered whether she was scared that she might be driven to touch if she stayed too close to him.

His whole body went into overdrive when he imagined her coming to him, unable to fight the force of their mutual attraction.

'What are your plans for the day?' Sammy thought that if she didn't change the conversation he would carry on looking at her with those brooding, amazing, fabulously sexy eyes and she would go up in flames.

'*My* plans?'

'I thought as we aren't due to meet Adele until lunchtime that you might want to get some work done.'

'Why would you think that?'

'Because you obviously have a lot on your plate. I mean, you don't get to bed until very late and you're up early so that you can catch up.'

'A wild number of misconceptions in that statement,'

Leo said lazily. 'I'm my own boss. I'm not a hamster on a treadmill, running furiously for fear of getting left behind. And yes, I don't happen to need much sleep but I assure you that I would be more than happy to hit the sack early and get out of it late if the incentive was right...'

'Will you stop doing that!' But it turned her on. Why bother to pretend otherwise? She *liked* the way his eyes on her made her feel. She *enjoyed* the slow, crazy burn she got when he talked like that, saying things that made her feel sexy and feminine, which were two things she had never felt in her life before. He was the equivalent of a slab of wicked, wicked chocolate. You wanted it so much but you knew that you had to fight the temptation because one bite wouldn't be enough and it certainly wouldn't be good for you.

'I wouldn't dream of leaving you to your own devices today,' he said, pocketing his cell phone and heading towards the door. 'We'll get breakfast, then do some city exploring and get back here in time to meet Adele.'

Sammy knew when she was beaten. She hoped he wouldn't wage his devastating assault on her senses. She found herself fast-forwarding to conversations they might or might not have. She braced herself to keep pushing him back.

She was disproportionately disappointed when the morning passed with him being the perfect gentleman.

He held her hand but he didn't try to kiss her. He looked at her, but those looks didn't linger longer than necessary. She had expected to spend three hours rigid with tension but he seduced her into talking about herself and, afterwards, she couldn't imagine how he had done that.

How had he managed to bypass her guard?

'Are you nervous?' she asked as they were making their way back to the hotel.

'About what?' Leo looked at her with a frown. It had taken more willpower than he knew he possessed not to touch her.

'Seeing Adele.'

'The only thing I'm nervous about is this custody battle not going in my favour. My father wouldn't recover.'

'Have you spoken to him?' Sammy's voice softened for she was hugely fond of the elderly man.

'Two emotionally charged emails and one phone call where he sounded as though a nervous breakdown wasn't far away. This has to work out. There's no choice.'

'Do you have much experience of children?'

'Is that a necessity?'

'It helps.'

'I don't.' He turned to her as they entered the cool of the hotel lobby. 'So it's just as well that I have someone by my side who can make up for my shortfall, isn't it?'

He looked past her and then pulled her close to him and dropped a kiss on her head.

Sammy had followed his eyes and almost immediately her heart went out to the child sitting on one of the long grey sofas in the lobby, next to a man she recognised as one of the lawyers from the other side.

Adele was a pretty little thing, with long dark hair caught in two braids which ended in pink ribbons, neatly tied into bows. They matched her dress and her shiny patent plastic shoes. She was sitting ramrod straight, her hands folded on her lap and next to her was a bright pink bag. Not a backpack but a handbag. Her face was small and serious and she looked terrified.

Leo hadn't seen her for well over a year. Suddenly, the enormity of his undertaking was brought home to him. This wasn't a deal. There was no company involved, no stock market to follow in the wake of a deal, no factory that might or might not need to be closed, no redundancies to be handled and workforce to be relocated. This was a living, breathing child and he tensed.

Sammy felt it. He had faltered. No one would have noticed, but *she* did. She looped her arm through his without looking at him, took a deep breath and headed directly for the little girl who was primly sitting on the grey sofa.

'Hi.' She ignored the lawyer, who had risen and taken Leo to one side so that they could have a confab. 'I'm Sammy.' She knelt down so that she was on eye level with Adele. She was accustomed to young children. She was comfortable around them and she knew how to make them feel comfortable around her. It was part and parcel of being a good teacher.

Leo watched her. The lawyer was busily telling him about the arrangements that had been secured for the day and the outcome of the long meeting they had the day before. Leo heard everything but his attention was riveted to the woman kneeling in front of the little girl. All her natural warmth was on show. She was very tactile, was resting her hand on Adele's arm, and he could see the way the child was being drawn into whatever she was being told.

Compared to her, his girlfriends of the past, with their frantic self-absorption, now struck him as somewhat brittle.

There was an earthy, engaging and entirely uncontrived sexiness about his fake fiancée that kept turning him on. He dragged his attention away to finalise details of handing Adele back to the lawyer and then, lawyer gone, he joined the twosome, standing above them until Sammy straightened.

Introductions were made. Adele stared at him with huge navy blue eyes and noticeably cringed back.

'What now?' Leo asked roughly, on the back foot for the first time in his life.

Sammy gave Adele's hand a tiny reassuring squeeze. 'Leave it to me.' She stood on tiptoe and impulsively kissed the side of his mouth because he looked uncertain and weirdly vulnerable and she liked that. She liked knowing that, for the first time in his life, probably, he wasn't quite in control of a situation.

They had Adele for lunch and the remainder of the afternoon, and Sammy allowed the little girl to choose what she wanted to do. They lunched at a popular restaurant where everything was geared towards children, from what was on the menu to the colouring books and games they could enjoy while they waited for their food.

Then they went to the Melbourne Aquarium.

'Do you do stuff like this often?' Sammy asked casually at one point during the day, and Adele shook her head and whispered that sometimes Sarah would take her out but mostly she stayed in and played with her toys.

'Sarah?'

'The girl who looks after me,' Adele said. 'Nana Gail doesn't have much time because she goes out a lot and she's busy all the time.'

Leo tried to involve himself but he was so clearly

making an effort that it had the opposite effect of scaring Adele away. The bigger the effort he made the more alarmed she seemed to get. And the more frustrated he became. By the end of the day, there was a tentative hug from Adele for Sammy and a polite handshake for Leo. Pink plastic bag dangling on her tiny wrist and feet beautifully turned out because, she had confided haltingly, she did ballet lessons three times a week because it suited her grandmother who met friends for early evening drinks then, she looked like a miniature queen politely bidding one of her subjects goodbye.

'Well, that was a complete fiasco,' was the first thing Leo said as they headed up to the suite. 'I need a drink. Actually, scratch that. I need several drinks.'

Sammy was on a high. She had had a wonderful time. She had been as nervous as a kitten about meeting the lawyers, about meeting Gail and about the whole pretend charade, and Adele had been a shining light, returning her to her comfort zone. And it had felt good to find herself in the leading role for the first time, rather than tumbling around on a roller coaster ride into which she had suddenly been plunged.

'It wasn't a fiasco,' she said, stepping into the lift and then turning to him as they were whooshed up to their suite. 'It went really well.'

'It went really well for *you*,' Leo amended, lounging against the mirrored panel, thumbs hooked on the waistband of his jeans. 'You're obviously a natural when it comes to children.'

'It's my job. Besides, I really liked her. She's been through a rough time. That's why she's so quiet and scared. I can't imagine what it must have been like having two very young and irresponsible parents and then, when they're no longer around, having to cope with a grandmother who clearly doesn't particularly want her around.'

'You're really…' He looked at her, head tilted to one side until colour crawled into her cheeks.

'I'm really *what*?'

Leo opened the door with his key card and pushed it, stepping back so that she could brush past him. She smelled of sun and the outside—a flowery, healthy, clean, natural smell that filled his nostrils, making him want to take a step back and close his eyes.

'Caring.' He took up where he'd left off.

Over the years, he had heard all about her from his father, who was her number one fan. It had mostly gone in one ear and out the other. But he remembered things he had been told now, about how good she was at her job, how popular she was with her pupils, the sort of girl who took in stray animals and nursed them back to rude health. Privately, it had all sounded like the perfect description of a bore with whom he couldn't possibly have anything in common. Pious and saintly, which had always been the image he had been fed, couldn't have been further from the sort of person who could engage his attention.

But she was nothing like that image he had built in his head. She didn't set about drawing attention to herself like most women he knew were prone to doing, but she was still curiously capable of holding his attention in ways he didn't really get.

And she was naturally empathetic. He had seen that for himself with Adele today, if it hadn't already been apparent.

She was feisty but caring, argumentative and stubborn as a mule but had what it took to gain the trust of a suspicious five-year-old. She didn't strut her stuff and blushed like a teenager. He couldn't imagine anyone less likely to make a pass at him, even if she wanted to. She believed in true love and was seriously romantic.

In all respects, she managed to tick none of the boxes that he had always thought counted when it came to women.

But the more he was in her company, the more turned on he was by her.

Sammy thought that he had succeeded in turning *caring* into *as boring as watching paint dry*.

'You mean I'm dull!' She laughed off the knot of hurt that tightened inside her.

He was pouring himself something from the well-stocked minibar and she accepted a glass of wine because she was still smarting from the *dull as dishwater* description she had read into his words.

It wasn't yet six-thirty. She guessed that the plan would be for them to go somewhere for dinner. After two nights, she no longer felt awkward about the whole sharing a bed situation. He seemed to have an amazing ability to detach. He might tell her that he found her sexy, but he didn't feel any compulsion to follow through.

Thank heavens, was what she firmly told herself.

'You're anything but dull.' Leo had opted for red wine over his instinctive choice of something a lot harder and he looked at her as he sipped it.

The day's outing had done great things to her satiny skin, which was fast acquiring a pale gold colour and turning her blond hair even blonder. The ponytail had disappeared at some point during the day and her hair now tumbled in curls and ringlets over her shoulders. She was the picture of health, the perfect image of someone who didn't care about what the weather was doing to her make-up or her hairstyle. Once he'd started staring, he found that he couldn't stop and he had to physically turn away and prowl towards the floor-to-ceiling window that overlooked a park that was bathed in the last of the sunshine.

'I just want to say…' He frowned and tried to locate the right words.

'What?' The wine was delicious and Sammy wandered to where he was standing and absently looked outside before turning her attention to him.

'I want to thank you.' His voice was gruff and she gazed at him, bewildered.

'Thank me for what?'

'You took charge today.' He drained his glass, twirled it thoughtfully between his fingers and then gently placed it on the squat glass table next to him. 'Quite honestly, I'm not sure how things would have gone if you hadn't been there.'

'You would have… You…er…'

'I can tell you're confused because you can't decide which of the many things I did today made just the right impression on Adele. You're spoilt for choice.'

Sammy blushed and laughed because he was incredibly endearing when he was being self-deprecating.

'You would have coped. I have a lot of experience when it comes to dealing with young children and you don't have any. I guess it was always going to be easier for me. I also don't have any emotional investment in the situation whereas you do.'

'That's a very generous take on the situation. I like that about you.'

'What do you mean?'

'You give the benefit of the doubt to people.'

'And you don't?' Her heart was beating like a jack-hammer because the conversation was so personal. She liked the feeling of playing with fire. She liked not caring whether she got burnt or not.

'I really want to make love to you.'

Sammy froze. Her eyes widened and her breathing slowed to a near stop. His voice was thick with intent.

'I mean,' Leo continued huskily, 'we could carry on pretending that there's nothing between us. I could work out here until I'm certain that you're asleep and then I can creep into the bed and wake up before you start surfacing from your beauty sleep and we can both kid ourselves that we haven't shared the same bed at all and that, even if we did, it doesn't matter because we're just two business associates on a job and that if there's some chemistry then we can choose to ignore that. I can make sure not to look at you for too long and only touch you when we're in public. I can pretend that I don't feel you tremble when I do touch you. I can pretend that you don't sigh softly when I kiss you. The alternative, however...'

He allowed that to stretch out into the silence between them while he continued to pin her to the spot with his eyes.

'This isn't real.' Sammy heard the desperation in her voice as she tried to cling to sanity.

'We're not really engaged,' Leo agreed in a rough-ened undertone. 'And we won't really be walking up the aisle with stars in our eyes. But *this*...' he cupped the side of her face with his hand and then caressed her smooth skin, dropping his finger to her mouth and tracing the outline of her lips '...*this* is real.'

'We shouldn't...'

'You're preaching to the converted,' Leo confessed with raw honesty. 'I know that making love isn't what either of us had planned. I know I'm probably the last guy in the world you would actively hunt down...' He wasn't even aware of leaving a pause after he said that but he was piqued when she didn't rush to fill it with a denial.

'I'm not the kind of girl who falls in bed with someone.'

'No.' Her skin was so soft and silky. It was torture trying to suppress his very natural urge to take and conquer.

'In fact,' she said awkwardly, 'I'm not the type of girl who has ever fallen into bed with someone.'

His hand stilled and he frowned as his brain tried to compute what she had just said. And failed. Was she admitting to being a virgin? A woman in her twenties?

'You're kidding.'

Sammy stared off into the distance. If her heart were to beat any faster she would be in danger of it cracking a couple of ribs. She'd always known that she would have to have this conversation with whatever guy she eventually fell into bed with, but in her head the conversation had never been with a man like Leo. In her head the conversation had always been with a kind, gentle guy who would clasp her hand and understand where she was coming from because he, like her, if not a virgin, would have been discriminating with his women.

Leo enjoyed women unabashedly. He took what he

wanted, always drawn to the prettiest and the most tempting, and he moved on quickly from one to another.

The fact of her virginity was just something else that separated them.

Actually, there were so many things separating them that she could start counting now and probably not reach the end of the list by the time they left the country.

'Why would I be kidding?'

'Because...' Leo was lost for words. 'Because... How old are you?'

'Twenty-six.'

'You're *twenty-six* and you've *never* slept with a man?'

Sammy flushed but she wasn't ashamed of that and never had been. She'd never been part of any crowd, growing up, who had giggled and ticked off the days on a calendar before they could lose their virginity and, once she had left her teens behind, the subject had never arisen with her girlfriends. If anything, she had seen enough broken hearts from friends who had become hopelessly involved with the wrong type of guy to have known that when she did decide to sleep with a man it would be with the right man.

What a joke, as it turned out.

Because she wanted to sleep with *this one* and *wrong* didn't begin to describe the category he fell into.

'Why not?' Leo asked bluntly. He still couldn't get his head round that idea but now he was looking at her in a slightly different light. *A virgin?*

'Because it just never happened,' she muttered under her breath, red as a beetroot and furiously wishing she had never said anything. She should have just carried on keeping him at arm's length and not softened at that glimpse of vulnerability.

'I get it…' Leo said slowly, his beautiful mouth curving into a smile of lazy intent. 'You thought that sex was something you could control. You'd fall in love and sex would follow as a tidy little afterthought. You believed that love and sex came as a package deal…'

'I never said that.'

'But you're attracted to me and that doesn't compute.' He'd never experienced any woman fighting an attraction to him. 'You've discovered that lust doesn't necessarily go hand in hand with love, and you've found out that it's powerful enough to make minced meat of common sense. Welcome to the real world.'

'There's nothing real about what we have.'

'You can keep fiddling around with words, Sammy, but you still won't be able to turn the chemistry between us into something else because it makes you feel uncomfortable.'

'This is crazy!' she burst out, looking at him with agitation. 'It doesn't make any sense. It would be madness to…to…'

She didn't get to finish the sentence.

Because he pulled her towards him and kissed her and he kept on kissing her until all thought faded away and what was left was pure sensation.

CHAPTER EIGHT

AT THIS STAGE in the proceedings, Leo would have marked his boundary lines out very clearly. He didn't feel that he needed to with Sammy, though. She got them. She had entered this contract with her eyes wide open and she knew him for the man he was—a man who wasn't going to ever offer her anything but the gratification of a physical need.

She wasn't a woman rushing to climb into bed with him as a prelude to trying to stake a claim. She was a woman who had done her best to avoid climbing into bed with him and staking a claim was the last thing on her mind.

She wasn't losing her virginity to him because he was the man she had been looking for all her life. She was losing her virginity to him because, like a minnow caught in a riptide, she just couldn't help herself.

The chemistry between them, for all sorts of reasons he couldn't understand, was overpowering.

'Sometimes crazy is good,' he broke away to rasp. Without giving her time to find an answer to that observation, he picked her up and she gave a soft little gasp because they were heading for the bedroom and that king-sized bed.

She'd definitely overestimated her ability to hang on to her self-control when he was around!

If they'd buried this and not brought it out in the open, she might have been safe but, as it stood…

She spread her hand flat against his chest and felt the hardness of muscle. If she stopped to think about whether it had anything to do with love or affection or wanting to discover more about her, then she would go mad. It was all about sex and lust and he was right—she had never predicted how powerful a physical urge could be.

He deposited her on the bed and then stood back and looked down at her with an expression of masculine satisfaction.

'Hot day out there…'

'Huh?'

'I'm thinking we should start with a bath. How does that sound?'

'Maybe we should just get it over and done with.' Sammy looked at him anxiously and he burst out laughing.

He raked his fingers through his hair and gazed at her with lively amusement. 'That's the first time any woman has ever said that to me. *Maybe we should just get it over and done with*…' He shook his head and dropped onto the bed to sit next to her and she scrambled up so that she was hugging her knees, her eyes wide with a mixture of apprehension and hot longing.

Both did unheard of things to his body. His erection was so hard it was painful. He had no idea how he was going to get through a leisurely bathing session but sating their needs fast and hard was going to have to wait.

'Is this the first time you've ever made love to a virgin?' she asked quietly and he touched her cheek briefly.

'It is, but don't be scared, Sammy. I'll be gentle. I just need to make sure of one thing—I need to know if this is really what you want.' His voice was utterly serious. This wasn't quite what she had expected. She had summed Leo up as the typical wealthy, good-looking businessman who could have any woman he wanted and so took without thinking of consequences. She'd assumed that he was selfish sexually, happy to pick up and discard women without any thought to whether he left them with broken hearts or not.

His account of what had happened behind the scenes with Vivienne Madison had subtly changed that opinion but perhaps her opinion had been changing before that.

Assailed by a moment of confusion, her mind went blank for a few seconds and then she slowly began processing that the three-dimensional man was nothing like the cardboard cut-out she had had in her head.

'Really what I want?' she parroted weakly.

'You've spent your life saving yourself for the right man,' Leo told her roughly. 'I'm not the right man for you and I never will be. I'm not on the lookout for love—I don't have time for the complication of emotions. If I were to describe my ideal life partner, it would be someone whose view of the institution of marriage was similar to my own. A man like me would be no good for you any more than a woman like you would suit a man like me.'

Sammy hugged her knees tighter to her chest. She was being given an out. She looked at him, chin tilted mutinously at an angle. 'You were right,' she told him.

'I thought sex and love went together. I hadn't banked on being swept off my feet by…by…lust.'

Leo was impressed because it was brave of her to admit that. It would have been much easier to have buried her head in the sand, stuck it out here for the next week and then pocketed the money and put the whole thing down to experience rather than facing up to something she found uncomfortable and bewildering.

'Is that you telling me that you want this?'

Sammy nodded and he grinned. 'You're going to have to do better than that, Sammy.' He sifted his fingers through her hair and gently tugged her towards him. His kiss was long and deep, their tongues meshing, driving her wild.

'Let me hear you say it…' he encouraged, breaking apart to look at her.

'I…I want this.' Sammy felt heady and reckless. She felt as though she had one foot hanging off the side of a precipice. In a minute she would leap into the air and free fall. She was terrified and excited all at once.

'In that case, stay right where you are.'

He padded off to the en suite bathroom, where she heard the sound of the bath being run. When she thought about the two of them in that bath she shivered. But she wasn't going to back out.

Her mind was frantically trying to deal with images of them together when he reappeared at the bathroom door, leant against the door frame and gazed at her with his arms folded.

'Rule number one,' he drawled, 'is to relax.' He strolled towards her and she followed his lazy progress with wide blue eyes. 'Rule number two is to stop thinking that what we're about to do will be anything but exquisite. And rule number three...' he ran his fingers through her hair and gently tilted her face upwards so their eyes met, his reassuring, hers needing reassurance '...is that you trust me.' He stood back and held out one hand and she took it mutely and then he led her to the bathroom, where the bath was a mass of fragrant bubbles.

'Now...' Leo positioned her in the middle of the bathroom and stood back, gazing at her with the eyes of a connoisseur. It was an exaggerated pose, finger lightly resting on his mouth, head tilted back, eyes half closed, and she wanted to laugh, which relaxed her.

'What are you doing?'

'Where to start?' he murmured. 'With your top, I think...'

'No—no!' She hurriedly stepped back and hooked her fingers under the stretchy fabric. 'I can do that myself.'

'Should I turn my back and only look around when you're safely concealed under a metre of bubbles?'

'Hardly a metre!'

'You're not going to get away that lightly,' he teased, enjoying the novelty of a woman who wasn't flinging herself at him. He walked towards her and when she opened her mouth he gently placed one finger over her lips. 'Now, remember those rules of mine?'

Sammy nodded meekly.

'Okay. Let's focus on rule number three, which is *trust me*.' He lightly tapped her hands away from the top to replace them with his own and slowly, tantalisingly slowly, he pulled the top over her head, keeping his eyes on her face, and then he tossed it on the chair by the door.

Sammy's mouth was dry. 'I know I'm not exactly skinny,' she breathed huskily and he tutted under his breath. 'My breasts are way too big,' she continued, just in case she hadn't already made it perfectly clear that making love to her wasn't going to be like making love to one of his superslender models or waif-thin actresses, and not just because she was a virgin.

Leo was finding it very hard to step back from the searing urge to rip her bra off and feel those lush breasts for himself. The last thing his aching erection needed was a description from her about just how generous they were in size.

'You're perfect,' he ground out, briefly closing his eyes to get a grip.

Sammy would have launched into a question and answer session about his definition of *perfection* because she had eyes in her head and knew that *perfect* was the last thing she was, but he had slid his hands behind her back and was unclasping her bra.

She gasped and squeezed her eyes tightly shut as the bra joined her top on the chair. Her body was as rigid as a plank of wood but not for long, as he curved big hands around her breasts and then, slowly and expertly, rubbed his thumbs over the stiffened peaks of her nipples.

Leo wasn't sure he was going to be able to keep up the pretence of the sophisticated lover in control of the situation when he felt as though he was on the brink of exploding. He was hard as a rock and throbbing. When he looked down to those heavy, abundant breasts with their circular pink nipples, he could easily have been a horny adolescent on the verge of losing his virginity. That was how turned on he was.

He continued to massage them, to play with her nipples, while she moaned softly under her breath, as if a little embarrassed to be making any noise at all.

Her inexperience hit him like a dose of adrenaline and he fumbled, in a very uncool way, with her trousers, which he somehow managed to get down her legs without his usual aplomb.

She stepped out of them. Sammy's eyes were still squeezed shut and, whilst everything was melting, she just didn't quite know what she should do next. Her whole body went up in flames when she thought of those fabulous dark eyes scrutinising her body. She took a peek and daringly made some halting attempts to get him to the same state of undress as she was.

'Shh…' Leo murmured, as though she had spoken. He stayed her hand.

'This feels weird,' Sammy said shyly. Their eyes met and he nodded. He had never made love to a virgin in his life before. Had she ever seen a man naked? He was well built. Would his sheer size intimidate her? He stepped back and began undressing, his dark eyes fixed on her as she watched him with unabashed fascination. Without thinking, she had covered her breasts with her arm. It was curiously erotic.

Shirt off, he began unzipping his trousers.

Sammy couldn't take her eyes off him.

He was the most sensationally beautiful man she had ever seen and all of a sudden she knew, with some kind of unerring instinct, that she had been looking at him all her life. He'd never noticed *her*, but she had spent her life noticing *him*.

And now here she was…

She was so turned on that she had to briefly close

her eyes and, even with her eyes closed, she could still see his image imprinted on her retina. Broad bronzed shoulders, muscled arms, narrow waist and washboard-hard stomach.

When she opened her eyes he was stepping out of the trousers and she gasped, her mouth forming a perfect oval, and Leo grinned.

'I can't remember the last time I had such a dramatic reaction from a woman at the sight of my naked body,' he drawled wryly.

Sammy's cheeks were burning. Her eyes flicked down to his substantial, impressive manhood and then back to his face. He was still grinning.

'Don't worry—' he read her mind without her having to say what was on it '—male and female bodies are engineered to fit together.'

He urged her into the bath. It was huge, big enough for them both, but he knelt at the side and lavished his attention on her, taking his time as he soaped her, massaging her neck until her bones turned to water and then moving on to massage her breasts until she was so relaxed she just wanted to sigh and moan and enjoy the intense pleasure of his hands on her.

Her self-consciousness had disappeared some time between sinking into the hot water and hearing the sound of him lathering soap between his hands.

By the time his big hands were moving over her breasts, her legs were limp and her eyelids fluttered as he worked his way down her body, urging her to sit up so that he could soap her back, his thumbs pressing against her spine in a way that was quite, quite delicious.

'Enjoying?' he whispered and she nodded and muttered something that was meant to signify a resounding *yes*.

'Still nervous?' he questioned, and she flicked drowsy eyes at him.

'Not so much,' she confessed. 'You're good at this, aren't you?'

'I've never been in this position before. It's as new to me as it is to you.'

'But you have heaps of experience.'

'There's another rule I should have added,' Leo mused. 'I should have added the *no chatting* rule.'

'I mean—' Sammy ignored him completely '—I always imagined that when I was, well, in this position… You know what I mean, that it would be with someone less…er…'

'There would be something a little weird about a guy in his mid to late twenties who was still a virgin. Or am I being a little fanciful here? Now, stop talking!'

His hands moved over her body, massaging gently, exploring gently, finding her inner thighs and separating them…also gently. His caresses were unhurried and measured and she physically felt herself relaxing more and more until all the apprehension had seeped out of her.

She received his finger with a shiver as it slid between her legs. Maybe it helped that she was covered in warm, sudsy water. Or maybe because the lighting was dimmed in the bathroom and her eyes were closed so that she couldn't see that lean, beautiful face. Or maybe she was just, weirdly, relaxed. She didn't understand how or why but she was. Everything was happening so slowly.

Leo stroked her between her legs, building up the

rhythm. He knew that this would be achingly intimate for her, and he half wondered whether some kind of prudish instinct would kick in and she would push his questing hand away, but she didn't and he was inordinately pleased by that.

It mattered to him that she open herself to him and that was what she was doing. Her breathing quickened and her cheeks became flushed with hectic colour. She was moving in the bathtub, bucking ever so slightly so that the water lapped around her, enabling him to see the slick wetness of her big breasts rising and falling. He kept up his gentle but insistent rhythm until, with a deep groan, she arched up and spasmed against his finger.

Sammy was shocked and mortified at the way she had just *let go*. She had been so caught up in the waves of pleasure rolling over her that she would not have been able to stop herself if she had tried.

When she opened her eyes, he was smiling and she struggled up into a sitting position. 'I'm sorry…' She could barely get the words out. He stroked her face, stood up and helped her to her feet.

'You should be,' he admonished, 'because I'm so turned on I feel as though I'm about to explode. I had planned this bathing experience to be very long and very leisurely but I'm going to have to revise that plan.'

'Why's that?' She smiled shyly because she knew what he was saying and yet she could hardly believe it.

'Fishing?' Leo grinned, outrageously masculine in his nakedness. If he didn't have her, and have her fast, he wasn't going to be responsible for whatever his body decided to do.

'Yes,' Sammy confessed honestly. He helped her out of the tub and wrapped her in a towel and she was bemused to find herself suddenly settling onto the over-sized bed—the same bed which had filled her with dread when she had first arrived.

Leo laughed. 'I like that,' he confided, and she looked at him with a puzzled expression. 'The way you have of saying exactly what's on your mind,' he elaborated. 'You don't care what impression you make.'

'And that's a good thing?' Sammy asked lightly.

'Refreshing. The women I date have always taken great care to say what they thought I wanted them to say.'

'I thought all men liked women who agreed with them.'

'Maybe,' Leo murmured, 'or maybe that's just a lazy response. Now, enough talk.' He sank onto the mattress and guided her hand to his throbbing erection, drawing in his breath sharply as she wrapped her fingers around him.

She asked him what to do. She was anxious that he enjoy himself. Her frank honesty and hesitancy was refreshing.

'Don't worry about me,' he told her roughly. 'This is about *you*. I want this first time for you to be special. I want you to remember it forever.'

Sammy's heart swelled as he angled her underneath him, pinned both her hands together above her head with one hand and then instructed her to leave them there.

If he was as turned on as she was, then his whole body would be on fire, just as hers was, and yet he was willing to sublimate his urges so that he could take his time with her. He nuzzled the side of her neck and she wriggled and sighed, her eyelids fluttering as he then proceeded to work his way downwards, sprinkling a trail of delicate, feathery kisses along her collarbone, then lower to the soft swell of her breasts.

She opened one eye and the sight of his dark head, the intimacy of where it was placed just there by her nipple, made her stifle a squeak of edge-of-the-seat excitement.

She closed her eyes. She felt like the cat that nabbed the cream. His mouth edged down to her nipple and he suckled on it, drawing it in and teasing it with the tip of his tongue. Sammy groaned out loud. Her hands itched to burrow into his dark hair and propel him harder against her sensitive nipple but instead she clasped her fingers together and squirmed as he continued to send her body to heaven. She was still tingling between her legs and the tingling was building momentum, wanting satisfaction all over again.

He caressed her breasts, torturing her by taking his time as he explored first one then the other. He licked her nipples, traced them with his flicking tongue, nipped them and sucked them until she barely recognised the low, shuddering moans coming from her.

Those moans grew deeper when he cupped her between her legs and very gently pressed down in lazy circular movements.

Leo felt her impatience, felt her body yearning to receive him and he wanted nothing more than to yield to the siren call of desire, to satisfy his driving need to feel her tight and hot around his hard, painfully erect manhood.

It took immense willpower to leave her breasts so that he could taste the flat planes of her stomach, so that he could circle the delicate indentation of her belly button with his tongue, so that he could breathe in the musky, sexy scent of her womanhood.

He knelt between her legs and took his time, first licking the soft underside of her thighs and then, when her panting was raspy and hoarse, gently inserting his tongue along the crease and then delving deeper to taste her wet, slick sweetness.

Sammy bucked against him. She couldn't keep her hands obediently clasped above her head and instead curled her fingers into his dark hair, driving his mouth deeper against her so that the starbursts of pleasure became sharper and sharper until she was rolling on a tide of pure sensual delight.

She hitched her legs up, intensifying the pleasure, and then cried out when he inserted two fingers into her so that he was caressing her with his mouth and his fingers.

Leo could feel self-control slipping fast. He wanted and *needed* to be inside her.

'I need you *now*.' He barely recognised the shaky tenor of his voice. He reared up and their eyes met. Sammy nodded wordlessly. Even in the midst of searing passion, she noted that he took time out to put on a condom. She was a virgin so perhaps he assumed that she wasn't on the Pill or maybe, even if she *was* for whatever reason, he was a man who never took chances.

He had brought her to the brink and had taken her to a place where nerves at taking him inside her had miraculously vanished. Yes, she still registered that this was going to be a whole new experience for her, but she literally couldn't wait to feel the bigness of him inside her.

He ran a finger along her, delved briefly into her

wetness, then nudged her tentatively with the tip of his shaft.

'Leo…' She whispered his name in a voice that was halfway between a gasp and a plea. Her hands were on his shoulders, her body arched up, ripe and ready, as he edged into her, inch by glorious inch.

The feeling was exquisite. Sammy had never actually dwelled on what sex might *feel* like. It had always been a blurry, rosy image wrapped up in the comforting haze of love with a capital *L*. There was nothing blurry or rosy about this. The sensation of his hardness plunging into the very depths of her was mind-blowingly erotic and raw. She pushed against him and that was all Leo needed to ramp up his rhythm. He thrust deeper and harder and felt her whole body quiver around him, their bodies fused.

Sammy was scarcely aware of a brief twinge of discomfort. His need mirrored her own and it was proof of his mastery that he had been able to get her to a point of relaxing enough, trusting enough, to give herself to him without fear of stepping into the unknown.

The feel of her tightness was amazing, as was the heat of her body, the lushness of her feminine curves, the naked desire that had darkened her eyes and caused her nostrils to flare.

He held on, tuned in to her every whimper and cry, knowing just how to drive and angle his big body to intensify the sensations pouring through her as her cries became higher, more uncontrolled.

Her whole body tensed and arched up and only then did he allow himself to let go. The timing was impeccable as their bodies convulsed in unison. It was the most sensual experience Leo could remember having and he wondered whether the fact of her virginity had been a mental turn-on as well as a physical one.

Sagging against him, utterly spent, Sammy wondered what happened next in this scenario. She hadn't given that a moment's thought. She'd been way too busy rushing into Leo's arms. Now, her nudity embarrassed her and she made tiny movements to distance herself from him and put the sheets between their damp bodies. Leo wasn't having any of it.

'Don't tell me that you're going to go all modest on me,' he murmured, firmly lifting the sheets she had tried to stuff between them and pulling her close against him so that she was in no danger of pretending that what had happened had been a blip she could swipe away. 'I've seen you naked now so trying to cover up is just shutting the stable door after the horse has bolted.' He grinned and lay back flat, tugging her onto him and then draping his arm over her.

Sammy quivered. Her automatic instinct was to analyse what had happened and discuss what would happen next. This was a big deal for her. It was slowly trickling into her that the lines between what was real and what wasn't had become blurred. Where did that leave her? She had handed her virginity to Leo. What did that mean? Was this the beginning to an affair? She'd never considered herself to be *affair material*. Or maybe this was just a one-night stand, something that had happened because they had both been overwhelmed.

She knew that he was not being afflicted by similar internal angst. He wasn't confusing lines or frantically wondering what happened next. When it came to sex, Leo was a man who lived in the moment. He had wanted her, she had wanted him and one and one made two—it was as simple as that.

If she told him that this was a one-off, a mistake, then she knew that he would shrug those broad shoulders of his and put it down to experience. Their charade would continue unimpeded.

And for her...

Would it be so bad for her to snatch a little bit more of this while it lasted? Instead of reacting like Chicken Little with the sky falling down? Leo was offering *fun* and the fact that they were supposedly engaged was an added bonus because it just added verisimilitude to the charade. What was wrong with fun?

She had had a hellish year and a half and now she had a chance to lighten up and enjoy herself for a little while. Where was the crime in that?

His phone buzzed and he rolled to his side and she watched his broad, tanned, muscled back as he read whatever message had been texted to him.

Daringly, she traced a pattern with the tip of one finger. It was probably the least wanton gesture she could have made but she was gratified when he moved and then turned back to her and swung her against him.

'Nice,' Leo growled, turning back to her and catching her finger, sucking it, while keeping his dark eyes firmly fixed on her face. 'I can tell you're destined to be an excellent pupil.'

'What makes you say that?' For someone as forbidding as he was, she was discovering that he could be incredibly engaging.

'You've already picked up rule number four before I've even had a chance to tell you what it is.'

'Have I? What is it?'

Still grinning, Leo primly tucked the sheet under her breasts and circled one of her nipples with his finger. Instantly, it peaked into hot arousal. He moistened his finger and returned it to her nipple and absorbed the little reactions of her exquisite body.

'You're making the first move,' he drawled. 'I like that, but before we have fun—' he settled her against him '—we're going to go downstairs and have something to eat and then we're going to talk about tomorrow.'

'Why?' She flashed him a reckless smile. 'Weren't you the one who mentioned something about no chatting? Wasn't that one of your rules?'

'Like I said, a fast learner. But you're going to have to be the teacher for a while,' he told her wryly. 'The text I just received was from my lawyer. We're going to have Adele solidly for the next four days. A test, it would appear, to judge whether she can adapt to us.'

'Day and night?'

Leo nodded. 'I gather that this is Gail's attempt to throw her granddaughter in at the deep end to prove a point, after which she will repeat her case for having the child stay in Melbourne with her, while she continues to collect even more money from me, no doubt, than she already does, unless she can convince the court that Adele is incompatible with my lifestyle, whether you're on my arm or not, then her case is over and the money will stop.'

'My goodness! And how on earth is it going to be possible to prove anything at all? Is she going to have spies with binoculars peering from behind the bushes and writing reports on what we're doing?'

'A child psychologist will establish how well Adele

is likely to cope in the UK and how comfortable she feels around us. So…'

Sammy could see a flicker of anxiety in the depths of his bitter-chocolate eyes although his voice remained neutral.

'So?'

'So I propose we escape to somewhere a little less busy. Head to the coast. I can get my lawyer to source somewhere we can rent. A villa by the sea.'

Without crowds around them and a deadline to meet before Adele was returned to her grandmother, it was going to be much harder for their charade to hold water, especially with a child. Sammy knew, from experience, that most children were a heck of a lot sharper than adults thought when it came to assessing situations and people. Leo wouldn't have to pretend to be in love with her for the sake of lawyers and the public at large. This was going to be a much more difficult task.

'And,' she said slowly, 'you want me to teach you how to relate to Adele? How on earth can I teach you something like that?'

'I didn't come this far to fail at the final hurdle.' He slid out of the bed, prowled naked towards the window, then returned and leaned over her, caging her in, his arms on either side of her body.

'Children aren't like adults,' Sammy told him softly. 'They don't judge and they respond the more natural and open you are with them.'

'Then natural and open is what I will have to be.'

Sammy gazed at him and she thought that it was going to be a lot more complicated for him than merely being natural and open. He would have to relinquish his desire to control everything around him. He would have to go with the flow.

Somehow the thought of that made it easier for her to accept that she wanted him even if it meant stifling her urge to analyse where that *want* would take her. They would both be functioning out of their comfort zone.

She laughed and then sobered up when she saw that he was dead serious. 'Sometimes, it's hard to believe that you and your father share the same genetic pool.'

Leo slipped back into bed. 'I know,' he said drily. 'I guess I'll just have to learn how to operate a little on his emotional level for a while.'

'Is that going to be possible for you?'

Leo didn't answer. The enormity of this undertaking was hitting home—and hitting home hard. To leave Adele in the care of her grandmother would be a disaster but bringing her back with him was going to require changes to his life he had not considered in depth. Would he be able to cultivate an emotional bond with the child? He'd had a good childhood, he thought, even though he had hardened over time as he had watched the destructive path his father's emotional excesses had taken him down.

He relaxed.

He might have trained himself to put his emotions on ice when it came to the opposite sex—he had seen for himself the catastrophes that could occur to the hapless bugger who wore his heart on his sleeve—but there was no reason to think that he wouldn't make a perfectly acceptable guardian to Adele and, besides, what he lacked his father would make up for in spades.

'Perfectly possible.' He smiled lazily. 'Especially with you at my side, applying a little discipline whenever you notice me slipping up.' He dropped a kiss on her parted mouth and the kiss deepened until she was throbbing between her legs for him. He pulled back. 'I'll get the ball rolling for somewhere by the sea.' He flicked on his cell phone and began scrolling through his address book. 'And you can get dressed and start thinking of ways of turning me into a good little boy who can pass the next big test.'

CHAPTER NINE

SAMMY LAY BY the pool, her eyes hidden behind the oversized sunglasses she had bought two days previously, shortly before they had collected Adele from her grandmother's lawyer.

Everything had to be done by the book.

'One foot out of place,' Leo had said grittily, 'and she'll run screeching to her lawyers that we're flouting the rules.'

In the past couple of days she had heard things about Gail Jamieson that had conclusively done away with any lingering doubts about what they were doing. Leo had clearly been loath to part with the information but maybe because they were now more than just partners in a business arrangement he had felt inclined to open up.

Pillow talk.

'Sean was a weak man,' he had told her pensively late at night after their first successful day with Adele, the little girl tucked safely in bed hours earlier. 'An only child, spoiled and indulged, with almost no discipline, and I tend to agree with my father that he found himself swept along on a riptide over which he had no control whatsoever. He was completely taken in by Louise and it wasn't hard for him to fall off the bandwagon completely after his mother died. From his communications with my father, it would appear that whilst he knew well enough that neither he nor Louise were equipped to take care of the child they had produced, neither was Gail. There were stories of her leaving the baby unattended while she went out at night and, on one occasion, an actual admission to hospital when Adele was little more than a toddler, after her *falling down some stairs*—although Sean hinted that some corporal punishment had been inflicted by the grandmother.'

'Why on earth didn't he take Adele and leave?'

'Because,' Leo had told her with a wry grimace, 'he was a drug addict. His best intentions were never going to come to anything. Nor could we have undertaken a snatch and grab rescue mission. No, the only way my father felt he could help was to send money over to make Adele's life more comfortable and to sponsor rehabs that never seemed to come to anything.'

'If Gail has been responsible for physical abuse, then surely that would make it easy for you to…'

'Hearsay,' he had told her bluntly. 'To outside eyes, she is the grandmother who rose to the occasion when her daughter couldn't look after her own child.'

Now, looking at Adele in her swimming costume at the side of the pool, Sammy could make sense of the child's personality.

Since they had arrived at the villa, which was an exquisite masterpiece of modernism with spectacular views down to the Surfers Paradise Coast, Adele had barely spoken to Leo at all. She was a cautious, watchful five-year-old, without any of the spontaneity she should have had at her age. There was no running around, no bursts of laughter, no mess made, no noisy intrusions into adult conversations.

Her clothes were neatly worn and never seemed to get dirty. She was the most background child Sammy had ever encountered and her heart went out to her.

And it went out to Leo because she could tell that he was trying hard. Unfortunately, whilst his questions were politely answered, there was minimal eye contact made and absolutely only essential interaction. Now, he was doing lengths, his lean, well toned bronzed body cutting a swathe through the crystal-clear water while Adele stared out into the distance as she clutched the side of the pool.

Sammy could predict the way the rest of the day would go because she was sure that it would follow the pattern of the other days they had had in the villa.

They would enjoy the sun and the swimming pool and then venture down to the town for something to eat and take in another of the local sights. Yesterday had been a stroll on the beach, where they had watched surfers ride the soaring waves. The day before they had paid a visit to the animal park, where Adele had been encouraged to pat a koala, which she had seemed to enjoy. Today they would do something else, some other fun activity, which would end up leaving Leo restless and frustrated because he would, yet again, fail to break through the wall of Adele's politeness.

She smiled as Adele caught her eye and then levered herself up and began walking over. She was wearing a plain black swimsuit and had not removed her bright pink plastic beach shoes, which sloshed as she approached.

'I thought you were going to be a little fishy again—'

Sammy grinned '—and show me how you could do those flips underwater.'

Adele smiled and dropped her eyes. 'Leo's in the pool,' she said in a whisper and Sammy reached out and held the child's hands in hers.

'You can't let him be the only fish,' she said with a smile. 'Besides, you make a much prettier fish than Leo. Maybe today we could get you a nice fishy swimsuit. Would you like that? Something nice and colourful? And maybe an inflatable for the pool, as well?'

'Nana might get angry.' Adele chewed her lip anxiously. 'She says it's important not to ask for things. I can only have things if I don't ask for them.'

Sammy's ears pricked up because Adele rarely mentioned her grandmother. 'What if you *do* ask?' she questioned gently. 'Does your grandmother get cross?'

Adele shrugged and remained silent.

'You know,' Sammy said quietly, 'that you have a lovely grandpa over in England who really wants to meet you.'

Adele slid a sideways look at Sammy. 'Nana says that no one wants me but her.'

'Now I *know* that's not true.' She was still smiling, her voice soft and encouraging, but her heart clenched at the behind-the-scenes picture being painted. 'You have a very, very loving grandpa who would burst into tears if he heard you say that.'

Adele's eyes brightened. 'Old people don't cry!' she giggled.

'Just wait till you meet your uncle Leo's dad,' Sammy confided. 'He's a big softie. But maybe you *should* be cautious,' she mused thoughtfully. 'He's famous for hugging a lot. He might just get hold of you and never let you go. You'd be wrapped up in a big bear hug for the rest of your life!'

'How would I eat?' Adele giggled again. It was an unusual sound.

'Your uncle Leo would have to sneak you titbits.'

'How would I go to the bathroom?'

'You'd be allowed to go to the bathroom but you'd have to follow that trail of bread back to his arms.'

'Like Hansel and Gretel.'

'*Just* like Hansel and Gretel.'

'Running away from the bad witch.'

'Who is the bad witch?'

Adele shrugged and her face grew serious, and Sammy knew when to leave things alone.

Later, she repeated the conversation to Leo. It was a little after eight in the evening and Adele was asleep. She never kicked up about going to bed. Indeed, she had to be persuaded on night one to stay up beyond six and as soon as Leo had looked at his watch, at a little after seven, she had jumped to her feet, her teddy clutched to her chest, ready to head upstairs.

She never asked for a bedtime story. She never asked for anything.

'It's almost as though she's too scared of the response she might get.'

'Does that surprise you?' Leo looked at her. The sun had worked magic on her skin, turning her flawless, milky whiteness a toasted golden colour. He couldn't get enough of her. Hours were spent in anticipation of bedding her as soon as they were together. He guilt-ily wondered whether he was devoting the amount of attention he should have to his little charge when his thoughts always seemed to be wrapped up in images of Sammy and her hot, willing body under his, when his eyes seemed to follow her every small movement. Right now, with the meal finished, he took his time as he watched her over the rim of his wine glass.

She wasn't wearing a bra.

He'd told her that just the thought of being able to reach under her top and feel her glorious breasts was enough to make him harden and she had teasingly threatened to dispense with the bra, a threat he had been extremely keen to take her up on.

'You're looking at me.' Sammy blushed. Her nipples tightened into hard pebbles and she felt that wonderful, familiar dampness between her legs. She had never thought that her body could respond to anyone the way it responded to Leo. His eyes on her made the hairs on the back of her neck stand on end, made her skin prickle as though someone had run a feather over it. The sound of his voice, deep and dark and velvety, could trigger a series of graphic images in her head that made her pulses quicken and her heart beat faster.

She blinked as her sluggish brain began to make all sorts of connections that had been there all along, waiting to be unearthed.

She'd agreed to a phoney relationship and then had agreed to a sexual one because she had been unable to deny her body the thing it seemed to crave.

She'd been swept along on a rosy wave of thinking that she was having fun and not doing anything that any girl her age wouldn't have done. Namely, falling into bed with a hot guy she found irresistible. She was only acting her age!

Had she been especially vulnerable because Leo had

been an adolescent crush? Had that added to the thrill? She hadn't stopped to question it.

Of course, it wasn't going to last and that was fine. They were as different as chalk and cheese and if fate hadn't thrown them together then their paths would never have crossed in the way that they had. They would have remained two people who met now and again and exchanged a bit of this and that conversation.

In time, she would have met someone to settle down with. Mr Right. He would have been reliable, kind and with a gentle sense of humour. In keeping with the fact that she had never placed much importance on looks and bearing in mind that she was never going to be asked to sashay down any catwalk, he would have been pleasant enough looking. No gargoyle but no movie star.

So what was she doing falling in love with a billionaire who was out of her reach? A guy who wasn't into commitment, who had thought nothing of throwing money at her to get what he wanted and who had not once mentioned having any feelings for her even though they were sleeping together?

Because fall in love with him she had. Hook, line and sinker, and now the thought of returning to life as she knew it held no appeal, even though she would be getting everything she had dreamed of that money could buy, including the freelance career she craved.

It was a nightmare. What on earth would he think if he could read her thoughts? If he could see into her heart? He was having a fling and she was busy experiencing the greatest love of her life.

'You make me want to stare,' Leo confided roughly.

'Huh?'

'Penny for them.'

'Penny for what?'

'Whatever it is that's going through your head.' He smiled lazily, the smile of the predator sure of its willing prey. 'Is it me?'

Sammy blinked. Her heart was thumping so fast that her ribcage felt threatened. She tried to match his sexy smile with one of her own. It wobbled. 'You're so egotistical.'

'Come and sit next to me.' He patted the space next to him. 'I can't look without touching.'

'Adele's upstairs!'

'And have you ever known a child to sleep as soundly as she does?' Leo asked drily. 'When I looked in on her half an hour ago she was snoring like a trooper.'

Besides, the way the house was designed, it was unlikely that they would be disturbed. It was a clever configuration of all glass at the front, so that every bit of the spectacular view was captured, from the soaring surf of the ocean to the vast blueness of the sky, an uninterrupted panorama because the house was built into the side of a cliff. On the lower floor, everything was open-plan. When one of the immense glass panes was opened, the sea breeze reached every corner of the house. On the veranda, which was railed in with steel, the view was breathtaking.

They were in the snug, which was the only enclosed room on the lower floor and was on a raised, floating mezzanine that afforded them a bird's-eye view of the entire floor but, thanks to one-way glass, no one inside could be seen. A useful office space, Sammy assumed, from which family life could be observed whilst absolute privacy within was maintained.

Not, as Leo had pointed out, there was the slightest

chance of Adele surprising them. It was apparent that surprising anyone was something she had been trained never to do.

'We were talking about Adele.' But her voice was tellingly feeble.

'I can't talk with you sitting so far away.'

'Don't be silly.'

'Shall I come and get you? Do you want a demonstration of my caveman capabilities?'

Sammy could think of nothing she wanted more but now her every move was invested with the pain of knowing that all too soon this would be gone. She padded the few feet separating them and sat primly next to him and he pulled her so that she was sprawled against him, lying on top of him but on her back, her body cradled between his powerful thighs.

He slipped his big hands under her tee shirt and she released a sigh of pure pleasure as he massaged her breasts, rolling his fingers over the stiffened peaks of her nipples and rubbing until the wetness between her legs made her want to wriggle.

'We were talking about Adele,' Leo reminded her.

'I… Yes…' Sammy panted. His erection was pressed like a rod of steel against her back, tangible proof of how much he was turned on. 'She… It's a difficult situation for her but, in a strange way, it's, um, actually… I can't think when you're doing that…'

'Playing with your breasts? I'd quite like to take them into my mouth. Think you could flip over so that I can taste them?'

'Leo!'

'You know you want to.'

She did and so much more besides. She flipped over

and arched up over him so that her breasts quivered tantalisingly above his mouth and she flung her head back and closed her eyes as he took his time suckling on her nipples, feasting on them, in no great rush. Eyes shut, teeth clenched, she endured the exquisite agony of being teased until she couldn't stand it any more, at which point she settled back down in her original position between his legs, breathing hard and fast.

She wriggled into a comfortable position and her legs dropped open.

'Take off the shorts,' Leo commanded softly into her ear.

Sammy wriggled out of them but when she made to remove the lacy briefs he stayed her hand. Her body was on fire. This was what he did to her. He took away her ability to think and to behave sensibly. He'd done that from the start and he would carry on doing it until he walked away from her. Until they walked away from one another. Except he would continue having an effect on her long after she had disappeared from his life. She couldn't imagine how it would feel to see him the way she had before, in passing glimpses, with Adele.

He pressed his hand flat between her legs, over her knickers, and caressed her until she was moving against his hand, wanting those lazy movements to pick up tempo.

Then he slipped his hand under the lacy cotton. When he inserted his finger and began stroking, she felt like passing out because it felt so good. Her breathing quickened as she savoured the feel of him touching her, the even rhythm as his finger slid up and down, pushing against her core.

He moved and began licking her, revelling in her

wetness on his mouth, sliding his tongue into her and feeling the gasp she uttered transmitted directly to his own body, stirring him up. He wouldn't let her come against his mouth like this. But he would fire her almost to the point of no return and then take her.

Their bodies were slick with perspiration when, as she balanced precariously on the cusp of coming against his mouth, he levered her off, pausing only to don contraception while she watched him impatiently, cupping herself between her legs with her hand to alleviate the ache there. Their eyes tangled and he smiled because he knew exactly what she was thinking and what she was feeling.

He nudged at her sensitive opening and then eased himself inside her, his girth filling her up, and when he began to thrust in deep, rhythmic strokes she could only close her eyes and let sensation carry her away.

Their bodies moved as one. Sammy couldn't imagine that sex could ever feel as glorious as this with anyone else, but then how could it when she had given her heart away to him? She came, her body stiffened and then arched up as it splintered into a thousand heavenly pieces and she felt his own orgasm matching her own.

She was as limp as a rag doll as he rolled off her so that they were lying side by side, shoulders and arms lightly touching, both of them staring up at the ceiling. She idly wondered whether the size of the sofa in the room, wider than a single bed, had been fashioned with this sort of activity in mind. Work and play in sound-proof silence, invisible to outside eyes. There was something a little naughty about the design of the room and its position inside the house.

She turned onto her side to say something of the sort

to him, only to find him staring at her intently, expression speculative.

'What?'

'I expect you're going to be a little shocked at what I'm about to say.'

'What? What are you about to say?' He was so long in answering that her heart had time to gather pace and her nerves had time to start jangling and her brain had time to work out a thousand possible scenarios.

'Will you marry me?'

Sammy's mouth dropped open and she stared at him. She wondered whether her ears had been playing tricks on her but the way he was staring at her, his dark eyes serious with intent, made her pause.

Piercing happiness shot through her. She hadn't dared hope that he might have returned her love! He had been so adamant in his opinions on commitment. He had been so clear-cut when he had laid down the rules of this charade. But if she had been wrong-footed by Cupid, then who was to say that he hadn't been, as well?

'Marry you?'

'I can see that my proposal is shocking but—' he slid off the sofa, flexing his muscles, and slung on his trousers, zipping them up but not bothering with the top button and not bothering with his shirt, then he returned and perched on the sofa next to her '—I don't think I considered this whole thing when I embarked on my mission to rescue Adele from her grandmother.'

'What do you mean?'

'My father was desperate to make sure that his granddaughter was brought to England. He'd read between the lines of Sean's infrequent communications to fear the worst and I was inclined to agree with him.

The fact that Sean wanted the child to live in England was another argument for the defence, so to speak.'

Sammy was barely following what he was saying. She was too busy wondering where the marriage proposal had been buried. The breathless excitement that had raced through her was giving way to confusion.

'Yes…'

'I expected,' Leo confessed, 'that the difficult part would be getting the grandmother to acquiesce. In other words, I had focused exclusively on winning the custody battle and, with that in the forefront of my mind, all other considerations had taken a back seat.'

'Okay…' It seemed ridiculous that he had put his trousers back on while she remained on the sofa in her birthday suit, so she, likewise, stuck on her shorts and her tee shirt although she could still smell the tang of sex on her body and could still feel the powerful throb of him inside her.

She sat up straight, hands primly on her knees, and watched him.

'Of course, I did understand that having a child around would alter the dynamics of my life.'

'Did you really?'

Leo grimaced. 'I deserve your sarcasm,' he conceded with a graceful gesture of rueful surrender. 'I was naïve.'

'You're way too accustomed to having everything your own way.'

'I also thought that Adele would be…less stubborn. I have no experience with young children but, in my head, I naturally assumed that this would, indeed, be a rescue mission and the object of the rescue would be overjoyed at being saved.'

'And instead,' Sammy filled in slowly, 'you got a little girl with problems and anxieties. And despite the fact that remaining in this country with her grandmother will probably be the worst thing for her, despite the fact that she probably, from the sounds of it, doesn't even *enjoy* living with her, it's still all she's ever known and she's going to cling to the familiarity.'

'I frighten her,' Leo said bluntly. 'The second I try to engage her in conversation, she clams up. The minute I get too close, even if I'm obeying your teacher theory of stooping down to her level, she looks as though she's going to have a panic attack.'

'She just needs to get used to you and she will. Wait and see.'

'Whilst I deeply appreciate your stirring words of encouragement,' Leo said wryly, 'I don't have a great deal of time left over here before the case is decided one way or another. If the outcome is that she is allowed to come back with me, and I very much think that it will be a favourable outcome, then it doesn't give me much time for the bonding process to be solidified.' He looked at her speculatively. 'She likes you. She feels safe with you.'

Sammy didn't say anything. The marriage proposal and that brief flare of thrilling, wonderful joy had withered fast. She knew where he was going and it made her feel faint.

'And so you want to marry me because marrying me would make your life easier with Adele.'

Leo flushed darkly. 'That's not quite how I would have put it.'

'Then how would you have put it?'

'What started as a necessary charade to win this

custody battle has stopped being a charade. We're lovers and we both know the sex between us is amazing. On top of that, you have won Adele over. She trusts you and it would certainly make things easier for her if you were to be around when we return to London. Provided, of course, that we return mission accomplished,' he amended dutifully.

'You've paid me a great deal of money,' Sammy said coolly. 'You could just have asked me to stick around for a couple of weeks until she settled in to life over there.'

'I could have,' Leo admitted, 'but it occurred to me that marriage might be no bad thing. I cannot expect to resume my old life as I knew it with a child on the scene.'

'So what you're proposing is a business arrangement.' Sammy's voice had dropped from cool to positively freezing.

'Since when can sex ever be classified as part of a business arrangement?'

Restlessness consumed her and she paced the room, prowling to stand by the glass pane overlooking the living area, distractedly appreciating the fabulous symmetry of the house while she fought down the hurt and anger of being offered a marriage of convenience.

'I don't suppose it's occurred to you that I might want a little bit more for myself than a marriage of convenience?'

Leo's jaw clenched. He wondered whether he had approached this matter in the right way but how else could he have broached the subject? And why was she now attacking him? He had asked her to marry him. It was a proposal that made sense and not just for him but for her, as well. They got along and the sex was great.

She would make a terrific surrogate mother to Adele. Was the prospect of all of that, with unlimited money thrown in for good measure, so appalling?

She was a virgin when she had met him. So obviously the man of her dreams had not sauntered by waving a wedding ring in his hand and patting a cushion in preparation for his bended knee, and surely she was practical enough to wonder whether such a man existed anyway.

Whatever line of reasoning he used, Leo knew that he was aggrieved because he had offered her marriage, the single thing he had never offered any other woman, and she had turned him down, which no other woman— not one, not a single one—would have done.

'You only want to marry me because it makes sense.' Bitter disappointment made her sound shrill. She hated herself for actually imagining, even for a second, that he had been about to follow up on his marriage proposal with a confession of love. She had truly forgotten the game they'd been playing. She'd truly forgotten that he hadn't jumped into bed with her for any other reason than passing lust and, now that they were lovers, she made sense as a wife because of the relationship she had fostered with his charge.

'Remind me what's wrong with a marriage based on good sense,' Leo gritted. 'Look at my father's disastrous union with Sean's mother and Sean's disastrous union with Adele's mother. The list could go on and on and on. Emotions have a nasty habit of sabotaging good intentions.'

'No.' It would be pointless going into lots of reasons why she wouldn't marry him but for her the biggest one was that he just didn't love her and, when it came to spending the rest of her life with someone, love had to be on the menu.

And he could quote as many disastrous unions as he wanted—that was *his* learning curve, not hers.

He wanted her to be a fixture in his life because he would be inheriting a small child and having Sammy around would enable him to return to his normal life without too much difficulty. She would be there to take the brunt of the childcare away from him. She would be working freelance and could so devote her time to ensuring that Adele settled in as best she could. Leo might have sidelined work a little whilst he was in Melbourne but as soon as his feet hit British soil he would once again immerse himself in his job and if she were around as the dutiful wife he would be unfettered by having to compromise his time.

Marrying her was the lazy, selfish solution to a complex situation he had not given much thought to.

She could understand that he might think that he was conferring a great honour on her because the women he dated would all have probably walked on a bed of burning embers to get to the other side if the ring had been on offer. He wasn't to know that she was in love with him. He wasn't to know that the thought of being with someone who couldn't love her back would have been torture.

Plus, whilst he might be attracted to her now, what was to say that he wouldn't lose interest in a few weeks' time? Without love there to provide the necessary glue to a relationship, would he consider it acceptable to have affairs with women because he had married a woman to basically look after his charge? How could the commitment ever be there between two people locked in a marriage that was an arrangement? When would she start to become a liability? In time, he would form a firm bond with Adele and her usefulness would be at an end. Would he then start regretting his impulsive proposal?

The arrangement he had proposed had more holes than a colander but she still felt sick because she knew that if she turned him down then what remained of their stay in Melbourne would be awkward and stilted and she had become so accustomed to the easy, sexy, flirty rapport they had developed.

But turn him down she would.

'I can never marry you,' she explained quietly. 'I want more from life than being harnessed to someone for all the wrong reasons. If you're worried about how Adele will adjust if you win this fight and get custody of her, then you just need to employ a nanny.' She looked him straight in the eye. 'If you employ a good-looking one, you might even find that you want to hop into bed with her. You really don't have to stick a ring on my finger to get what you want. Now, if you'll excuse me, I think I'll go have a shower…and an early night.'

CHAPTER TEN

LEO STARED, SCOWLING, at the computer in front of him. The office was, as was usual late in the evening, quiet. Under normal circumstances, he would have relished the peace and solitude to catch up on the enormous amount of work that required his undivided attention.

Unfortunately, normal circumstances had not been in evidence for some time now.

And yet current circumstances couldn't have been more *normal* in the great scheme of things. He had won custody of Adele. The child psychologist had done a thorough job, had spent time assessing Adele through the child-friendly means of drawing, paper tasks and games. Unbeknown to Leo, it emerged that some testing had previously taken place and had indicated some areas of concern with her grandmother. These areas of concern were not in evidence when it came to Adele's experiences with Leo and Sammy. The process of bonding had begun and the psychologist had been gratified to note that, thanks to her interpretation of the various tasks set, under that quiet five-year-old's exterior was a child who was tentative but keen to face the future with a couple who would allow her to be a child without fear of reprisal. Ironically, the act they had instigated had convinced everyone that the love between them would provide just the security that Adele needed.

Furthermore, the parting of ways between the child and her grandmother had been less nightmarish than expected, thanks to the vast amount of cash he had gifted the woman. Along with assurances that contact would be maintained between her and her granddaughter, with one trip a year being paid for so that they could physically meet. With defeat staring her in the face, Gail had tactfully backtracked from her belligerent stance to become the epitome of helpfulness.

That had been over two months ago.

He had, before even leaving Melbourne, instructed his PA to supervise the redecorating of the room Adele would call her own and, with money thrown at the project, it had been completed in record time.

A week after the agreement had been reached, they had arrived back at his penthouse apartment to a wonderfully child-friendly environment.

Sammy had even gone beyond the call of duty and stayed on the scene for a couple of weeks after they'd returned.

Leo's scowl deepened. She'd thrown his marriage proposal back in his face, politely told him that circumstances had altered and she would no longer feel comfortable being his lover and had then proceeded to act as though nothing had ever happened between them. She had blanked out the amazing sex and turned into a distant friend, acting the part she had been hired to play. She had spent the remainder of their time at the villa keeping Adele occupied, smiling and chatting politely to him and reading her book in the evenings, out on the front deck that gave on to the spectacular ocean views.

He hadn't been able to comprehend why she had turned him down.

What he *did* comprehend, what had become patently clear over time, as she had gradually extricated herself out of his life, was that she had left some kind of ridiculous void.

She was on his mind all the time.

He couldn't focus.

There were many times he wanted to talk to her about Adele, ask her opinion on the child's progress. He knew she'd have been pleased at how *his* progress with Adele had been and he caught himself wishing she was around to congratulate him, with that warm smile that he missed so much.

He had got a top child psychologist on board to come for little 'chats' three times a week, so that he could spot any problems in the making, of which there were, thankfully, none. She would have approved of that. He had taken his time and, with Sammy's help during those first couple of weeks, had employed a young nanny who worked part-time at the school into which Adele had been enrolled. He had made a big effort to try and curtail his working hours and he had spent every weekend with his father, who had been over the moon to have his granddaughter back in England.

Indeed, this was the first late night he had had at the office and only because Adele was in the country staying with his father for a long weekend.

He would be joining them at lunchtime the following day.

It irked him to acknowledge that he couldn't stop wondering whether Sammy had spent the day with Adele and his father. He knew that she was building up her fledgling career as a freelance artist because his father had told him so in passing.

Pride had prevented him from asking for more detailed information.

But pride made a very cold bedfellow and his bed was the coldest it had been since he had reached adulthood. He had no interest in inviting any woman to share it.

With a groan of pure frustration, Leo glanced at his watch to register that it was a little after eight and he had managed to achieve very little on the work front.

This couldn't continue. Accustomed to assuming that for every single problem there was a solution, Leo made his mind up on the spot. It would take him several hours to get down to Devon but the only way he would ever get the wretched woman out of his head was if he actually confronted her.

They had parted company with too many things left unsaid behind the polite smiles and courteous, remote conversation and cornflower-blue eyes that had refused to quite meet his.

He needed to tell her...

Leo's mind braked to a halt and he frowned because he had to dig deep to find the answer to that and digging deep when it came to anything emotional was not in his nature.

So instead he focused on the logistics of getting down to Devon on a Friday evening, debating whether to get his driver to do the honours so that he could try and work in the back of the limo, or else driving himself.

Moving and thinking at the same time, he opted to drive down himself.

He enjoyed driving and being behind the wheel of his high-performance sports car might just clear his head.

There was no need to pack for he kept a wardrobe in his room at his father's house so he didn't have to return to his apartment.

He hit the road and as soon as he cleared the chaos of late-evening London traffic his head also began to clear. Just leaving London behind induced a rush of freedom and he realised that this, at least in part, was down to the fact that he was going to do something about the messy tangle of emotions that had afflicted him ever since Sammy had walked out of his life.

In the morning he would talk to her.

He would pay her a civilised visit. He would ask her how she was doing. Ask to see the studio, maybe talk about her work. Having a civilised conversation with her would fill the nagging hole she had left in his life. It would remove her from the pedestal on which she had somehow managed to get herself placed and he would once again see her for what she was—a nice, uncomplicated and rather ordinary young woman who was ill suited to have any place in his fast-moving, high-octane London life.

She had been a temporary blip and because of the way things had ended, because she had been the one to walk away, he had been left with his nose out of joint.

Wounded pride and a dented ego were curable ailments but he would have to re-establish some sort of normality between them instead of the frozen silence that currently existed.

Frankly, he just felt that he needed to see the woman to get a grip on his wayward emotions.

Adele would be pleased to see him and he found himself smiling. Every shy smile she directed at him was worth its weight in gold.

He had never had much of a paternal streak in him and he had accepted that having the child in his life would be the equivalent of taking on an honourable duty, but Leo was beginning to taste the sweet beginnings of unconditional, uncomplicated love.

He was discovering that there was nothing boring in looking at a three-line story written in oversized letters that were misspelt. Nor was it a waste of his time fumbling to try to braid her hair and secure the braid with the bright pink ribbons she seemed to like so much. She still didn't talk much but she no longer darted into hiding whenever he appeared. The nanny and the psychologist had worked miracles but the miracle had really started in Melbourne, under the attentive eye of Sammy.

Thoughts flitted through his head as he steadily burned up the distance between London and Devon.

He didn't allow any of them to settle for too long. He knew that at one point he toyed with the crazy notion that the only way he would get her out of his system would be if he slept with her again.

It was beyond incomprehensible because he couldn't conceive of ever chasing behind any woman who had turned him down, especially one who had turned him down when the offer had gone way past the bedroom door and up the aisle in a church.

But the memory of her responsive, hot body still burned a hole through all his attempts at shutting down the temptation to try it on with her again.

He was barely aware of the darkness gathering as he drove fast and smooth past Bristol and into the West Country.

He was also barely aware that he had bypassed the usual route to his father's mansion and was instead following the less travelled road to where Sammy lived with her mother.

He knew the route.

He had taken it on two occasions, the first when they had both arrived down in Devon with Adele and had taken her first to see the grandfather she had never known and then to Sammy's mother. The second time he had managed to find some excuse to take his little charge there. It had been only two weeks previously and Sammy had not been there. He had made a point of not asking where she was.

Leo found himself parked outside the cottage, which was in predictable darkness at a little before midnight, and he honestly couldn't work out at what point his plans for a civilised chat first thing in the morning had changed.

Sammy heard something outside and woke up instantly, although it took her a few seconds to register exactly what it was she was hearing. When she *did* register the source of the noise, she was too alarmed and, frankly, confused to do anything but sit up in bed and hold her breath.

Just in case she had imagined the whole thing and she had, in fact, been awakened by a bad dream. One of the many that plagued her largely restless nights since she had returned to Devon.

Her life should have been a bed of roses. Leo had fulfilled all the financial obligations as promised and more. She now had a fabulous studio in which to work, was right there for her mother, whose health was improving hourly because there were no money worries distressing her to bring her down and cause her sleepless nights. She had arranged a part-time teaching job at a nearby school, just so that she could continue having adult company because freelance work could be a solitary career. Two evenings a week, she went into the school and helped with additional lessons for some of the children. The atmosphere at the school was lively, the teachers were young and she loved it there.

But behind the smiles and cheerful façade of the perfect life, she couldn't stop thinking about Leo and the brief relationship they had shared.

She knew that she'd done the right thing in turning down his marriage proposal but, where that clear-cut decision should have helped her move on, she seemed caught in a halfway house of muddled emotions and dissatisfied longings. And she also missed Adele. They had formed a bond in the time they had spent together and, although she had seen her a few times since she had returned to pick up the pieces of her life in Devon, she wished that she could see the child more, could play more of a part in her growing life.

The sound of something hitting her window snapped her back to the present and she warily sidled towards the window, making sure not to turn on any lights in the room, and pulled back just enough of the curtain to peer out without being seen.

Her heart began to thump and her mouth went dry because although she hadn't known *what* she had been expecting, it certainly hadn't been Leo.

And definitely not Leo, the epitome of everything that was an alpha male, throwing pebbles at her window. How did he even know *which* window was hers? And then she worked out that it wouldn't have been difficult. The cottage was tiny and only her mother would have occupied, for health and mobility reasons, the bedroom on the ground floor.

She yanked back the curtains and raised the sash window.

'Leo!' For a few seconds her brain seized up. 'What the heck are you doing?'

Good question, Leo thought. He shoved his hands into his pockets and glared up at her, his midnight-black eyes narrowing on her face with the sort of accusation that had Sammy's bewilderment turning to sudden anger.

How dare he show up at her house and throw her into turmoil when turmoil was exactly what she was so desperate to run away from? What gave him the right to mess with her head by just appearing out of nowhere? And why was he here anyway?

At midnight?

When the whole world was asleep?

She flew down the stairs, as silent as a ghost for fear of waking her mother, which was unlikely because she was nothing if not a deep sleeper. Still, it was better to take no chances. When she had returned, mission accomplished, engagement off, she had had the sneaking suspicion that her mother had been disappointed. Although when she had lightly raised the subject, her mumbling concerns had been laughingly waved aside.

But were her mother to wake up and find her daughter caught in a mysterious tryst with Leo, then who knew what idiotic ideas she might start conceiving?

Which brought her right back to wondering what he was doing on her doorstep, as she pulled open the door and, not seeing him there, carefully stepped out into the night.

Dressed in just her thin oversized tee shirt and with only fluffy bedroom slippers on her feet, the cool early spring air instantly made her shiver. She wrapped her arms around her body and tentatively circled to the side of the house to find him leaning against the wall, so tall, so lean and so ferociously masculine that she felt the breath catch in her throat.

'L-Leo,' she stammered, taken aback by his body language and by the sideways glance he slung in her direction at the sound of her approach. 'What on earth are you doing here?' Her breathing was raspy and uneven, her heart thundered inside her, her eyes were riveted to his lean face, drinking him in the way a starving man might eye up a banquet.

His lack of self-control in ending up here, bringing her outside by a thirteen-year-old's ploy of throwing stones at her window, slammed into him with the force of a sledgehammer and made him stiffen in automatic self-defence.

He had never done anything like this before or ever acted with such a lack of discipline and even now, as his gaze swept over her scantily clad body, he could feel his self-control drop another notch.

'Going to invite me inside?' He pushed himself off the wall but kept his hands firmly in his pockets. 'I decided not to ring the doorbell in case your mother was sleeping.'

'Why are you here?' she breathed shakily.

'I...' He looked away. 'I had to talk to you.'

'At *this* hour?'

'I drove straight down from London,' he said in a non sequitur.

'You could have just called me.'

On the back foot yet again, he bunched his fists and fought down his instinctive urge to try to take command of the situation in any way he could think.

'I needed to see you. I needed to talk to you face-to-face and I thought that if I phoned you, you might be tempted to ignore my call. I wasn't taking any chances.' His glare challenged her to take issue with what he had said but Sammy was so shocked at his raw honesty that she could only stare at him.

She spun round, heart beating fast, and led the way back into the house. She was scarcely conscious of the fact that she was dressed in next to nothing or that the stiffened peaks of her nipples were poking against the soft jersey cotton of her tee shirt.

She'd tried hard to forget the impact he had on her but just seeing him here now, as she shut the kitchen door behind her and leant against it, was reminding her of her aching weakness for him—a weakness she didn't want.

'Surely whatever you have to say could have waited until tomorrow. Is it to do with Adele? I know you've been looking at schools for her in London.'

Don't let your imagination run away with you.

Don't start reading anything behind that intense, disconcerting expression on his face.

'How do you know that?'

'Because your father told me.' Face flaming red, she turned her back on him to put the kettle on for some coffee, hands shaking.

'You've been talking to my father about me?' Leo asked quickly and, he was forced to admit to himself, hopefully.

'No!' Sammy spun round to face him and leaned

against the counter by the sink, arms folded, very conscious now of her legs on display. 'He mentioned it in passing. I can't think of any reason for you to have just shown up here unless you had some pressing need to ask my advice on schools since I taught in one for quite a while. And that doesn't make sense anyway! That's the sort of thing that could easily have waited until tomorrow. Why won't you just tell me what brought you here?' The atmosphere had shifted and her skin warmed as his eyes roved over her and suddenly she just *knew* why he had come under cover of darkness, *knowing* that he would find her mother fast asleep!

Except surely he wasn't arrogant enough to think that because *she* had been the one to walk away from him that the scales wouldn't be balanced until she warmed his bed again and *he* was the one to walk away? The way he always walked away from women? It seemed incredible but why else would he have descended here at this hour of the night? She truly couldn't think of any other explanation and was frankly appalled when she actually gave houseroom to the tempting idea of taking him up on any advances he might make because she just missed him so much.

'I…' Leo surprised himself by faltering. 'I had to,' he said in a driven undertone and Sammy's brow pleated in consternation. 'You turned down my marriage proposal.'

'You came all the way here and threw stones at my window to tell me *that*?'

'I told you why I didn't ring the doorbell.'

'But I still don't know why you're here.'

And it's not fair to spring yourself on me because I'm not strong enough to withstand your impact.

'I haven't been able to stop thinking about you.' His fabulous dark eyes held hers. 'I couldn't believe it when you turned me down.'

'Because you're so accustomed to getting your own way,' Sammy said painfully, lowering her eyes and sipping some of the coffee. She noticed that her hands were shaking a little and hoped that he hadn't noticed that, as well. Every nerve and sinew and pore in her body was reacting to his presence, putting her on hyperalert and touching her in places she didn't want. It wasn't fair!

'You can't just show up here and say stuff like that!'

'It's the truth. You make me lose sleep.' He groaned, impatient with the way he suddenly couldn't find the right words to express what he wanted to say. 'When you rejected me I thought that it was something I would be able to shrug off without too much difficulty. I had never let my emotions get in the way of my private life. I had always known where my priorities were. My father had set me a good example when it came to being wary of the pitfalls of acting on impulse and flinging yourself into situations because you were being guided by your heart and not your head. The truth is that I've been thinking about you every day. And every day I managed to convince myself that common sense would reassert itself and I would actually be able to get on with my work and with my life…'

Sammy fought down a wave of disappointment because he was simply confirming what she had already concluded for herself. He had been driven to show up because he hadn't been able to accept the reality of being turned down, especially when it had involved something as serious as a marriage proposal.

'I'm not going to fall into bed with you because…

because you miss me,' she said on a hitched breath and Leo flushed. Yes, he missed her. Another weakness of which he was not proud but a weakness, he now realised, he had never had a hope in hell of combating.

He found that he was hesitant to ask her whether *she* missed *him*. What if her answer was *no*? Never before had Leo felt himself treading carefully on such uncertain ground.

Lush lashes shielded his gaze as he lowered his eyes. Sammy itched to reach out to him and she knew that it was just the effect he had on her. He made her want to touch.

'It's not just about missing you.' He recognised what was at the very heart of the restless turmoil that had been undermining his usual single-minded focus for the past few months. 'It's more than that. I feel things for you.'

'You feel *things* for me? What sort of *things*?' Sammy refused to be drawn into feeling hopeful because she had been down that road once and wasn't going to be lured down it again.

'I need you in my life, Sammy.'

'You think you need me because of Adele.'

'This has nothing to do with Adele. My relationship with her is improving by the day. I—no, this is to do with how I feel about you. You came into my life for reasons I could never have predicted and you changed my life and all my priorities. You're warm and funny and smart and all those things should have alerted me to the real reason why I proposed to you.'

'What real reason?' Sammy drew in an expectant breath and held it.

'I love you, Sammy. I fell in love with you out there

in Melbourne but I didn't wake up to that because I had always associated falling in love with the kind of excesses I had witnessed, not just in my father and my stepbrother, but in friends, as well.'

'You love me?'

'I love you with all my heart.' His dark eyes were intense with emotion. 'I'd locked away the simple truth that my father adored my mother. I'd sidelined it because the impact of my father's second marriage occurred when I was older and perhaps that's why it was the example I processed more easily. He lost a fortune to that woman who used him ruthlessly and took advantage of his emotional nature. Indeed, he only went into that marriage because he hadn't been able to cope with my mother's death. All in all, I'd resolved from an early age to approach life a lot more phlegmatically than my father had always been prone to do. So when I started loving you it was easy for me to write it off as lust. Lust was something I could deal with. I should have known the minute I proposed to you that I should sit up and take notice.'

'I turned you down because I needed you to love me,' Sammy said, heart full. She reached across the table and they linked fingers. 'I knew that I had fallen for you and I knew that if all you wanted was a suitable mother figure for Adele then it would just be a matter of time before you got fed up having me around and started regretting the fact that you were stuck with me if we married. You don't know how many times I asked myself whether I made the right decision to turn you down.' She grimaced. 'I had to keep reminding myself that you didn't love me and that I would end up getting terribly hurt because you didn't. When you showed up here tonight…' She looked at him with love in her eyes. 'I actually thought that you might have come to try to seduce me. And, if you had, I knew I would have been so tempted to have just caved in.'

'Will you marry me, Sammy? Because I can't live without you. Because you give my life shape and meaning.'

Tears glimmering in her eyes, Sammy smiled and moved round the table to sit on his lap and entwine her hands tightly round his neck. 'I will.'

The following day they announced their engagement— their *real* engagement—to Adele and their parents. They had expected surprise and had anticipated a few seconds of shock. Instead, Sammy's mother exchanged a smug smile with Leo's father.

'I told you,' she said comfortably.

'You win.' Harold chuckled. 'Remind me,' he told his son, beaming, 'never to make a bet with a woman again. This lady never doubted that you'd end up together.'

Adele, sitting pressed between the adults, looked at them for a few seconds and then said tentatively, her little face alive with pleasure, 'When you get married, can I wear pink?'

* * * * *

HIS MAJESTY'S
TEMPORARY BRIDE

ANNIE WEST

This is my 30th book for Harlequin Mills and Boon! Thirty stories would not have been possible without the support of my fabulous editorial team in London and all the other staff who work hard to ensure my published books are the best they can be. My family, who are gracious and supportive despite my mind often being elsewhere. My writing friends, who know how to celebrate and motivate and make even the tough days fun.

And above all you, my readers, who enjoy the books and encourage me to keep dreaming.

Thank you so very much!

PROLOGUE

CAT VAULTED OVER the low wall, her blood singing at the sheer joy of running *parcours*. Her breathing was fast but her movements measured as she and Paolo raced through the abandoned warehouse.

She vaulted, then made a tic-tac of her feet on a wall as she built momentum and leapt, grabbing the edge of an empty skylight. Swinging, Cat hauled herself up and over the edge. It was there Paolo passed her. She was fast and agile but he beat her hands-down in upper body strength.

With a whoop he was away, across the roof to clatter down an empty stairwell while she raced to draw close. Bounding off stairs, walls and a balustrade, she'd almost caught him when they reached the perimeter fence.

'Mine today,' he gasped.

Cat nodded, bracing hands on knees. Her ponytail swung over her shoulder as she breathed deep. 'That *passe muraille* of yours was faultless.'

He grinned. 'Something for you to aim for?'

She punched his arm. 'Almost up to my standard.'

They headed for the exit. 'Same time next week?'

'I may have a job out of town. I'll call.'

He nodded and unlocked his car. 'You need a lift?'

Cat shook her head. 'No. I'm heading to the gym.' The outwardly dilapidated but excellent gym they used was around the corner. She wanted to check on the kids she'd been coaching after school. They were troubled teens, like she'd been. But they showed promise and while she was between jobs she enjoyed being with them.

She turned into the dog-leg alley shortcut, head full of teenagers and their prickly pride. Which was no excuse for the few seconds it took to scope danger. The shiny limo was out of place in this part of New York. But it was the tall guy with the bulge under his jacket, peeling away from the wall, she should have noticed instantly.

He moved fast as a professional. But so was she. When he reached for her she ducked, grabbed his wrist and used his forward momentum to crash him to the ground. Knee between his shoulder blades, she took his gun.

'Ms Dubois!'

She turned, hearing the man beneath her groan as her knee swivelled. Standing in the doorway of the limo was a slim man in a dark suit, eyes wide.

'Ms Dubois, please. I only want to talk.' The air expelled from her lungs in a rush. Because the man didn't speak English but the distinctive patois of her native tongue—a modified version of French. Alarm bells rang, leaving her more rather than less alert.

'Who are you?' She eased back, giving the guy beneath her room to breathe, keeping a hand locked on his wrist.

The man at the limo stepped closer. 'I'm the St Gallan ambassador to the US. I'm here with a job offer. If I may show you my credentials?' Slowly he approached and Cat read his ID. It was genuine.

Tucking the gun into her waistband, she rose. 'If you want to talk, why send *him*?' She gestured to the big man clambering to his feet.

The ambassador grimaced. 'I was told you might not welcome an approach from St Galla and I needed to be sure you'd listen. His instructions were to bring you to the car so we could talk.'

His bodyguard straightened, rolling his shoulder to test it and nodded. 'Tactical mistake. I knew you were one of us but I didn't expect…' He shrugged, then winced.

'I'm not interested in a job in St Galla.' She'd left her island home at eighteen after her mother's funeral. The place held nothing for her after she lost the one person who'd ever loved her, the only one *she'd* loved.

The ambassador nodded. 'There's someone who could change your mind. The Prime Minister is waiting.'

Cat's eyes darted to the limo's tinted windows.

'A long-distance call. Allow me to offer you the privacy of my car while you talk.'

Angry and confused, Cat was in no mood to comply. But curiosity won and she found herself alone in the vehicle, looking at a screen and the thin, clever face of the St Gallan Prime Minister, Monsieur Barthe. He looked shocked.

'By God, you *are* like her! I saw the photos but...'

Cat's skin crawled. That feeling of a thousand ants swarming. She hadn't felt it in years but it was back with a vengeance, dredging a lifetime's painful memories.

'Who are you talking about?' As if she didn't know.

'Princess Amelie.' He shook his head. 'The similarity is astonishing.'

Cat remained silent. She'd learned there was nothing she could say. As a kid, the taunts and snide accusations had grown unbearable. She'd tried turning the other cheek, ignoring them, even fighting back when the bullies got physical. All that had got her was more trouble. On the upside it led to an interest in martial arts that had eventually been her key to escape.

She set her jaw, hating the feeling of powerlessness after all these years and a continent of distance. It was as if ten years had vanished in an instant, all she'd achieved a mirage.

'Ms Dubois, I have an important, confidential assignment for you.'

'I'm always discreet.' As a bodyguard to the famous it was a necessity. 'But I'm not interested.'

'This is for your country.'

Her country could go hang. She hadn't been able to shake its dust soon enough. Her first eighteen years had been tor-

ment, defending herself and her mother's reputation endlessly in public. Then at home, watching the man she'd had
to call father grind her mother down.

'I'm still not interested.'

'Even though Lambis Evangelos recommended you?'

Lambis? He was the best in the business. His company
ran the best in the business. They'd met in Chicago when
she worked with Afra, the superstar singer. Cat had been
pleased at his interest, his offer of an open door if ever she
wanted work.

But to work in St Galla? She shuddered. 'I suggest you
find someone else.'

Shrewd eyes surveyed her. The next question would be
why she wouldn't return to her homeland. As if she'd share
that with anyone. The only people who'd known the truth
about her were dead. She wasn't about to let anyone else in
on her sordid secret.

'There are plenty of other bodyguards.' Though she
prided herself that those who employed her asked for her
again and again, particularly women who felt more comfortable with a female shadowing them.

His voice dropped. 'We need your special…attributes.
Mr Evangelos suggested you if we ever needed a body double for Princess Amelie.'

Cat sat back, pulse racing. 'She's in danger?' Her voice
was inexplicably husky. She'd never met the Princess yet
still she felt a connection.

'Not…danger. Though the situation is delicate.'

'What situation?'

'The Princess is…away.' He paused as if choosing his
words. 'We're not sure when she'll return. Meantime it's
vital she appear at a small palace reception. This event *must*
go ahead, for the nation and the Princess herself.'

Cat stared. 'You want me to impersonate Princess Amelie? You can't be serious!' She'd grown up being compared

with the Princess. The woman was charming, elegant, graceful, accomplished in ways Cat wasn't. She wore jewels and formal gowns. Cat was allergic to high heels and had never worn a full-length dress in her life.

'Deadly serious.' His tone chilled her and again that shiver of preternatural connection, of anxiety, passed through her. 'You wouldn't have to face anyone who knows the Princess well. All you have to do is make an appearance, chat a little, then withdraw.'

'It's not possible.'

'Not even for a very generous settlement?' Monsieur Barthe named a sum that made her goggle.

'You can't be serious.' Shock stretched her voice.

His mouth tightened. 'Completely. Money is no object.'

Cat blinked. With that money she could achieve her dream. Bodyguard work had been good to her but she couldn't do it for ever. Already she wondered how long her knee would hold up long-term. Last year she'd been injured saving Afra from a car driven by a crazed stalker. It had been a long slog to get back to something like her previous fitness.

Cat had no other qualifications, no career path. But working with kids, diverting their negative energy into physical endeavours and a positive outlook—*that* she could do. Developing a centre either in the wilderness or in a city gym devoted specifically to kids—she'd give so much to achieve that. For the kids and herself.

'Half the money in advance and half on completion.'

She jerked her head up, meeting steely eyes that had read her momentary lapse.

Cat shook her head. 'I might look superficially like her, but I'm no princess. Everyone would know.'

'Not a problem. You'd stay at the palace in advance of the event to be tutored in everything you need to know.'

He paused, surveying her set features. 'Look on it as your chance to see how the other half lives.'

Cat stared as the words insinuated themselves into her brain. How often in childhood had she wondered what it was like to be Amelie? To live the cosseted life of a rich, beloved child, adored by her father and the nation? It had been a fantasy she'd retreated to when reality grew unbearable. She'd put it behind her years ago, yet to her amazement shreds of that yearning still lingered.

'I'll double the fee.'

Cat goggled. The amount was ridiculously huge. What on earth was going on?

'The Princess…is she safe?' Again, that sixth sense niggle of concern.

'I'm not in a position to say. But you'll help her enormously by doing this.'

Cat didn't need Princess Amelie's gratitude. She could get by without the money, even though it represented more than she'd earn in the next several years. It shouldn't matter if it brought her dream to reality.

Returning to the country of her birth would betray the vow she'd made at eighteen never to look back.

Yet something stopped her refusal. The possibility that Amelie genuinely needed her? Or that the bastard half-sister finally had a chance to discover what life would have been like if she'd been born legitimate? To experience the life she might have had?

No, it was far more than that. This wasn't curiosity to see how the other half lived. It was a desire, deep down in her secret self, to connect with the family she'd never known. To find a way to meet her sibling. For years she'd told herself no good could come of connecting with her royal relations, yet still that yearning remained. To belong.

Cat cleared her throat, hating the tug of emotion turning

her voice hoarse. Hating the neediness. She'd thought she'd conquered it years ago.

Maybe this is your chance to do that.

And still that snaking anxiety for the half-sister she'd never met. 'Send me a contract to consider.'

His smile told her he knew he'd won. 'You won't regret it, Ms Dubois.'

She already did. But she had to do this and silence once and for all the voices of her murky past.

CHAPTER ONE

ALEX STRETCHED, STARING out over the azure depths of the Mediterranean.

He hadn't wanted to come. If he'd been able to avoid the celebration in St Galla he'd have done it, especially as his mother had stitched up a half-baked proposal that Princess Amelie would make him the perfect bride.

He was only thirty-two, had only been King for three years. He had more important things to grapple with than marrying, no matter what his advisers thought.

Giving up a career he loved to rule Bengaria hadn't been in his plans. Alex's fists clenched as he leaned on the gleaming rail of the yacht.

It should have been his cousin, Stefan, on the throne. Except for the accident that had snuffed out his life and propelled Alex's father into his place. His late and unlamented father. The man who'd almost bankrupted Bengaria in the years he'd been Stefan's Regent and later the King. The man whose chicanery and double-dealing had milked the nation almost to a standstill, leaving Alex to haul an economic nightmare out of the red and into the black.

No wonder everyone wanted Alex to marry Amelie. St Galla was wealthy and could help Bengaria, even though he was hopeful his country was beginning to recover now.

He sighed and forked a hand through his hair. He'd only agreed to the visit because of his mother. She'd suffered long and hard through her marriage. Alex had at least escaped his father's control by leaving Bengaria and pursuing a career as a pilot. She'd been stuck in a loveless marriage to a despicable man.

A familiar chill rippled down his spine at the thought of his father.

In the circumstances, meeting Amelie, the daughter of his mother's best friend, was little recompense for all she'd put up with. He'd attend the reception to commemorate five hundred years of friendship between their countries then return home and report that Amelie wasn't the woman for him.

Now, with the early sun warming his bare back and the prospect of no civic duties, he felt a lightness he hadn't known since he'd given up flying. These couple of days were his first vacation in three years. Even though he'd spend most of it working from his office on the yacht, it felt like freedom. Temporary but glorious.

He sauntered along the deck, contemplating a dip, when a shout rang out. He swivelled to face the shore.

Another shout. A splash.

Alex narrowed his eyes against the sun's golden dazzle. In the distance he made out a capsized canoe and flailing arms. Another shout and a submerging head.

'George!' He raced along the deck. 'Get the tender! Someone's in trouble.' For the people—two of them—weren't swimming. One floated near the hull of the canoe and a second floundered mere metres from it.

Alex dived, the cool water a shock after the warmth of the sun. He surfaced and powered towards the accident.

How had they capsized in such still waters?

Why weren't they wearing life vests? Obviously they weren't since one was sinking.

Hauling in air, Alex forced himself to concentrate on the quick, hard rhythm of his strokes, forging through the water with a speed that might, he hoped, save a life and hopefully two.

A gurgling cry told him he was close and he stopped to discover he was only metres away.

A third head bobbed in the water but he realised with re-lief this woman could swim. She held a boy under the chin, propping his face above water as she sliced back through the water towards the canoe.

'You're okay?' he gasped.

Her head lifted and his gaze collided with gleaming green, the colour of mountain meadows.

'We will be,' she said through gritted teeth, 'when he stops fighting me.' The teenager was flailing, one long, thin arm reaching back, grabbing at her head.

Alex moved towards them but she was already disen-gaging the kid's grasp, telling him firmly but calmly to lie still and let her do the work. Seeing she had things under control, he turned to the canoe where another dark head bobbed precariously low in the water.

Swearing under his breath he raced across, hauling a body up under the arms till the kid started coughing water. No hope of righting the canoe with a dead weight in his hands. Instead he shoved the kid high, so high he lay sprawled over the hull, arms flopping down its other side.

Satisfied he was safe, Alex turned and found the other swimmer had successfully brought the second boy up be-hind him.

'Let me give you a hand.'

She nodded and told the kid what they were going to do, again in that clear, calm tone. Then she held the canoe steady while Alex hauled him up onto the hull beside his companion.

Alex's chest and shoulders burned from the effort. Both teens were lanky and getting purchase in the water had taken a lot of strength. He grimaced. He needed to get out of the office a whole lot more.

'You'll be okay.' He blinked and realised the woman wasn't reassuring him but the two boys. She'd moved round to the other side of the canoe and was inspecting them.

Alex joined her, relieved to see both kids breathing, albeit in rough gasps.

In the distance he heard a motor start. 'Help's on its way. That's the tender from the yacht.'

She nodded, her attention fixed on the youngsters, and Alex found his gaze dwelling on her high-cut cheekbones, straight nose and plump bow of a mouth. Mermaids were supposed to be beautiful and this one didn't disappoint.

Abruptly she turned her head, catching his stare. Alex felt their gazes mesh, a palpable connection, and wondered if it had been so long since he'd been with a pretty woman that his brain had turned to mush in the interim.

'What?'

'Nothing.' He shook his head. 'It will be easier to transfer them from the other side. I'll go round and help George if you can stay here and reassure them.'

'Of course.' Her voice had a lilt that tugged at something deep inside and told him English wasn't her first language. He wondered how his name would sound on her lips.

Alex swam around the canoe. First her eyes, now her voice. Had it *really* been so long since he'd been with a woman?

He banished the thought as George cut the engine and the pair of them worked to get the kids aboard. Once more his golden-haired mermaid proved quietly efficient, easing their burden.

'Here.' He beckoned her over when the others were aboard the small boat. 'I'll give you a boost up.'

'No need.' She flashed him a smile and his pulse kicked hard.

Number three. First the eyes, then the voice. But that smile surpassed the rest. It turned his cool, capable, impervious mermaid into a beckoning sea sprite. That smile was pure mischief and again he felt that draw in his belly, hard and urgent.

Before Alex knew what she intended, or George could offer her a hand, she planted her hands on the side of the tender and pulled herself up smoothly and easily.

He was treated to a view of neat breasts against a saturated T-shirt, a slim waist, baggy shorts and long, shapely legs of pale gold.

Four. Alex clutched the boat, breathing hard. Despite the cool water, this time his response wasn't belly-deep but lower, stirring his groin. He'd always had a weakness for great legs.

'Want some help?' She leaned out, ready to offer a hand, that smile dancing at the edge of her lips.

In that instant Alex knew if he was still the impulsive guy he'd once been, carefree and unencumbered by a crown, he'd have curled his hand around her neck and tugged her close. He'd have kissed her till she planted those small, capable hands on his chest and begged for more.

And he'd have given it.

'I can manage.' He hauled himself up.

It was as her eyes rounded that he remembered he'd dived naked into the sea. With the yacht's crew on shore leave and only he and George aboard, he hadn't bothered dressing when he woke.

Her gaze stayed low on his body a fraction too long, making his blood surge south in response.

Her eyes flashed to his. 'I'm guessing you weren't expecting company.' Her lips twitched.

Five. Most women he met these days lacked a sense of humour. He missed that. In his old life he'd been part of a close-knit team where humour made a demanding job easier.

'I was thinking about an early morning dip, but not like this.' He was responding way too much to the glint of humour in her bright eyes and the husky edge to her voice.

He moved further into the small boat and stood. Alex was fully aware the movement laid his back and buttocks bare to her gaze—he'd swear he could feel the prickle of her regard right now. But it was better than presenting her with what could too easily turn into a promising erection.

He hunkered down at the side of the boat, motioning for George to start the motor. One of the kids had a gash on his temple and there was a first aid kit on the yacht. To his relief though, they seemed to be improving by the minute.

By the time the five of them were on the yacht Alex knew they'd be okay. He got the first aid kit then left it in George's capable hands while he went below to dry off and dress.

Yet as he tugged on old jeans and a shirt, Alex could recall exactly how he'd felt when the mermaid's gaze dropped to his chest, lingered a second and then kept moving to his abdomen and groin. The prickle under his skin was a prelude to something he could *not* afford to give in to.

The timing was all wrong.

So was the place. The person.

Imagine the complications if he followed his instincts and pursued an affair with her right here, offshore from the palace! Especially when there were so many people in both countries promoting a royal wedding.

Alex shuddered and zipped his jeans. Marriage was *not* on the agenda.

'There's Alex now,' George said and Cat looked up. Alex, the owner of the beautiful vintage yacht, strolled towards them. His gait was loose-hipped and easy, shoulders back as if he hadn't a care in the world. Definitely the walk of an assured man. One too sexy for his own good.

Fire spiked in her blood as she recalled his lazy, half-lidded expression when she'd seen him naked. The devastatingly attractive way the corners of his mouth curled up, the gleam in those indigo eyes.

She liked a confident man. One assured enough not to bolster his ego at the expense of others.

He was athletic too. That tall body was strong and taut and oh-so attractive, with powerful thighs and sinewy forearms and a classic male outline that tapered from wide shoulders. She had a sudden recollection of the bunch of his rounded, perfect glutes as he'd walked away. Cat forced her attention back to the bandage she was securing.

'There, that should do.'

'Good work, Cat.' George, the yacht's captain, closed the first aid kit.

'Cat?' The lazy drawl was like fingertips dancing down her spine. She told herself it was the breeze cooling her ancient T-shirt against her skin but she feared it was his luscious baritone.

'Alex, this is Cat. Cat, Alex.'

'Nice to meet you... Cat.'

She looked up to read curiosity crinkling his broad brow. A flare of his nostrils brought that chiselled, patrician nose to life and his dark blue eyes narrowed as he surveyed her.

Was that tension in the pulse flicking beneath his squared jaw? No, she'd imagined it. His body language spoke of easy confidence. And a bone-deep, almost indolent sex appeal that played havoc with her hormones.

'Nice to meet you, Alex.' She kept her voice blank. The fact he'd obviously towel-dried his black hair and not bothered to comb it, leaving it appealingly dishevelled, shouldn't make her itch to touch. As for the fact he was still barefoot, and hadn't buttoned his shirt, which showed a tantalising strip of taut skin...

'How are you boys feeling?' It was easier to concentrate on them than this sudden rush of attraction.

They murmured that they were okay, one even venturing a smile. They'd be fine, now the fright wore off. But she'd feel better when a professional checked them.

Alex stopped before her. 'Why don't you dry off while we take care of the boys and rustle up a warm drink? Downstairs, second cabin on the left. There's an en suite shower and I put out clean clothes you can wear till yours dry.'

Cat was about to refuse then thought better of it. George could put her ashore using the tender so she didn't have to swim back. She'd feel better knowing she didn't look like a drowned rat. Especially as her nipples were peaking insistently against her bra and she suspected her white T-shirt was transparent.

'Thanks. I will.' With a smile for George and the boys, she made her way downstairs.

The yacht was unlike any she'd seen. In her years as a bodyguard she'd been on massive, ultra-modern motor cruisers. Huge edifices several storeys high that housed not just a small boat, but a car and even a helipad. Those cruisers were built for socialising, for glamorous parties and sybaritic self-indulgence.

This yacht was nothing like that.

Cat passed through a wide cabin that was comfortable and stylish rather than *look-at-me* trendy, though no expense had been spared. Her hand slid down a polished teak rail as she followed the stairs into a roomy corridor. On either side were gleaming timber doors finished with brass touches. Everything was pristine yet the style belonged to an earlier, more gracious era.

She pushed open the second door and found an exquisite cabin, more wood on the walls, a deep plush carpet of dusk blue and a vast bed covered in crisp white and blue.

Wary of dripping onto the carpet, Cat moved quickly into the bathroom, where the luxury continued with marble and mirrors. It was hard to believe she was on a yacht, till she looked out the window and saw the sea and the shore bright in the early light.

Quickly she stripped and showered, tying back her hair with a band she found in the cupboard. There were clothes too. A brief black bikini and an oversized white shirt.

Cat frowned. But her shorts were sodden and she rejected the idea of putting on her wet T-shirt, knowing how it clung.

The bikini fitted surprisingly well and Cat felt a moment's annoyance that Alex had calculated her size then raided his private store of women's swimwear, no doubt kept especially for his lady friends.

Shoving her arms through the shirt sleeves, she rolled them up to her elbows, relieved at the way the oversized garment fell well down her thighs. Cat hadn't missed the way Alex's eyes had gleamed as he surveyed her.

In other circumstances she might have been interested. But not now, not here, not while she was in St Galla on the most challenging job of her life.

Not while she was impersonating her royal sister.

Cat shivered and she hugged her arms around herself, rubbing away prickling gooseflesh and grateful for the soft fabric of the shirt she sincerely hoped was George's and not his boss's.

She'd had a bad feeling about this contract from the first. But it was only when she was installed in an exquisite guest apartment a corridor away from Princess Amelie's that Cat realised how completely she was out of her depth. They might share their father's royal blood but that was all.

No one would believe she was Amelie, not for a second.

Worse was the awful ache-in-the-belly certainty that it had been a mistake returning to the country where she'd been so desperately unhappy. Or to have anything to do with her distant family. She'd never belonged to them and they'd brought her nothing but trouble.

Buttoning the shirt as high as it would go, she avoided the mirror and swivelled away, grabbing her sopping wet clothes.

She'd tell the Prime Minister she couldn't go through with it. He could have his deposit back. She hadn't spent a cent. He'd probably be grateful—the lady-in-waiting who'd been trying to tutor her in etiquette, deportment and the like had made it clear Cat wasn't fit for the role.

It would be a relief to get out of this place where even the scent of the sea and the pines crowding the rocky slopes evoked painful memories.

Cat emerged on deck with a determined step but pulled up when she found it deserted.

Everyone had gone, and so had the tender, she saw when she crossed to the rear of the vessel. The shower must have masked the sound of the motor.

'There you are.' That deep, smooth voice tantalised, trailing along her skin like a caress. 'Coffee or fresh juice?'

'Neither, thanks. It's time I left.' She glanced at her waterproof watch. It was still early.

Racked by doubts, she'd got little sleep and had gone running through the palace's private grounds as the first glimmers of dawn appeared.

She swung round and caught Alex's eyes on her bare legs.

Slowly, so slowly it must be deliberate, his gaze rose from her feet to her knees, then her thighs, lingering at the hem of the shirt before surveying her body so thoroughly she knew the shirt was transparent. By the time those blue eyes collided with hers, her arms were crossed over her breasts and her mouth was pursed.

'Do you do that to every woman?' Her chin hiked. She chose to ignore the little shiver of excitement that stirred in her belly at his obvious appreciation. For once the attraction was mutual.

He shook his head and Cat caught the curl of his mouth at one corner. 'Never. I'm making an exception with you.' His lips stretched into a full smile that did devastating things to her pulse. She should be furious at such a sexist attitude but strangely her anger was hard to hang on to. 'I'm returning the favour. You took your time looking at me.'

His stare defied her to argue and Cat clenched her jaw.

She *had* got an eyeful of bare, some would say awesome, masculinity and she hadn't been eager to look away. She was in no position to object that he gave as got as he got.

Except that standing here in a brief bikini and see-through shirt, she felt vulnerable in a way she hadn't felt with any man.

Cat had spent a lifetime ensuring she was unassailable, emotionally and physically.

'Where are the others?'

'George is taking them to the recreation camp further up the coast. It turns out they took the canoe without permission and they started to think the staff might worry when they found it and them gone.'

'So how do I get ashore? Is there another boat?'

Alex shook his head. 'Just the tender. But George won't be long. In the meantime I'll get breakfast.'

'I really need to get ashore.'

'Well.' He tilted his head, appraising her. 'You could swim to the island. But you'd get wet all over again. Why don't you relax and let me cook for you?'

Cat turned, calculating the distance to the shore. She'd already run ten kilometres before shucking her shoes and diving in to help the boys. But she could swim back easily.

There was no reason to remain, not when she'd made up her mind to resign and turn her back on St Galla once and for all.

It hit her with a punch of disbelief that the only reason she hesitated was the man behind her.

She'd never known such instantaneous, full-on attraction. The humour in those stunning eyes and his upfront attitude appealed as much as his hunky masculine body. Even the dark stubble shading that hard jaw made her want to touch him.

Cat had spent a lifetime learning how to keep guys at a distance, as colleagues or friends rather than lovers. This surge of awareness, the sudden feeling of connection was unique.

She turned back and found he'd moved closer, his bare footsteps silent. He was a mere arm's length away.

Cat hauled in a sharp breath. The combination of that half smile, the hint of citrus and warm male skin in her nostrils, and the certainty he felt the spark too, froze her to the spot.

It was there in the dilation of his pupils and the widening of his nostrils. He leaned towards her as if forced by the same compulsion for nearness. Yet he didn't touch.

The air vibrated as if an invisible cord tightened between them. Cat swallowed, her throat dry.

Abruptly he stepped back and the air emptied from her lungs in a whoosh.

'Breakfast? I do an excellent pancake.' His smile was easy, the intensity wiped from his expression. Yet his eyes were watchful. For all his overtly casual stance, he was alert, aware of every tiny tell-tale movement she made.

Like a predator scoping its prey.

It would be out of character but so easy for her to respond to his sexual pull. To laugh over breakfast and fall under the spell of that indigo gaze. For once in her life not to be prudent but to dive into what she knew instinctively would be a hot, steamy, thoroughly satisfying affair.

But it *was* out of character.

Plus she had enough on her mind with the need to escape the claustrophobic confines of the palace and the role she'd accepted. She wasn't cut out for deceit—masquerading as her half-sister and hiding her very personal reasons for wanting to visit the palace.

As much as her suddenly active hormones protested, Cat had to focus on setting things right.

'I'm sorry,' she said, not bothering to hide her regret. 'But I can't stay.'

She dropped her wet clothes and grabbed the hem of the

shirt she wore, reefing it over her head then tossing it to Alex. He caught it one-handed against his chest.

His gaze didn't drop from her face but she *knew* he was aware of her every contour. She was aware of *him* from the soles of her feet to her peaking nipples and hammering pulse. And everywhere in between.

'I have to go.' Forcing herself to break his gaze, she turned, raised her arms and dived into the clear depths of the azure sea.

CHAPTER TWO

LEAVING ST GALLA wasn't as easy as Cat had hoped. How had she thought, after the lengths they'd gone to, and the money promised, they'd release her from her contract?

'Impossible.' The Prime Minister's voice over the phone was severe. 'I expect you to finish the job.'

'I'll return the first payment. Since arriving I've realised I can't pull this off. I'm a security professional, not an actor.'

'As a professional you'd know we wouldn't resort to this charade unless absolutely necessary. There's no other option.'

Silence hung between them.

'Princess Amelie isn't in danger, is she?' She'd asked before but got no answer.

The nation was still mourning the death in an accident of Amelie's younger brother, King Michel, and his wife. Cat had been stunned by the emptiness she'd felt after hearing the news, knowing she'd never have an opportunity to know her half-brother. Not that she'd anticipated *ever* meeting her half-siblings. Yet she'd followed the news with a fascinated dread, reading how, after the double funeral, Princess Amelie had cancelled her public appearances to spend time with her orphaned nephew, Sébastien.

Where were Amelie and the young Prince? Given the freedom Cat had to explore the beautiful Belle Époque palace and its grounds, they weren't here.

Cat regretted never knowing her brother. That sense of loss only strengthened her longing to meet her last living relatives: Amelie and Prince Sébastien.

'That need not concern you, Ms Dubois. Concentrate on

the task for which you've been employed.' He paused. 'Remember the penalty clauses in your contract.'

Oh, she remembered. Massive financial penalties should she divulge the secret of what she was doing here. And for leaving before the requisite period was over.

But she hadn't yet begun the masquerade. 'Surely it's better to pull the plug now than when people realise we're trying to fool them? I've tried, but my tutor will tell you I'm a disaster in the role.' The woman made that clear with each sniff of her thin patrician nose.

'On the contrary, I've heard you're a quick study and you've made good progress.'

'Nevertheless—'

'Let me be clear, Ms Dubois.' Monsieur Barthe's voice was glacial. 'You will complete this assignment. If not, by the terms of the contract you have seven days to pay the penalty.'

Seven days to pay money she didn't have. The penalty payment was even larger than the total she'd earn.

'I trust you'll see the wisdom of staying.' He paused, but Cat couldn't think of a thing to say. 'Good. I'll see you at the reception.'

The phone went dead. Cat put it down, her stomach cramping. There was no way out. She shouldn't have agreed to take this on. Hadn't she known it from the first?

Never had the massive chasm between herself and the siblings she'd never known seemed wider. And her little nephew. Her heart had gone out to the tiny mite she'd seen on the news. His big, troubled eyes had tugged at her, but she was crazy to think she could help either of them.

Cat shook her head. She'd let sentiment and curiosity overcome sense.

Now she had to face the consequences.

She stared out the huge arched window of her room. Beyond the manicured gardens, the pools and fountains and arbours, lay the wooded private royal reserve that encompassed the whole southernmost peninsula of the island nation. Beyond that was the sea.

Where Alex had his beautiful yacht.

For a second she let herself imagine she could simply walk out the door, swim to him and ask him to take her away. For she couldn't shake the bone-deep fear that in coming here she'd opened a door that should have remained firmly bolted. Like Pandora opening her box and releasing forces she'd never imagined.

Cat shivered, as if someone walked over her grave.

Nonsense. She didn't like it here because it reminded her of the father who'd rejected her before she was born. And the shame she'd been made to carry through no fault of her own.

But she was strong and capable. She'd do the job, then leave without a backward glance. Simple.

Twenty-four hours later Cat walked carefully down the long ground-floor corridor, heels tapping on the beautiful parquetry floor. At her tutor's insistence she wore stockings, heels and a silk dress that swirled to her knees. Lady Enide had declared Cat would never convince anyone till she learned to walk in a dress.

Apparently she walked like a boy. Even if she did keep her shoulders back and her chin up.

Cat set her jaw and concentrated on balance. Teetering on stiletto heels was harder than *parcours*. Harder than karate. No wonder Lady Enide had left her to it, informing her crisply that they'd meet in forty minutes, by which time she expected to see Ms Dubois moving like a *lady*.

Cat's mouth curved in a mirthless smile. She'd always been a tomboy, rebelling against the inevitable comparisons between her and the graceful, ultra-feminine Princess who lived at the far end of their island nation.

It was easier for tomboys to pretend not to hurt when

insults and innuendos rained down. And tomboys gave as good as they got when the insults became blows.

She didn't fancy her chances of convincing anyone she was an elegant lady.

Butterflies the size of kites twisted in her stomach. The Prime Minister had lied. Cat had just learned next week's event wasn't the simple affair he'd said.

Restlessly she pushed open a door and entered a grand reception room. It was white and gold, with ornate couches that looked as if they'd break if you sat on them. The mirrors were huge antiques, the chandeliers, she'd learned, brought from Versailles centuries ago. The paintings…she tried to recall which monarchs were in the paintings and failed.

Another black mark against her. She had to memorise everything about these rooms for the reception to celebrate five hundred years of amity between St Galla and distant Bengaria. It would be a glittering event.

And she'd been told minutes ago that the King of Bengaria would attend!

Her stomach cramped in horror. How did the Prime Minister expect her to fool a royal? It was madness. If she'd known she'd never have come. Which was no doubt why Monsieur Barthe hadn't broken the news earlier. He'd even tried to convince her their royal guest wouldn't see through her disguise since he'd never met Amelie!

As soon as she got a chance she'd look up the Bengarian King. For the first time her avoidance of all things royal worked against her. She shunned celebrity gossip about aristocratic families. She could so easily be fodder for those stories!

Cat shuddered. If she'd needed proof that this masquerade was desperately important for Amelie, this was it. Clearly Cat was covering for a crisis of some sort.

Maybe she could stand at the top of the elegantly curling staircase and wave her hand at the King without getting close? If she could keep her distance, and not talk, there was the slimmest chance she could bring off this charade.

Cat grimaced. From a distance no one would notice she was a smidgeon shorter than Amelie, her nose not quite as straight and her mouth a fraction wider. Or that she was smaller in the bust.

But to convince a king? Cat shook her head and pushed open the door to the next room.

On the threshold she stilled. Someone stood, silhouetted in the vast arched window.

A sensation, as if she rode a runaway roller coaster, plunged her stomach to the floor. Her hand clung to the door as she took in the tall figure, straight-shouldered, slim-hipped, long-legged.

Over his shoulder through the window a familiar yacht, streamlined, vintage and luxurious, lay anchored in the palace's private cove.

'You!' Cat's eyes rounded as he turned and that dark blue gaze snagged hers.

She'd told herself memory had exaggerated yesterday's sizzle of attraction. She'd been wrong. One look and sparks flashed under her skin, igniting heat deep within.

The instant of recognition stretched out and out.

Intriguingly, he now looked like an ad for some exclusive men's fashion house instead of a laid-back, sinfully sexy beachcomber. His dark hair was brushed back in a severe style that made her gaze linger on the sculpted perfection of his even, chiselled features. From head to toe he was suavely elegant, assured and breathtakingly male. Only the light dancing in those indigo eyes betrayed a hint of something else.

Despite her shock and instinctive caution, delight quivered through her as she read that look. He'd watched her that way yesterday. As if she were a delicacy he wanted to bite into.

'What are you doing here?' Her voice was stretched and too high as she stalked across the room, for once ignoring the sensation she was walking on stilts. 'How did you get in?'

'Through the front entrance. The butler asked me to wait here.' He smiled, a slow curl of the lips that fed a silly little shiver under her skin.

'I mean, *why* are you here?'

He lifted a hand, holding out a paper bag.

Hesitantly Cat took it and peered inside. Within lay her old running shorts. She recognised them from the frayed hem, and her ancient T-shirt, not only folded but ironed, if she wasn't mistaken. George had washed and ironed her gear. She couldn't imagine Alex doing anything so mundanely domestic.

Her gaze shot to his as she put the package down on the grand piano a few steps away.

'Thank you.' She paused, wondering how to handle this. 'That's very thoughtful.' Could she get rid of him quickly? She wasn't ready to play the part of Princess Amelie and admitting her real identity was impossible.

But how had he known where to find her? She'd said nothing about staying at the royal palace. She'd been running through the private royal reserve but assumed he'd think she'd trespassed, like the boys in the canoe who'd ventured into the palace's private zone.

Anxiety stirred. This scenario was wrong. There'd been no reason for Alex to look for her here.

'You don't look pleased to see me.' His voice was easy, low enough to hum through her bones in a way that disturbed as much as it appealed.

Cat was no pushover when it came to men. It took more than a dark velvet voice and a hint of humour to win her over. Far more than a sexy, athletic body and stunning eyes.

Yet there was something about Alex that broke through a lifetime's reserve. She didn't like it one bit.

'I'm…surprised.' She drew a quick breath. 'I didn't expect to see you again.' If circumstances had been different she'd definitely have wanted to pursue their acquaintance. But not like this.

If anyone discovered who she was the fallout would be disastrous.

Something about the lazy speculation in his eyes told her Alex saw far too much.

'I'm afraid the palace is closed to visitors at the moment.'

'So I gathered. The butler seemed surprised when I arrived.' Yet Alex made no move to leave. That speculative gaze was heavy as it took her in from head to toe.

Instinctively Cat drew herself up. She'd have to usher him out the door. 'I think it best if—'

'Why Cat?' He spoke at the same time.

'Sorry?'

'Your name. Is it a nickname because of your eyes?' When she didn't immediately answer he went on. 'I've never seen eyes quite that colour.'

'Cat's eyes?' She blinked. She'd never thought of that. People told her she had beautiful eyes but she'd never been convinced. Probably because through her early years they'd been the bane of her life. Such a distinctive colour, always commented on. Royal St Gallan it was called here because every member of the royal family for generations had inherited eyes that colour. Yet it was extraordinarily rare in the rest of the population.

When her mother had given birth to a girl only seven months after her hasty marriage to a man she'd never shown a preference for, and when that baby had eyes of Royal St Gallan green, there had been talk. People commented on how suddenly she'd left her job at the palace, and how it was whispered that the King had a roving eye despite his gorgeous wife and obviously happy family life.

'Cat?' He'd moved closer. The fresh scent of citrus and warm flesh invaded her nostrils. It sent tendrils of feminine pleasure curling through her.

She stiffened. This was *so* not good.

'It's what my friends call me.' That at least was true. She'd never been Catherine except to her stepfather, the man who'd treated her mother as a drudge and her as a disgusting burden despite the largesse he'd received for giving them his name.

'An unusual choice, but it suits.' His eyes crinkled at the corners as he smiled. Even in heels she was no match for his rangy height. Cat found herself wondering why she even noticed. She worked with guys all the time, some even taller than Alex.

'It was lovely of you to take so much trouble. Really.' Her muscles stretched taut as she forced a smile. 'But this isn't really a good time.' She stepped away, holding his gaze, inviting him to accompany her as she moved to the door.

'I understand.' Abruptly the hint of humour in his gaze disappeared. 'I should have begun by saying how very sorry I am. It must have been a tough time for you.'

'Sorry?' Cat frowned. From the moment she'd crossed the threshold nothing had made sense. Not seeing Alex here, looking urbane and remarkably at home, nor his interest in her name, nor the trouble he'd taken to return her ratty old running gear. And now he was sorry…?

'For your loss.' His mouth flattened and he raked a hand back through his hair, which immediately fell back into place. 'I'm not doing a very good job, am I? I should have offered my condolences when we met but you left so abruptly.'

The hair at Cat's nape rose as she read the sympathy in his eyes, the sincerity in the grim expression bracketing that generous mouth.

Anxiety stirred and doom-laden foreboding.

A large hand captured hers, long fingers enfolding it, warm and reassuring. 'You must be going through a hellish time, losing your brother and sister-in-law. You have my sympathy and my mother's. If there's anything I can do—'

He broke off when Cat stepped back, heart thundering, tugging her hand from his.

He thought she was Amelie.

The knowledge pressed down on her, stopping her breath, making her ears buzz and her head whirl as she stared up into that handsome, now sombre face.

Finally, hand to her sternum, she managed to gasp in air, sucking it deep and filling starved lungs.

Did he know Amelie? How well? How long before he realised Cat was an imposter?

And somewhere deep in her psyche, buried so deep she almost didn't register it, was a part of her that wanted to reach out and grab his hand again, feel that rush of heat and fortifying strength, because, absurdly, she *did* feel grief for the half-brother she'd never known and would now never know. Even though she had no right to feel anything.

She'd always been an outsider. These people weren't really her family, no matter the blood they shared.

'I…' She paused and forced a brittle smile. 'Thank you. That's very kind.' Her lips felt stiff and the words sounded stilted.

She wished she'd never got herself into this tangle of deceit. It went against everything she'd made of herself. Forced to hide her true identity since childhood, there'd been freedom and a welcome dignity and strength in building a life for herself that had no taint of subterfuge. Where she was simply Cat Dubois, capable, professional and open.

'I—' Cat broke off as the door opened behind her. Swinging round, she saw Lady Enide, immaculate as ever in a navy suit and pearls, her silver hair a testament to good taste and a personal stylist. The other woman paused on the threshold, her features morphing into a mask that even for her looked pinched and full of concern.

She stepped into the room and, to Cat's amazement, bent deep into a curtsey. The sort of curtsey she'd tried and failed to teach Cat.

'Your Highness. Welcome to St Galla.' Her eyes weren't on Cat but on Alex. Cat felt once more that enervating sensation as if her stomach had disconnected and plummeted at speed towards her toes.

'My apologies that you weren't greeted appropriately. The palace has only a skeleton staff during this period of mourning and we weren't expecting you yet.'

Colder and colder, Cat's spine froze vertebra by vertebra till it felt as if her backbone and neck were clamped in an icy vice.

Slowly she turned back to see Alex smiling. 'No need for apologies. As you can see, Princess Amelie has made me welcome.'

Eyes of rich blue met and held hers. She read curiosity and something that might have been satisfaction there. But she was too busy revisiting their conversation, wondering if she'd betrayed herself, to interpret his thoughts.

For the issue now wasn't merely her identity, and whether she could maintain a royal masquerade.

Worse was the fact Enide had called him 'Highness'. That the haughtiest, most proper woman she'd ever met had practically scraped the floor with her curtsey.

Which meant Alex wasn't merely a layabout yachtie.

Cat's brain galloped ahead to the guests expected for the St Gallan-Bengarian celebrations. Celebrations to commemorate an old alliance between the two nations, forged when St Galla fought annexation by both its mainland neighbours, France and Italy. Celebrations which the King of Bengaria would attend.

King Alexander.

Her breath stalled and for a horrifying moment she thought she'd crumple as her knees gave way.

Cat dropped her eyes from his bright, enquiring gaze and found herself staring at a pair of glossy hand-made shoes. She kept her eyes fixed on them, forcing down the surging rush of panic.

He was King Alexander of Bengaria.

And he believed her to be Amelie.

Could it get any worse?

Cat found herself sinking into a deep, perfectly executed curtsey. The sort of curtsey that had eluded her for days.

It was amazing what adrenaline and sheer panic could achieve.

'Welcome, Your Majesty. It's a pleasure to have you here.'

CHAPTER THREE

ALEX TWIRLED THE stem of his water glass, surveying his lunch companions. Lady Enide who, according to his mother, was warm-hearted despite her frosty demeanour, kept the conversation rolling. They'd skated over the tragic deaths of King Michel and Queen Irini to discuss Alex's mother's health, upcoming celebrations, trade talks, the economy, the weather and even his yachting holiday.

His query about young Prince Sébastien, now an orphan, was met with the news he was staying with family friends away from prying eyes. The news surprised Alex who'd assumed, like everyone else, that the boy was being cared for here by his aunt. All reports indicated the two were close, had been close even before the tragic accident that killed the boy's parents.

Alex picked up tension in the room, camouflaged by the polite small talk. Tension because he was here, sooner than expected? Or because of something else?

The fact Princess Amelie… Cat clearly had no intention of mentioning they'd met already intrigued him. Why hide something so innocuous?

Unless the sudden blaze of attraction between them made her uncomfortable. *Something* did.

Beside Enide, Cat sat silently cutting her meal into ever smaller portions. It was only occasionally he managed to catch her eye.

What had happened to the confident, fascinating woman he'd met in the bay? She hadn't been daunted by an emergency situation or the sudden lightning strike of desire hammering the air between them. Instead of shrinking away, she'd returned his regard with clear interest.

Now, on the rare occasions their eyes met, she inevitably looked away first. She seemed in some way diminished, despite how beautiful she looked in a pale green silk dress that rustled provocatively when she moved.

Those soft sounds as she shifted interfered with his concentration. Alex kept remembering her sleek curves in the black bikini, tempting him through the light cover of his shirt.

'Do you swim often, Amelie?' He forced himself to use her proper name, sensing she wouldn't appreciate his use of her nickname here.

Her head jerked up and her eyes widened. Was that fear in those green depths? Again, she made it obvious she didn't want Enide to know they'd met. Fascinating.

At twenty-nine Amelie was a capable woman, soon to be proclaimed Regent for Prince Sébastien till he came of age. Surely there was no reason to hide their unconventional meeting.

'I enjoy swimming but I don't get a lot of time for it.'

'Perhaps while I'm here you could show me your favourite swimming place.'

She paused and Enide answered first. 'The cove immediately below the palace has always been the royal family's favourite.' She turned to the younger woman and Alex read a hint of stiffness. 'Hasn't it, Amelie?'

Amelie nodded. 'Yes, it's beautiful there.'

What it was about the exchange that put him on alert, Alex didn't know. Yet he knew something was wrong. There was a constraint about Cat... Amelie that hadn't been there before.

'And I see you have an extra-large swimming pool. Which do you prefer, the sea or the pool?' He was talking idly, trying to fathom what was going on.

Did he imagine Cat's flickering gaze towards their chaperone? For it had become clear Lady Enide was just that—

keeping a watchful eye on them. Alex didn't know whether to be amused or annoyed.

Did the St Gallans think because they'd suggested a royal marriage, he'd take that as carte blanche to scoop Cat up and into his bed before the banns were read? He wasn't that medieval.

Yet the idea was ridiculously tempting.

Despite not wanting a wife.

'I usually do laps, but there's a freedom about swimming in the sea, don't you think?' This time when her gaze met his there was the hint of a smile and response tugged deep in his belly. Whatever this was between them: lust, fascination, the temptation to cut loose after three long years with his nose to the grindstone, it fired his libido like flame to pure alcohol.

'I couldn't agree more. There's nothing more invigorating than an early morning dip in the sea.'

Was it imagination or did something ignite in that clear gaze? Did she too remember how it had been between them—he naked and she as good as with her sopping clothes—as arousal roared into life?

Alex wanted that again. Wanted it more than he'd wanted anything for years.

Because he'd denied himself so many things since inheriting the throne? Because his responsibilities didn't leave time for anything as selfish as uncomplicated sex with a beautiful woman?

Or because there'd been something about Cat that he'd connected with instantly?

How long since he'd bantered with a woman, flirted and enjoyed that frisson of sexual desire? He'd been too busy delving into the murky morass of his father's financial affairs, the contracts given to friends and those offering back-handers. His father had run the country as if it were his personal piggy bank to be plundered. Alex had spent three years turning the tide, avoiding national bankruptcy by the skin of his teeth and slowly clawing back control of the national finances from his father's grasping cronies.

Now, on vacation for the first time in years, he was ready for a little dalliance. The problem was he'd set his sights on the woman his mother and all his advisers had pegged for his wife.

No way would he make a move on Cat… Amelie. Not when it would be construed as a statement of marital intent.

An affair, on the other hand…

A mutually enjoyable short-term affair for the length of his stay…

Lust corkscrewed through his belly as their eyes met and that high-octane blast of awareness reverberated.

'Perhaps we could swim together tomorrow?' he suggested.

Cat opened her mouth but Lady Enide spoke swiftly, her tone cool. 'Unfortunately the Princess will be busy tomorrow.' Alex stared and, seeing his surprise, Enide hurried on. 'It's regrettable, Your Majesty. Unfortunately we weren't expecting you quite so soon.'

There was more to it than that. But what? There was something more than officious about the way the older woman hovered over Cat. It reminded him of the anxious way his mother had watched his father when he was in one of his moods. As if preparing to deal with his freak tempers.

More and more intriguing.

Cat seemed anything but highly strung. She'd impressed with her calm competence in the water, her self-assurance and capability. Today, though subdued, she'd given no signs of the self-absorption and unsteady ego that had characterised his father.

'Another day, then. I'm here for some time.' Alex leaned back, watching the ripple of consternation on Enide's face.

He sensed a mystery.

'You're not travelling on and then returning for the festivities?' Cat spoke, her voice calm yet with a telling husky edge that sharpened his libido. Surprising how arousing it was to sit across a formal dining table from a woman dressed in silk and heels and imagine her in his bed, naked and eager.

Even the dragon guarding her was a challenge rather than a real obstruction. Alex might be out of practice, but he'd always been successful with women, even before it looked as if he might inherit a throne.

He just needed to discover if Cat felt the same undertow of desire.

'I'm afraid any plans to sail on to Italy have been put on hold. The yacht has to go into dry dock for repair.'

George would be surprised, but Alex sensed dragon lady's unwillingness to have him in the palace and he was determined to find out why. And give her no chance to deny him. The fact she was so obviously on edge at having their guest of honour arrive early set him on alert. Besides, George *had* talked about the need for work on the yacht one day.

'In that case you must stay here.' Lady Enide's mouth curved in a smile as welcoming as hoarfrost.

Beside her, Cat swallowed. Did he imagine it or did her pupils widen?

'Amelie?' Despite his burning curiosity he wouldn't thrust himself into her home, especially after her recent loss, if *she* objected.

'I'm sure you'll be more comfortable here than in the city. There's plenty of room, after all.' Her jaw angled infinitesimally higher, banishing the earlier hint of reserve. 'I'll ask the chef to make pancakes for breakfast while you're here.'

A hint of a smile softened her mouth and understanding passed between them, the memory of him offering to cook her pancakes on the yacht.

'Pancakes?' Lady Enide looked perplexed.

'I heard somewhere that His Highness is fond of pancakes.'

'Alex, please.' He relaxed back in his seat, pleased Cat was taking the lead. Her silence had puzzled him. 'Yes, I'm fond of pancakes. I acquired a taste for them when I worked in the States.'

It wasn't till the next day that he managed time alone with her. Time enough to wonder if he'd acted too rashly, inviting himself to the palace he'd originally planned to visit for only the shortest of official visits.

Yet it was too late for second thoughts.

He'd been installed in a guest suite with views on two sides to the manicured gardens and the sea beyond. He had everything he could wish for, except the company of his hostess.

It was only a couple of months since Cat had lost her brother. She had other priorities. Yet he was disappointed when a staff member showed him the palace. And when Lady Enide, with a posse of senior diplomats and the Prime Minister, met him for afternoon tea in one of the grand rooms. There was no sign of Cat, merely a murmured reference to a previous commitment she couldn't break.

At dinner they sat with the full length of the long table between them. Afterwards his attempt to talk with her was stymied by the Prime Minister, inviting him to discuss trade opportunities Alex couldn't afford to ignore.

Strange behaviour for a woman who'd consented to the idea of marriage, should he agree. It felt, bizarrely, as if she didn't want to be alone with him.

Now, so early that dew clung to the grass and the sun's rays sprayed apricot and amber across the sea, he intercepted Cat on her morning run. He'd woken early and dressed in jogging gear. He'd seen her don running shoes after swimming ashore from the yacht and guessed she was an early morning runner. Now he peeled away from his vantage point and joined her.

Startled, she looked over her shoulder. Her expression was unreadable as she nodded acknowledgement. Yet she didn't break stride as she headed for a path descending into the forest reserve.

Alex followed, adapting to her pace. It wasn't a jog but a long-legged run, quickly eating up the distance. He found himself needing to concentrate on his breathing even as he enjoyed the flash of her smooth golden legs and the sway of that long ponytail over her slim back.

She moved like an athlete, not a royal who spent her days glad-handing VIPs and hosting formal dinners.

Princess Amelie was a poster girl for modern royalty. Losing her mother early, she'd become her father's official hostess, the pretty face of royalty in St Galla, often filling in for the King at openings, community events and charity occasions. She was a consummate diplomatic hostess and the media loved her for her warm heart and cool elegance, citing her as a modern-day Princess Grace.

Word had it she'd virtually raised her younger brother, Michel, and that she had a special fondness for children. It was this maternal side of her nature that had particularly appealed to his mother. As if he was ready to settle down with a brood of kids!

It wasn't Cat's assets as a mother that focused his attention as they ran the waterfront path through the forest. It was imagining that supple golden body wrapped around him, those soft lips on his, and that voice, throaty with desire, murmuring his name.

Even her hair made him want to tangle his fingers to draw her close. It pleased and intrigued him that it fell in abundant golden waves, so different to the photos he'd seen and the way she'd looked last night, hair tight and straight in a formal style. There was a hint of wildness about it now that suited her. Like the flash and sizzle he'd read in her the day they'd met.

Each time he saw her Alex was struck by how different the Princess was in the flesh, compared with her photos. In those she always looked refined and charming. But the real woman also had a vitality and undeniable sex appeal that drew him.

Drew him! It was a smack to his chest, stealing his air.

'You run well.' She'd stopped, hands on knees, drawing slow breaths, though he noticed she wasn't panting. Her T-shirt clung to her breasts and abruptly he was aware not only of the trickle of sweat down his backbone but the heat stirring in his belly that had nothing to do with exertion.

Hands on hips, he hauled in oxygen, chest expanding hungrily. How long since he'd had a good run instead of a snatched gym workout after a long day?

Cat's eyes dropped to his chest then roved up to his shoulders before cutting away to the glassy sea.

'So do you.' Alex tried and failed to divert his attention from her pert breasts and the pulse beating at the base of her neck where her skin glowed, damp and inviting.

Okay, maybe he didn't try very hard.

He lifted his eyes and met her clear gaze.

His lungs constricted. What he read there was unequivocal. Interest. Attraction. Desire.

She didn't hide it coyly. There were no slanting sidelong looks or fluttering eyelashes, just an appraisal that seared through his self-control and made him want to punch the air in victory.

So he hadn't imagined it. Despite the distance she'd put between them yesterday, Cat's direct gaze spoke of a need that answered his own.

A breeze stirred loose tendrils of her hair and he'd swear

he tasted her fragrance on his tongue. Something crisp and sweet like ripe pears.

She swallowed, the tip of her tongue swiping her bottom lip, and his mouth dried.

He forced himself to keep his hands anchored at his waist, fingers digging into taut flesh.

Cat blinked and stepped away, turning to look across the bay where his yacht had been moored yesterday. She wrapped her arms around herself.

'When did you recognise me? You never called me Amelie that first day.'

'On the yacht.' Not as soon as he should have. He'd been too distracted by the urgent hum of hunger. A hunger so sudden and complete it outclassed anything he'd ever felt for a woman. If it weren't for the fact he was coming out of a prolonged sexual drought it would worry him. Fortunately he knew this must be his libido's response to recent abstinence and a remarkably intriguing woman.

'You didn't say anything.' Was it imagination or did her mouth tighten?

He shrugged. 'Was there any need? It was clear we were going to get to know each other.' He hadn't intended it, but his voice hit a gravel-deep level at the thought of how well he'd like to know her. 'You're easily recognisable, even in wet clothes.'

The clinging clothes had merely turned the picture-perfect Princess into a real flesh-and-blood woman, much more appealing than in any of those posed photos. There was an aura about Cat, a vibrant authenticity, that drew him. He felt it now, when at last night's dinner it had been subdued.

'Cat… Amelie.'

She swung to face him, her expression grave. 'Yes?'

Alex cleared his throat. Absurd to hesitate. He needed to clarify his position, even if it scuppered the chance to know

Cat as he wanted to. He refused to lead her on. He could forgive most things but he abhorred falseness. Growing up with his conniving, deceitful father, Alex was upfront in all his dealings and expected that from others.

'I need to clear something up.'

'Yes?' She squared her shoulders, her chin tipping as if waiting for a blow.

'About the marriage proposal.'

She blinked, her pupils widening as if they might engulf her eyes.

Alex hesitated. Could she really have invested so much in the idea of a match between them? She struck him as down-to-earth, not the sort of female who'd languish waiting for her advisers to arrange a dynastic match.

But how well did he know her beyond the sexual attraction saturating the air between them?

'The marriage proposal?' Again that quick swipe of her bottom lip. Alex's belly curled in on itself, heat quickening.

'I know your advisers thought a match between us was desirable. I know you thought so too or it would never have been raised with my staff.'

Her features froze into blankness and he paused. He didn't want to make it sound like he was rejecting *her*. Far from it. It was the idea of marriage he wasn't ready for.

'There *are* advantages.' He paused and hated his hesitation. 'But the truth is I'm not interested in marriage. Not yet.'

She said nothing. Her expression was unreadable. Only the flickering pulse at her throat and the rise and fall of her breasts under the thin cotton proved she hadn't frozen in place.

Because she was insulted? Disappointed? Despite his scrutiny he could read nothing in her body language.

'You don't want to marry,' she said at last. Her voice held

an off-key note he couldn't place. Not disappointment or hurt, but *something*.

He nodded. 'I thought you needed to know straight away.'

Cat nodded, her head jerking as if pulled by some unseen puppeteer. It was all she could do to keep her features blank as she hid horror.

What had she walked into?

What had they deliberately dropped her into?

The Prime Minister had said she'd only need to appear at one small official function. It was only after arriving that she'd discovered King Alex of Bengaria would also be at the reception. Now he'd arrived early, before she was anywhere near ready to play the role, and she discovered there were plans for an engagement. Had Monsieur Barthe planned to break that to her too?

She locked her knees as they wobbled and her heart somersaulted crazily against her ribs.

How could anyone expect her to fool the man who was going to marry Amelie?

Or, it seemed, who wasn't going to marry her after all.

Cat's emotions were an unholy tangle as she met that intense blue stare. There was dismay and, yes, fright, at how easily she might have betrayed her identity.

Plus…was it relief that Alex wasn't planning to marry her half-sister?

Guilt twisted her insides.

Sternly Cat told herself this was none of her business, except to the extent he never realised her true identity. Behind the easy attitude she sensed a core of steel, and pride. No man, especially one like that, would want a stranger listening to words meant for his fiancée, or almost fiancée.

Were they actually engaged? Or hadn't arrangements got that far?

A sudden sick feeling in her stomach made her step away

and prop herself one-handed against a tree, inhaling the sharp scent of pine needles and saltwater. Rough bark bit her palm and she focused on that, rather than the rush of confusion and fear.

'Cat?' Concern edged his deep tone, feathering her skin in a wash of goosebumps. 'Are you okay?'

'Of course.' She hauled in sustaining oxygen and raised her gaze. He stood close. Too close. His brow crinkled. There was regret in his expression.

'I didn't mean to hurt you.'

She straightened, chin rising. 'You didn't.' Except, strangely, that's how it felt. As if he'd rejected *her*.

It didn't matter that she wasn't who he thought. Or that never in her wildest dreams would she fantasise about marrying someone like Alex. Her illegitimacy was a stain that had destroyed her mother's life and made Cat's early years hell. Pure bloodlines were paramount to the aristocracy. She'd never fit into that world and didn't want to.

'Apart from anything else, I'm not a fan of arranged marriages.' He paused and she read tension in his face. 'It's not common knowledge but I know I can trust you. My parents' marriage was an utter disaster. They didn't know each other before the wedding and then had a lifetime to regret their mistakes.'

His broad shoulders lifted and fell. 'It didn't matter to my father since he only wanted my mother's money and a suitable hostess. My mother suffered but felt obliged to stick it out, especially after I was born.' His mouth twisted. 'I'd never marry a woman I barely knew. It wouldn't be fair to either of us.'

Cat stared, torn between shock at his revelation and a gush of emotion, hot and heady, as she realised how much she liked his honesty and attitude.

'So, where do we go from here?' She was wary of saying too much, afraid to mention an engagement if there wasn't one.

He shrugged. 'Nowhere. I'll simply have my people tell your people that we won't proceed.' He ducked his head a fraction as if trying to read her expression. But Cat had donned her professionally impervious look. The one that deflected the most aggressive intrusion. She'd had plenty of practice. Stonewalling prurient curiosity was a tactic she'd learned in childhood.

'Cat? Say something.'

'What do you want me to say? It seems pretty straightforward from where I'm standing.'

But what about Amelie? Was she in love with Alex? Did she have her heart set on marriage? Surely that was impossible. Yesterday had confirmed Amelie and Alex had never met. Their countries lay half a continent apart and Alex hadn't expected to inherit the throne till recently. There'd been no connection between them.

Which made her wonder anew what her half-sister was like. Why agree to marry a stranger as if she were a piece of merchandise on approval before purchase?

Cat couldn't imagine any circumstances where she'd agree to such a cold-blooded arrangement.

But she hadn't been raised royal, had she?

'You're okay with this?'

She opened her mouth to say it wouldn't matter if she wasn't. He'd made up his mind and that was the end of it. But she thought better of it. Truly, she didn't know what to say. Any mistake could unmask her.

'Cat?' A large hand cupped her cheek and tilted her face till she lost herself in eyes the colour of a twilight sky. She dragged in a sharp breath alive with the aroma of citrus and hot male skin. It was a heady combination. Too heady. She made to step back but instead came up against the trunk of a pine tree.

'I mean what I say. This isn't about you; it's about me. I'm not up for marriage yet, despite what my mother thinks.'

'Your mother?' Cat swallowed hard, trying to ignore the heat of his hand and the detonations of pleasure where his hand touched her flesh. She'd never known anything like this instant, consuming response to a man. It distracted her when she needed focus.

He smiled, his taut features softening in a way that made her pulse quicken and her hormones wake. With his black hair flopping over his brow and that smile tugging his lips he was too charismatic. Handsome as Prince Charming but with a lethal edge of sex appeal more raw and real than any make-believe hero.

'Strange, isn't it, that after her experience she's trying to arrange a marriage for me? She always said your mother was a sweetheart, one of the nicest, kindest women she'd known. She was convinced her daughter would make a perfect wife, even without the political advantages of a match. That's why she proposed the idea.' He shrugged. 'Of course the fact St Galla's treasury could put Bengaria back in the black isn't to be sneezed at.'

So what would Amelie have got from the deal?

Marriage to Alex. That's what.

With his hand still cupping her face, his eyes twinkling and his long, lean body hemming her in, Cat felt a ripple of longing. Not for a royal marriage but for this man who awoke desires she'd sublimated too long.

Move away. Break his hold. Say something.

The orders from her brain came loud and clear but Cat found herself simply holding his gaze, listening to the unsettled thrum of her pulse and watching the amusement in his eyes die.

His touch tightened and need quivered through her.

It should be impossible. He was a stranger. A danger to her job here, a man she knew next to nothing about.

Yet what she felt was real and strong. Pure and true as the swell of the sea on the pristine beach nearby.

'Tell me you understand.' His breath warmed her lips. His thumb stroked back and forth across her cheek.

Cat nodded. 'You don't want to marry.'

'I've got too much to do. There's still so much work to get Bengaria back on track. I haven't got time for a wife. I'm not ready to be a father.'

Yet Alex didn't draw back. If anything, he seemed closer.

'If I wanted a bride it would be different.' His voice was husky.

Cat didn't trust herself to speak. His expression held her spellbound, though logic screamed that she needed to put distance between them.

'If I wanted a bride I couldn't go past those big green eyes. Or those lips. I'd be suggesting we got to know each other *much* better.' His thumb dipped from her cheek to her mouth, pressing her lower lip and dragging it down. Cat exhaled, lungs tight, nipples budding against the constraint of her bra as his thumb stroked her lip, once, twice, till she couldn't resist and tasted him with the tip of her tongue. He was salt and spice and frighteningly addictive.

His eyes dilated, his breath warm on her face, he crowded closer, long legs bracketing hers. His other arm stretched out to the tree trunk behind her as if Alex too felt the sudden need for safe anchor as the ground seemed to ripple and swell.

'And as for this body...' To her dismay his hand dropped but before she could frame a protest she felt his touch, tantalising and soft, brush her collarbone then trace the wide neckline of her T-shirt, before sliding down.

Cat's breath stalled as his knuckles brushed the outer swell of her breast, slowing then tracing down her ribs then splaying at her waist. Those long, hard fingers made her aware of how small she was compared with him. Of how much strength resided in those large capable hands and that taut athletic body.

Her mouth was parched but she had to find words to make him back off. This was too dangerous. To her masquerade but also to *her*. She teetered on the brink of feelings that made a mockery of all her training, her strength and control. She swallowed and moistened her lips with her tongue then opened her mouth to speak.

But the words didn't come because Alex's mouth settled on hers and the world exploded.

CHAPTER FOUR

A SHUDDER OF satisfaction ripped through him as he delved into Cat's mouth. The hairs on his nape lifted and his flesh prickled in a wash of excitement.

Yes.

This.

He angled his head for better access and found his eyes closing as he concentrated on the lush, moist warmth of her. Cat tasted like no other woman. A flavour he couldn't name, yet had surely craved all his life.

He let go of the tree and cupped her jaw, caressing, holding her still when she would have moved. A mighty shudder racked her. He heard the swift intake of her breath and knew she felt that slam of recognition too.

Instinctively he crowded her against the pine tree, not hard, but enough to stymie an easy escape. He needed her here, where he could explore the *rightness* of them together.

It must be an illusion. Yet it felt as if their bodies recognised and welcomed each other.

But he'd never met Cat till two days ago. Neither at an official function or even incognito in the years he'd worked as a pilot. He'd have remembered her taste, those stunning eyes, and the vibrant challenge of her.

He'd swear he'd be able to identify this woman even if he were blindfolded.

She refused to kiss him back, standing rigid. But he'd heard the hum of pleasure she hadn't been able to stifle, felt that initial tremor of delight. He loosened his grip on her waist and dragged his fingers up over her ribcage and a shudder ripped through her.

Alex stifled a smile of satisfaction.

He should resist this as she tried to. Getting tangled up with Princess Amelie at the same time as rejecting an offer to marry her was fraught with potential disaster.

Yet the tug of need was so compelling he couldn't shut it off.

Didn't want to shut it off.

This was about sex, not dynastic machinations. It was raw and real, not finessed.

After years of royal duty this was a lungful of clean air after claustrophobia. Like putting a new jet through its paces, the freedom of skimming to the horizon on a slip-stream of pure adrenaline.

He slid his hand from her jaw, across that smooth cheek to her thick, silky hair. Desire spiked, driving heat through his belly as he dug his fingers in, revelling in that rich soft-ness and enjoying her tell-tale movement as she tilted her head into his caressing hand.

Deftly he pulled away the tie that kept her hair up and again she moved, helping him. Then his hands were cup-ping her skull as he deepened the kiss.

Her hands rose to his arms. He felt her tight grasp as if she'd wrench his hands away. Her chest expanded mightily, pushing those ripe breasts against his torso and sending his blood south in a sudden rush.

Tension held him immobile, knowing and hating she was about to break away when he wasn't ready to stop.

But she surprised him. Her hands slid up his shoulders, clinging tight and strong, tugging him closer, not push-ing away.

With a soft sound that might have been relief or possibly dismay, she leaned in. Her breasts crushed against him, her lithe body supple and urgent in all the right places.

Then she was kissing him back with an urgency that sent the last of his control spiralling into nothingness.

She was flame and silk and cushioned invitation against

him. Her ardour matched his as she kissed him back like she wanted to fuse to him.

Cat welcomed his tongue into her mouth, melting against him. Her kiss was so sensuous, so eager, it knotted him with sexual hunger. Her barely-there sigh of delight, almost drowned out by the rough punch of his pulse, made him crazy.

Sex was fun, satisfying and sometimes urgent. It was never out of control. Never like this.

Whatever this was with Cat, he refused to give it up. Not yet.

Cat had never felt like this. As if a volcano of need exploded inside her, disintegrating every boundary, every thought.

Mouth welded to Alex's, she felt pure desire, urgent, mind-blowing.

She tried to pull back, to stop. But how could you stop a force of nature? It was cataclysmic yet wonderful. Sinfully dangerous yet searingly pure and real. Impossible to resist, though she'd done her best.

For this instant there was no gulf between them, no difference in social strata, no hidden identity, no lies. Nothing but bliss and a driving urgency to take this man as hers. An urgency she'd never known with anyone. It was utterly foreign to her cautious nature and the control she always strove for.

Was that why it felt like heaven to lose herself so completely in his arms? Because it was letting go as she'd never allowed herself to do?

She pushed against him, imprinting the rich, intense flavour of him on her sense memory. Everything about him, from his size to his hard masculine muscle and the slight prickle of his unshaved jaw, incited her to a level of sexual recklessness that was utterly unfamiliar.

Her knees turned liquid and she dimly realised it was

only his body and the tree behind her that kept her upright. Yet instead of a warning siren in her head all she registered was that she wanted more. She wanted—

Alex's hands dropped to her shoulders and, before she knew what he was about, he'd pulled back, holding her where she was so that a waft of sultry sea air drifted between them.

Her eyes snapped open and she lost herself in his cobalt stare. Did she imagine a kick of adrenaline as their gazes met and held? He looked ridiculously handsome, like a fantasy made flesh, yet his hard grip on her shoulders and his hot breath on her face were real. As was the desperate, clawing need to have him kiss her again.

Cat drew a shaky breath, then another, telling herself sanity would return if only she could break away.

But the dreadful truth was that she didn't want to get away.

Alex leaned in, lowering his forehead to hers. One hand cupped her cheek, his thumb stroking back and forth as if driven by the same restlessness that coiled within her.

'Cat.' Just that. But that deep voice whispering her name sounded like a benediction.

She shivered and lifted her hand to his jaw, exulting in the scrape of bristles across her palm. Excitement juddered through her, tightening her nipples and making her press her thighs together. Never, even working in the male-dominated world of personal protection, had she been as deliciously, exultantly conscious of the tantalising differences between male and female.

'We can't do this.' She hadn't been aware of the words forming and almost didn't recognise that husky whisper as hers.

She sucked in a breath that tasted of him. For a dizzying second she was afraid she'd tilt her head up to his, begging for another kiss. But she needn't have feared. A second later he was gone, moving out of reach. She slumped against the rough-barked tree. Cat clamped her teeth against her instinctive protest.

Alex stood, apparently watching the wind ruffle the pearlescent sea. Only the ticking of the pulse in his jaw and the deep rise of his chest as he dragged in air hinted that he too felt the effects of their kiss.

Determined, Cat tried to shut her mind to that. It was too subversively enticing. Yet she couldn't stop eating him with her eyes, from the solid plane of his jaw to the strong line of his aristocratic nose. From the width of his shoulders to the heavy muscle of his powerful thighs.

'There's a solution.' He raked his hand back through hair the colour of midnight and Cat felt a squiggle of delight that she, Cat Dubois, was the one who had him on edge. It was stupid. Any connection between them must be disastrous, but it would have been intolerable if she'd been the only one experiencing this.

'There can't be.' She pushed herself off the tree. She needed to put more distance between them. But she couldn't get her feet to move.

He swung around and there it was again, a zap of energy arcing between them as real as if he'd reached out and caressed her.

Cat swallowed and worked on making her face unreadable. She had to stop this madness.

'Forget our positions for a moment.' His voice was low, coaxing. 'Forget the idea of a royal marriage.' He paused, his gaze drifting over her before returning to hold hers. 'You deserve more than an arranged marriage anyway. You've got such passion, Cat. A woman like you deserves to marry a man who loves her, not some bridegroom chosen for his pedigree.'

Cat bit down a mirthless laugh at the idea of anyone ar-

ranging a marriage for her. As for the question of pedigree…
hers was irredeemably tainted by illegitimacy.

Alex couldn't have said anything that highlighted more
starkly the gulf between them—he a blue-blooded noble
with all the benefits of a privileged upbringing and first
class education and she… She shook her head, her hair
brushing her cheeks, reminding her of his hands there,
moulding, caressing.

'You said there's a solution.' Anything to resolve this
diabolical situation would be a godsend. She'd realised she
was in over her head pretending to be Amelie even before
Alex arrived. But now…she didn't have a clue how to go on.

'It's simple.' His smile was slow and bone-melting. 'We
have an affair.'

'Sorry?' Had her hearing been affected as well as her
body and her brain?

'You heard me.' He shifted his weight as if about to close
the gap between them then apparently thought better of it
and rocked back on his heels. 'There's no reason we can't
be lovers. I'll be gone next week, as soon as the festivities
are over, and I won't return. It's unlikely we'll see each
other again, except maybe in the distant future as guests at
someone else's royal wedding or coronation. In the meantime, why not enjoy ourselves?'

Cat gaped up at him. Enjoy themselves? As simple as
that? As if scandal and subterfuge didn't surround them
on all sides?

It wasn't just the threat of discovery and disaster that
worried her. There was the fact that her initial, overwhelming response was eagerness. She wanted to lie in this man's
arms, feel him possess her, take him inside her and feel
him come apart. She wanted to orgasm from his touch and
drown in the dark blue depths of his eyes.

She wanted him so profoundly, she knew instinctively
it was perilous. Her most important life lesson had been to

trust in no one, rely only on herself. Isolation had shaped her from the day she could understand the condemning whispers about her mother and the resentment in her step-father's eyes.

With Alex she was in danger of wanting too much.

Yet she barely knew him! How much more would she want if they became lovers? She feared this man could make her dream of things she could never have, and should never want.

'No!' She straightened, moving away to look across the sea, searching for calm. 'It's not possible.'

'Of course it's possible. Given the way we were a couple of minutes ago, it's a miracle we're not busy making it a re-ality right now, here on a bed of pine needles.'

Cat's head whipped around at the raw note in his usu-ally smooth voice. Their gazes met and clung and sud-denly, shockingly, she could see it clearly—the pair of them, naked, straining together in the peachy early morning light. His long, strong form blanketing hers, his hands running restlessly over her, hauling her ankles up over his hips as he plunged deep with a single, sure thrust.

Fire spread in her veins. She felt it crimson her throat and cheeks and knew he read its significance. His gaze dark-ened as if he shared the same erotic image.

Cat snapped her gaze back to the brilliance of the sun on the sea. 'I wouldn't have let it get that far.'

He didn't reply. He didn't need to. They both knew he, not she, had been the one to pull back.

'Just because there's…attraction.' She paused, wondering if any word could adequately describe the primitive need that had roared to life within her. 'That doesn't mean we have to follow through. We'll go our separate ways after next week's celebration.'

If she ever made it that far. Cat couldn't imagine main-taining this charade for another hour, much less a week.

'That's exactly why we should become lovers.' Alex's voice slowed and deepened on the last word, as if he savoured it. Prickles of awareness rippled across her skin. 'We both want that. You can't deny it. Lovers for a week with no strings attached—it's the perfect solution.'

'Do you always give in to temptation?' She tried to dredge up anger at his casual attitude, remind herself how disciplined she'd had to be to achieve what she had—independence from St Galla and a successful career. But it did no good because, despite a lifetime's training in self-denial and focus, she craved the same thing he did—relief from the most potent sexual craving she'd ever experienced.

His eyes bored into hers. 'You of all people must know I don't. I spend all my time doing my duty. I spend days locked in meetings and too much time at gala functions and official ceremonies. I suspect not even our advisers truly know what it means to be responsible for a kingdom and carry that burden under the full glare of public attention. That's something we have in common.'

Alex rolled his shoulders and for the first time Cat saw a hint of weariness in the grooves beside his firm mouth. Devastatingly, that only made him more, not less appealing.

He laughed but there was no humour in the sound. 'I never expected to be King, you know, even though my father was Regent for years. My cousin Stefan should be on the throne.' He frowned and she glimpsed a serious man behind the devastating charisma and charm. Cat leaned closer, responding to the sadness she heard behind his clipped words.

'Unfortunately Stefan died suddenly and my father became King.' Something about the way he spoke made her wonder what his father had been like. There was none of the affection she'd heard when he spoke of his cousin.

'When *he* died I had to give up the career I loved to return to Bengaria and the throne. It's been a steep learning curve.'

After a couple of days trying to walk in Amelie's shoes, literally, Cat was in awe of anyone coming in cold to a royal role and making a success of it. And she'd been learning the easy stuff, not how to lead a country.

Admiration stirred, making Cat tense. If only she'd learn something about him she *didn't* like.

'You want me to feel sorry for you?' She planted her hands on her hips. Yes, he'd had to give up his career but there were far worse things in the world.

Like always being an outsider. Never belonging. Even in her chosen profession Cat lived and worked on the fringes of other people's lives, keeping them secure. Alex had privilege, a real family. He belonged.

'Would sympathy make you sleep with me?' A flashing grin tore at the indignation she strove to shore up. She discovered she was no more immune to the devilry she read there than she was to the shimmering invitation in his eyes. She rubbed her hands up and down her bare arms as a crop of goosebumps covered her flesh.

'Of course not.' She tried to sound dismissive but the effect was more grumpy than superior. Like a woman forced to deny herself what she most wanted.

The trouble was that, despite every logical argument, Alex's outrageous proposition was too tempting.

'The morning we met was my first day off in three years.' Alex's expression sobered. 'I'd planned to sail on to Italy for a short vacation before returning for the festivities. I didn't intend to visit the palace till later.' His jaw tightened and Cat saw his hands clench. 'But then I met you.'

Cat frowned, filling in the silence that followed his words, not quite believing what it meant. 'You said your yacht—'

He lifted those powerful shoulders. 'It's getting some maintenance work. But it wasn't urgent.' He paused and Cat's blood pounded in her ears.

'The only reason I stayed was you.' His mobile lips quirked up at one side and something tumbled over inside her. 'I met you and had to see you again.'

Denial clawed its way up Cat's constricting throat. He couldn't mean that. It was preposterous. The sort of over the top compliment given by a sexy man intent on seduction.

Yet the Internet search she'd done last night indicated that, despite his charm and humour, King Alex of Bengaria wasn't a flagrant womaniser. He worked hard and was generally credited with turning around his country's ailing prospects. The only photos of him with girlfriends were ones taken before he'd become King. Cat had learned he liked slim brunettes and, to her disgust, had felt jealous when she saw him with one after another glamorous, ultra-feminine beauty glued to his side.

Cat's hair swung round her cheeks as she shook her head. 'That can't be. You've made it clear you're not interested in marriage.'

How bizarre that sounded. As if there were any circumstances in which *she* could ever be courted by a king. From bastard tomboy with skinned knees and prickly pride to royal bride via a career in martial arts and close protection? Not even Hollywood would take on such an outlandish story.

'That doesn't mean I'm not interested in you.' His eyes glowed in a way that made heat squirm through Cat's insides and her breath catch. 'Interest doesn't do justice to what I feel. I want you, Cat. Want you so badly I ache. Just standing here, not touching you, hurts.' He stopped, hefting in a huge breath that lifted his powerful chest against his plain black T-shirt. 'Tell me you feel it too.'

She opened her mouth to tell him she didn't know what he was talking about then snapped it shut.

The same ache rode low in her belly, tightening internal muscles and tensing her thighs.

The only times she'd lied in her life were when she'd

taken this job and in her youth when she'd denied the identity of her royal father. That had been for her mother's sake. Her gentle mother had never been able to shrug off the cruelty meted out to her by the townspeople and most especially the man who'd been paid to marry her yet subsequently treated her like dirt.

Her mother who'd fallen in love with a king, who had seduced and abandoned her.

She'd just been a passing fancy to a jaded man. When she'd inconveniently got pregnant the King had bundled her out of her job at the palace before the Queen or anyone else could learn of the affair. As for contacting her later to learn about their child…there'd been utter silence.

How often had Cat heard her stepfather predict she'd come to a bad end? *The apple doesn't fall far from the tree*, he'd say, leering at her, or more often backhanding her across the cheek when she dared defy him or stick up for her beloved mother.

'Cat?' Alex's low, rich voice sent longing shivering through her.

Was this how her mother had felt all those years ago? Overwhelmed by an instant, irrevocable attraction?

Her mother had called it love but Cat wasn't a romantic. This was lust, blazing hot and terrifying because she'd never before experienced anything that so threatened her self-possession. Even the time she'd been shot at and again last year when that madman had tried to run her over with his car. Cat had been calm, her brain in control of a body trained to disarm any threat.

But not a threat like this.

'Don't say any more!' She heaved a breath into tight lungs. 'I don't want to hear.' She spun away.

'Blocking your ears won't make the truth go away.' His tone wasn't cajoling but serious, almost sympathetic, as if he understood her internal battle.

'Nothing is going to happen between us.' She had to use all her self-control not to swing around and look at him. 'Now, if you'll excuse me, I'll finish my run. Alone.'

Her legs were leaden but she forced herself to run, increasing her pace as she followed the coastal track.

Yet, no matter how fast her pace, Cat couldn't outrun Alex's voice in her head saying he ached for her, or the tension still drawing her limbs tight and stiff.

She'd never been promiscuous. Her mother's fall from grace probably had a lot to do with that, but frankly she'd rarely met a man who attracted her enough.

But with Alex, *King* Alex, the one man it would be utterly catastrophic to get mixed up with, her libido was a raging fire, incinerating doubts, caution and logic.

She couldn't do that to Amelie, even if her half-sister was a stranger and always would be. Cat couldn't sleep with the man Amelie was thinking of marrying.

But was she?

Cat hadn't found out where Amelie was, except that neither she nor her nephew Sébastien were at the palace. Lady Enide had spoken of a private holiday while they recovered from losing King Michel and Queen Irini. Surely if Amelie was going to marry Alex she'd be here.

More—according to Alex, they'd never met. How could Amelie be serious about a marriage?

But there's not going to be a marriage.

Alex had made that absolutely clear. He would leave next week and never return. He and Amelie wouldn't marry. They wouldn't even see each other.

Which meant he'd never discover that Amelie and Cat weren't the same woman.

The thought struck like lightning out of a clear sky, jolting her to a stop, chest heaving and legs shaky from the long sprint. Cat braced her hands on her knees and bent, sucking in great draughts of salty, pine-scented air.

She could accept Alex's offer of an affair, knowing she wasn't hurting Amelie or wrecking her chances with him. Knowing that within a week he'd walk away and so would she. Their paths would never cross again.

What harm could there be in a fling? In giving in and letting this blaze of attraction burn itself out?

Cat grimaced, recognising the voice of temptation. She was stronger than that. For a long time inner strength had been all she possessed. And a determination not to let her illegitimacy make her accept second best.

She fumbled in her pocket for a spare hair tie and wound it round her thick, wavy hair, feeling more like herself with her face bare.

If she'd known she was going to meet Alex she'd have straightened her hair. But it wasn't the first time he'd seen her with it curling around her shoulders. She could only hope he assumed Amelie straightened her hair for every public photo.

Maybe if she concentrated more on pretending to be her sister Cat could thrust aside this terrible, thrumming need. Forget Alex with his *come-to-me* eyes and engaging smile. And how he'd kissed as if he wanted to consume her.

With a groan of despair, Cat felt her breasts tighten and her feminine core soften.

Forgetting Alex and his proposition was impossible. She'd have to settle for being strong in the face of adversity. That was her specialty after all.

Sadly, she'd never felt so weak in her life.

CHAPTER FIVE

'NO, THANKS.' CAT shook her head at the offered tray, taut muscles protesting even that small movement.

She was so on edge she was as brittle as old glass. The elegant dress of smoke-grey lace scratched at skin turned hyper-sensitive and she had to fight not to shift restlessly in unfamiliar stockings and heels. The string of flawless pearls at her throat felt heavy, as if protesting their use by an imposter.

After avoiding Alex all day, she'd found herself unable to escape dinner with him. Lady Enide hadn't been happy about it but even she conceded they couldn't leave their guest to eat alone.

'You don't like oysters?' he murmured as he helped himself.

Cat shuddered and looked away from the shell in his hand. 'Shellfish allergy.' The memory of her trauma as a child when she'd thought she'd never breathe again was still fresh.

Sympathy tinted his look. 'I won't ask how you discovered that. I understand it can be frightening.'

Cat nodded. 'You can say that again.'

'Do you—?'

'Your Highness.' Lady Enide leaned forward, her smile making her look like a grimacing horse. 'I hear Bengaria will be hosting a new international car race next year. How are plans proceeding for that? It must be very exciting.'

Despite her nerves at the charade she played, and at being so near Alex, Cat fought not to smile. Enide, with her silver hair and severe formality, looked like she belonged in another era. As if her idea of excitement was a new blend of Oolong for high tea with a group of other matrons. Not the deafening roar and blood-pumping adrenaline of motor sports.

But Enide was doing her gallant best to deflect any *tête-à-têtes* between Alex and Cat. Cat was grateful. Every time she met Alex's eyes, or felt his gaze settle appraisingly on her, fear notched taut as a garrotte, stopping the flow of small talk she tried desperately to maintain.

It was a relief to turn to the diplomat on her other side. A youngish man who seemed perfectly at ease. Cat assumed he knew about her deception and was part of the scheme to make it a success. He seemed suave and safe, unremarkable compared with Alex's striking looks and character. There was no lightning bolt of attraction whenever *he* looked at her.

The evening wore on, with the handful of guests taking turns to deflect Alex's attention. Yet they were only partly successful. Though Alex responded adroitly to every conversational gambit, charming even stiff-necked old ladies, Cat knew he watched her with a gaze that bordered on predatory.

Yet what terrified her wasn't the possibility he'd discover her true identity. It was that for the first time in her life she felt the urge not to fight on but to surrender. To accept this terrible yearning and let it run its course.

Madness, sheer madness!

Cat pushed her chair out from the table, on her feet before she could have second thoughts. 'I'm sorry but I must excuse myself.'

The men at the table hurriedly rose and across from her Lady Enide's features took on a pinched look that indicated Cat's manners were appalling.

'I hope you'll forgive me.' Cat's look encompassed the guests, skating past Alex before it could settle. 'I'm afraid I feel rather unwell.' It wasn't a lie. She was sick to the stomach at this duplicitous game and the tight way her hair had been styled gave her a headache. 'Lady Enide, you'll act as hostess in my absence?' It emerged as a statement, not a question, and Enide nodded, looking shocked at Cat's authoritative tone.

That was another reason this masquerade grated. Cat was used to being in control, assessing threats and dealing with them, an expert in her field. Being continually on the back foot, judged as less than capable by everyone, except Alex, didn't suit her.

Cat turned, only to find him beside her, his dark brows furrowing in a V of concern. Between them, out of sight of the rest of the guests, his hand claimed hers and a little jolt of energy shot up her arm.

Their eyes met and power arced between them, tugging her towards him. She made herself resist, but couldn't look away.

'Do you need anything?' His thumb stroked hers in a circular, soothing caress.

Silently she shook her head. Ridiculously, the tenderness in his tone made her throat close over a hot tide of emotion.

This was stupid. There was nothing between them but sexual attraction.

Yet his concern spoke to a part of her she'd forgotten existed. The girl who'd hidden her need for affection since childhood, when she'd witnessed her stepfather's anger whenever her mother dared to cuddle her or show her tenderness. The man had never got over the fact his wife hadn't borne him a child, so he was left with only another man's cast-off bastard to raise.

Cat swallowed and slid her hand free. 'I'll be okay after a good sleep,' she lied. Then, with a strained smile, she hurried out the door.

Though she tried, sleep was impossible. Cat was stuck, caught by her devil's bargain with the Prime Minister. If she pulled out he'd ruin her and she'd be in debt for the rest of her life. If she stayed…

She squeezed her eyes shut, wondering how long she could keep up this charade when all it took was the stroke of Alex's hand to make her want—

No! She refused to think about it. Instead she turned to something that always calmed her—physical activity. There was a pool on this side of the palace, screened by hedges. Minutes later she padded barefoot along a paved garden path. Only the faint swish of the sea and the rustle of a bird in a nearby tree broke the silence. It was well past midnight. The guests had gone and the palace was silent. She had the garden to herself.

Cat reached the pool terrace and dropped her robe on flagstones still slightly warm from the day's sun. She hadn't packed a swimming costume and wore the bikini Alex had provided. The memory of his stare when he'd seen her in it sent a shiver through her, making her wrap her arms around herself, suddenly self-conscious.

Cat didn't have hang-ups about her body. It was fit and streamlined. It did what she wanted. She rarely thought of how a man might view it. Now, suddenly, she was wondering if her breasts were too small, her…

'Enough!' she growled and strode across to flick off the underwater lights.

Blackness blanketed the terrace and she looked up, eyes adjusting till she found herself staring at a brilliant wash of stars across the velvet sky. That was better. She'd swim in starlight, lose herself in the rhythm of her stroke, drive herself till exhaustion washed everything from her brain so she could sleep.

One lap became two, became twenty, and Cat's pace didn't slow. She felt the tension drain, the deep-in-her-stom-ach ripple of sexual desire ease, the knotty problems filling her brain fade as she drove herself through the water, enjoying the familiar feeling that here, now, she was in control.

As she approached the end of the pool she sensed a change. She grabbed the tiled edge and lifted her head, flicking water from her face.

'Hello, Cat.' The deep voice came from the corner of the pool. Instantly her hard-won peace disintegrated. Tension hugged her, drawing every sinew and muscle tight.

'Alex? What are you doing here?'

He moved closer with an easy stroke that ate up the space between them. 'I couldn't sleep. I thought a swim might relax me.'

Cat bit down a retort that he'd followed her. Maybe it *was* true. 'I'll leave you to it.' She put her hands on the edge, ready to lever herself from the water.

'No. Don't go.' The urgency in his tone made her pause, muscles tense in mid-movement. 'Don't run away.'

Cat sank back into the warm water.

She never ran away. She prided herself on facing problems head-on. First her stepfather, then the schoolyard bullies, then starting from scratch in a new country. She'd been a fighter all her life, driven by pride, obstinacy and the belief that, despite what the world thought, she had nothing to be ashamed of simply because of the accident of her birth.

'I've finished my laps.'

In the dim light she saw him shake his head. 'No. You were still going strong till you realised I was here.' He paused. 'I don't want to chase you away.'

Cat's hand tightened on the pool's edge as she caught the gleam of his eyes on her. Her body hummed with excitement, being close to him.

This was dangerous. She spent her professional life protecting people from danger. Every instinct screamed that she needed to leave. If not for her sake, then for Alex's. For

Amelie's. Because this was a tangled mess which would unravel into disaster if she wasn't careful.

'This isn't a good idea.' She was turning away when he smiled. Even in the gloom she caught the flash of his grin. Its impact shot straight to her belly.

'Can't we forget everything for half an hour and swim? We don't even need to speak,' he cajoled. 'We'll be Cat and Alex, burning off unwanted energy.'

Cat paused, knowing she should move.

'Come on, Cat. Let go for half an hour. I promise not to tell Lady Frosty. Anyway, you owe me for leaving me with her this evening.'

Despite herself, a giggle bubbled up at his description of Lady Enide. It suited her perfectly.

Cat watched as Alex pushed off from the edge in a long, easy freestyle and somehow, without planning to, she found herself following. His lazy-looking stroke ate up the distance and she had to concentrate to keep up.

Relief filled her, and elation. He was as good as his word, not hassling her with questions, or invading her space. Simply keeping her company as she lost herself in the rhythm of the swim.

Except, even as she entered that almost meditative state of steady exertion, she was aware of his long body cleaving the water beside her, the soft splashes and the arc of his powerful arms as he picked up pace.

It dawned on her that he was pulling ahead, cutting faster through the inky water. Cat quickened speed, determined to catch him.

Up and down the pool they went, he using his superior size and strength to lengthen the gap between them, Cat catching up at every tumble turn with a burst of sheer energy and superior technique.

Finally, when she thought her lungs would explode, Alex

slammed to a stop at the pool's end. She slapped her hand against the tiles a couple of seconds later.

'You're quick.' He panted. 'Quick enough to have been a professional.'

She nodded, pulling air into burning lungs. 'Thanks.'

She heaved in another breath, ridiculously delighted at his praise. Despite her swimming talent, there'd been no money when she was young for training, and after she left St Galla she'd had to support herself. Professional swimming couldn't do that so she'd had to abandon that dream. 'So are you.'

'I was fresh and you weren't.' She heard him draw another deep breath. 'And I've got the advantage of being bigger and stronger.'

Cat turned, one hand anchoring her to the pool edge. As she watched he rose, broad, straight shoulders sluicing water like some legendary sea god emerging from the depths. His face was in shadow but she made out the magnificent V shape of his torso, the masculine beauty of his body.

She was so busy staring it took a moment to realise they were at the shallow end and he'd risen to his feet.

Feeling foolish, glad of the darkness hiding her expression, she dropped her feet to the tiled floor and stood.

As she did she realised her error. They were no longer separated by distancing water. With the water sliding around her hips she felt a waft of air, a sweet-scented night breeze that, despite its warmth, prickled her skin and turned her nipples to hard points.

Or maybe it wasn't the breeze. Maybe it was Alex. She heard his sigh, watched his shoulders dip and hitch as he drew another breath, and felt his gaze on her. Her skin tingled as if he touched her.

That was bad. Shockingly bad. Yet it felt—

He brushed a lock of saturated hair over her shoulder and

Cat shivered, not from cold but from the riot of sensations cascading from his touch.

'I have to go.' It didn't sound like her voice. It was thick and husky. Reluctant.

'I won't hurt you, Cat. I'd never do that.'

He thought she was scared of him? The idea was so appalling she didn't stop to censor her response. 'Of course you wouldn't.' In the short time she'd known him she'd realised he was a good man. Patient, decent, but with a wicked sense of humour and a lethal sexiness that would undo her if she didn't leave *now*.

Abruptly she turned towards the end of the pool just as he stretched out his other hand. He'd been reaching for her arm but now accidentally grazed her breast.

They froze.

Dimly Cat heard the soft trill of a night bird over the thundering pulse in her ears. She sucked in a desperate breath but that only made her breast rise against his open palm, her nipple budding tighter at that gentle scrape.

There was a moment, a long, infinite-seeming moment of stillness. Then a sigh, his or hers, she didn't know, as his fingers curled around her breast, gentle yet sure and possessive, and her eyes fluttered shut.

Just a second longer. A second to conquer the potent pleasure of his touch there. She squeezed her thighs together, trying to stop the pooling heat between her legs and the hollow ache that throbbed deep inside.

'Cat.' It was a groan. She felt a shudder rip through him, his touch tightening on her breast. Shock held her unmoving—it was so good. 'Cat. Tell me you feel this too.'

'I shouldn't,' she breathed, trying to ignore the glory that was his touch on her body. 'I can't.' Her brain buzzed with all the reasons this was wrong.

'But you do.' His voice was closer and she felt his breath on her bare skin. She snapped her eyes open to find him leaning close. 'You can't pretend about this, Cat. This is about you and me, Alex and Cat. Not diplomatic arrangements.'

Cat looked up into the darkness that was his face, her imagination filling all the details as if she saw him in a spotlight. That high forehead and sweep of black hair. Straight brows, proud nose and glinting, humour-filled eyes. Though there was no humour now. Tension radiated from him, and purpose. His other hand slid down from her shoulder, burning a sizzling trail till he reached her hand and captured it, threading his fingers through hers.

'You want me.'

Cat swallowed.

'Say it, Cat.' His other hand lifted from her breast and she had to stifle a cry of protest. Yet she couldn't prevent herself leaning in, instinctively seeking more.

She was rewarded with the touch of one finger, lightly circling her nipple in a slow, devastatingly seductive caress. Cat went into meltdown and there was nothing she could do to prevent it. She grabbed at the side of the pool with rigid fingers, her other hand gripping his so hard it shook.

'Cat!'

Finally, trembling with the effort, she admitted the truth. 'I want you, Alex.' It was torture and bliss to admit it. 'I've wanted you from the first.'

Powerful arms swept her close to his big, rigid body and his head dropped to her neck, his voice raw as he muttered something in his own language. It sounded anguished, like a man in extremis.

Cat wrapped her arms around him, absorbing the fiery heat beneath his cool, slick skin, burrowing closer to the wall of muscle and bone that made her senses overload in sheer delight.

It was an embrace of comfort as much as desire. For the tension humming between them made even breathing hurt. Cat was bombarded with impressions, her skin hyper-sensitised to the brush of his flesh against hers, the caress of his lips at the base of her throat, the solid weight of his thigh between hers.

She didn't intend to but suddenly her hips were tilting up, drawing her tight against him so she rode his thigh as she'd imagined riding him.

'Cat.' One hand tugged her head back, then his mouth was on hers and it was as if they'd known each other an eternity. As if that kiss by the sea hadn't ended. As if this was how they were meant to be.

His big body was impossibly familiar, and the taste of him, tangy and addictive, made her hungry for more. The lap of warm water against overheated skin only height-ened the sensuality of his embrace. She slid her hands up and down his back, tracing the ripple of muscles, the slick arch of his back, right down to the taut curves of his back-side. Her fingers dug in hard as his hands cupped her bottom, lifting her so she felt the rampant swell of his erection.

Heat doused her. Then, before she could recover, he nipped the sensitive flesh where her shoulder curved into her neck and Cat shuddered as a wave of ecstasy took her.

'Alex!' Was that will-o'-the-wisp voice hers? 'We mustn't...'

She slipped her hands around his hips and up his heav-ing chest, intending to push him away. But somehow the racing thud of his heart against her palm distracted her, and the curve of his pectorals, intriguing with the rough-ness of hair.

His mouth covered hers again and thought dissolved. Cat was lost in a blast of sensual connection. When she came to her hands were anchored on the back of his skull, clasp-ing him tight, wanting to burrow into him. Her back was to the pool wall with her legs hooked over Alex's thighs.

A quick hand tugged at her bikini bottom, yanking the

fabric aside in the water and there he was, searingly hot, bare and virile and perfect. She hadn't been aware of him shucking his swim shorts. Yet she wasn't shocked. For this was what she craved. She tilted her hips and sheet lightning lit the darkness behind her closed lids.

Alex groaned her name, the sound vibrating through his chest to hers as if they were already joined. He kissed her hard, pushing her against the tiles and she kissed him right back, shifting restlessly as he explored the slick flesh he'd exposed between her legs. A pulse beat there, urgent and needy, as he feathered a caress across her most sensitive spot and she jolted in his embrace.

His touch slid lower, deeper, probing, and Cat thought she'd explode with wanting. She needed him *now*.

She slipped her hand between them, encircling his thick length, exulting in the way he twitched in her hold, his hips bucking up against her. Another dazzle of lightning, another—

A firm hand loosened her grasp, pushing her away. Before she could protest he was there, nudging her entrance, hot and bold and—

'Yes!' Did she gasp it out loud or merely think it?

Cat didn't know or care. All she cared about was the perfection of his long, slow thrust of power right to her core. She wanted to revel in it, to rejoice and savour every sensation. But already the tumult was upon her.

It began as a ripple of delight up her backbone. A tingle of pleasurable friction through her body where he filled her. Then the ripple became a wave, a surge of delight so intense she had to dig her nails into him as the tide threatened to sweep her away.

But then Alex moved. He pulled back then bucked forward, hip to hip, filling her to a point she'd never reached before.

Suddenly the surge was a mighty rip current, sucking her

down and out into an ocean of rapture. Waves crashed and thundered. Lightning struck. She was sure it did. Felt it in the bite of electricity that tingled from her soles to her scalp.

She hung on and prayed it would never end. That she'd survive intact.

It was the single most glorious, frightening, wonderful experience of her life.

Alex lowered her to the wide day-bed, falling half over, half beside her, their bodies super-heated from sexual satisfaction.

It should have been impossible for him to walk, much less carry Cat out of the shallows and over the flagstones into the pool house. In the pool it had felt as if his bones as well as his muscles had dissolved in that shattering climax. He should be floating, boneless with satiation.

Except Cat had collapsed against him, murmuring snatches of fractured French against his neck, nuzzling him as if she couldn't get close enough. Exhaustion had vanished as his body quickened again.

He couldn't remember needing a woman so voraciously. Once had been nowhere near enough. Whatever the explanation for this stark hunger, Alex knew it would take more than a quickie to sate. He doubted even a week sharing her bed would be enough. But he was willing to try. So willing.

Already his erection lay heavy along her thigh.

His naked erection.

Hell! Alex rolled away just as Cat opened her eyes.

'We didn't use a condom!' Dismay roughened her voice as she made the same realisation.

Their eyes met. Despite the horror surging through him at the thought of unprotected sex, Alex felt again that gut-deep throb of desire.

'I'm sorry.' His voice was so thick he could barely get the words out. 'I didn't think.'

He shook his head. *Unbelievable!* Guilt and disbelief slammed him. Thirty-two and he'd acted like a reckless kid.

He was *never* reckless. He took risks, calculated risks, especially in the years when he'd been a test pilot for experimental jets. But he was never stupid. 'I've never had unprotected sex in my life.'

Yet to his chagrin saying the words made him remember how magnificent sex with Cat, utterly naked and unprotected, had been. To add to his confusion, he realised it wasn't the lack of a condom that made the difference. It was Cat. Cat and him together.

'Neither have I.' Her stunned eyes held his, making him want to reassure her. Her jaw firmed. 'I don't sleep around so you're not in danger from me. And I'm on the Pill for other reasons, so there won't be a pregnancy.'

It took a moment for Alex to process her words. He was stuck trying to hold himself back from touching her again. When he did take in her meaning, relief hit full force. 'Then we're both safe.'

He gave in then to the compulsion to touch, stroking her cheek and watching her eyes flutter closed.

The shock of having unprotected sex should have quenched his desire. That alone should make him pause and rethink what was happening here.

Instead all he felt was renewed urgency.

'Cat.' Her eyes snapped open, holding his. His hand paused in its rhythmic caress. Again that shimmer of heat passed between them, as powerful as a seismic quake. He had no name for it. No explanation.

An inner voice of caution told him to beware, to walk away and take the time to dissect these unprecedented sensations.

Caution be damned.

'Are you okay?'

She nodded. 'I've never behaved this way.' She swallowed and something inside Alex squeezed hard at her distress. Just as another part of him discovered her pale, slim throat was mouth-wateringly seductive.

He pressed his lips to the base of her neck, tasting her trembling pulse.

'I haven't either. You probably won't believe it but I'm never careless.' A childhood spent under his father's roof had seen to that. His father had liked nothing better than exploiting weakness. As a result Alex had grown up utterly self-contained, only learning to relax and enjoy life when he'd left Bengaria.

Cat nodded, the movement jerky. 'Me too.' She swallowed again. 'This...I can't explain what happened.'

Alex let his hand slide down her damp skin to her collarbone. She had a sensual allure that spiked his attempts to regroup and think this through.

With Cat he felt elemental longing, an urge to meld himself with her in the most primitive way possible.

'Pheromones,' he suggested gravely, knowing the answer, if there was an answer, was more than that.

A hint of a smile caught the edges of her lush mouth and heat pooled in Alex's belly.

'Biorhythms?' she offered. 'Hormones?' She sighed and his attention dropped to the rise of her breasts, barely covered by the skimpy bikini.

'Abstinence,' he whispered, enthralled as he skimmed his hand over the saturated fabric and felt the taut nub of her nipple tickle his palm.

'You could be right,' she sighed, arching her back, pushing her breast into his hand.

'It's been a while?'

'Years.' She sucked in her breath as he stroked his thumb across her nipple. He loved the answering jolt of response that passed through her, making her body taut with longing.

'Me too.'

'Really?' Her eyes rounded in astonishment and he'd have laughed out loud if sexual tension wasn't clamping every muscle tight.

'Really.' Their gazes held and it was like the unseen but palpable backdraft of a fire, sucking them both closer.

She swallowed, her hand clamping his wrist. He felt the strength of her grip and remembered the clean, athletic way she'd cut through the water. The way she'd gripped him with her legs as they'd come together.

'Not a good idea.'

Alex shook his head. 'Sorry?'

'We should stop. Now.'

Alex knew he should be thanking her. Far from reading too much into what had happened, she was telling him their tryst was over.

'Are you involved with someone else?' As he asked it, he tasted sourness on his tongue. He didn't want marriage, but he discovered a streak of jealousy at the thought of Cat with another man.

'I told you, there's no one.' Her brow puckered and to his surprise he found even that endearing.

'In that case—' he lifted his thigh over her hip '—there's no reason we shouldn't enjoy ourselves.'

She firmed her mouth and he knew she was going to argue, despite the way she shifted eagerly beneath him.

Alex stifled her protest, stroking his tongue along her lips once, twice. He was rewarded on the third stroke when she opened for him, sucking his tongue deep into the sensual haven of her mouth.

Alex slid his hand to her bikini bottom he hadn't bothered to remove in the pool, only to find his fingers tangling with hers as she wrenched at the slick fabric.

Satisfaction and anticipation pulsed through him. It was going to be a long, delightful night.

CHAPTER SIX

Alex sat on his balcony, feeling the early sun on limbs that were lethargic after a night's energetic loving. A smile widened his mouth as well-being enveloped him.

Clearly he shouldn't have abstained from sex so long, despite his taxing workload and the fact most women seemed attracted as much by the glamour of his title as by him. Glamour! Repairing the damage his father had done to the country by selling national assets for his own gain and favouring cronies in shonky deals. Despite the pomp and glitter, Alex hadn't found much glamour in being royal.

Cat changed that. Though *glamour* wasn't quite the word. Exciting was more like it. She was classy and sexy in a way that had nothing to do with court protocol or public show.

Her allure cut through the red tape surrounding them. He'd responded to it the morning they'd met and again last night. He'd been charmed by her directness. And something he couldn't name—a quality that made her stand out.

That was why, after saying goodbye to her half an hour ago, he was sitting watching the sun come up, searching the Net for information on her. Not the information his mother and his advisers had provided, focused on her family ties and official work.

After a night in her arms, a night of the best sex in his life, he needed to know more. Last night, away from the hangers-on who chaperoned them, he'd glimpsed the real Princess Amelie.

He mightn't want to marry her but he needed…more.

A huff of laughter escaped as he hit enter on his laptop. Okay, he wanted more sex with her. He wanted a flaming affair that would last as long as he was here, hopefully burning out the compulsion he felt for her by the time he left.

The connection between them was unprecedented. They'd spent the night exploring each other's bodies. They should have been limp with exhaustion. Yet when they'd parted downstairs they'd devoured each other all over again, Cat with her back to the wall and her fingernails digging into his shoulders and he with his hand between her legs and his body aflame.

He was hard now, wishing he'd followed her to her suite instead of returning to his.

Alex surveyed the images he'd found. In every photo she looked charming and well-groomed, with that lovely smile and perfect poise. He preferred her passionate and naked beneath him. And her hair. Why bother straightening it for every public appearance? He enjoyed the way it curled around his hand as if it had a life of its own. It was sexy, like Cat herself.

As ever, Alex was struck by the difference between the woman in the photos and the one he knew. It was something indefinable, but nevertheless real. Strange he should feel it with every picture he found.

He scrolled, looking for something more informal. And suddenly there she was, not smiling but grinning. It was another official event and she was dressed to the nines but the photographer had caught her in a moment of genuine delight as she lifted something to her mouth.

Alex clicked on the link and discovered a short piece about her opening a local seafood festival. There was a blessing of the boats with feasting and—

He blinked and backtracked, rereading the text.

A cloud must have covered the sun for a chill ran through him, dousing the warmth of sexual gratification and lazy expectation.

Alex sat straighter, searching for a simple explanation and knowing there was none. Not an honest one.

His gut tightened and his jaw clamped. He detested deception. He'd lived with it all his life. To outsiders his parents' marriage had been loving and stable. Only those caught within had known his father Cyrill had been an unfeeling autocrat, showing a smiling face to the world while he made his wife and son's lives hell.

As Regent, Cyrill had managed Bengaria for his own ends. Then he'd undermined Alex's cousin, Stefan, when he'd come of age and inherited the throne. He'd bullied Stefan's sister, Marisa, when she wouldn't kowtow to him. And when Stefan died he'd pretended grief while systematically pillaging the country's wealth for his own gratification.

Alex frowned. His father cast a long shadow, but he was dead and gone. This deception was about Cat.

No, not about Cat, but *by* her.

There was a buzzing in his ears, a fullness in his chest as he thought of the woman he'd made love to all night— so honest in her desire, so open and generous. The woman he'd connected with as no other. Deceiving him.

He looked at the photo of her grinning as she lifted an oyster to her lips.

Shellfish allergy. That was what she'd said last night.

Which meant the woman in the photo couldn't be Cat.

Cat wasn't Princess Amelie.

She even had to straighten her hair to play the part, he realised. No wonder she didn't quite look like her photos!

Anger, the slow-burning sort that hadn't ignited since his father's death, sparked deep inside. He'd spent his early years manipulated by a ruthless liar. He'd believed he could identify deception better than most, yet still he'd been taken in. Taken in and made a fool of.

She'd listened as he'd all but apologised for not wanting to marry. Worse, he realised with a prickle of foreboding, he'd spilled family secrets. Believing her to be Amelie, he'd revealed the truth of his parents' marriage.

His mother had found precious little happiness in marriage but still had her pride. The idea he'd blurted her private pain to someone who might sell the story to the press was untenable.

The photo of the smiling woman before him blurred as a red mist descended.

Cat slipped her feet into the elegant shoes that matched the hyacinth-blue dress. If only it were as easy to put on the persona of a princess as to wear these beautiful clothes.

But Cat didn't feel like a gracious royal. She didn't even feel like herself this morning. Her skin was tight, her pulse too quick as excitement effervesced in her blood.

She hadn't slept, yet instead of exhaustion she felt invigorated by a night spent sharing her body with a stranger.

A man who believed she was her half-sister.

Her stomach dipped and she pressed a hand to it, as if she could prevent the welling emotions. Worry, shame and, despite those, excitement. For last night had been unlike anything she'd experienced. What she'd felt with Alex...

She pulled herself up. She couldn't go there. Instead she surveyed herself in the mirror: a fake royal, right down to the carefully straightened hair and high heels she'd never have chosen for herself.

She had no right to think about the joy of her stolen night with Alex. For it *had* been stolen.

Would he have slept with her if he'd known who she was? Logic said no. Yet her heart hoped.

Hoped what? That there was a way around this horrible mess? That somehow they'd find a way to connect again, not just sexually, but—

'No.' Saying it aloud shut down her circling thoughts.

But it didn't stop the regret. She'd done wrong, withholding the truth. Even if he didn't plan to marry Amelie, he deserved to know who he'd been with, and who she wasn't.

The knowledge of what she had to do was a weight dragging at her belly, making her wish she could stay in her room and not face him. But it had to be done. Pride, fighting spirit, call it what you will—she'd always faced problems head-on. It was one of the reasons her bullying stepfather had hated her—she'd stood up for what she believed was right. It was the way she was made and she couldn't change now.

It was one thing to keep her role here a secret. It was something else, something sordid and unpleasant, to deceive Alex after last night.

Cat set her chin, spun on one spindly heel and walked to the door.

'Alex?' Despite herself she couldn't keep the excitement from her voice, or repress the anticipation curling her insides tight.

He swung round, silhouetted against the huge windows at the end of the room. Cat's mouth dried as she took in his long-legged, wide-shouldered form. Last night she'd explored every inch of him with an unfamiliar hunger that hadn't abated. She could still taste the warm tang of his flesh on her tongue. The sense memory weakened her knees.

Cat had never thought of herself as a sensual woman, but last night had been an eye-opener. She'd never craved a man like she'd craved Alex. The way she still did.

She couldn't read his expression but felt his eyes on her and that was enough. Her nipples puckered and between her legs she felt a lick of damp heat. Nervously she clenched her muscles, trying to regain control.

'Princess.'

Her brows gathered close. Of all the outrageous things

he'd called her last night, that hadn't been one of them. How grateful she was. The word was a reminder of all that lay between them.

Cat swallowed and forced herself to walk slowly towards him. She wanted to kick off the spindly heels and run barefoot to him. To launch herself, confident that he'd catch her and sweep her up for a kiss.

Except she didn't have that right. She wasn't who he thought. She needed to get the truth off her chest. Surely she could rely on his discretion not to let the Prime Minister know she'd revealed the secret of her identity.

Her heart beat too high, as if it had leapt into her throat. 'Will you—?'

'We need to talk.' He sounded tense.

Cat peered at him, trying to make out his expression against the light. He didn't sound like the same man she'd made love to through the night. Maybe lack of sleep made him grumpy.

'Yes, we do. I was about to ask if you'd walk with me in the garden.' If they went now they'd avoid Lady Enide and have a chance of privacy.

'Lead the way, my lady.' His tone, and the way he called her *my lady* instead of Cat or even Amelie, sent anxiety skating down her backbone. Or maybe it was the fact he made no move to touch her—so different from last night when he couldn't get enough of her.

Cat squashed disappointment and turned to the door. 'This way.'

Silently she led him outside, down gravelled paths and past mirror pools that reflected the azure sky and pale pink palace with its delicate white frosting of decorative work. Past fountains and the knot garden and the rose arbour, heavy with scent. Through the French garden and the Italian garden to the secluded nook she'd discovered that wasn't overlooked.

A waft of salty air teased her nostrils as she sank onto the bench overlooking the forest and the gleaming Mediterranean. Cat turned, drawing a fortifying breath.

Alex stood, arms crossed, legs planted wide. Despite his tailored jacket and trousers and his crisp cotton shirt, he looked dangerous rather than suave. His eyes were stormy not laughing, his mouth thin-lipped and jaw clenched.

She blinked. She'd never seen him like this. 'Alex? What's wrong?'

A voice inside told her she was delaying because once she told him the truth there'd be no more smiles. No more intimacy.

'What could be wrong?' Yet his voice was as tight as the muscles bunching beneath his sleeves. It reminded her of what she'd discovered last night. That he was potently masculine, with a powerful body that made her glad she was a woman.

Cat sucked in air, trying to focus. 'You seem…different today.'

'Really? Not what you expected?' He lifted his eyebrows. 'I could say the same of you.'

'Sorry?' Cat froze on the bench seat. Something was wrong. She had such a bad feeling.

He tilted his head as if to get a better view of her. Yet he'd already seen more of her than anyone in the world.

'You can stop the innocent act. It makes me sick. All I want is the truth. Who the hell are you?'

Cat gaped. 'You know?' Yet hadn't she known she'd never fool anyone?

What had given her away? Did it matter? The fact was he knew. It was there in his scornful stare.

'That you're not who you pretend?' His nostrils flared and he looked down his straight, well-bred nose with all the hauteur of his aristocratic ancestors.

This time his searing stare didn't sizzle so much as slice

at her unprotected flesh. Gone was last night's ardent lover, gone the charismatic man whose humour and potent sex appeal had drawn her into behaving totally out of character.

Cat shivered, her hands running up her bare arms as they prickled.

What had she expected?

'I was going to tell you—'

'Really?' One slashing eyebrow lifted in patent disbelief.

'Yes!' She shot to her feet then didn't know what to do with herself. She wanted to reach out to him, bridge the gulf widening between them. But that was impossible. The man surveying her wasn't the man she'd fallen for so hard and fast. He was an imperious stranger. 'That's why I wanted to talk with you privately. To explain.'

'Explain away then, Ms…?'

'Dubois. Cat Dubois.'

'So Cat is your real name?' Even now he sounded disbelieving.

'Catherine. But I don't use my full name. I've been Cat for years.' Since she'd escaped this country. It had been her mother's pet name for her, the one remaining link she had to the sweet woman taken too early by cancer.

Besides, Cat suited her more. Catherine was gentle and delicate, like her mother—so feminine and beautiful. Cat was strong and independent. As for femininity, that was something she'd spent her life downplaying. It had been her mother's downfall and in Cat's job it was a definite negative when people wanted someone to protect them.

Alex said nothing, merely stared stonily. She breathed deep, regret knotting her insides. Regret and guilt. She should have told him. Should never have let herself be swept away.

Shame bit. Had she let herself go because she'd known he'd never have made love to her if he knew who she really was?

'I was coming to tell you the truth—'

'I'm not interested in what you *meant* to do.' His brusque tone killed off hope he might eventually understand her predicament. 'I want to know who you are and why you conned me.'

Cat nodded and swallowed, trying not to wince when it felt as if her throat was lined with broken glass.

'My name is Cat Dubois and I live in the US. I'm a bodyguard.'

'A bodyguard?' He frowned. 'Princess Amelie's body-guard?'

'No. I've never met the Princess.' And never would now. Why had she given in to curiosity about her royal rela-tions? She'd been crazy to hope she'd meet them, or under-stand their world by entering it for a couple of weeks. She looked at Alex's censorious expression, the aggressively bunched arms and tendons taut in his neck, and knew she'd destroyed whatever fragile connection had briefly flared between them. Desolation engulfed her.

'I don't usually work in St Galla.'

'But you're from here.' When she frowned up at him he explained. 'At dinner the other night I heard you speaking with the diplomats. It wasn't pure French but a version I've only heard here.'

Of course he'd know the difference. His French was per-fect and cultured. With his privileged upbringing he'd prob-ably been tutored in half a dozen languages.

'I was born on the island, but I haven't lived here for a decade.'

He said nothing and she forced herself to go on, though every word weighed like lead.

'A couple of weeks ago I was approached to do a job here as a body double.' Still not even a flicker in those cool, dark eyes. 'It was an offer too good to refuse.'

Bitterness welled. She'd told herself that with the money

she could open the centre for teenagers she'd dreamed of. But it had been her yearning to connect with Amelie that persuaded her. How self-destructive! You'd think she'd have learned years before that a connection with that side of her family could cause only pain.

'You work for the Princess?'

'I told you, I've never met her.' She looked out to sea, preferring the view to his cold eyes. 'Apparently she's... away, I assume with little Prince Sébastien. I was employed to attend a function in her place next week. I've been here learning how to act the part.' Her mouth twisted. She might be able to walk in heels now, just, but, as far as Lady Enide was concerned, she was a hopeless princess.

He said nothing and she swung round, her chin lifting so she could look him in the eye. 'Then out of the blue you turned up. I didn't even know who you were at first. No one mentioned you'd be visiting. If I'd known I had to meet the Princess's fiancé I'd never have taken the job.'

'I'm not her fiancé.' If possible he looked even more forbidding than before. Cat's shoulders tightened and her skin iced but she stood her ground.

'Almost fiancé then.' Cat bit out the words, reminding herself that was none of her business. She'd had a bone-melting one-night stand with him but that was all. She'd never been in his league and had always known it. 'It's been hard keeping up the pretence of being Amelie with you here.'

'So you decided to sleep with me to distract me from the truth?' Contempt honed his features. If his face grew any tighter he'd be able to use that jaw as a blade.

'Distract you?' Cat couldn't help it. Her voice rose in outrage. Fury was a relief after the shame and nerves that racked her. 'Who did the seducing? Who's the one that wouldn't ignore the...attraction between us?'

Her pulse beat loud as silence stretched between them.

'If you'd told me who you were instead of leading me on—'

'What? If I'd told you I wasn't royal you wouldn't have kissed me, is that it?' Cat couldn't rein in her anger any more. She'd spent half a lifetime weathering the hurts inflicted by others. She'd learned not to show pain. But this… this was a raw, bleeding wound. She'd actually believed there was something special between her and Alex despite coming from different worlds. That he was attracted to her, Cat, the real woman, not the persona she played.

Her hands found her hips and her eyes narrowed on that gorgeous, aristocratic face. 'Because a prince couldn't possibly be attracted to a commoner, could he?'

Except she was wrong. Her father had been a monarch, her mother a maid.

'That's got nothing to do with it.' Fire blazed in his expression and Cat was almost grateful. Facing that cool, condemning stare took more bravery than she'd expected.

'It's got everything to do with it. You'd never have—'

'You're skating on thin ice, Ms Dubois. Don't pretend to know me based on a few hours of sex. You've done nothing but lie since I got here.'

Cat rocked back on her feet, her hands sliding down to clasp in front of her. He was right. She'd stupidly felt there was more to the connection between them. There *was* no connection. He was a virile man and she'd caught his eye. Maybe he'd viewed sex with Amelie as an amusing way to pass the time while stuck here.

For all she knew he had a string of affairs wherever he went. Maybe he was just good at keeping the gossip out of the press.

Cat was torn between horror at her naiveté, shame at her behaviour and despair that even now, confronting his utter contempt, she craved the fantasy she'd let herself believe last night.

She'd never felt so lost.

'Did you lie about being on the Pill too?' His harsh voice grated her nerves. Dully she wondered how deep the degradation could go.

'No.' Once more she looked away, finding no comfort in the gorgeous sea view. 'I take it to manage my cycle.' The erratic, sometimes painful periods had been tough to deal with on some jobs. 'And I don't have any diseases.'

'If I can believe you.'

Cat's shoulders hunched but she said nothing. His doubt made her feel tainted. She'd striven so long to become someone she was proud of. In one night she'd put herself in a position where he diminished her self-worth.

No, not one night. It wasn't all down to him. She shouldn't have this job. She hated deception, even if this masquerade had seemed harmless, actually helping Amelie through a crisis. Cat had betrayed herself as well as Alex.

'So all I have to worry about is a kiss-and-tell story in the press.'

Cat's laugh, an abrasive, husky sound, escaped before she could stop it. 'If you think I'm going to breathe a word about last night, you're completely wrong. I can't think of anything worse than sharing my mistake in public.' The thought sent a shudder down her spine.

'Mistake?'

Cat swung around. Something in his tone was unexpected, something other than disdain and disbelief, but she couldn't identify it.

'Surely that's the one thing we agree on. Last night should never have happened. It was a dreadful mistake.'

She watched emotion cross his face—too fast for her to read. Yet she was left with the impression her words angered him even more.

'You're assuring me you're not interested in blackmail—

your silence for a fee? Then there's the chance to sell the press an inside scoop on my parents' marriage. Too good to miss, surely?'

Cat drew herself up so high her taut muscles twanged in protest. 'I'm not in the habit of lying.' She saw his lip curl and hurried on. 'Which is why I'm not good at it. I won't talk to the press about you *or* your family. I believe in respecting people's privacy. As for money, my contract with the Prime Minister provides more than enough.'

'The Prime Minister?' His eyes narrowed.

Cat hesitated. She shouldn't tell Alex these details. The penalty for discussing her contract was heavy. Yet he knew the main part already. Why prevaricate?

'He hired me to be Amelie for a short time.' She frowned. 'For the period you were expected to visit, in fact. Why would…?' She shook her head. She had enough to worry about without concerning herself with the Prime Minister's reasons. 'He hired me for a substantial fee. I have no interest in getting money from you as well.'

Given the choice, she'd leave the money behind if she could walk away right now. Instinct had been right. She should never have returned. The place was poison to her.

'He told you to have sex with me?' Alex's deep voice was harsh, rougher than she'd ever heard it.

'What sort of woman do you think I am?' Cat wrapped her arms around herself as pain sliced through her middle. She'd thought the shame could get no worse, but she'd been wrong. How could he look at her as if she were something filthy he'd picked up on the bottom of his shoe when a couple of hours ago…?

'Don't answer that.' She hefted a deep breath that smelled of sunshine and pines, the sea and hot male flesh. Longing quivered through her, longing for Alex as he'd been last night—sexy and fun, warm and tender, passionate and generous. Not the man who watched her with disdain. Devastation engulfed her.

'No one told me to have sex with you. It was my own stupid idea. Not that it was an idea,' she muttered. 'If I'd thought about it properly I'd never have done it.'

So she said but she wasn't sure she believed it. She'd been in Alex's thrall from the first, despite her attempts to pretend she wasn't.

'But you kept pushing and pushing.' She was shifting the blame for her weakness but it hadn't all been her fault! 'I kept thinking of the Princess but you insisted you weren't planning to see her again. It wasn't as if I was stopping you and her—'

'So that made it all right? The fact I wasn't planning to marry Amelie meant you felt free to deceive me?' There was such ire in his expression, with another man she'd be concerned he'd turn violent like her stepfather.

But Alex wasn't like that. Cat noted the fact and told herself it meant nothing. He still despised her.

Wearily Cat pressed a hand to her temple. Stress and lack of sleep made her head thump.

'You're right. There's no excuse. I should never have slept with you, no matter what the circumstances.' No matter how her body had been aflame with need. Or that she'd never felt such a response to any other man. 'As for deceiving you, it wasn't honourable. I can only apologise.'

Alex looked down into wide sea-green eyes and realised she'd taken the wind from his sails. His lashing fury stalled in the face of her patent regret.

Regret that she'd spent the night giving him the most intense sexual pleasure of his life.

No, that wasn't what he wanted her to apologise for.

It was the deception he hated. The way she'd played him for a fool. That rankled.

But her frank apology and talk of honour disarmed him. Was that a ploy to deflect his anger?

Damn the woman. He'd revelled in the simplicity of last night's pleasure, only to uncover a murky web of dishonesty. That infuriated him. When he looked at her jaw set hard, her eyes fixed on his as if waiting for punishment and her arms clasped protectively around herself, he wanted to believe everything she said. Believe her and let it go.

'I signed a secrecy clause, you see. The penalty for telling anyone the truth would ruin me financially.' She swallowed. 'I thought I was helping the Princess. I didn't think there'd be anyone else with a...personal interest in my masquerade.'

A personal interest. That was one way of putting it.

The remarkable thing was that, despite this morning's revelations and that sick-to-the-gut feeling of having been duped, Alex was still interested, physically at least.

What did that say about him?

'What happens now?' She dropped her arms, standing like a soldier at attention. In her feminine purple-blue dress and narrow shoes she should have looked ridiculous. Instead something caught in his chest at the sight of her.

'Nothing.' He made a snap decision. 'We continue as before.'

As her eyes bulged he realised she was remembering them together through the night, their slick bodies so attuned that every touch, every taste was bliss.

'You pretend to be Amelie. I pretend to think you are. Under no circumstance are you to tell anyone I know the truth. Or what happened between us.' It was clear this charade had been to fool him and he intended to find out why. 'And you don't breathe a word about my mother to anyone. Understood?'

She nodded but it wasn't enough.

He reached out and gripped her jaw, keeping his touch

firm, ignoring the silky invitation of her soft flesh and the hitch in her breath that reminded him how responsive she'd been to his touch.

'If you betray me again you won't just have to worry about a financial penalty. I'll make sure you never work again, in the States or anywhere else.'

CHAPTER SEVEN

'THERE'S BEEN A change of plan. I've been speaking to Monsieur Barthe.'

Cat watched Lady Enide's lips pinch and realised that for once she wasn't the cause of the woman's disapproval. After this morning's confrontation with Alex Cat felt so dreadful she expected to be held responsible for whatever this new problem was. The disdain in Alex's eyes…

'You spoke with the Prime Minister?' Cat moved to the edge of the antique gilt chair. She'd tried to contact him too, to beg him to release her from her contract. She hadn't got past his secretaries.

'Didn't I say so?' Enide snapped. Then she blinked and sat back, looking for the first time old and frail. Her brow puckered. 'I'm sorry, Ms Dubois. I'm finding this situation…more difficult than I'd imagined. That's no excuse for taking it out on you.'

'What did you imagine it would be like?' Cat leaned closer.

The older woman's mouth thinned and she looked at her hands. 'A one-off event to buy the Princess more time…'

'The Princess. Is she all right? They wouldn't tell me.' Despite her own worries, Cat's concern for Amelie rose again. Why would a royal walk away from her life? Her obligations? Especially Princess Amelie—a poster girl for duty and responsibility.

'You care?' Enide swung back, eyes rounding. She stared at Cat as if she'd never seen her.

'I…' It was Cat's turn to look away. She couldn't stifle the belief that Amelie needed her help. 'I've wondered if she's okay. The situation is so odd I can't shake the feeling there's something badly wrong.' Everything pointed to a major crisis if Amelie didn't attend the reception.

A muffled sound of distress made her turn. Enide pressed an embroidered handkerchief to her mouth.

'Lady Enide? Can I get you a glass of water?' Cat rose.

The woman shook her head, indicating with a blue-veined hand that Cat should sit. 'Thank you, but I'm fine. I'm just an emotional old woman.'

After a week of icy stares Cat thought of her as stern, impatient, haughty—not emotional. This was a new side to Lady Enide. 'You care about Princess Amelie.'

'Of course! Her mother was my younger cousin and Amelie is just like her—sweet-natured, caring…'

'And you're worried about her.'

The older woman met her eyes. 'It's been a very difficult time for the family—for Amelie and especially little Sébastien. They desperately need time before they have to face…' she waved her hand to encompass their plush surroundings '…what's required of them.'

Cat frowned. Did she mean resuming their normal life or something more? Instinct said something more.

'You're not what I expected, Ms Dubois. You continually surprise me.'

'I do?' Did Enide suspect what had happened with Alex? Cat's stomach dropped. At the time, being with him had seemed the most natural, beautiful thing that had ever happened to her. But, faced with his fury and caught in this masquerade, Cat wished it had never happened.

'I made assumptions about you based on what I guessed of your background.'

Cat stared at the other woman and was surprised to see her cheeks flush.

'My background?' Her stomach roiled.

'Forgive me, I—'

'What do you know about my background?'

Enide folded her handkerchief in her lap. 'Only what I was told. You were born in the north of the country, your parents ran a bakery, and you now live in the US.'

Her eyes lifted. 'But I remember a young woman from the same town who worked in the palace years ago. Her name was Catherine. Very pretty and popular. Everyone was surprised when she left without explanation. She had a way of tilting her head when thinking, a way of looking at you as if she saw right to your thoughts, that I haven't seen in years. Till now.'

Cat sank back, her chest pounding.

'I knew the old King better than many. His reputation as a devoted husband wasn't what it seemed.'

Cat's insides knotted. Her hands turned clammy. She'd thought no one knew her secret. She'd believed it had died with her mother and stepfather.

'Who else—?'

'No one.' Was that sympathy in the old lady's eyes? 'You wouldn't have been brought here if anyone suspected.'

Cat looked away. Sympathy was better than the disgust she remembered from childhood, but still it felt invasive, like prodding a hidden bruise. She thought she'd left this behind. The feelings of shame, of being tainted, of being an outsider.

'I apologise, Ms Dubois. I thought at first you were here to make trouble for Amelie.'

Cat's mouth twisted. 'Revenge because she had what I could never have?' There'd definitely been a desire to discover what her half-sister's life was like, maybe even a little envy at having everything handed to her without hardship. 'I'm not like that.'

'I realise that now.'

Cat's eyebrows rose in surprise.

Enide smiled. Her first genuine smile and it transformed her from icy harridan to a careworn woman with surprising warmth. 'I may have been biased but there's nothing wrong with my powers of observation. You've conducted yourself wonderfully in difficult circumstances. It's a daunting task and you've thrown yourself into it without complaint. Even with the complication of King Alex being here.' Her expression sobered. 'And hasn't that disrupted everything?'

'Lady Enide? Why was I brought here?'

The other woman blinked and refocused. 'The Prime Minister is determined Amelie will marry the King of Bengaria. With Amelie…away indefinitely it's possible she wouldn't return in time for next week's celebrations. Which would kill any hope of a royal match since King Alex is here specifically to meet her.' She shook her head. 'Having you here keeps the possibility of a match alive till Amelie returns, even if it means moving heaven and earth to keep you and King Alex at arm's length so he doesn't recognise the deception later.'

Cat's head whirled. 'She hasn't been kidnapped?'

Enide's mouth turned up at the corners. 'She's safe, I promise you. But for once she's setting her own priorities instead of doing what's expected. The powers that be don't know where she is and, even if I knew for sure, I wouldn't betray her.' Her long chin jutted. 'She has other things to concentrate on. She doesn't even know you're here.'

'I see.' Amelie was about her own mysterious business. The authorities were going to extraordinary lengths to promote a marriage between her and Alex—a match Alex had no intention of accepting. It was a tangled mess.

Cat's instinct for self-preservation urged her to walk away and return to her own world.

Except she'd be ruined financially. And Alex had promised to see she never worked again. Did he have the power? She shivered. A black mark against her name by a VIP like Alex would damage her reputation irreparably.

Would he really do it?

'You said there's been a change of plan?'

Enide sighed. 'King Alex has contacted Monsieur Barthe with a list of visits he intends to make. He seems to have decided to end his vacation and turn this stay into a business opportunity. In the circumstances it would appear odd if you don't accompany him on at least some of those visits.'

Nausea rose again. Along with a frisson of excitement that worried her more than anything. Surely, knowing how he felt about her, Cat's attraction to him should have withered?

'You want me to spend time with him? What about the danger of being unmasked?'

'It's unfortunate. But—'

A door snicked open on the other side of the sitting room. 'Ah, there you are, Lady Enide. And Princess Amelie too. How delightful.' Alex's smile was charming. It was only when she met his eyes that Cat read steely anger.

So Cat had her answer. He'd meant every lashing word. She was stuck here, for good or bad.

Ire still seared his belly. Yet as Alex sat with Lady Enide and Cat over afternoon tea, watching the tension in Cat's slim frame and the effort the older woman made to keep the conversation rolling, he felt an unwanted flicker of sympathy for them.

He couldn't understand it. His father's conniving and manipulation had given him an abhorrence for liars. There should *be* no sympathy.

He didn't know what had made Enide take part in this outrageous con. He respected her, not just because of his mother's recommendation but because he'd come to enjoy her incisive observations and dry humour. As for the fake Princess Amelie—the shadows beneath her eyes and the tight line of her mouth made her appear ridiculously vulnerable. He told himself he didn't care.

Yet when she entered the fray, engaging him in conversation when Enide faltered and pressed a hand to her forehead, Alex mentally applauded her grace under pressure. Even when he deliberately turned the conversation to people and places she couldn't know, she didn't back down. With a flash of those stunning eyes she surprised him with her apparently easy answers. She *had* been doing her homework.

What's more, she didn't by so much as a flicker of expression indicate she knew he was deliberately aiming to catch her out. Only the flat quality of her smile betrayed the effort it took to keep up the performance. That and her concern as she watched Lady Enide.

Since when had the pair been friends? That wasn't the vibe he'd got.

Alex didn't know whether to be pleased Cat hadn't collapsed in a heap now he'd confronted her, or concerned at how easily she disguised her true self. Was she really such a consummate liar? Last night he'd have sworn he'd never been with a more honest, open woman.

Before he'd discovered she'd done nothing but lie!

Yet he couldn't ignore that fizz of awareness when she handed him a coffee cup and their fingers brushed. Wildfire raced through his veins and the low cadence of her voice caught at his libido.

'Excuse me, Your Highness, Your Majesty…'

'Yes?' Cat turned to the chamberlain at the door.

'There are visitors from the recreation camp along the peninsula—the camp director with two boys. They have no appointment but were hoping to speak with you.' His disapproval was clear. 'I told them it was most irregular to request an audience but he was very persistent.'

Cat's gaze slewed to his. Alex could hear her thoughts

as if she'd spoken aloud. The boys they'd rescued had been from the camp.

'Please show them in.'

Cat turned to Lady Enide, her tone matter of fact as she explained about the incident a few days previously. Alex noted she avoided mentioning her own part in the rescue, making it sound as if she'd been merely a bystander. Buttering him up? Or not interested in the limelight? In the circumstances he found the latter hard to believe.

Minutes later the trio were introduced and seated stiffly. Sure enough, Alex recognised the boys they'd rescued. One, good-looking and well-groomed, who'd been briefly unconscious, sat taking everything in with a mix of awe and excitement. The other, a smaller teen with baggy clothes and dark hair spilling over his face, looked surly.

'It was good of you to see us,' the camp director, Monsieur Vincenti said. 'I believe it important the boys apologise in person. Especially since the camp is funded by your personal generosity, Your Highness.' The smile he gave Cat was eager and admiring. So admiring Alex knew a sudden, unreasonable urge to send the guy on his way.

That dog-in-the-manger jealousy took Alex by surprise. He stiffened, appalled. Hadn't he washed his hands of the woman? Yet here he was, annoyed that some smarmy, yes, definitely smarmy bureaucrat toadied to her.

He was so caught up in his thoughts he barely heard the boys apologise for trespass and the trouble they'd caused. But he noticed the triumphant sideways glance the taller boy gave the dark-haired one.

'I was wary of accepting him at the camp, since he's caused trouble before, but our remit is to be accessible to all.' The camp director pursed his lips. 'Again, I can only apologise. Please be assured he won't have a chance to lead anyone else astray. I've decided to send him home.'

The slouching boy reacted to that. An abrupt stiffening,

a widening of his eyes before he bent his head even lower, hiding his expression.

Instinct—the instinct of someone whose own home life had been a sore trial, despite the public façade his parents fabricated—told Alex the kid was horrified at the idea of going home.

Cat saw it too. She shifted in her seat, leaning forward.

'How do you know he's the one doing the leading astray?' Both kids stiffened at Alex's tone.

'Thomas came to us with a reputation, Your Majesty. For fighting and insubordination.' The director puffed himself up. 'It's obvious that—'

'It's not obvious at all.' Alex shouldn't have enjoyed cutting the guy off. But his pomposity and his fawning on Cat annoyed him.

'Tell me—' he turned to the bigger of the boys, the neat, good-looking one '—can you swim?'

'Yes, sir.' The kid darted a look at the man beside him and sat straighter. 'I'm fastest in my school at the hundred metres.'

'And you, Thomas? Can you swim?'

Thomas shrugged.

'Come on, boy,' the camp director scolded. 'You've been asked a question.'

'It's all right, Monsieur Vincenti. We know the answer. When the Princess and I found Thomas he was floundering to keep afloat. Clearly he can't swim.' Alex pinned the director with his gaze. 'I find it unlikely a boy who can't even keep himself afloat would dare or bully someone else into stealing a canoe and paddling it around the headland, don't you?'

For the first time Thomas lifted his head, his eyes meeting Alex's in a swift stare of astonishment, before looking away.

Cat swung round in her seat, eyes wide. 'I hadn't thought

of that.' Her voice was husky with dismay. 'I should have realised.' She frowned, her teeth catching her bottom lip.

'Your Highness—' Vincenti spread his hands '—I'm sure there's a reasonable explan—'

'There's nothing at all reasonable, *monsieur*, in hosting children at a seaside camp and not ensuring they can swim.' Cat shot to her feet, rigid with outrage.

Vincenti stumbled out of his chair to stand before her, dismay on his smooth features.

'Tell me, *monsieur*,' she continued. 'Have you checked if there are any other children at camp who can't swim?'

'No, Your Highness. Our policy—'

'Your policy needs to change immediately. I will not fund an institution that puts the lives of children in danger.'

The man blanched but Alex hardly noticed. All his attention was on Cat, taut and sparking with indignation. This was no charade. She was furious yet totally in control of herself and the situation. She intrigued him.

'You will take instant steps to assess who at the camp can swim, and to ensure all future attendees are safe in the water.'

'Immediately, Your Highness. I'll personally ensure that only those who can swim are invited.'

'And leave out those children who haven't had the luxury of swimming classes?' She shook her head and the light caught the golden tones of her hair. 'I expect you to introduce swimming classes as a priority.'

'Of course, Your Highness.' Vincenti clasped his hands. 'Though at the moment we don't have a qualified swimming instructor...'

'You run a recreation camp on the coast and you don't have a swimming instructor?' There was no missing the blaze of outrage in her fine eyes. Energy radiated from her. Even the sullen Thomas lifted his head to watch.

Cat paced to the window then back and with each step Monsieur Vincenti's consternation grew.

'I have grave concerns about the way your establishment is run, *monsieur*.' She looked so stern, so unconsciously haughty Alex found it hard to believe she wasn't the Princess she pretended to be. His curiosity intensified, and his admiration.

Technically this was none of her business. All she had to do was receive the apologies, smile at the director and send him away. Instead, she was taking responsibility as if she *were* Princess Amelie. But this was no stunt for his benefit. Alex guessed she'd all but forgotten his presence.

'An immediate review is required. I'll report my concerns to…'

'To the Board of Governors.' Lady Enide sat forward. 'I'll take care of it on your behalf today, Your Highness.'

A look passed between the two women—one he couldn't read, but there was definitely understanding there. 'Thank you, Lady Enide.'

Cat swung back to the director. 'Your first priority, *monsieur*, is to identify who else in the camp isn't safe in the water, and hire an appropriate teacher for them. In the meantime, I expect Thomas here at eight tomorrow morning, with any other children needing instruction. There will be a qualified instructor here to tutor them till you fill the post.'

She cut across Monsieur Vincenti's response and turned to the boys.

'Thomas?'

The kid met her eyes, his face expressionless.

'Do you want to stay at camp? Or would you rather go home?'

'Camp.' He mumbled the word, the sound almost drowned by Vincenti's demand that he stand.

Cat ignored the man and concentrated on the boy. 'I'll

see you tomorrow. In the meantime, stay away from the water. Understood?'

Thomas nodded. His gaze was fixed on the vibrant, beautiful woman before him as if he couldn't look away.

Alex knew the feeling.

CHAPTER EIGHT

'THANK YOU FOR speaking up back there.' Cat kept her eyes on the driver beyond the glass partition as the limo slid through the palace gates and turned towards the city. 'I can't believe I didn't pick up on the relevance of Thomas not being able to swim.'

'I didn't either.' As ever, Alex's deep voice stirred wanting deep inside. Cat fought to stifle it. 'We had other things on our minds.'

Like the instant burn of desire.

Lust. Call a spade a spade. It was lust and it would burn itself out quickly.

Just not quickly enough.

Despite everything, Cat still experienced that trembling hyper-awareness when he was near. The way he'd dealt with Monsieur Vincenti and uncovered the truth about the boys had only increased her respect. It would be easier if she could detest him for his privileged life and über-confident demeanour. Or not care what he thought of her.

But he worked hard for his people and, as for his deceptively lazy air of being able to meet any challenge—that wasn't a front. Without his formidable strength in boosting the boys to safety over that upturned canoe, Cat suspected one of them would have drowned.

Alex was competent, sexy and honest. No wonder she was attracted!

Yet he viewed her with complete contempt.

Or did he?

'Why did you want me to come with you to this meeting?' Was this a little thawing?

'I didn't.' His voice was clipped and a sideways glance

revealed a set profile, jaw tight above that beautifully tailored jacket and silk tie. 'I presented a list of the places I wished to visit. I didn't know I'd have the pleasure of your company.'

So she was attending for appearances. Because it would be natural for Princess Amelie to accompany her suitor occasionally. The PM must be sweating, hoping she was up to the charade at such close quarters with Alex.

Cat's shoulders pressed back into the upholstery but she didn't let disappointment show. She was used to being the outsider, the one hiding pain. Yet she was surprised how much Alex's dismissive tone hurt.

She turned to survey the city. She'd only been here once before, the day she'd travelled to the capital for the sole purpose of leaving and never returning. Dully, she noted the pretty pastel-coloured buildings with their terracotta tiles and wrought iron balconies, the bright flowers spilling from window boxes. And beyond them the glinting sea.

But Cat couldn't summon excitement. Not with regret plaguing her. Was it stupid to wonder if, in different circumstances, she and Alex might have—?

No! He was a king. She was a commoner. Not just any commoner, but the illegitimate daughter of a king. The scandal if anyone found out would be appalling.

She was well past the age of believing in fairy tales. Her stepfather had ensured she lived in the real world, not a fantasy one, the day he'd first back-handed her for standing between him and her mother.

'This laboratory, why are you going there?'

He didn't turn his head. 'Because I'm interested.'

Cat refused to react to his dismissive tone. She'd hoped for some hint about what the place researched. The visit had been sprung on her so suddenly she'd had no time to prepare.

The professional in her hated that. Preparation was the

key to maintaining control. Worse, the thought of visiting a scientific laboratory evoked memories of her struggles at school, leaving a sour metallic taste on her tongue. The taste of failure. That ancient shame.

Would it be obvious she hadn't even completed high school? That she was incapable of understanding what they were talking about? Her science teacher, a friend of her step-father, had made it abundantly clear whenever he'd sent her from the classroom for some imagined infringement, that she hadn't the capacity to grasp the most basic concepts.

A shiver scudded across her skin. She had an awful feeling she was about to make an utter fool of herself.

Wouldn't His Majesty enjoy that?

'We're particularly excited about this new project.' The facility director spoke quickly, emphasising each point with enthusiastic gestures. 'I'm sure Your Highnesses will find it fascinating.'

He was right. Alex was intrigued by the possibilities nanotechnology provided, especially now he was considering establishing a similar centre in Bengaria.

Yet his attention kept straying to Cat who, for the first time since they'd met, looked awkward. It struck him that she was an intensely physical person. There was her uninhibited sexual passion—making love with her whole body and that fierce focus, so a night with her had felt like a life-altering experience. Plus the way she moved. She had an easy grace, a command over her body he recognised from the elite athletes he'd known.

Yet now she looked ill, not poised but cramped, her skin paler than he remembered against the purple-blue of her dress. Her eyes were wide, fathomless green wells that flickered to his then away.

She was nervous. He felt her anxiety like a vibration in the air.

Alex frowned. Why was she nervous? All she had to do was smile and nod and ask a few questions.

Yet she'd said virtually nothing since they'd arrived. This was the woman who'd easily parried Alex's earlier conversation, which he'd deliberately littered with references to people she hadn't met, to make it tough. She'd wiped the floor with that sorry excuse for a camp director to champion a kid many would write off as difficult.

'Don't you think so, Your Highness?' The director turned to Cat and Alex watched her swallow hard.

She opened her mouth, but took for ever to murmur, 'Yes, of course.'

Instead of triumphing in her discomfort, Alex found himself stepping closer, drawing the director's attention. 'I'm afraid you may have to explain the basic premise again, in words of one syllable.'

Beside him Cat stiffened. Was that sudden intake of breath indignation or because he'd hit the nail on the head? Yet she made no move to confront him or laugh off his words. What had happened to the confident woman he knew?

'My understanding of nanotechnology is virtually nothing,' Alex continued, as if he hadn't taken a special interest in the field's recent developments. 'If you could explain in lay terms it would make it much easier for me.' He turned to Cat. 'Unless that would bore you, Princess?'

'Not at all. I'm afraid I'm not…scientifically inclined either.' Cat smiled and Alex guessed he was the only one who recognised the strain in her features.

'Of course. Forgive me. I get wrapped up in my work and forget this is outside most people's understanding. Basically we're talking about science and technology at the smallest imaginable scale, so small we're viewing and controlling individual atoms and molecules.'

'It sounds…incredible,' Cat said.

The director nodded. 'I feel that way every day. Incredible but with so many possibilities. Work has been done on developing particles that will attract toxic metals found in water after an oil spill, so they can be removed more easily. And on combating water-borne bacteria.'

'That's what you're looking at here?' Cat's interest was caught. It was there in her voice as she leaned closer.

'Our research is a little different.' The scientist invited them to follow. This time Cat didn't hang back.

By the time they finished Alex had acquired the insight he needed to make a better decision about a similar lab in his own country.

Even more interesting, he'd seen Cat transform from nervous to enthusiastic. What had she been afraid of? All he could put it down to was discomfort at being out of her depth in the lab. As if anyone expected her to be an expert!

Yet her anxiety had been real. He'd felt it like an electric charge arcing from her body and it had made him feel… bad. He'd wanted to protect her.

Crazy for a guy who'd been duped by her.

He watched her shake hands with the staff. Cat had won them over. She was a natural at the meet and greet.

That didn't come easily to many royals. His father had been abysmal at it. Perhaps because in person people sensed he wasn't trustworthy. But Cat had an openness—

What was he thinking? Cat had lied straight-faced. She couldn't be trusted.

Still he had to admit she had a way with people. Not just here but at those dinners they'd shared. He'd seen guests light up when she turned her attention on them. Even Thomas, the brooding kid who looked like he'd turned teenage rebellion into an art, had responded.

This visit proved something else, he realised as they headed to the limo. The staff were St Gallans. They knew Princess Amelie from years of media reports and possibly even personal sightings. Yet they accepted Cat without question.

Alex had decided he'd fallen for this scam charade because he'd never met the Princess or taken a particular interest in the St Gallan royal family. For most of his life his focus had been on building his career in aeronautics. He'd never imagined he'd one day be forced to accept the throne.

Clearly Cat was enough like Amelie to fool the public. It wasn't just the blonde hair and stunning eye colour. That could be achieved with dye and coloured contacts. The similarity between them was bone-deep. Beyond the boundary fence the press vied for photos. Yet there was no frantic jostling as if they suspected Cat was an imposter.

Who *was* this woman, settling so sedately on the limo's back seat?

Alex's gaze lingered on the inviting curve of her calves and the way her dress rode high for a moment, showing toned thighs. Thighs that last night had encircled him as he'd powered into her, losing himself in bliss. Fire raced through him, drying his mouth and igniting need in his belly.

He yanked his eyes to the closed window between them and the driver. Alex shifted, willing away the hardening of his groin.

Better to concentrate on the puzzle she presented. Anything to distract from memories of how good it had felt when she'd taken him inside her body. Or the trace of sweet, fruity perfume making his nostrils twitch.

Why did she look so like the Princess? Surely there was a family connection. A cousin?

That had to be the answer, though it surprised him Amelie's cousin worked in the US as a bodyguard. On the other hand, hadn't he lived there too, carving out a career while his cousin then his own father sat on the throne?

But even a cousin of the ruling family would be used to

the limelight. Such royal connections brought public attention from birth.

'Why were you anxious?'

'Sorry?' She smoothed her hands down her dress. Deliberately drawing his attention, or because she was nervous?

Damn. He wished he could read her better. She'd taken him in so completely, now he second-guessed every impression of her.

'Back there.' He nodded to the building as the large car moved out into the traffic. 'When we arrived you were nervous.'

He didn't miss her swift glance at the driver, assuring herself he couldn't overhear. 'I'm not…comfortable in this role.' She kept her eyes averted.

'You could have fooled me. Last night you were comfortable enough to give yourself to an almost stranger.'

Her hissed breath filled the silence. In her lap her hands clenched, white-knuckled.

'We all make mistakes.'

A mistake because he'd uncovered the truth or for some other reason? The sex had been stunning, so it couldn't be that. Part of the magic had been *because* they were strangers with no long-term expectations.

But now that wasn't enough. Alex needed to understand her. Maybe then, when she was no longer an enigma, he could shove aside all thought of her.

'It was more than that. What was wrong back there?'

'I have a headache.' Her head was turned so he couldn't read her expression. 'I'd rather not talk.'

'You're a rotten liar, Cat.' It was the first time he'd called her that since he'd kissed her, when desire was a fever in his blood and he couldn't get enough of her. Her name in his mouth was a reminder of how wonderful they'd been together.

Of how she'd deceived him.

Yet now, without seeing her face, he knew she lied. As if she wasn't an adept liar after all. Or because he'd finally wised up?

'You're afraid to tell me? Is this some other elaborate scam?'

Her head swung round, her eyes brilliant with fierce emotion.

'I'm not scamming. I've told you everything I know.'

'Not what happened at the laboratory.'

She swallowed, her slender throat working, but there was no change in her expression. 'It's personal. It's got nothing to do with you or…anything else.'

Alex crossed his arms and leaned back. 'I'll be the judge of that. Tell me or I'll ask your employer.'

She blinked. 'But if you ask him he'll know—'

'That I know you're a fraud.' He paused, letting that sink in. 'Then you can say goodbye to your payment. And wasn't there something about a fine for disclosure?' It wouldn't make any difference, he was sure, whether Cat had disclosed the truth or not. If Alex's assessment of Monsieur Barthe was correct, the man would show no mercy to someone who let him down.

Alex watched, fascinated, as her expression turned blank. No hint of vulnerability or anger. It was as if a mask had dropped down and cut her off from him. Instantly he thought of Thomas, the teen who so ostentatiously distanced himself.

Alex's curiosity intensified.

'I was…out of my depth,' she said finally. 'I know my way around the palace now and Enide has been drumming lessons in etiquette and deportment into me so I'm reasonably confident meeting a few people there.' She paused, leaving him to ponder how comfortable she'd feel next week at the gala to mark the anniversary of the special relation-

ship between St Galla and Bengaria. Did she have any concept how significant that would be?

Of course she did. She'd agreed to the job.

'Go on—why were you out of your depth?'

Her mouth tightened. 'You sprang the visit on me. I didn't
have time to prepare. I wasn't hired to go on tours of inspection!' Her voice rose, revealing what her closed expression hid.

'No, you were hired to fool me.' It was a guess but he
knew he was right when her eyes widened. 'So, you knew
all along.' Why did he feel disappointed? Because she'd
claimed not to know?

'I didn't.' That slim neck lengthened as she sat straighter.
'Lady Enide told me this morning. She said the Prime Minister is determined Amelie will marry you. I was brought
in because she's away doing something personal—don't
ask me what because I don't know. They were afraid if she
wasn't here for next week's celebration that would be the
end of the match. I think they thought you'd be offended if
she didn't show.'

Alex frowned. There wasn't going to be a match. Though,
to be fair, he'd kept that to himself, wanting to tell Amelie in person.

Why was Barthe so set on the marriage? After Alex's father's depredations, Bengaria wasn't as rich as it had been.
Nor did he and Amelie have a personal relationship to build
on. Was the man like Alex's father, believing royals could
only marry royals?

'I still want to know what happened at the laboratory.
What was wrong. If you can chat with diplomats, listening
to a couple of scientists shouldn't faze you.'

Silence stretched then, abruptly, she slumped as if the energy drawing her tight had switched off. She sagged against
the seat, her gaze shifting to the houses on the outskirts of
the city.

'*I* was wrong.' Her hands twisted in her lap. 'It was silly of me, a hangover from when I was a kid.'

Alex waited, shifting his gaze from her restless hands to her face before he was tempted to reach out and cover them.

She laughed but it didn't ring true. 'If you must know, I felt intimidated by the fact it was a science lab. I'm not academic and science was my worst subject.'

'You can't be good at everything.' Alex had always loved science but history had sent him to sleep.

Cat's mouth twisted down. 'I wasn't good at anything at school. Except getting detention.'

Alex digested that. It didn't gel with what he knew of Cat. She'd learned a lot in the time she'd been here. She couldn't have done that unless she was clever and focused.

'Are you dyslexic?'

This time the curl of her lips was almost a smile. 'Looking for excuses for me?' She shook her head. 'No, I'm not. School and I weren't a good match. My science teacher gave up even trying to teach me and I left school as soon as I could.'

'Sounds like you had a poor teacher.'

Eyes bright as gems locked onto his and he felt again that hit of sensation. 'Don't try to make excuses. The fact is I couldn't hack it.' Her jaw angled up the tiniest fraction, defying sympathy. It struck him as an interesting attitude from the woman who'd championed Thomas.

'Did you understand what you were told about the lab today? Or were you pretending?'

'I understood. I thought it was interesting. But that's different. I didn't have to learn it.'

Alex was bemused by her attitude. 'It's not different. If you could understand complex scientific principles today you could cope with high school science—in the right environment.'

For a second longer she held his eyes, then looked away

towards the glimpses of sea visible through her window. 'I doubt it. And it doesn't matter now.'

Clearly it did, but there were other things he wanted to know.

'Tell me, how is it you and Amelie look so similar? Are you cousins?'

If she'd been tense before, it was nothing to her reaction now. She was so rigid she didn't even appear to breathe. Her only sign of animation was the fierce flick of a pulse below her jaw.

'Sheer coincidence.'

'As if. Come on, Cat. The truth.'

Slowly she turned and met his eyes. That blank mask was back. But more, there was a change in her eyes, as if someone had doused the inner fire he'd always seen there. For the second time in minutes he felt the compulsion to comfort her.

But who would he be comforting? He didn't know this woman. No matter how they'd shared themselves, how close to her he'd felt. He didn't know what was real and what was sham.

'I'm not the Princess's cousin. If you stay here long you'll see quite a few people with similar colouring.'

But that didn't explain the uncanny resemblance.

'If you're not related, how did they find you for this job?'

'Lambis Evangelos. He runs a multinational security firm—one of the best in the world. We met last year and he took an interest. He offered me a job if I wanted one but I was happy where I was. Apparently—' she paused and her breasts lifted as she breathed deep '—he noticed a superficial similarity to the Princess and passed on my details in case she ever needed a body double.'

Superficial similarity! Did she think he'd buy that?

'Where's your family? In America?' If her siblings were there it would explain her move across the Atlantic.

'I don't have family.' She caught his eye as he opened his mouth. 'None at all.'

Her tone was so final, her gaze so direct, he was tempted to believe her. Except he'd seen the shadow of something else in that defiant stare.

'Tell me about your parents, then. Who were they?'

For a second he thought she wouldn't respond.

'Mathieu and Catherine Dubois. He was a baker. A big man, with hands the size of dinner plates. She was much smaller, more…delicate. She ran the bakery, in a small town in the north of the country.'

'And why—?'

'That's enough!' The words fired from her, overloud and husky with emotion. 'They're dead and I don't want to talk about them. My family is none of your business.'

So her family was the key to understanding the real Cat Dubois. That was clear. Yet instead of pressing her he held back, because the expression shadowing her features now was pain.

'You're uncomfortable.'

'Not uncomfortable, tired of your probing. You have no right…'

She stopped when he raised one interrogative eyebrow. Understanding pulsed between them. They both knew he had a right to the truth about who she was.

It had been like this from the first—an understanding that leapt, lightning-quick between them, often without the need for words. That was why her deceit had taken him by surprise. He'd felt as if he *knew* her.

CHAPTER NINE

'You know what makes *me* uncomfortable, Ms Cat Dubois?' That indigo gaze raked her. She felt the abrasion on her skin and deeper, down where her secrets were buried.

She shook her head. In the confines of the car the air thickened and her throat dried. She couldn't have found her voice if she'd tried. Never had anyone got so close to her—not physically but crowding her very being, beating at the trapdoor she'd used to cover her past, with its disillusionment and hard-won lessons.

Cat swallowed, hating this choking feeling.

Alex leaned nearer. She could make out the thick black lashes framing his eyes, the minuscule scar on his temple, the hint of a shadow darkening his sculpted jaw.

'Deception.' His nostrils flared and she wondered if he inhaled her fragrance just as the scent of citrus and warm male skin invaded her senses. 'I loathe deception.'

Guilt spidered through her. But what more could she do? She'd apologised. She'd told him everything she knew about the reason she'd been hired.

'And I loathe bullying.' She told herself that's what he was doing, looming over her, trying to intimidate her into spilling the story of her past.

Except she wasn't scared of Alex. She hated that he saw her as an enemy and a liar. She hated the disappointment in his eyes, but he didn't frighten her. Staring into his hard-chiselled features, it was wanting she felt, not fear.

That realisation gave her strength to turn away, severing the connection between them. She felt the tension snap and ease and drew a deep breath, trying to focus on the city streets beyond the window. But she didn't feel better. How could she, when he thought her a cheat?

'Why?'

'Sorry?' She stared dully at the back of the chauffeur's head through the glass partition.

'Why do you loathe bullying?'

Cat shook her head. 'The usual.' She refused to give him chapter and verse on her early years.

'You were bullied?'

Was that regret in his tone? Surely not. Even if it was, it was far too late to make a difference.

'It was a long time ago. I learned from it.' Learned to defend herself and be strong. It had been that or live down to everyone's expectations and she'd refused to give them the satisfaction. 'I can stand up for myself now.'

'Is that why you became a bodyguard? Why you chose to make a profession of protecting people?'

The question sliced through her indignation.

'I'd never thought of that before.' It was like a light going off in her head, illuminating part of her she'd never recognised. One of the things that gave her satisfaction was knowing her clients were protected from physical harm in a way she hadn't been.

How could Alex, who'd known her such a short time, see that when she hadn't? It made her feel naked. As if he'd stepped inside the defensive walls she'd spent years building, seeing her as no one else did.

'You've got it wrong.' Though he was partly right. 'I was good at self-defence. Very good.' The free community martial arts classes had been her saviour. 'I dropped out of school with no qualifications. Fitness and martial arts skills were all I had. I fell into personal protection.'

Cat didn't mention the years of hard work, the gruelling training and the sheer determination that had driven her to the top of her field—an elite professional trusted with some of the world's most well-known VIPs.

'Why do you hate deception?' she asked before he could dig further.

'Because of my father.'

His candour surprised her, especially as he'd been so concerned for his mother's privacy. Maybe he finally believed she wouldn't blab to the press. Or perhaps, given his grim expression, he didn't care about protecting his father's memory.

Cat couldn't tear her gaze from him, even when they passed a square and the sound of music intruded. She'd been curious about the capital where her royal relatives lived, the places they knew so well and the lives they led. But Alex was more fascinating.

'Your father? King Cyrill?'

'The one and only.' Alex sat back and instantly the tension thrumming between them eased. But, as she watched the crooked line of his mouth, Cat saw he wasn't relaxed.

'You didn't like him.'

Alex shook his head. 'My father was an unprincipled liar.' His mouth tipped up into a grim smile as he saw her surprise.

'He was greedy for power and recognition. For wealth too. He hated that he was the younger son and that the throne passed to his older brother's son, Stefan, before him. My father was Stefan's Regent for years, and every one of those years he schemed and cheated to accumulate as much power and wealth as he could from what rightly belonged to my cousin and the nation. I've been working for years to put right some of the damage but it's a long haul.'

Alex tugged at his neatly knotted silk tie, pulling it askew so he could flip open the top couple of buttons on his shirt. There was a restless energy in his movements that spoke of strong emotion. 'Shocked? You thought kings were above that kind of behaviour?'

'Not shocked at all.' Cat thought of her father seducing her mother, a palace maid, just after his honeymoon. 'I'm not awed by royalty.'

'So I gathered.' Alex's mouth turned up in a tight smile that made her heart kick. Or maybe it was the sudden heat in his eyes that reminded her of things she was trying to forget, like the feel of his arms around her, their hearts hammering as he made slow, devastating love to her.

'My father was a cold-hearted bastard.' Alex's words interrupted her reverie. 'He married for money and didn't care about his wife or son but insisted we put on a show of being a happy family. He's the reason I left Bengaria to study then found myself a job in the States. I couldn't bear the sight of him. Or the smarmy way he pretended to be a careful regent while all the time he was taking backhanders. He even—'

'Yes?'

But Alex seemed to gather himself. 'He was utterly two-faced. Living with him gave me a distaste for deception. I don't like being conned and no one fools me more than once. When my trust is betrayed that's the end.'

Yet that didn't stop him thinking about Cat. About the contrast between the laughing, confident woman he'd first met and the one petrified by the idea of talking to a few guys in lab coats.

She'd lied to him, something he abhorred, but he had to admit the Prime Minister had left her in a no-win situation. If what she'd said was true…

Alex lengthened his stride as he jogged back up the coastal track from his morning run.

What did he know of her? She and Lady Enide seemed

to have developed an understanding. He respected Enide's acuity. And it seemed she, in turn, respected Cat.

What else? Cat had a strong protective streak. Look at her career choice and the way she'd championed Thomas, a kid who on the face of it was a teenage troublemaker. Except Cat, like he, had been quick to guess there was more to the boy. The way she'd faced down that pompous camp official had been magic. She'd left him with no option but to give in to her scheme for the boy.

Alex glanced at his watch. Nine. Had the swimming class finished? Would Cat be there?

He turned towards the pool. He was curious about Thomas. But if Cat happened to be there…

He'd spent another evening watching her across a polished dining table. In sea-green silk and with her hair swept high she'd looked every inch the regal Princess. Yet he'd wanted to plough his hands into her smooth wheat-blonde hair and tug it free till it rippled in waves down her back. Wanted it with a quiet savagery that had stunned him. As had the hard need pulsing through his lower body as he'd watched her smile and chat to the man beside her.

Alex had wanted her mouth on his, her hands not on the heavy silverware but on *him*.

His brain told him to wash his hands of her. She'd made a fool of him. But instinct or hormones, *something*, refused to let him ignore her.

He stopped, drawing a hand over his face. He needed a long shower, preferably ice-cold.

'That's it. Like that.' Cat's voice, soft yet enthusiastic, came from beyond the hedge around the pool. 'Hey, good work! I bet you didn't think you could do that.'

Suddenly the idea of a cold shower and a few hours preparing for his industry visits held no allure. Business could wait. After all, hadn't he originally slated this week as a long-overdue vacation?

He entered the pool yard and came to a stop under a vine-shadowed pergola. Thomas floated, arms wide, on his back at the shallow end of the pool. Metres away two little girls, arms outstretched to hold body boards, propelled themselves across the water with enthusiastic kicks.

Standing in the pool with them, wearing an encouraging smile and a familiar black bikini, was Cat, her wet hair the colour of dark honey.

Alex's pulse revved as he watched her high breasts jiggle and the water lap around the streamlined curve of her hips. He had instant recall of how her slick skin had felt when he'd grabbed her hips in this pool and hauled her close. How she'd tasted as she all but climbed up him, as eager for him as he was for her.

This couldn't go on.

Instead of fighting Cat, using her deception as a reason to maintain his distance, he had to face the fact this gut-deep attraction wasn't dead. Wouldn't be dead till…

What?

He had no idea.

Every cell in his body screamed that he wanted this woman. Anger, and disgust at his own gullibility, had made him despise her as a liar. But things weren't so simple. Cat wasn't so easily pegged.

If he looked past his damaged pride he saw a woman more complex than he'd imagined. Not complex like his conniving, self-centred father whose crocodile smiles and smarmy charm had hidden soul-deep corruption. Complex in ways that intrigued and, yes, attracted. There was real courage and grace in this woman, a woman who cared for a stray kid yet fiercely hid her own fears, that tugged at something deep-seated in Alex.

He crossed his arms and leaned back against a pillar. There was time before his next business meeting. He'd spend it adding to his store of knowledge about Cat.

* * *

'That's brilliant, girls.' Cat smiled. 'You're naturals. Now, get changed in the pool house. The car will be waiting for you.'

'But we can come tomorrow, can't we?'

'Absolutely.' She grinned. 'Off you go. And tell the driver Thomas will return a little later.'

'Don't tell me,' Thomas said, his voice stiff with challenge. 'I've got detention.'

Cat saw the teen on his feet, scowling. His clenched fists and hunched shoulders spoke of aggression but also— was she right?—an attempt not to show disappointment. He hadn't quite been able to hide his enjoyment of the session. Not from her. At his age she'd perfected the art of sullen posturing and studied indifference.

She ignored the hint of menace in his stance.

'There's no detention here, Thomas. Besides, you did far better than I expected from a first-time swimmer. You floated for over ten minutes without once reaching for the side. That's some achievement.'

Instead of gushing over him, Cat turned to collect the body boards. From the corner of her eye she caught a ripple of emotion on the boy's face.

Her throat tightened. Was he so unused to praise?

'Thanks for lending a hand with the girls. They wouldn't have done half as well if you hadn't showed them there was nothing to be scared of.' Cat paused. 'They trust you.'

He shrugged. 'They know me. We live in the same place.'

'The same town?' Cat stacked the boards on the side of the pool then hauled herself out, deliberately casual.

'Yeah. And the same orphanage.' That confirmed what she'd suspected from a few things the girls had said. Cat heard the challenge in his tone, the expectation of a reaction. Was he disappointed when she didn't give one?

'That explains it. They know you won't hurt them.' She

turned and caught his grim expression as he climbed from the pool. Too grim for a boy his age. But she knew he'd reject sympathy. Even though the bruises on his ribs and back told their own story.

Were they from the camp or earlier? Either way, with Enide's help, and with the power that came from pretending to be Amelie, she'd make sure whoever was responsible wouldn't get another chance. Enide had backed her up when she'd confronted the camp administrator. She'd back her up in this too.

'Of course I'd never hurt them!' Outrage tightened his voice.

Cat nodded. Thomas might have a reputation for being difficult but the younger girls liked him. Which meant he wasn't violent. Who'd beaten him? Another teenager, or an adult? Anger prickled her skin.

As soon as he left she'd take steps to uncover the truth and ensure the kids at the orphanage and the camp were safe. There'd be no more beatings. But she could do more.

'They obviously look up to you. I bet you protect them when you can.'

Again that shrug.

'It must be tough though.'

'Why?' He looked suspicious, as if she'd tried to catch him out.

'Well, you're like me—a bit on the small side. Sometimes people think that means you're weak.'

'As if! I can protect myself.'

Cat met his eyes. 'Can you? How well?' She didn't let her gaze stray to the bruises fading on his ribs but they both knew she'd seen them. 'Have you learned self-defence?'

He stiffened. 'I don't need—'

'Of course you do.' Cat planted her hands on her hips. 'Everyone should know how to defend themselves.'

'I can manage.' His lower lip jutted.

'You could manage better. Not just for yourself but for the younger kids.'

'What do you think I am, some unpaid bodyguard?' Yet, despite his offhand tone, Cat saw the spark in his eyes.

'Well, if you're not interested...' She picked up a towel and headed to the pool house. She'd reached the steps when finally he spoke.

'Wait. Would you...? Are you serious?'

'Of course. I could teach you—'

The sight of a long, lean figure approaching from the far end of the pool stopped her words.

What was Alex doing here?

In sweat pants and a black T-shirt that emphasised his long-legged stride and straight shoulders, with his hair ruffled and his unshaved jaw deliciously dark, he reminded her of a pirate, stepping ashore for a bit of swashbuckling R and R.

Cat stared, aghast at her wayward imagination. An imagination that envisaged her plastered to that hard chest, offering herself for his pleasure.

Her heart hammered even harder when he met her eyes and his mouth curled in a smile. She'd missed that smile, despite its devastating effect on her internal organs. Surely something vital inside was melting?

'Taking the class yourself, then?'

'It seemed easiest.' Was that breathy voice hers? She sounded like a swooning teenager, not the competent woman people turned to in a crisis.

'How was the swimming, Thomas? Good?'

The boy nodded, his expression wary.

Damn. He'd been about to ask her to teach him and now with Alex here he'd retreat again behind the walls of his teenage pride.

Cat couldn't help every troubled teen. But she could no more turn away from this bruised boy than fly.

Alex's drawl cut off her thoughts. 'Did I hear you offer to give instruction in self-defence?'

Cat blinked. She read a gleam of intent in Alex's expression. A gleam at odds with his laid-back demeanour.

How long had he been here? Even if he'd just arrived he couldn't miss the discoloured skin on Thomas's skinny frame. Maybe that explained why he'd buried the hatchet, for now at least.

'Princess?' Alex waggled his fingers to catch her attention.

'I was indeed. Are you interested?'

'I'm always interested.' His baritone drawl ignited that spark in her belly she'd been trying to ignore. The spark that reminded her how she'd gone up in flames and glory all through that long night with him.

Alex turned to the boy. 'But I'm not sure she's up to teaching us defensive moves. What do you say, Thomas? She's a bit on the puny side.'

Cat quelled a smile, sure now. Alex was playing into her scheme.

It felt good to have him on her side, however briefly. Like yesterday when he'd spoken up about Thomas being unable to swim. Her wariness crumbled. He didn't *need* to help, especially since it meant spending time with *her*.

'The Princess is stronger than she looks.' Thomas straightened his shoulders and lifted his chin and another layer of Cat's defensive wall eroded. No wonder the younger girls accepted the boy. He had a protective streak a mile wide, despite the chip on his shoulder.

'Thank you, Thomas.' Was that a blush on his sallow cheeks? She turned to Alex. 'Or do I have to convince you I'm up to the job?'

'I'm sure you have some moves.' His lazy smile told her he'd chosen his words deliberately. Yet she felt as if the laughter in his eyes wasn't *at* her but *with* her. 'But I'm not convinced you could handle someone my...size.'

To her amazement Cat felt heat prickle her chest and creep up her throat, making her abruptly aware she wore only a bikini. All she could think about was how it had felt to accommodate Alex's size. Remembered pleasure washed through her as she recalled the heavy thrust of his body inside hers and how he'd taken her to heaven.

Alex's eyes held hers. It was clear he remembered too. His cocky smile reminded her of the day they'd met and how much fun it had been bantering with him, underscored as it was by undeniable attraction.

Did this mean Alex had forgiven her?

No time now to find out. She grabbed her oversized T-shirt, hauling it on so it hung loose down her thighs.

Was that disappointment on Alex's face? The idea boosted her mood.

'It's not size that matters.' Deliberately she let her gaze skate low over his hard-packed body. 'It's how well you use what you've got.'

His laugh sounded choked and Cat swung back to the boy. 'I could teach you how to ward off a punch.'

'I'd rather learn how to punch back.'

Cat sympathised. It took everything she had not to let her gaze stray to his bruises.

'Anyone can start a fight,' Alex's deep voice said. 'Ending it takes far more guts.'

It sounded as if Alex spoke from personal experience. For some reason she'd imagined a member of a royal family wouldn't have to defend himself. But what did she know?

'Come on, Thomas, grab a towel and your T-shirt and we'll show you.'

'Both of you?' The kid's eyes widened. 'Really?' Of course he was stunned. A king and a princess teaching him to defend himself? Even to Cat it seemed bizarre. Living in a pastel-pink stucco palace with its own helipad and private bay was bizarre too.

But she refused to let Thomas go back till he knew how to deflect an attack long enough to call for help.

Cat led the way to some thick turf. 'I know His Highness looks a little soft—' she bit down on a smile '—but I'm hoping he's up to it.'

'Oh, I'm up to it.' That baritone drawl from just behind her made Cat's bones shiver and a pulse quicken between her legs. Alex's breath feathered her neck as he continued in a whisper for her ears alone. 'If you cast your mind back you'll remember being soft isn't a problem I have.'

Cat swallowed hard. What had begun as a bit of fun, a little banter that was heady relief after the tension of the last few days, had turned into something too dangerous.

She had no right flirting with Alex, or he with her, while he looked on her as an enemy. Especially not in front of an impressionable boy.

She stepped away and turned. Alex stood a few steps away, smiling. Thomas hung back.

'Come on, Thomas. Over near me.' Cat gestured to a spot to one side. When he was in place she beckoned to Alex. 'Now, punch me.'

Thomas stiffened in shock and even Alex frowned.

'I know you're…capable,' he said at last, 'but I'd hurt you if I connected. How about I grab you?'

She shook her head. 'We'll get to that later. Thomas, what do you notice about the way I'm standing?'

'Nothing. You're…' He paused. 'You have your feet apart and your knees a little bent.'

Cat nodded. 'And I'm watching him, looking for signs of how he's going to move. Being alert is important.'

She beckoned to Alex but, instead of throwing a punch, he lunged for her. She shifted, grabbed, turned, and was surprised that he was ready for the movement. Instead of using his momentum to toss him Cat was forced to rethink. This was a guy who could hold his own, she realised in a flurry of pleasure, her body locked against his. She twisted again and, using all her skill, upended him with merciless technique that left him lying on the grass.

'Not bad.' His mouth kicked up at one side and his eyes glinted in appreciation.

Cat stared. Many men hated being thrown by a woman. Of course Alex was taking part for Thomas's sake, but the fact he'd anticipated and parried her first move showed he'd aimed to best her. Yet still he smiled.

It wasn't fair. It would be easier if he was grumpy, like when he'd discovered her deception. When he smiled she liked him too much.

He lifted his hand and automatically she reached out to tug him up. His hand was large, the palm callused, making her recall its tender scrape on her flesh.

Cat turned away, but not before she saw Alex's smile widen. 'Now,' he said, 'you come at me.'

Cat shrugged. 'Okay.' She moved forward, half her attention on Thomas to see if he was watching. Alex's next move was unexpected, unorthodox, and ended with her on the grass, looking up into shining indigo eyes.

'You've done this before,' she gasped, refilling her lungs with a deep breath.

'I trained in martial arts.'

'Really?' She couldn't help her smile. With his dark hair flopping over his forehead and a smile teasing the corners of his sculpted mouth, he was far too gorgeous. It struck her how much she wanted him to look at her this way, not with disdain. Was his good humour all for Thomas's benefit or was it possible Alex had forgiven her? She told herself it was too much to expect.

'When did you start training?' He pulled her up.

'I was eight.'

He looked like he was about to comment but then turned away. 'How about it, Thomas? Want to try?'

Through the next hour Cat was thankful Alex was there. She taught every week back home. But he had a rapport with the boy, far easier than her own. Cat put it down partly to the fact Thomas showed an aversion to fighting a female. Plus Alex, when he put his mind to it, could be incredibly likeable.

Interesting that Thomas had no qualms about standing up to a man whose shoulders were twice as wide as his. In fact the boy was surprisingly eager. Which made Cat all the more determined to get to the bottom of those bruises.

At the end of the session he murmured goodbye and headed to the car waiting to take him to the camp.

'He's not effusive, is he?' Alex towelled his face.

'He's learned not to trust. It will take more than a morning to break down those barriers.'

'You sound like you know something about it.'

She shoved her feet into sandals. 'At home I teach self-defence and fitness to kids. Kids you'd probably class as tough.'

'Home? You mean the States, not St Galla?'

She flicked him a glance, then had to peel her eyes away from the way his damp shirt clung to that powerful chest. Looking at him made her long for things she shouldn't. Things that were no longer possible.

'This isn't my home.'

He heard the snap in her voice. 'You weren't happy here?'

She stared across the garden towards the delightful palace, looking like some fanciful concoction in palest pink with decorative white frosting around its large arched windows and doors. Would she have been happy if she'd lived here? Was Amelie?

She wrenched her gaze away. 'I hated it. I couldn't wait to leave.'

'Because of the bullying?' Alex's quiet question slipped through her defences like a stiletto to the heart. 'Is that why you're determined to protect Thomas?'

'Someone has to care. Someone has to give him a chance.' She saw the curiosity in his eyes and hurried on. 'Thank you for this morning. You didn't have to give up your time for this.'

'Neither did you.' Something in his tone made her suddenly self-conscious.

'It's what I do. One day I plan to open a centre especially for teens. Somewhere they'll enjoy going that helps them develop their self-esteem and...' Her words petered out. She couldn't believe she was telling him this. He wouldn't be interested.

Yet when she darted another glance his way Alex's stare was thoughtful, not bored.

'Anyway, thanks again. I think Thomas opened up more, having a man to relate to.' She drew a quick breath. 'I know the last thing you want is to spend time with me—'

'That's an exaggeration.'

Her eyebrows arched. 'You don't have to spare my feelings.'

He chuckled, the sound like rich chocolate, teasing her. *She had to get out of here. Fast.*

'I'm not.' His smile died and for the first time this morning he looked utterly serious. 'Despite the way you lied I find I quite...like you, Cat Dubois.'

CHAPTER TEN

I QUITE...LIKE YOU.

Cat grimaced. That wasn't what she wanted to hear from Alex. Though it was a lot better than his frosty outrage. She wanted—

'Try it again, Ms Dubois. If you manage without counting aloud that would be an improvement.'

Cat turned to Lady Enide, sitting on a chair so gilded and majestic it looked as if Louis the Sun King might have used it. Unlike Cat, wobbling on spindly heels on the polished ballroom floor, Enide looked poised, though there was a worried pleat on her pale forehead.

'I'm no good at this. You must see that.' Cat gritted her teeth, willing her desperation not to show.

'Rubbish, my girl. You're an expert in martial arts and fit enough to sprint around the peninsula every day. You have enough co-ordination to manage a waltz.'

'Not in heels and a long dress.' A borrowed ball gown of Amelie's that was loose around the bodice and dragged on the floor, a reminder that her royal half-sister was taller and better endowed. No doubt she waltzed perfectly too.

'You're making excuses. You've set your mind against this because you're scared.'

'Scared?' Cat stared, arrested.

Enide's eyes narrowed. 'I'm no fool, my dear. I realise how different all this—' she gestured to their plush surroundings '—is from your usual life.'

Cat straightened. 'Not so. I go to posh receptions all the time. To boxes at the opera and the ballet and to billionaires' parties in penthouses and private cruisers.'

'As a bodyguard—not a guest.' Those pale eyes surveyed her with something like sympathy.

'If you're suggesting I secretly yearn for a life of luxury you're wrong.' She'd worked hard for everything she had and could hold her head up in any company.

'I simply meant it must be difficult to be thrust out of the shadows and into the limelight. Into *Amelie's* life.'

'No one ever took the time to teach me to dance, but I got by.' And she didn't care. Really, she didn't. Being a tomboy, without the pretty dresses, make-up and nail polish had been no hardship. From her teens she'd tried to be as different as possible from the graceful, beautiful half-sister who appeared regularly in press reports.

She hadn't needed or wanted sleepovers with the other girls, or gossipy sessions about boys and fashion that she'd never been invited to join anyway.

Cat turned and saw her reflection in one of the mirrors. She'd never owned a pink dress. Her hand splayed over the deep carnation pink folds. Wearing this gown with its strapless, glittery bodice and cinched-in waist she looked like a stranger.

'Every girl should learn to waltz,' Enide said crisply. 'There's nothing like being whirled around the ballroom by the right man, a man with strong hands and the devil in his eyes, to make a woman feel…all woman.'

Cat turned to see the older woman smile reminiscently. 'Enide?'

'Don't look so shocked. I wasn't always this old.' She flapped one elegant ringed hand. 'Now, try again.'

Cat shook her head. 'It would be better to change the arrangements. It's too late to teach me to dance. I was told a small reception.' She'd said it before but it had made no difference. She'd been deliberately misled about this job—a job she couldn't wriggle out of. Cat felt caught in a vice—

pressure from the Prime Minister, from Alex, from the need not to let Amelie down the only time her sister needed her.

Enide sighed. 'If I could, I would. But any change now would cause talk and that's what we're trying to avoid. I blame myself for not checking you could waltz.'

'But if I have to dance with lots of people someone will realise I'm not Amelie. You must see that!'

She was tempted to blurt out that Alex already knew the truth, but she couldn't risk the penalty clause in her contract, or the threat of being blacklisted.

Enide nodded, her mouth turning down. 'I agree. However, it's not as bad as you think. Open the dancing with King Alex. One waltz only, then retire to watch. You'll have done your duty. Everyone will understand that, so soon after the tragedy in your family, you're not ready for a night of dancing.'

Cat opened her mouth to object, then clapped it shut. That fragile look was back on the older woman's face. Clearly she was deeply affected by the deaths of Amelie's brother and his wife. Clearly too, she had no more enthusiasm for this royal reception than Cat.

Every demand placed on her came from the PM. Enide was doing her best to ensure that Cat and Amelie didn't come unstuck.

Cat could only try to fill her half-sister's shoes and hope no one noticed Cinderella had two left feet.

Alex strode into the palace, his mind on his meeting. He wouldn't do business with the company he'd visited. He didn't like its ethics. But the real reason he'd cut the meeting short was the issues he had to sort out here.

His pace slowed as music reached him. Waltz music. Curious, he turned from the curving marble staircase and followed the sound to a pair of large doors, slightly ajar.

He'd been right. The *Emperor Waltz*—his mother's favourite. Alex remembered seeing her years ago, swirling around the dance floor in some VIP's arms. She'd been graceful, gorgeous and more animated than he'd ever seen her with his father. She loved dancing, but Cyrill had never partnered her. He'd never spent time with his wife. He was always too busy working on his next shady deal.

Curious, Alex pushed one of the doors wide. Golden, late afternoon light slanted in, gleaming on the polished floor and spotlighting the woman dipping and twirling, arms raised as if resting on an invisible partner. There was no one else in the room.

Her hair was up in one of those oh-so-neat bun arrangements that he'd detested ever since he'd seen her gorgeous locks rippling across her bare shoulders. She wore a grimace and a ball gown that displayed enough flesh to send lust quaking through him.

For days he'd been with her each morning while she taught Thomas self-defence. Each evening he spent with her and Enide and a variety of tame guests. And every day that gnawing urge grew stronger—to forget she'd duped him and relieve his burning frustration with her sweet, sexy body in his bed.

'What are you doing?' He shut the door behind him. 'Stupid question. But why dance alone?'

Cat swung round, her skirt belling around her. She was breathing hard. Alex's throat dried as he imagined tracing a line along—

She yanked the bodice of her dress up. Flags of deep rose pink painted her cheeks, almost matching the colour of her dress. Though from the fit it clearly wasn't *her* dress.

'What are you doing here?'

'I'm staying here, remember? You haven't answered. Why are you dancing alone?'

She shrugged. Alex watched those bare shoulders rise stiffly and was struck abruptly by her vulnerability.

It wasn't something he naturally associated with Cat. She could take on most comers in physical combat and she had a sharp tongue when riled. He guessed if she had any idea how he responded to that forlorn look in her fine eyes she'd be horrified.

She turned away to switch off the music, her movements quick and far more fluid than when she'd been attempting the waltz. Strange how someone so supremely active should look uncomfortable dancing.

'It turns out there will be dancing at the reception.'

'You're out of practice?'

Her laugh was humourless. 'I've never danced in my life. Now they want me to open a royal ball, with you.' Was that panic underlying her clipped words?

A frown tightened Alex's forehead. 'How can that be?'

'Because I'm taking Amelie's place, of course.'

'I mean how can you never have danced?'

Her mouth flattened. 'You sound like Lady Enide. Not everyone grows up attending balls.' With her hands on her hips she was helping gravity tug her dress lower. Alex fought to keep his eyes on her face, not those delicious curves. 'There's no need to look so smug!' Her gaze flashed fire and perversely he wanted more of that crackling energy. The alternative—seeing her looking almost lost—bothered him.

'You must have gone to some sort of dance.'

She shook her head. 'Never.'

In her ill-fitting gown, and her hair dressed in someone else's style, it struck him how hard it must be, playing Cinderella in another woman's place.

What had Cat's life been? She'd never danced. She'd been bullied and hated talking about her family. His suspicions had been roused when he'd seen her fierce determination to protect young Thomas and recalled her saying her father had hands the size of dinner plates. Surely that wasn't the first thing that should come to mind when describing a parent?

But what did he know? His father had been a slimy piece of work. Instead of using his hands, he'd cut people down to size with his tongue and made them pay in other ways for disrupting his plans.

'I'll teach you.'

Instantly she stepped back. 'There's no need.'

'You'll never master it alone.'

Predictably that chin lifted. 'Enide partnered me for a while but—'

'But you need a man.'

'I don't need...' Her voice stopped as he curled his arm around her waist and took her hand. She fitted him exactly.

'Don't argue. Put your other hand on my shoulder and follow my lead.'

'But I don't...'

'Don't argue, Cat. Or this will take even longer.' Not that he minded longer. Looking into her dazzling eyes, breathing in her scent, holding her close, was the best he'd felt since their tryst at the pool.

'You're holding me too tight.'

He shook his head. She was right but he was damned if he'd put a proper distance between them now.

'Stop twitching.'

'But it's uncomfortable. Enide insisted I wear heels and stockings. I *hate* stockings. They're even worse than pantyhose.' She was talking too fast, her breath nervous little puffs that landed on his chin.

She was right to be nervous.

Alex shut his eyes, fighting the urge to forget dancing and seduce her here, where anyone could walk in. He'd start with those stockings. A shudder ripped through him at the thought of Cat's long, toned legs in stockings. Of her smooth upper thighs above wispy nylon, then the warm silk of her—

'Alex? What's wrong?'

'Nothing.' He cleared his throat and opened his eyes. Hers looked huge and uncertain.

Did she feel the same shuddery need? And more—that too-tight feeling in the chest? He'd never known it with any other woman. Even when he'd been furious with her, he hadn't managed to conquer it.

'Thank you for volunteering to teach me,' she said solemnly. 'And for helping Thomas. I appreciate it.'

Alex tried to smile but his mouth was too tight. Absurd how tense he was.

'It's nothing. And I haven't taught you yet.'

'I know it's asking a lot. Even now that you *quite like* me.' A hint of a smile curled her lips.

'Witch.' He rubbed his thumb over the centre of her palm in a deliberate caress that made her breath hitch and her pupils widen. He loved how receptive she was to his touch. That at least had always been real between them.

'If we're going to dance we need music.' She broke away abruptly.

Madness, sheer madness, to let him hold her like that.

But what option did she have? Her lesson with Enide had been a disaster. Somehow she had to learn the right dance moves.

The trouble was with Alex it wasn't dance moves she had in mind. Especially when he touched her that way.

What did he mean by it?

It was difficult enough when they met each morning, helping Thomas. Especially as she found herself *liking* him as he took the boy under his wing. He was a natural role model for the kid—apparently easy-going but with an inner strength that demanded respect.

Cat switched on the music. It started softly but her nerves

sparked at the thought of being held in Alex's arms as he swept her around the room.

As if that was going to happen. More like she'd lame him with these spiked heels.

'Cat?'

She drew a deep breath and spun round. He opened his arms invitingly and it was the most natural, scary thing in the world to walk into them. This time he didn't hold her too close. She registered a sliver of disappointment at the distance between them. Yet the feel of his hand pressing her waist through the silk gown made her skin flush.

'First up, don't look down at your feet. You can't see them anyway in that skirt. Look at my face.'

Reluctantly Cat shifted her gaze. There was a fizz of sensation as their eyes met.

'How am I supposed to see what I'm doing if I don't look?'

'You don't. I'll look out for both of us. That's why I lead.' He paused, his mouth curling in a smile that made her heart kick. 'You have to let yourself go completely and trust me. Can you do that?'

All too easily.

That night in the pool house she'd trusted her instinct and followed blindly where he led. It had been the single most amazing experience of her life. The ease with which she'd given him her trust was terrifying.

'Come on, Cat. Take a risk.'

The music was an enticing rhythm and Alex moved. She followed, moving backward, silently counting the beats and trying to anticipate the direction of his turn.

Her knee bashed his and her foot came down on his shoe.

'Sorry.' She bit her lip, stepping back, but Alex stepped with her, pulling her nearer.

'Don't apologise. You don't let Thomas apologise when he doesn't get something first go.'

'That's different.'

'Not different at all. You're learning. Cut yourself some slack. If you relax a little you might enjoy yourself.'

Enjoy making a fool of herself in front of him? 'I doubt it. I don't have the knack.'

Another smile. This one sent flames roaring through her blood. 'Of course you do. Let me make all the moves.' He leaned closer, his voice a rumbling whisper. 'Waltzing is like making love. Didn't you know?'

Cat's eyes popped wide but before she could respond his grip firmed and the music swelled and suddenly they were moving. Not the tentative, carefully measured steps Enide had taught her, but a wheeling, whirling circle of movement that turned the rest of the room into a kaleidoscope blur.

Cat's grip tightened on Alex's broad shoulder for balance. Her long skirts belled out around her in a soft swoosh of silk. His knee and thigh pressed against hers then retreated then touched again, prompting her to move, to step and spin. It was a miracle but somehow, without actually trying, Cat was dancing.

She wasn't pressed up against his body but she was close enough to feel his breath warm on her face and inhale the scent that was his alone. She saw the pulse at his neck and the way his mouth curved and understood what he meant about the intimacy of the dance. They were fully clothed. Anyone seeing them would notice nothing untoward. Yet the way her body responded so completely to his, receiving and reacting to each tiny message about the direction of the dance…it was completely instinctive. Just, as he'd said, like sex.

Round and round they went, down the length of the ballroom and back. Cat caught glimpses of them in the mirrors over his shoulder, a blur of blush pink against sober charcoal grey. Like figures in some fairy tale—elegant and handsome.

'Look at me.' Again that deep voice. But this time the command was a growl.

Cat looked up and instantly was lost in the dark sea of his eyes.

Alex twirled her faster, the momentum threatening to spin her out of his arms, except his hold, like his gaze, was steady, keeping her with him. He was totally in command, easy but firm and precise in every movement.

For only the second time in her life Cat revelled in ceding total control. The first time had been when Alex had taken her on a trip of sensual discovery that shattered her habitual barriers, leaving her naked in a way that had little to do with her lack of clothes.

This should scare her.

Instead she was thrilled. Exultant.

The hand at her back urged her nearer to that hard-packed heat and muscle. His mouth curled in a smile that held nothing back. It shot delight right through her.

Suddenly Cat found she was laughing. Spinning and twirling as the music soared and swooped and the mirrors and windows flashed by. She felt like she was flying. She felt—

They slammed to a halt, her long dress swooshing around her legs, her heart pumping hard, her breasts pushing up against the ill-fitting bodice.

Alex released her hand, lifting his warm palm to her cheek as his arm tightened on her waist. His breath was rough, like hers, as the joy in his blazing eyes faded to something that made her gulp.

She should step away. Say how remarkable it was that she'd been able to keep up.

But the expression on his face, or perhaps the strange fluttery feeling deep within, stopped her words.

'Cat.' It was a soft breath of air. A caress. The single

word in that impossibly deep register rippled through her in endless waves.

She swallowed, sought for something to say, but instead found only a yearning, melting sensation as she looked into eyes the colour of twilight.

'Beautiful Cat.' His hand slid up, fingers spearing her hair, massaging her scalp in slow, delicious caresses till the tightly secured tresses loosed and fell. She heard hairpins scatter on the floor.

'That's better.' Alex smiled and the impact made it hurt to breathe. 'Now you look like you.'

'Alex?' She planted her hand on his chest, trying to anchor herself, for his words made her knees wobble. The steady thud of his heart beneath her palm should have reassured but the intimacy of touching him made her more, not less unsure. 'I don't understand.' What had happened to his censure? His distrust?

'I can't get enough of you, Cat.'

She sucked in a shocked breath, struggling to process his words and the intent look on his face.

Despite caution, despite pride, she felt herself glow. An answering need rose within her, urgent and unstoppable.

'You don't want me! You made that clear.' Pride made her lift her chin, as if neither of them heard the tell-tale hitch in her voice. As if she was as strong as she pretended to be, when all the while her silly heart jolted against her ribcage and excitement and anxiety knotted her stomach.

'I explained and apologised but it didn't make any difference.' She shouldn't care what he thought, or what he wanted. He'd rejected her.

Yet she did care. Despite everything, she did.

She'd discovered far more than Alex's charisma and sex appeal. He was patient but firm with Thomas, giving his time freely without being asked. With Enide he was amusing and solicitous, especially when the older woman was stressed and looking fragile beneath her armour of formidable hauteur. It had struck Cat that though he knew Enide was part of the scheme to dupe him, he treated her not as an enemy but as an old lady carrying a heavy burden of stress.

With Cat he'd been…understanding. She knew he'd asked their guide at the lab to speak simply solely for her, because he hadn't quite managed to hide his own level of knowledge. He'd pushed her to talk about her past but his response to her revelation about dropping out of school had made it seem unimportant. Then he'd opened up about his family and she'd found herself feeling that connection she'd thought severed between them. And since he'd begun helping her with Thomas's lessons she'd found herself enjoying his company, admiring him, and…

'What are you thinking?' His deep voice cut off her thoughts.

'That this is a bad idea. You need to let me go.' Because the appalling truth was Cat didn't have the power to break his gentle hold. What had Alex done to her? How had he sapped her willpower?

Slowly he shook his head. 'I can't, Cat. I've tried, ever since I realised you lied to me, but it's not working. The more I'm with you, the better I know you, the harder this is.' His words were an uncanny echo of her thoughts.

'I was angry. Too angry.' Yet he didn't look angry now. Her heart gave a single mighty thump then raced on.

'Because I deceived you.' They were back where they'd started. Despite her hurt, Cat couldn't blame him for his anger. No one liked to be made a fool of.

'It wasn't all your fault.' His words surprised her. 'I believe that you didn't know I'd be here. I followed up what you told me with some discreet digging. It turns out the Prime Minister is the one pushing the royal marriage. He's a ruthless, conniving man and he's convinced the regency shouldn't go to a single woman like Princess Amelie. He wants her married to a *suitable* man who can be a role model for the young Prince.'

As he spoke Alex combed his fingers through her hair, drawing it around her shoulders and breasts, all the while holding her gaze. It was one of the most sensual, arousing experiences of her life. Pleasure exploded across her scalp and shoulders, sending shockwaves through her, making it hard to concentrate on words.

Her tongue felt thick and clumsy but she forced herself to speak. 'That doesn't excuse what I did.'

'We all make mistakes.'

'Alex?'

His mouth tipped up in a hint of a smile and his arm tightened around her waist.

'Lying is a hot button for me. When I discovered the truth...' He shrugged. 'I held you equally to blame with those behind the charade. But what I conveniently blanked from my mind was that you hadn't set out to seduce me. I was the one seducing you. And that, whatever this is between us, it was close to irresistible.'

Alex paused, his eyes searching hers. 'It still is.'

Cat gasped, and inhaled that familiar warm, citrus tang she remembered from when she'd kissed him all over. A terrible trembling started deep inside.

'Cat? Tell me it's not just me feeling this.'

'Feeling what?' she croaked, fighting the undertow of longing that threatened to sweep her away.

His gaze was steady. 'Attraction. Desire. Respect. Liking.' His hand slid from her hair to her face, cupping her cheek; his thumb swiped the corner of her mouth and Cat struggled not to dissolve at his feet.

'Not just sex?' Her voice was unrecognisable.

'Not just sex.' His gaze pinioned her. 'I've seen who you are, Cat Dubois. I don't pretend to know everything but I like what I see. More than I'd thought possible.'

He swallowed and she saw his Adam's apple bob in that strong throat. 'I *want* what I see, despite how this started. The question is, do you still want me?'

Dazed, Cat felt herself drowning in his darkened gaze. She read heat, hunger and honesty. He liked her, he wanted her. He *respected* her. He was offering the chance to continue where they'd left off with an affair that would be short but intense and oh-so satisfying.

Cat licked dry lips, trying to find words. Instantly he zeroed in on the movement. A second later he lowered his head. But, instead of taking her mouth, he pressed a kiss to her cheek, then another on her jaw, then more, tracing her jawline and down her throat.

'It has to be your decision, Cat. I won't push you.'

No, he'd make her lose her mind with devastating kisses.

Cat inhaled deeply and was suddenly conscious of the silk bodice sagging across her breasts. Conscious she wore another woman's finery. She was in unfamiliar surroundings and out of her depth.

She told herself none of that mattered. What she felt for Alex was real, whether she wore jeans or gym gear or borrowed stilettos.

But she no longer trusted her judgement. Not when Alex—*King* Alex—made her feel things she'd never before experienced.

With a gasp of disbelief at her own actions, Cat pushed him back. Their eyes locked and she felt the compulsion to slam her mouth to his, let him sweep her into mindless delight.

Instead, with a strength she hadn't known she possessed, Cat spun away. Reefing up her billowing skirts, she stumbled to the door. She needed time to think. Time alone.

It was only as she stumbled up the wide staircase that she realised she'd left her satin shoes behind.

CHAPTER ELEVEN

CAT LEANED OVER the balustrade, looking down into the palace foyer where staff bustled, carrying massive flower arrangements and chairs, preparing for tonight's festivities. The front doors were open and two men unrolled a carpet of royal St Gallan green edged in gold.

She rubbed her hands up her arms as nerves prickled. Already her hair was up in a style that looked frighteningly regal. When she'd looked in the mirror she'd seen a stranger. How would she look after a session with the make-up artist and wearing the amazing dress, made to measure, that had been delivered?

Knowing Alex was at yet another meeting, she'd aimed to clear her head with a quick walk through the palace galleries. But she felt as muddled as before.

Yesterday Alex had held her close and told her he wanted her. That he'd forgiven her deception and more. So much more. Cat had spent last evening in her room, pleading a headache. It hadn't been much of a lie. Her head had swum and she'd felt wrung out.

His words, his expression as he'd held her, had made Cat want to surrender to her feelings for him. Feelings she hadn't been able to eradicate, even when he'd hated her.

She felt a foreigner in her own body, her own mind. Romance had been scarce in her world. But that didn't mean she was a pushover.

Yet, even as she thought it, she recalled the expression on Alex's face, the roughened timbre of his voice as he spoke about needing her. He'd said this wasn't just sex, despite the thrumming sexual attraction, and she'd been on the brink of giving him whatever he wanted.

Yet what more could they share? And if it was simply sex, was she ready for such a brief liaison? Could she walk away, heart whole afterwards? She was due to leave tomorrow. She wasn't naïve enough to imagine a king would carry on a long-distance relationship with a bodyguard. He in his palace in northern Europe and she in New York or wherever work took her.

That was without the complication of her true identity. If fairy tales happened and he did want her even then, sooner or later someone would discover her past and reveal the sordid truth for the world to devour over morning coffee.

Cat shivered at the thought. Not merely of facing her past, but of how the scandal might affect Alex and Amelie.

So, all they could offer each other was sex. A steamy liaison for a week in Bengaria if she followed Alex before she took up her next job.

She was so tempted. She told herself she was fascinated by what he'd told her of his people's fierce pride and warm hearts and how, when things looked grim, they'd pulled together. Under his leadership, Bengaria was now becoming a centre for innovation and investment.

But it wasn't Bengaria that drew her. It was Alex.

Hers was a blood-deep craving.

Cat shook her head and hurried to her room. The sooner she—

'There you are.' Enide was at her door. She looked tired but there were spots of colour high on her cheeks.

'Lady Enide. Are you all right?' This situation was so difficult. She'd been increasingly worried about Enide, despite her self-contained air.

'I have someone who needs to speak with you.' She glanced around as if checking they were alone. Cat followed her gaze, wondering where the visitor was. She hoped it wasn't another demand from the Prime Minister. Despite the penalty if she walked away from the job, Cat was close to pulling the plug on this whole masquerade.

'Not here.' Enide opened the door to Cat's suite and ushered her in. It was only then Cat saw the slimline phone in the other woman's hand.

Enide put the phone to her own ear. 'I have her here. Are you absolutely sure—? Yes, of course. I will. But please, take care of yourself.'

Cat stared. It couldn't be the Prime Minister's office, not with Enide sounding clucky as a broody hen.

Enide straightened, putting her hand over the phone. She opened her mouth then closed it. Cat's curiosity rose. Then Enide held the phone out. Cat took it and was bemused when the older woman briefly clasped her other hand and squeezed. Then she left the room, gently closing the door behind her.

'Hello?'

'Ms Dubois?' The voice was female, warm and young. Cat relaxed a fraction.

'Yes.'

'It's Amelie here. Princess Amelie.'

Cat staggered and groped for a seat, plopping down into a velvet-covered chair near the window. She heard her blood rush in her ears, felt the quick hammer of her heart. She'd waited all her life to connect with her other family; even in the years when she'd told herself she didn't *want* any contact, the desire had still been there, hidden beneath her pride.

'Your Highness.'

'Amelie, please.' There was a pause so long Cat wondered if the line had dropped out. 'May I call you Cat?'

'Of course.'

'Thank you.' Another pause. Cat wondered at the sudden certainty Amelie was nervous too. Almost as nervous as her. But how could she possibly know that? 'Are you all right, Cat?'

'I'm sorry?' Cat pressed a hand to her forehead, confused.

'I asked if you're okay.' There was a soft sigh on the other end of the line. 'I've just found out about this scheme for you to take my place at tonight's reception. I had no idea. The event should have been cancelled when I told the Prime Minister I wouldn't be there. I believed it *had* been cancelled.' Steel underscored her words.

'I haven't been watching the news, you see, and I haven't been in regular contact with anyone at the palace so I didn't know you'd been brought in. Are you all right?'

Amelie was asking *her* if she was okay?

'I'm fine. I…well, I'm not very good at being a princess, but I'm muddling through.'

'Even with King Alex in the palace?'

Cat rubbed her hand across her brow. She was on thin ice no matter what she said.

'Cat? Are you sure you're all right?'

Cat didn't know if it was tiredness or frustration at being in such a situation, hemmed in by other people's demands. Or the totally unexpected concern in Amelie's voice. Her *sister's* voice. But suddenly she'd reached breaking point.

She dropped her hand and stared at the view beyond the window. From here she could see one end of the pool where she and Alex had made love all night long.

Her jaw tightened. She was sick of pretending.

'I'm fine. And Alex knows the truth. He guessed some time ago.'

'Yet he's still there?' Cat heard Amelie's astonishment.

'He knows it's not your doing. He blames Monsieur Barthe. But he's willing to go along with the pretence so there's no public scandal.' She paused, wondering how to say what needed to be said. 'But there's something else you need to know. He made it clear, even before he found out who I was, that he wasn't interested in marriage.'

'Thank God. That's one thing less to worry about.'

'You're pleased?' Cat was confused.

'I agreed to entertain the idea, but my heart wasn't in it.' Amelie's laugh sounded bitter.

'Are *you* all right? I've been worried you might be in trouble.'

'That's kind of you.' She sighed. 'Things haven't gone quite as I'd expected but I'm coming home. I'd like, very much, to meet you. I…' There was a long pause. 'I didn't know you existed till Enide told me.'

Cat felt a lump choke off her breathing. Amelie knew or guessed they were half-sisters and still she wanted to meet. It was more than Cat had ever dared hope.

'I'd like that.'

'Good. I'm looking forward to it too.' She paused. 'Now, about tonight. I'll see if I can get there in time. Transport is a bit limited from here and—'

'It's all right. I can do it. It's only for a couple of hours and with Enide and Alex watching out for me I'll be fine.'

She would too. She could do this. Afterwards she'd leave and take up her own life again. And she'd have the prospect of meeting her sister to look forward to.

'Alex?' What had Amelie heard in her voice?

'He's been…helpful.' She opened her mouth to say he'd taught her to waltz but the memories of their dance were too personal, too intimate to share.

'I see.' Amelie paused. 'Are you absolutely sure? I couldn't guarantee I'd get there exactly on time but—'

'I'm sure. I'll manage. I'm sure you have other things on your mind than tonight's reception.' It must have been something major to take her from her kingdom. 'I hope Prince Sébastien is well.'

'He's fine.' The warmth in Amelie's voice was obvious. 'Much better than before.' A man's voice sounded in the background. 'I'm sorry. I have to go. Are you sure about tonight? I can try—'

'Absolutely.' If Amelie arrived late, missing the opening of the event, questions were sure to be asked. Better that she, Cat, play the part one last time.

'Thank you, Cat. If you can manage tonight it will give me a little time to…organise things. But we'll talk soon and arrange to meet, either in St Galla or elsewhere.'

Alex stood in the echoing foyer, smiling and greeting guests entering the palace on the carpet that stretched to the white gravel driveway. On his left stood Lady Enide in silver and pearls, and on his right was the St Gallan Prime Minister, taking the temporary role of host.

Since the royal family was still mourning the recent deaths of King Michel and his wife, the official line was that Princess Amelie wouldn't formally host the event.

It was a clever way of reducing the chances of Cat being recognised as an imposter. Alex had to admire Monsieur Barthe's deft control of a tricky situation. Except the more he saw of the man's methods, the more he disliked him. He reminded Alex of his own father—a man who'd shamelessly lied and manoeuvred situations to his own ends.

This was the man responsible for Cat's charade, for the lies Alex had been fed. He intended to ensure the man paid a high price for his devious tactics, as soon as tonight was over and Cat was safely away from here.

Cat. As he smiled and shook hands he acted on autopilot. His mind was on her.

Twice she'd run from him. That first day on his yacht when she'd dived into the sea rather than admit the attraction between them. Then yesterday when he'd told her he wanted her, cared for her.

She'd looked like a doe caught in headlights. Her eyes huge with shock. But he'd known, or thought he'd known, she felt the same. The sound of her laughter as they'd danced, the way she responded to him, the light in her eyes.

He'd *felt* the connection, as strong and true as ever. It had withstood his fury and hurt pride at her deception. It made a nonsense of his intention not to get involved with anyone till he'd achieved what he needed to in Bengaria. It turned him, and his plans, upside down.

Yet she'd spent the last twenty-four hours avoiding him. Because he'd been wrong and she felt nothing? Or because she felt too much?

It *had* to be the latter.

Every instinct told him Cat was in as deep as he. It was only that understanding that had stopped him invading her privacy to force a discussion. She needed time. She needed—

A ripple of excitement passed through the crowd. Faces turned up and those in the receiving line stopped to look.

Alex turned and his heart stalled.

She was magnificent.

Poised at the top of the staircase was a slim, breathtaking woman in a dress that looked black till she shifted and the light from the chandelier caught a gleam of darkest green. Her shoulders and arms were bare and from her hips soft folds fell to the floor. Gems glinted in her blonde hair and diamonds glittered at her throat.

It wasn't the gems or couture gown that stopped his breath. It was Cat. In baggy running shorts and an old T-shirt he wanted her. In a bikini she was sexy and enticing. But here, now, facing an evening, and a crowd, that must be utterly daunting, she was composed and elegant.

Her bravery knocked him sideways. Her determination. He'd seen her nerves yesterday and guessed enough about her past to know she was out of her depth in this environment. Yet she'd promised to do this and here she was, utterly superb.

'Excuse me.' Ignoring protocol and curious stares, he

left the receiving line and cut his way through the crowd, taking the steps two at a time till he reached her.

This close he saw the fear in her eyes. When he reached out and took her hand in his it trembled, then, to his delight, squeezed back.

'You look beautiful.'

She shrugged, and her necklace, a solid circle of diamonds with pendant diamond stars, winked and flashed. 'It's the dress.'

Alex took his time scrutinising the velvet bodice, cut to accentuate her slim figure and tiny waist, and the delicate layers of lightweight fabric that made up the skirt. She shifted nervously and a sprinkle of diamonds winked from the folds.

'It's not the dress. It's you.'

He watched rosy colour cover the upper slopes of her breasts, then climb to her throat and cheeks. Her response to that simple compliment made Alex want to haul her to him and never let her go.

Face it, you always want that.

He'd given up lying to himself about it.

'Alex? What is it?'

He shook his head. This wasn't the time.

'About what you said yesterday—'

He stopped her words. 'It can wait.'

'I shouldn't have run from you.' Her chin angled in an endearingly familiar movement. 'I was...overwhelmed but it was cowardly of me.'

Staring into her stern, slightly bewildered features, Alex felt something tumble in his chest. The hubbub of voices at the bottom of the stairs faded as he read her confusion. He wanted to carry her off in his arms and leave the Prime Minister explaining *that* to the crowd below.

'You look fierce. I thought you weren't angry with me any more.'

'I'm not.' It was true. Finally he'd been able to move past his knee-jerk hatred of lies—enough to see the fix she was in and the woman she was.

He'd spent so long wondering which was the real Cat and if there even *was* a real Cat. Till he realised he'd known her all along but let himself be blinded by anger.

From that first day he'd responded to her. Cat was the delicious mermaid with the quick tongue who was so capable in a crisis and made a living protecting others. The woman who championed kids. Who made love with her whole being—body and soul. Who was scared of failure but brave enough to befriend the formidable Lady Enide.

Alex lifted her hand to his mouth and pressed his lips to her wrist. She tasted unique. No one else in the world tasted so good. He stroked his thumb over her fluttering pulse and was rewarded with a soft hitch of her breath. Her pulse was as uneven as his.

'I'm wrestling the urge to abduct you. To take you away from this crowd so we can continue yesterday's discussion. But that will have to wait till later.'

She nodded. 'When we can be private.' Her eyes blazed so bright, Alex almost abandoned his good intentions. But the murmurs from the crowd grew louder. They were attracting gossip.

'Come on, Cinderella. Time for your ball.'

To Cat's surprise, she enjoyed the evening she'd been dreading.

She was used to blending into the background, being part of the invisible machinery that made events like this tick. Facing the blaze of attention should have been difficult.

Except one look at Alex's approving face, his half smile, and Cat felt as if she could take on anything.

Alex was at her side all evening, supportive as they mingled with the wealthy and privileged and high achievers from various fields. His ease and good humour were infectious. Or maybe it was the realisation she'd stopped fighting her feelings that made her giddy and excited.

When he'd loped up the staircase, his athletic stride somehow not at odds with his exquisitely tailored formalwear, her heart had stuttered. She'd never dreamed of Prince Charming, never needed one. But if ever a man fitted the role it was Alex of Bengaria.

With his chiselled features, glossy dark hair and wide-shouldered swimmer's body, he looked the part as no other could. But it wasn't that making her body hum. It was Alex the man. The charmer. The companion. The lover. The partner.

When he'd kissed her wrist then led her down the stairs she'd floated on air, like when he'd taught her to dance. She spent the next fifteen minutes in a blur of delight, so the challenge of entering the ballroom and facing the throng was over before she realised.

'Your Highness?'

Cat blinked and realised Alex was standing before her, proffering his hand. Behind him the richly dressed crowd had cleared space at the centre of the ballroom and from the end of the room came the sound of music. The orchestra played a familiar waltz.

Her heart knocked her ribs as she looked up into twinkling eyes.

'You trust me not to step on your feet this time?' she whispered.

He leaned in as she placed her palm in his. 'I'll brave even that for the chance to hold you.'

A laugh bubbled up. 'I knew from the first you were a smooth talker. Dangerous.'

He smiled. That private smile that was no more than a flicker of movement at one corner of his lips. Its effect was devastating, turning her insides over.

'But you don't run from danger, do you, Cinderella?'

He drew her into the centre of the room. Hundreds of eyes were fixed on them but Cat was aware only of Alex, the enticing promise in his look, and the mad yearning to enjoy what they had and forget tomorrow.

His strong arm curled around her waist, drew her close. His smile grew as she placed her hand on his shoulder. Beneath the fine tailoring he was all hot, hard muscle and bone. Cat had trained with him daily, touching him as she demonstrated defensive moves. But this was different. A thrill rippled through her as the music swelled and Alex stepped forward.

This time Cat didn't see them in the mirrors as they passed by. The crowd wasn't even a blur on the sidelines. Her eyes were locked on Alex's as they spun together, light as a leaf on the breeze. The soft layers of her skirt swished around her, the rhythm of the music becoming the beat of her blood while Alex's breath warmed her face.

Cat was euphoric. She couldn't explain it. There was nowhere she and Alex could go with this attraction except a short—far too short—affair. But her heart, her very essence screamed that this magic couldn't be ignored.

She spun and dipped and swayed in Alex's arms, more alive than she'd ever been.

It was crazy. She'd regret it. But she could no longer deny the *rightness* of being with him.

Alex swung them to a halt and Cat realised the music had ended. Her breathing was heavy, the diamonds rising and falling at her breast. Still he didn't look away. The flare of approval in his eyes should have singed her. Instead she felt exultation burst like sunshine in her veins.

Cat leaned in so only he could hear. 'You're right, Your Highness. I've given up running.'

CHAPTER TWELVE

CAT TIGHTENED HER robe then rapped on Alex's door.

Downstairs, staff still tidied up after the reception but up on this floor all was quiet. Lady Enide had left Cat half an hour ago, with a smile of relief at the evening's success, and the boxes of jewellery Cat had worn.

Standing barefoot in the corridor, her hair loose around her shoulders, Cat should have felt nervous. Physical intimacy with Alex would make their inevitable parting more difficult. Yet a force stronger than logic drove her. After being constrained to do others' bidding, it was freeing to make her choice and act on it.

Crazy to think she'd known him less than two weeks. He'd changed her irrevocably.

Or had she changed herself? Had coming here, taking the chance to connect with the part of her life she'd always denied, made a difference?

Cat had lived cautiously, every step planned, always on the defensive, never taking big risks. It felt glorious now to follow the voice of instinct, not caution.

She raised her hand again but, instead of knocking, she turned the handle and walked in, closing the door behind her.

Mellow lamplight spilled across the sitting room and a gauzy curtain riffled at an open door. Swiftly Cat crossed to the door then paused, her heart too big in her chest, as she took in the tall, broad-shouldered man standing there in the gloom of the balcony.

In the distance a final car rolled away down the gravelled drive and the high gates swung shut behind it.

'The Prime Minister has left.' Alex swung round, the play of shadows casting his face in stark lines. 'He wasn't happy.'

'Not happy?' Cat hesitated. She didn't want to talk about politicians. 'The evening was a huge success.'

'In more ways than one.' Alex opened his arms. 'Come here.' Cat didn't respond well to orders, but this one, in a husky baritone that sent delicious ripples down her backbone, was different.

Wordlessly she went to him. His arms folded her close and then his mouth was on hers, urgent, almost rough, as he leaned into her, prising her willing lips open, delving deep as if he hadn't eaten in a month and she was a banquet laid out for his delectation.

Cat wound her arms around his shoulders, swaying back in his arms as he bent over her. His thick hair was soft to the touch, his hard thighs hot against hers and the taste of him drove her wild.

'I thought you'd never come.' He nipped a line of kisses down her throat and wildfire flared. Her nipples tightened and puckered as she pressed herself against him.

'I had to get changed.'

A possessive hand stroked the silk of her robe from shoulder to thigh, then slipped round to clasp her buttock and haul her against him.

Cat gasped as she came in contact with his erection. It had only been days but it felt like a lifetime since she'd felt him against her, inside her.

'I thought you were beautiful in that ball gown, but I prefer you like this.' His hand captured the back of her head. 'You've let your hair down too.'

Cat opened her mouth to ask if he preferred it that way, but got her answer when he took her mouth again. His kiss was urgent, hungry, like the press of his body and the iron-hard arm lashing her to him.

Where they touched fire kindled and blazed. Every sense went on alert as she began to spiral into mindless delight. The small night sounds grew distant, eclipsed by their breathing and the throb of her pulse in her ears. Already her body was softening for him.

It took everything Cat had to tear her mouth away.

'Wait.' Her voice was an almost silent gasp yet he heard. She felt a tremor pass through his big, lean body then he stilled.

'Second thoughts?'

Cat leaned back in his arms, enough to see the too-tight clench of his jaw and the frown lining his brow. It struck her that, even now, Alex would pull back if she changed her mind. Her chest tightened. She touched his forehead, smoothing the crinkles with unsteady fingers.

'No.'

The instant relief on his features would have been balm to her ego except Cat couldn't relax yet. She had one last hurdle to face. A shadow that threatened to dull her joy.

'Cat? What's wrong?' His voice was sharp.

'We need to talk.' She shook her head. 'Things aren't as simple as you think.'

'Simple? Nothing about this situation is simple. Except that we want each other.' He paused, holding her gaze. 'Don't we, Cat?'

There was challenge in his tone, and something else. If she didn't know better, she'd think Alex nervous.

'Yes.'

His lips stopped speech and the taste of him, the warmth of his arms holding her, made her knees crumple.

Reluctantly she put her palms on his chest and stepped back on wobbly legs. He loosened his hold just enough that a sliver of chilly night air passed between them.

Alex stared down at that determined chin and froze. She couldn't deny him. Not now.

He could ignore her doubts and seduce her. From the first there'd been one truth neither of them could deny—the phenomenal, unstoppable attraction they shared. Cat went up in flames when they kissed.

Except he didn't want anything coming between them this time. Whatever the problem, he'd deal with it. He wanted Cat and he'd have her, no matter what it took.

'What's wrong? Is it the Prime Minister?'

Cat blinked up at him, a little befuddled, and satisfaction filled him. She wasn't as in control as she pretended. Did she realise her hands were roving his chest? That slow caress made him want to return the favour. The thought of his hands on her sweet breasts dragged heat through his groin and he stiffened.

'You don't need to worry about him.' Alex's voice was rough. 'He left tonight thinking you'd fooled me, so you've fulfilled your contract.' He paused, thinking of the satisfaction he'd derive later, once Cat was safely away from here. Then Alex would deal properly with the man who'd schemed to deceive him.

'I did happen to mention, though, that there'd be no royal match.' It had been small compensation, seeing the man's hopes crumble—all those machinations for nothing.

Cat shivered in his hold. 'He won't like that.'

Alex drew her close. This time she didn't resist and unfamiliar emotion filled him when she met his eyes. Delight and protectiveness and something more.

'I won't let him hurt you, Cat.'

'It's not up to you to protect me. I can do that.' Then her mouth curved in that unstinting smile that made him catch his breath. 'But thank you; I appreciate it.'

'So if he's not the problem, what is?' He slipped his hand through her hair, drawing the silky threads back, watching her eyelids lower and her head tilt in sensual appreciation.

How he wanted her! From the crown of her head to her dainty feet that could fell a man with one kick. He wanted her passion and her smiles. Even the way her smooth brow knotted when she was troubled, her pride and strength when she faced things that made her nervous. The way her jaw angled, ready to argue. He wanted it all.

'I need to tell you about myself.' There it was, that clear-eyed, almost defiant look that he'd learned could hide nerves as well as determination.

'Can't it wait?'

'No. I don't want to keep anything from you. You need to know this first.'

That word *first* held a promise that made his heart race. Whatever Cat's problem, it was something more than nerves at not being able to dance or hold her own discussing science. Her whole body was tense.

Alex stilled, all except his hand, gently soothing her. 'Go on.'

'You asked who I was and I told you.' She paused and drew in a deep breath. 'What I didn't tell you is that Dubois was my stepfather. My mother was pregnant to someone else when they married.'

Alex nodded. So her biological father hadn't been a baker in a provincial town. Somehow it didn't surprise him.

'My real father was the King of St Galla. Amelie's father. I'm her bastard half-sister.'

That explained the remarkable similarity between them. Now it all made sense! He'd thought a cousin, but this—

'Why don't you say something?' The razor edge to her words caught his attention. In the dim light she looked pale and strained.

'Thank you for telling me. I imagine not many know.'

'No one. Though Enide guessed.' She watched him intently as if expecting more.

'Did he mistreat you? Your stepfather?'

Cat tilted her head as if to view him better. 'He was a bully who wasn't afraid to use his hands. He was bitter that my mother never gave him children of his own, and resentful of harbouring someone else's bastard even though he'd been well paid to marry my mother. Because he made his distaste clear, everyone else despised us too.'

There it was again. *Bastard.* Why not say 'illegitimate'? Or 'natural daughter'? It was as if Cat chose the most brutal description she could.

'I'm sorry.' He cuddled her close. 'No child should have to experience that.'

Now he began to understand. She'd been rejected by both the King and the man paid...*paid* to be her father! No wonder Cat held herself apart from everyone else.

It explained too, her early interest in self-defence.

His jaw tightened as he thought of her as a kid, ostracised in her own town and needing lessons to defend herself against her stepfather.

'I'm not looking for sympathy.'

Of course she wasn't. She was so fiercely independent Alex wondered if she'd ever leaned on anyone. It moved him that she'd confided in him. Would she turn to him if ever she needed help?

'You're not surprised?'

He shrugged. 'I guessed there was some close connection between the two of you.'

'And now you know?'

What did she want him to say? 'Did you ever meet your birth father?'

Cat shook her head. 'I was his dirty little secret. I never met him or his family.'

Her family too. Suddenly, urgently, Alex wanted to hold her close and never release her.

'I thought you needed to know the truth about me.'

'I'm glad you trust me enough to tell me.'

'Because if anyone guessed my true identity there'd be an uproar.'

Alex peered down into her set expression. '*That's* what's bothering you?'

'I'm a potential embarrassment to you and to Amelie for that matter.'

Alex stared. She was warning him off? She thought he cared so much for gossip? The idea pricked his pride. 'Amelie can look after herself and so can I.'

'You don't care?'

'I care that both the men who should have loved and protected you betrayed you. I care that your childhood was difficult and that you seem to expect rejection as a matter of course.' He lifted his hand to her cheek and felt her lashes flutter. 'I care that you think it would make any difference to us.'

'Alex?' Her voice was a raw whisper, so bewildered it sent something like grief scything through him.

'Is there anything else I need to know?'

'Isn't that enough?' Her voice cracked.

'Yes. I've had enough conversation.' He tucked his arms under her, lifted her against his chest and stalked into the sitting room. He intended to prove to her that not all men were as selfish as the ones she'd known.

Passing into the darkened bedroom he paused, giving his eyes time to adjust.

'You're sure about this?' Cat's voice feathered his neck.

He laughed, the sound too tight. 'I've never been more sure of anything. I need you, Cat. And unless you tell me you've changed your mind I intend to spend the night making love to you.'

He lay her on the bed and settled next to her hip, looking down into wide, solemn eyes. 'I need you too, Alex.' She reached for his shoulders and tugged.

But, instead of lowering himself to her, Alex made himself stay where he was. Already tension was razor-sharp.

Lying against her, even fully clothed, he wouldn't trust himself not to lose control.

He tugged the tie at her waist then peeled open her robe, first one side then the other, revealing tip-tilted breasts and fluid planes and curves that invited his touch.

'Take your clothes off, Alex.'

'Not yet.' He leaned down, kissing one darkened nipple that trembled at his touch. His tongue slipped out, circling it, tasting her unique, sweet flavour. He had to plant his hands wide on the bed on either side of her, so as not to touch. If he touched he'd be lost.

She cradled him with both hands, tugging him close, and he gave in to her silent pleas to suckle at her breast. Desire jolted, solid as a blade to his belly. His erection grew impossibly harder and he had to take a moment to gather his shredding control.

'Alex, I want you.' Her siren whisper curled around him, inviting him to release. But he wanted to treasure her, show Cat he cared enough to give without taking—yet. Show her she was important. He hadn't realised how important till she'd told him about her identity and her past and he'd wanted to do violence to someone for the pain she'd suffered.

He let his hand trail down her ribs, past her navel to the softness of her belly and lower, to the V of rough silk between her legs. Instantly her thighs parted and her sigh scattered his thoughts.

She was slick and needy, shifting with every minuscule circling of his thumb. When he probed deeper her hips jerked and she gasped his name in a sound that was part purr, part protest.

With one last lick at her breast he sat back, watching her hands drop to the bedspread and clench the fabric as his caress between her thighs deepened. Her eyes were closed and her lips open as if she couldn't get enough air.

He'd never seen anything so erotic in his life.

'Look at me, Cat. Open your eyes.' Finally they opened, slowly as if it took enormous effort. Alex smiled. He could grow addicted to the sight of Cat's pleasure. 'Now watch me.'

Spreading her knees with his palms, he settled himself between her legs and stroked her with his tongue. She would have shot off the bed but for the weight of his arms and shoulders forcing her down.

'Alex! Please! I want you.'

Her voice was a potent aphrodisiac and he had to pause, conjuring a mathematical equation to distract himself from the urgent need to shuck off his clothes and plunge into her.

'Soon.' The word was muffled against her body as he licked where his fingers had traced. She shuddered and shifted. Alex smiled as he caressed her with his hand and his mouth till he felt her tremble and she sobbed. Strong hands gripped him and her knees came up as the storm broke upon her. On and on it went, Alex gladly feeding it with deft caresses till, with a guttural cry, she collapsed back.

He lifted himself to survey her, a tumble of lithe limbs, hair splayed in waves across the bedding. She was the picture of abandoned sensuality but she was more too. That curious, too-tight feeling was back, as if his ribs had contracted against his heart and lungs. He wanted her but he wanted more too. He—

'Alex. Please. Come here.'

Gingerly, aware of the needy throb of his erection against tailored trousers that no longer seemed to fit, he moved up the bed to lie on his side next to her. Somewhere along the line he'd kicked his shoes off but otherwise he was fully clothed, his bow tie choking him. Propped on one elbow, he reefed the tie loose then began to open his shirt.

Movement tickled his abdomen. Cat, nimbly dealing with the fastening of his trousers.

'Not yet.' The brush of her hands there was delicate torture. But she was quicker than he'd imagined. A moment later a strong, slender leg curved round his waist and a hand tugged his shoulder, pulling him off balance so his weight rested on her.

Another slender leg rose to clamp his waist, tugging him down as she lifted her pelvis.

Stars sprinkled the blackness behind his closed lids as he tried to breathe through the tsunami of sensation. She'd undone his clothes enough so that, as she rose to him, he rested right at her centre. She rose again and fire trailed through his groin and exploded in his blood.

He'd meant to wait. He'd planned to give her climax after climax before satisfying himself.

'Open your eyes, Alex. Open them and look at me.' Her throaty voice was irresistible and he found himself snared by the sight of her. Another deliberate, slow lift of her hips and he couldn't help himself. With a groan of surrender he pushed his clothes out of the way, tilted his hips and slid down, down, right to her heart.

The world stopped. Even, he'd swear, the blood in his arteries paused for a second.

Cat's smile of triumph was short-lived when he took control, one hand planted on the bed, the other sliding beneath her, lifting her to him. She gasped as gravity fitted them even tighter together.

The sensations threatened to slay him. Especially when he leaned in and kissed her breast, tasting her again.

'Alex!' She grabbed his arms, eyes widening, and he felt the tremors of her climax around him. The world trembled and, with a roar of triumph, he spilled himself.

Through it all he held her eyes, and her shuddering body, and knew he never wanted to be anywhere else.

CHAPTER THIRTEEN

CAT HUMMED AS she packed. The day had dawned grey and wet, first sign of the winter that had already settled on the mainland peaks. But that couldn't dim her happiness.

She'd finish packing then cancel her flight to New York. Alex had invited her to Bengaria. She was nervous about visiting his home but she'd grasp what he offered with both hands.

Last night she'd realised why his trust mattered so much. Why she'd had to tell him about herself. Why she was taking risks she'd never dared take before.

She loved him.

She'd known him less than two weeks but she loved him!

Waking beside Alex, she'd realised what she wanted most was to wake beside him every day for the rest of her life. To share her life and be an integral part of his.

He'd taken the news of her identity better than she'd hoped, but the chances of a permanent relationship…?

A shiver raced down her spine but she ignored it. The die was cast—she couldn't change her feelings—so she'd grasp happiness while she could and worry about tomorrow later.

She'd never been in love, never known any love but her mother's and that had been overshadowed by her bullying stepfather who'd made their lives hell.

Fierce joy eclipsed Cat's fear. For once she'd embrace life rather than insulating herself against it. Soon too she'd meet Amelie, the sister she'd never known. She'd never felt so excited.

Someone tapped on her door and her heart lifted. 'Come

in!' She was hurrying across, expecting Alex, when the door opened.

'Enide? What's wrong?' The other woman looked terrible, her face grey. She clasped her hands in front of her and leaned back against the door for support.

Cat stared. Despite her age the old lady usually held herself ramrod-straight, her posture perfect.

'Are you all right? Please, take a seat.'

Enide shook her head. 'There's no time.' Her gaze took in the suitcase. 'You're almost packed. Excellent. Your flight to New York has been brought forward.'

'I'm not going to New York. I'm flying to—'

'Bengaria?'

'How did you know?' Cat looked at Enide's pinched mouth and foreboding slithered through her. 'Please, sit down. I'm worried about you.'

For a second the older woman's expression softened but the impression was gone in a blink.

'There's no time. The Prime Minister has ordered a private jet to take you to New York.'

'But I'm going to—'

'Bengaria? I'm afraid not. King Alex's plans have altered.' She drew herself higher. 'He's staying here to deal with a crisis. The last thing he needs is to be seen with you.' Enide wrung her hands. 'I saw the attraction between you but I didn't for one moment think—'

'What's happened, Enide?' Cat's belly roiled. She took the older woman by the arm and gently helped her to a seat. 'You're worrying me. Do you want a glass of water? A—?'

'Nothing.' Enide shook her head.

Cat wanted to scream in frustration. Her nerves stretched to breaking point. 'Tell me. Please!'

'There were paparazzi at the gate last night, photographing guests.'

That was expected. Photographers had pointed cameras at the royal limousine when she and Alex went to the city.

'One of them stayed after the ball finished. As if he knew it would be worthwhile.' Enide's gaze turned piercing.

'I don't understand. Can't you please explain?'

After a moment Enide nodded. 'I believe you. I told myself you weren't devious. You didn't organise this.'

'Organise what?' Cat glanced at the door. Maybe it would be faster finding Alex.

'Photos have been delivered to the palace—photos taken with a telephoto lens, of you and Alex on his balcony, kissing. Of him carrying you into his suite. It's obvious you're wearing nothing beneath your robe, and you're *not* talking affairs of state.'

Cat tottered to the bed and sank onto it. Photos of her and Alex? While they'd talked, kissed… While she'd shared the truth about herself and fallen even more in love with the man who'd accepted that revelation as if it was nothing…

All that time someone had been watching, photographing?

Cat shivered, hunching her shoulders and rubbing her hands over her arms.

'I feel sick.' She wanted to scrub herself under a hot shower to alleviate the feeling of violation. She'd seen Afra like this last year, when stalked by a crazed fan. Cat had sympathised and thought she'd understood. But nothing prepared her for this sick sensation of helplessness.

She lifted her head and read distress in Enide's eyes. 'Has Alex seen the photos?'

'They were sent to him too, with a request for an exclusive interview. The implication is that if there's no interview they'll be posted publicly.'

Cat pressed her hand to her churning stomach. 'This is a nightmare.' She stared at the carpet, the trailing pattern of gold on ivory, and a thought struck her dazed brain. Her head jerked up. 'They think I'm Amelie. That it was Alex and Amelie…'

Enide's nod confirmed the worst. 'I suppose I should blame you for putting Amelie in an untenable position. But I can't in all honesty blame you. This situation has been fraught from the start. And Alex is a particularly charming man.' Her mouth trembled. 'I just can't see a way out of this mess for either you or Amelie.'

'I have to make a statement. Explain.' How had something so wondrous and beautiful turned into disaster?

'No! That's exactly what we don't need. Bad enough that the paparazzi believe they have proof Amelie and Alex are in a relationship. We can't tell them what *really* happened. Amelie said she'll return soon and it's vital you're not here when she arrives.'

Cat shot to her feet, nervous energy filling her. 'But this needs to be set right.' Though how, she didn't know. She swayed as she thought of the fallout for Alex and for Amelie. Neither wanted to be shackled to the other yet now everyone would believe—

'I must see Alex.'

'You can't. He's not here. He left as soon as he received the photos.' The older woman's mouth twisted. 'He looked like he wanted to do someone violence. He's convinced the Prime Minister is behind the photos, trying to force him into a royal marriage.'

Cat's jaw dropped. 'You think Alex would let himself be *blackmailed* into a dynastic marriage?'

'I don't know what to think. Except it's the sort of devious trick Barthe might pull. As for blackmail…it's no secret St Gallan money would be welcome in Bengaria. Alex needs investment for major projects he's negotiating. A pragmatic man could decide the scandal of publicly rejecting our Princess would be too costly.' She paused. 'If anyone can sort this out, Alex is the man.'

Cat swayed as the room spun. Alex and Amelie wouldn't marry if they didn't want to. Even for the good of their countries—the idea was too medieval. But Enide was right; Alex had intimated the business investment he was brokering on this visit was vital.

She put a hand to her whirling head. 'I need to see him. As soon as he returns to the palace.'

'I'm sorry, my dear. I suspect he won't be back for quite some time. Which may be as well.' Enide grimaced. 'He needs time to cool down. I've never seen a man so furious.'

Pain stabbed Cat's heart. 'He couldn't believe I had anything to do with it.'

Yet Cat had duped him once under the Prime Minister's orders. And only last night Alex had told the PM the marriage was off so maybe this *was* a strategic move by Barthe. If there was a plot to force Alex's hand, he'd have to wonder about her role.

Cat's skin grew clammy.

Deception was Alex's hot button. And while he'd spoken of liking and respecting her, she guessed for him their relationship was mainly about sex. She'd be mad to read anything more into his invitation to Bengaria.

'Did he mention me?' Cat saw Enide's sympathetic look but couldn't afford pride. She had to know.

'Not a word.'

Cat's stomach dropped. She swung around and fumbled for her phone. Alex had given her his private number. Surely once they spoke—

She dialled. After two rings she got the answerphone. It hadn't gone straight there though. He must have seen who was calling and declined the call.

The phone fell from numb fingers as Cat's hopes shattered.

Alex had forgiven her once. But he'd never allow himself to be duped twice. Clearly he believed she'd been part of a scam to force his hand.

She stumbled, bracing herself on the wall as despair engulfed her.

A knock sounded and Cat's head came up, her heart slamming high in her chest. *Alex!*

'I'm sorry, my dear, but that's your escort to the plane. I'm afraid I don't have the authority to intervene.' The old lady looked so distressed Cat found herself nodding, her chest aching.

'It's okay.' She forced her lips into a grim smile. 'Once I talk to Alex we'll sort something out.' If she said it often enough she might believe it.

Enide opened the door to a pair of grim-faced men Cat recognised from the Prime Minister's security team.

So that was it. She wasn't being given a chance to see Alex. She could evade the two guards but there'd be more nearby. She couldn't outmanoeuvre them all.

Defeat hollowed her belly. She wanted to fight for herself and Alex, for what they'd so briefly shared. Yet how could she if Alex refused to listen?

It took thirty-five minutes to get to the private jet. Thirty-five minutes and sixteen calls to Alex's private line.

Each time she got the answer machine.

He was blocking her calls.

There wasn't even a two-word text saying he'd call later.

She remembered his words. More, she remembered the soft savagery in his voice. *'No one fools me more than once. When my trust is betrayed that's the end.'*

Cat crossed her arms tight across her chest as the plane hurtled down the runway, as if she could hold back the heart threatening to burst from her chest. The pain was so intense every breath hurt. Even thinking hurt.

Alex had decided she was guilty.

There'd be no second chance.

CHAPTER FOURTEEN

'CAT, ARE YOU OKAY?' Afra's eyes caught hers in the limo's rear-view mirror.

'Isn't it my job to ask you that?' Cat forced a smile, glancing at the chauffeur beside her. The guy had been surprised when she'd insisted on sitting up front. But she was Afra's bodyguard, not a VIP.

'You look tense.' Afra's voice didn't sound right.

Cat pushed her shoulders down, realising they'd inched up towards her ears. Tense was right. Tense and sick with nerves. How had she let herself be persuaded to accompany Afra on this extra stage of her new tour?

'Everything's fine.' *That* was how Cat had been persuaded—because Afra was still nervous after the horror of last year's stalker. If it weren't for that Cat would have refused point-blank to visit Bengaria, even if it was for a single benefit concert.

'It's a pretty city.' She turned to survey a cobblestoned square and charming old buildings. Despite the chill there were lots of people walking and cycling, enjoying the sunny Saturday.

Cat wished she were anywhere else in the world but here, in Bengaria's capital. It had only been ten days since she'd left Alex in St Galla and she felt stretched too thin by the enormity of her loss.

As if she'd ever really had a chance of a meaningful relationship with him!

Her nerves were shredded, waiting for the press furore to start when those tell-tale photos were published. So far they hadn't hit the media. Maybe they wouldn't. Maybe instead there'd be an announcement of a royal wedding.

Nausea cramped her belly.

'Hold on.' Her voice cracked as she pivoted to the driver, alert for danger. 'We're going the wrong way. This isn't the way to the concert hall.' Cat might never have been here but she'd learned the route by heart.

'Sorry. I forgot to tell you.' There it was again, that wobble in Afra's voice. 'There was a last-minute change. We're at a new venue.'

The hairs at Cat's nape lifted as they turned into a wide boulevard and she saw a massive building at the end of an avenue of trees. 'Afra?' She had a *really* bad feeling.

In the mirror their eyes met and Cat knew instantly she'd been conned. Afra wasn't afraid for her life, but she *was* on edge.

'Tell me.' Cat's voice was terse, her short nails digging into the palms of her hand.

'I'm performing at the palace. After all, it's for a charity sponsored by the royal family.'

Cat was still struggling to swallow the burning knot of tangled emotion blocking her throat when they swept through ornate wrought iron gates. A troop of royal guards marched by, the absolute precision of their movements as eye-catching as their ceremonial uniform of sky-blue tunics, tall fur hats and dark trousers.

Numb, she looked up to the huge grey palace before her and saw the Bengarian flag flying proud. The King was in residence.

Cat stood on the edge of the room, eyes flicking from the singer who'd performed for the Dowager Queen's charity, to the crowd filling the Mirrored Hall.

She stood out from the other women, in a black tailored jacket, low heels and slim trousers. There was no glint of jewellery at her throat or ears to draw a glance, yet Alex couldn't take his eyes off her.

Her pale hair glowed under the light of the Venetian glass chandeliers. It was drawn back from her face, falling in waves, and he wanted to reach out and touch it. He recalled the soft stroke of it on his bare flesh as they made love. The scent of it…

Hell, every detail of the time they'd spent together was indelibly tattooed on his brain. Including her vulnerable expression as she'd told him about her birth father and waited for rejection.

He'd *known* that and yet he'd been so swept up in fury that last morning he'd thought of nothing but stopping those photos. By the time he'd realised his mistake it was too late. The damage was done and Cat was gone.

She'd *run* rather than face him! An unholy brew of indignation, pain and guilt stirred in his belly.

Alex stalked towards her, grateful her attention was on Afra. Not once in the hour and a half since she'd arrived had Cat's eyes met his. Every time he looked at her she was busy scanning the crowd or checking on the singer, intent, it seemed, on everything but him.

She couldn't have made it more obvious that she didn't want to see him.

'Ms Dubois.'

She spun round, eyes wide. His heart catapulted in his chest. What was she thinking? More important—what did she *feel*?

Before she could retreat he took her hand. Instantly she froze, all except the runaway pulse fluttering at her wrist. A pulse that gave him hope after ten long days of regret and uncertainty.

Alex was tempted to kiss her hand but he needed all his focus. Kissing Cat, even the back of her hand, would be too distracting.

'Come. We need to talk.'

Of course she resisted, pulling back, but he didn't let her break his hold.

'I'm working.' Her tone was cool.

'You're relieved of duty.' He nodded to the two security men who'd followed him. Silently they positioned themselves, their focus on Afra. 'Your employer has accepted my offer of protection while in Bengaria. You're off-duty.'

'You can't—'

'I can and will.' He leaned in, inhaling her delicious perfume. 'Don't fight me, Cat, unless you *want* to make a public spectacle.'

Her mouth opened then closed. Fire blazed in her green eyes. 'Five minutes.'

Alex nodded and led her away. This would take more than five minutes. And if at the end she wasn't convinced? A vice clamped his lungs. He refused to consider that.

Her face was blank when he invited her to take a seat in his private chambers.

'No, thanks. I prefer to stand.'

Alex raked a hand through his hair. She wasn't going to make this easy, was she?

'You ran.' They weren't the words he'd planned, but that sharp tug of pain in his gut made them spill out.

'I didn't run. I left for New York as planned.'

'Not as planned.' He paced to the window, not seeing the view beyond. 'You'd agreed to come here with me.' Despite guilt at the poor way he'd handled things, it *hurt* that she'd left like that. 'I've never invited any other woman.'

He swung round and caught her stunned expression. 'It was obviously the only option.'

'Obviously? What about staying with me till we sorted everything out?'

'The way you stayed with me?' Her lip curled and, despite the jarring blow to his conscience, Alex applauded her spirit.

'I apologise for that. I—'

'Apology accepted. Now, if you'll excuse me—'

His hand shot out, capturing hers. 'We're not done.'

For an instant her eyes gleamed bright as lasers, then the fire in them was eclipsed, her face washed of emotion. Alex hated watching it.

'Please, Cat. Let me explain.'

She swallowed hard and he wanted to wrap his arms around her and not let go. 'I apologise. I shouldn't have left the palace that morning without speaking to you. I was just so incensed.'

'I understand. You had a right to be. I was.' Except her voice told him anger was the least of her emotions. She was hurting too.

His lungs compressed so tight he couldn't breathe.

When he found his voice it didn't sound like him. 'It's my weak point. With anything else I'm slow to anger, but when it's deliberate trickery…' He heaved in a deep breath. 'That's no excuse but you need to understand.'

'I understand.' Still that bleak expression. 'You thought I'd set you up.'

'No!' His grip tightened on her hand. 'That's not why I left. I went to see the St Gallan Prime Minister.'

'Because you thought I was in cahoots with him.' She tugged her hand free and loss engulfed him.

'I went to *protect* you!' He'd never known such anger as when he realised Cat had been the unwitting victim of such a brutally intrusive scheme. He remembered how vulnerable she'd been that night, baring her past, and how strong. It had wrenched his heart to think of anyone callously using her that way. His concern for her outweighed outrage at the invasion of his own privacy.

'You wouldn't be able to shrug off those photos if they appeared in print.' Her expression confirmed it. 'Not when eventually people would dig till they discovered your real identity.'

Cat stared up at him and Alex felt a glimmer of hope. 'I realised too late that I should have stayed and spoken with you first, but I saw red and I acted.'

She shook her head. 'You rejected my calls.'

'I was in a meeting with the Prime Minister. I planned to contact you as soon as I could tell you everything was sorted and you had nothing to worry about. I wanted to fix everything.'

'But you didn't. You didn't call.'

Alex spread his hands. He wasn't used to having someone call him on his every action. 'I got it wrong. Later, when I saw the number of missed calls, I knew I needed to speak to you in person. But you'd left the palace.'

It had been clear then that it was too late to convince Cat. She'd made up her mind and who could blame her? More drastic measures were needed.

'But still you didn't call.' Hurt rang behind the challenge and his heart squeezed.

'I tried, but by then you'd switched off. What I had to say was too important for a message. I had to *see* you. See you somewhere you couldn't simply walk away without hearing me out. That's why this elaborate set-up—because I needed a home ground advantage.' In his more desperate moments he'd even wondered about kidnapping her, long enough to make her listen.

'I brought you here to explain and apologise.' But her stony expression worried him. 'I didn't think you'd set me up, Cat. That's what you believed, isn't it?' It was there in her bruised eyes and tight mouth.

'Of course you did. It was an obvious conclusion, even if it was wrong.'

'I never for a second believed you knew about the photos. I remember what we talked about out there on the balcony,

Cat. What passed between us was too intimate, too real.' It had *moved* him. He'd never felt so connected to anyone as he had to Cat that night. Surely she'd felt the same.

He reached for her hand and read doubt in her eyes. Then she moved back a step and frustration rose.

'It doesn't matter now. Somehow you've managed to stop those pictures hitting the press so there's nothing more to talk about.'

'Nothing to talk about? What about us, Cat? Or did that mean so little to you?'

So little? Her breath snagged on a shard of pure pain. *If only.* Being in the same room was testing her to the limit. What did he *want* from her?

'How did you stop the photos being published, Alex?' Even saying his name was a forbidden delight. She shivered, wrapping her arms across her chest.

Alex mirrored her movements. On him the action emphasised his powerful male splendour. In formal clothes he was spectacular and she couldn't help drinking him in. This would be the last time she saw him. Once he got over his pique at her leaving. Because she knew now she couldn't survive what could only ever be a short fling for him. Even if he'd arranged today just to see her. Part of her was flattered, dangerously flattered.

'I told the Prime Minister to publish the photos and be damned.' Alex held her gaze, his strong chin thrust forward. 'I told him I had nothing to be ashamed of, being with the woman I intend to make my bride.'

Cat rocked back on her feet.

She'd half expected it but nothing had prepared her for hearing the words.

Alex intended to marry Amelie! They must have overcome their doubts about the marriage. After all, arranged marriages were common in royal circles, weren't they?

'Cat? Don't you have anything to say?'

Alex had moved closer. So close he loomed over her. There was nowhere else to look but into those stunning indigo eyes.

Cat tried to turn but her feet were cemented to the spot. She blinked and felt heat sear the back of her eyeballs.

'I hope you'll both be very happy.'

'Cat, did you hear what I said?' The deep resonance of his voice was like a touch trailing along her bare skin.

'Yes!' Anger vied with despair that he could affect her this way, even as he told her he was marrying her sister. 'You and Amelie are getting married and—'

Strong hands grabbed her elbows, hauling her up on her toes against him. Heat swamped her. Longing, confusion and shame that she couldn't conquer her feelings for him.

'It's you I want to marry, Cat!'

'What?'

She was drowning in sensation, revelling in his hard body against hers. Even the scent of his skin sent her hormones into overdrive.

'I told the St Gallan Prime Minister I was going to marry you. And that if those photos hit the press I'd immediately reveal you weren't Princess Amelie but my fiancée. I'd let it be known he'd tried to fool not just me but the people of St Galla by hiring an imposter.' He paused, his chest rising and dipping.

'It was a calculated risk. I know you didn't want your role there revealed but I couldn't see any other option. But I was right. He agreed to stop the release of the photos. He's about to announce his resignation, by the way. He was made to see he couldn't continue as Prime Minister.'

Cat gawked. She was stuck back on Alex wanting to marry her. 'You didn't have to say that, about marriage.'

'Why not? It's what I want. What I hope you want too.'

The world tilted abruptly and she swayed. Instantly Alex scooped her up against his chest.

'Put me down.'

'So you can faint at my feet?' Was that a hint of a smile?

'I'm not going to faint.' She should hate his managing attitude, carrying her as if she weighed nothing.

'Not while I'm holding you.' He sank onto a couch, still holding her close. Cat thought about breaking free but somehow couldn't find the willpower.

'Please, Alex. What do you want? Really?'

Instantly he sobered. 'You, Cat. I want you.'

'But we were just having an affair—'

His mouth covered hers and the world stopped spinning. Cat lost herself in the most perfect, sensuous yet gentle kiss of her life. When he lifted his lips she clung to him.

'What did I tell you, Cat? Do you remember? This is more than sex.'

'You said it was attraction. Desire. Respect. Liking.'

Alex grinned down at her and she'd swear she heard music playing and chimes ringing. 'You *did* listen! What do you think all that adds up to? *I love you, Cat.*'

The shock of it shuddered through her. How she wanted to believe. But miracles didn't happen. Cat lived in the real world, not some dreamland.

'You can't. We barely know each other.'

Instantly he sobered. 'I know everything I need to understand I want to be with you.' He paused. 'How do you feel about me? I thought you felt the same.'

'It doesn't matter what I feel.' She choked down the need to tell him she loved him. 'You're a king and I'm—'

'The woman I adore.'

She shut her eyes. It was too much, too tempting. 'I'm the illegitimate daughter of a king. I'm a scandal waiting to explode if you let me into your world.'

Alex's hand was warm as it cupped her face. 'I don't care. Nor does my mother.'

'Your mother?' It was close to a shriek.

'How do you think I managed today? It's her charity event. And, for the record, I don't give a damn who your parents were. All I care about is you. Times have changed and Bengaria has changed with it. You'll see. I can marry anyone I want. Yes, your identity would be news but that would fade with time. We'd ride it out together.'

Cat shook her head. 'I won't marry you.'

'But you love me?'

Maybe a stronger woman would have denied it. But it was impossible for Cat when she saw his bravado hid a worried man.

'Of course I love you. I fell for you like a ton of bricks.'

This time Alex's kiss was so thorough that when it ended her hair was loose, his tie had disappeared and they were both breathing heavily. Pleasure engulfed her. Not just pleasure but the warm glow of love.

'Tell me again.' His lips grazed her ear and she shivered.

'I love you, Alex. But I can't marry you.'

He pulled back and pinioned her with his darkening gaze. 'One thing at a time. You love me. That's what counts. And you'll come and live here in Bengaria, won't you? I can't promise it will be all balls and parties. I've got years of hard work ahead, but I promise I'll do everything I can to make you happy here.'

Give up life and her job to live here? As what? His mistress? His girlfriend? The old Cat, the one who'd never known love or risk, would have said no.

'Please, Cat. I want to spend my life with you. I want to share your life too. Always. Together. Give us a chance.'

His words were a perfect reflection of her own desires. They made her heart turn over.

'It's mad. We've only known each other—'

'Twenty-one days.'

She shook her head, trying hard not to respond to the smile curling his firm lips and failing. 'For ten of those we've been on separate continents.'

He nodded gravely. 'I blame you for that. You've got a lot of making up to do, Ms Dubois.' His hand moved, stroking down her side and around to pull her up against him. Arousal jolted through her and she arched into him.

'Say you'll move to Bengaria, sweetheart. I have connections.' He winked. 'I'm sure you can get a visa to work here.'

Her laughter covered the emotion choking her throat. 'You'd be seen dating a bodyguard?'

'So long as dating means I get to do this.' He kissed his way down from her mouth, grazing his teeth on the erogenous zone at the base of her neck, drawing her to breathless anticipation.

Alex drew back. 'I've found a place on the edge of the capital that might make an excellent youth centre. You'd have to check it, but if not there we'll find somewhere else.'

His expression made her heart dance. 'I've contacted young Thomas's new foster parents too. They've promised to bring him here for the opening, if you decide to go ahead. I thought you'd like a little St Gallan support.'

Cat stared, unable to take it in. 'You did all that? Really?'

He grabbed her hand and kissed her palm. Cat melted.

'Whatever it takes to make you happy. I want to marry you but I understand you're not sure. We'll take things as slowly as you like. As long as you're with me, that's what matters.'

Cat lifted her hand to his jaw, revelling in the feel of his clean-shaven skin stretched over strong bone, in the thrill of being here, with him, but most of all in the love she saw in his eyes.

It was time to take the biggest risk of her life.

'I can't think of anything I'd like more.'

EPILOGUE

CAT SMOOTHED A hand down the bronze silk of her ball gown. Outside fresh snow dusted the picturesque city but in the Mirrored Hall it was warm enough for a sleeveless dress. Alex's face when he'd seen her in it confirmed she'd chosen well.

'Shall we, Ms Dubois?' Alex stood before her, wearing a jacket of indigo and black trousers with an indigo side stripe—the dress uniform of his old regiment.

He was Prince Charming, except that knowing smile and the lascivious gleam in his eyes didn't belong in a children's story. Was he remembering why they'd almost been late for their own engagement ball? Fire fizzed in her blood. Even after months their passion was strong. Their love grew each day.

'Thank you, Your Highness.' Cat let him lead her to the centre of the room and the orchestra struck up a familiar tune. The 'Emperor Waltz'.

Suddenly the enormous changes in her life hit her. From imposter to almost royal. From alone to loved and cherished. Cat met Alex's intent gaze and smiled with all her heart.

He hauled her to him, his embrace warm and strong.

'Aren't you holding me too close?'

Alex shook his head, his expression suddenly serious. 'I want the world to know I love you. You've made me happier than I thought possible.'

As he'd made her. They spent as much time as possible together and Alex didn't keep anything from her. The highs and lows of his work. The challenges ahead. And he supported her as she painstakingly built the youth centre she'd dreamed of so long.

Together they'd faced the press and the Bengarian people. It wasn't easy but her adopted country had opened its arms to her, presumably because Alex was so obviously happy. After the flurry of headlines when, with Amelie's support, her identity was officially announced, the media was surprisingly positive. Most put an upbeat spin on the long-lost sister angle and the whirlwind romance.

She'd even met her nephew and begun to establish a relationship with him.

'You've made me happy too.' Cat smiled up into Alex's indigo eyes and seconds later was spinning and swaying, her skirts swishing around them as she clung tight and gazed up at the man who'd stolen her heart.

The ballroom was a swirling collection of snapshots. Alex's mother, elegant and smiling as she leaned close to Lady Enide. Alex's cousin, Marisa in vivid orange, beside her handsome Brazilian husband, Damaso. People she barely knew, wearing diadems and jewels. A sprinkling of friends from America, grinning.

Then, in a gown of pistachio-green, her sister Amelie, smiling. Beside her, inevitably, stood the big bear of a man who never seemed to take his eyes off her.

Cat had wondered what it was like to have family. Now she knew it was one of life's most precious gifts.

Almost as precious as the man holding her tight.

'Have I told you how much I adore you, Your Highness?' The words emerged husky with emotion.

Alex swung her to a stop in the centre of the floor, ignoring the music and their audience. 'Yes, but feel free to repeat yourself, darling Cat.'

Then his mouth claimed hers and the room receded till even the thunderous applause was eclipsed by Alex's kiss.

Cat knew, whatever the future held, she was home.

* * * * *

ONE NIGHT IN PARADISE

MAISEY YATES

To my very best friend, who I happened
to be married to. Haven, I love you.

CHAPTER ONE

CLARA Davis looked at the uneaten cake, still as pristine and pink as the bride had demanded, sitting on its pedestal. A very precarious pedestal that had taken a whole lot of skill to balance and get set up. Not to mention have delivered to the coast-side hotel that sat twenty miles away from her San Francisco kitchen.

Everything would have been perfect. The cake, the setting, the groom, well, he was beyond perfect, as usual. And everyone who had been invited had come.

There had been one key person missing, though. The bride had decided to skip the event. And without her, it made it sort of tricky to continue.

Clara eyed the cake and considered taking a slice for herself. She'd worked hard on it. No sense letting it go to waste.

She sighed. The cake wouldn't make the knot in her stomach go away. It wouldn't ease any of the sadness she felt. Nothing had been able to shake that feeling, not since the groom, who was now officially jilted, had announced the engagement in the first place.

Though, ironically, watching him get stood up at the altar hadn't made her feel any better. But how could it? She didn't like seeing Zack hurt. He was her business partner—more than that, he was her best friend. And also, yeah, the man who kept her awake some nights with the kinds of fantasies that did not bear rehashing in the light of day.

But secret fantasies aside, she hadn't really wanted the wedding to fall apart. Well, not this close to the actual ceremony. Or maybe she had wanted it. Maybe a small part of her had hoped this would be the outcome.

Maybe that was why she'd agreed to bake the cake. To stand by and watch Zack bind himself to another woman for the rest of his life. There wasn't really another sane reason for it.

She blew out a breath and walked out of the kitchen and into the massive, empty reception hall. Her heart hit hard against her breastbone when she saw Zack Parsons, coffee mogul, business genius and abandoned groom, standing near the window, looking out at the beach, the sun casting an orange glow on his face and bleeding onto the pristine white of his tuxedo shirt.

He looked different, for just a moment. Leaner. Harder than she was used to seeing him. His tie was draped over his shoulders, his jacket a black puddle by his feet. He was leaning against the window, bracing himself on his forearm.

It shouldn't really shock her that after being left at the altar he looked stronger in a strange way.

"Hey," she said, her voice sounding too loud. Stupid in the empty room.

He turned, his gray eyes locking with hers, and she stopped breathing for a moment. He truly was the most beautiful man on the planet. Seven years of working with him on a daily basis should have taken some of the impact away. And some days she was able to ignore it, or at least sublimate it. But then there were other days when it hit her with the force of ten tons of bricks.

Today was one of those days.

"What kind of cake did I buy, Clara?" he asked, pushing off from the window and stuffing his hand into his pocket.

She forced herself to breathe. "The bottom tier was vanilla, with raspberry filling, per Hannah's instructions. And there was pink fondant. Which I hand-painted, by the way. But the vanilla cake in the middle was soaked in bourbon and honey. And not a single walnut on the whole cake. Because I know what you like."

"Good. Have someone wrap up the middle tier and send it to my house. And they can send Hannah her tier, too."

"You don't have to do that. You can throw it out."

"It's edible. Why would I throw it out?"

"Uh…because it was your wedding cake. For a wedding that didn't happen. For most people it might…take the sweet out of it."

He shrugged one shoulder. "Cake is cake."

She put her hand on her hip and affected a haughty expression, hoping to force a slight smile. "My cake is more than mere cake, but I get your point."

"We've made a fortune off your cakes, I'm aware of how spectacular they are."

"I know. But I can make a new cake. I can make a cake that says Condolences on Your Canceled Nuptials. We could put a man on top of it sitting in a recliner, watching sports on his flat-screen television, with no bride in sight."

The corner of his mouth lifted slightly and she felt a small bubbly sensation in her chest. As though a weight had just been removed.

"That won't be necessary."

"That could be a new thing we offer in the shops, Zack," she said, knowing business was his favorite topic, aborted wedding or no. "Little cupcakes for sad occasions."

"I'm not all that sad."

"You aren't?"

"I'm not heartbroken, if that's what you're wondering."

Clara frowned. "But you got left at the altar. Public humiliation is…well, it's never fun. I had something like that happen in high school when I got stood up by my date at a dance.

People pointed and laughed. I was humiliated. It was all very Carrie. Without the pig's blood or the mass murder."

"Not the highlight of my life, Clara, I'll admit." He swallowed. "Not the lowest point, either. I would have preferred for her to leave me before I was standing at the altar, with the preacher, in a tux, in front of nearly a thousand people, but I'm not exactly devastated."

"That's...well, that's good." Except it was sort of scary to know that he could be abandoned just before taking his vows and respond to it with an eerie calm. She reacted more strongly to a recipe that didn't pan out the way she wanted it to.

But then, Zack was always the one with the zenlike composure. When they'd first met, over a cupcake of all things, she'd been impressed by that right away. That and his beautiful eyes, but that was a different story.

She'd been working at a small bakery in the Mission District in San Francisco, and he'd been scoping out a new location for his local chain of coffee shops. He'd bought one of her peanut-butter-banana cupcakes, her experiment du jour. His reaction, like all of Zack's reactions, hadn't been overly demonstrative. But there had been a glint in his eye, a hint of that hard steel that lay just beneath the outer calm.

And he'd come back the next day, and the next. She'd never entertained, not for a moment, the idea that he'd been coming in to see her. It had been all about the cupcakes.

And then he'd offered her twice the money to come and work in his flagship shop, making the treats of her choice in his gorgeous, state-of-the-art kitchen. It had been the start of everything for her. At eighteen it had been a major break, and had allowed her to get out of her parents' house, something she'd been desperate to do.

In the years since, it had been a whole lot more than that.

Roasted's ten thousandth location had just opened, their first in Japan, and it was being hailed a massive success.

Conceptualizing the treats for that shop had been a fun challenge, just like every new international location had been.

She and Zack hadn't had a life since Roasted had really started to take off, nothing that went beyond coffee and confections, anyway. Of course, Zack was the backbone of the company, the man who got it done, the man who had seen it become a worldwide phenomenon.

They had drinks, coffee beans and mass-produced versions of her cupcakes and other goodies in all the major grocery chains in the U.S. Roasted was a household name. Because Zack was willing to sacrifice everything in his personal life to see it happen.

Hannah had been his only major concession to having a personal life, and that relationship had only started in the past year. And now Zack had lost her.

But he wasn't devastated. Apparently. She was probably more devastated than *he* was. Again, cake related.

"I didn't love her," he said.

Clara blinked. "You didn't…love her?"

"I cared about her. She was going to make a perfectly acceptable wife. But it wasn't like I was passionately head over heels for her or anything."

"Then why…why were you marrying her?"

"Because it was time for me to get married. I'm thirty. Roasted has achieved the level of success I was hoping for, and there comes a point where it's the logical step. I reached that point, Hannah had, too."

"Apparently she hadn't."

He gave her a hard glare. "Apparently."

"Do you know why? Have you talked to her?"

"She can come and talk to me when she's ready."

Zack would have laughed at the expression on Clara's face if he'd found anything remotely funny about the situation. The headlines would be unkind, and with so many media-hungry witnesses to the event, mostly on the absent bride's side, there would be plenty of people salivating to get their name in print by offering their version of the wedding of the century that wasn't.

Clara was too soft. Her brown eyes were all dewy looking, as though she were ready to cry on his behalf, her petite hands clasped in front of her, her shoulders slumped. She was more dressed up than he was used to seeing her. Her lush, and no he wasn't blind so of course he'd noticed, curves complemented, though not really displayed, by a dress that could only be characterized as nice, if a bit matronly.

She did that, dressed much older than she needed to, her thick auburn hair always pulled back into a low bun. Because she had to have her hair up to bake, and it had become a habit. But sometimes he wished she'd just let her hair down. And, because he was a man, sometimes he wished she wouldn't go to so much trouble to conceal her curves, either.

Although, in reality, her style of dress suited him. They worked together every day, and he had no business having an opinion on her physical appearance. His interest was purely for aesthetic purposes. Like opting for a room with a nice view.

That aside, Clara was all emotion and big hand gestures. There was nothing contained about her.

"I'm fine," he said.

"I know. I believe you," she said.

"No, you don't. Or you don't want to believe me because your more romantic sensibilities can't handle the fact that my heart isn't broken."

"Well, you ought to love the person you're going to marry, Zack."

"Why? Give me a good reason why. So that I could be more broken up about today? So that I could be more suitably wounded if she had shown up, and we had said our vows, when ten years on the marriage fell on the wrong side of the divorce statistics? I don't see the point in that."

"Well, I don't see the point at all."

"And I didn't ask."

"You never do."

"The secret to my success." His tone came out a bit harsher than he intended and Clara's expression reflected it. "You'll survive this," he said drily. "Breaking up is hard to do."

She rolled her eyes. "I'm worried about you."

"Don't be. I'm not so breakable. Tell me, any big word on the Japan location go up online while I was busy getting my photo taken?"

"All good. Some of the pictures I've been seeing are showing that it's absolutely slammed. And everything seems to be going over huge."

"Good. That means the likelihood of expanding further there is good." He sat down in one of the vacant, linen-covered chairs. They had pink bows. Also Hannah's choice. He put his hands on the tabletop, moving his mind away from the fiasco of a wedding day and getting it back on business. "How are things going with our designer cupcakes?"

"Um...well, I was pretty busy getting the wedding cake together." Clara felt like her head was spinning from the abrupt subject change.

Zack was in full business mode, sitting at the trussed up wedding-party table like it was the pared-down bamboo desk he had in his office at Roasted's corporate headquarters.

"And?"

"I have a few ideas. But these are pretty labor-intensive recipes and they really aren't practical for the retail line, or even for most of the stores."

"Cupcakes are labor intensive?"

She shot him a deadly look. "Why don't you try baking a simple batch and tell me how it goes?"

"No, thanks. I stick to my strengths, and none of them happen to involve baking."

"Then trust me, they're labor intensive."

"That's fine. My goal is to start doing a few boutique-style shops in some more affluent areas. We'll have bigger kitchens so that we'll have the capability to do more on-site baking."

"That could work. We'll have to have a more highly trained staff."

"That's fine. I'm talking about a few locations in Los Angeles, New York, Paris, London, that sort of thing. It will be more like the flagship store. A bit more personalized."

"I really like the idea, not that you'd care if I didn't."

"I am the boss."

"I know. I'm just the Vice President of Confections," she said, bringing up a joke they'd started in the early days of the company.

A smile touched his lips again and her heart expanded. "A big job."

"It is," she said. "And you don't pay me enough."

"Yes, I do."

She gave him a look. One she knew was less than scary, but she tried. "Anyway, go on."

"I had made an appointment to speak to a man who owns a large portion of farmland in Thailand. Small clusters of coffee and tea. All of his plants receive a very high level of care and that's making for extremely good quality roasts and brews. My goal is to set up a deal with him so we can get some limited-editions blends. We'll sell them in select locations, and have them available for order online."

Her mind skipped over all the details he'd just laid out, latching on to just one thing. "Weren't you going to Thailand on your honeymoon?"

"That was the plan."

Clara couldn't stop her mouth from dropping open. "You were going to do business on your honeymoon?"

"Hannah had some work to do, as well. Time doesn't stop just because you get married."

"No wonder she left you at the altar." She regretted the

words the moment they left her mouth. "Sorry. I didn't mean that."

"You did, and that's fine. Unlike you, Hannah had no romantic illusions, you can trust me on that. Her reasons for not showing up today may very well have had something to do with a Wall Street crisis. There's actually a good chance she's at her apartment, in her wedding gown, screaming obscenities at her computer screen watching the cost of grain go down."

She had to concede that the scenario was almost plausible. Hannah was all icy cool composure, and generally nice and polite, until someone crossed her in the corporate world. Clara had overheard the other woman's phone conversations become seriously cutthroat in tense business situations. Threats of removal of tender body parts had crossed her lips without hesitation.

She admired her for it. For the the intense way she went after what she wanted. She'd done it with Zack. It had been sort of awe inspiring to watch. Mostly it had been awe-inspiringly depressing. Because Clara wasn't cutthroat, or intense. And she hadn't been brave enough to pursue what she really wanted. She'd never been brave enough to pursue Zack.

"I doubt that's what happened," Clara said, even though she couldn't be certain.

"There was a reason I asked how the designer-cupcake thing was going."

"Oh." Back to business.

"I was trying to make sure you didn't feel swamped by the amount of work you have to do."

"No. Creating recipes is the best part of my job. I've been having fun with this one. I've actually done most of the experimental baking and tasting with our panel, and I have a few standout favorites, plus some that need to be improved. And then I'll have to narrow down the selection, because it just won't be feasible to have too many different kinds on the menu at once."

"So that was the long, detailed version of you telling me you aren't too busy at the moment?"

She shot him a deadly look. Jilted or not, he didn't need to be a jerk. "No, I'm not too busy."

"Good, because everything was set for me to head to Chiang Mai tonight."

"And you need me to make sure everything is running smoothly at corporate?" That wasn't usually the role she fulfilled. She wasn't an administrator, not even close.

"No, I want you to get packed, because you're coming with me."

Her stomach honestly felt like it plummeted, squeezing as it made its way down into her toes. "You're not serious. You're not actually asking me to come on your honeymoon with you?"

"The trip is booked. I have appointments made. I'm not canceling the honeymoon just because my bride neglected to show up." He looked at her, like he had thousands of times, but this time felt… It felt different. The inspection seemed closer somehow, his gray eyes more assessing, more intimate. She swallowed hard and tried to ignore the fact that her heart seemed to be trying to claw its way out of her chest. "I think you'll make a more than fitting replacement."

CHAPTER TWO

IF he had physically hit her he couldn't have possibly hurt her worse. A replacement? The consolation prize. The stand-in for tall, lean, angular Hannah who possessed the cheekbones of a goddess. Not that Clara had noticed, or compared.

Well, she had. And in some ways, on some days, the fact they were so different made it easier because there was no question of what the other woman had that she didn't.

But she had never, never put herself in the position of trying to vie for Zack's attention, not in that way. Because she'd known that she would be the consolation prize if he ever did decide to look in her direction. And she'd decided that was one thing she couldn't do to herself. The one thing worse than watching the man who meant the world to her tie himself to another woman. Being the one he'd settled for.

And now Zack was shoving her into that position. It made her want to gag.

"I'm not a replacement for anyone, Zack. And if you're suggesting I am, then I think we've become a little bit too comfortable with each other."

She turned and walked out of the reception hall. She left the cake. She didn't care about the cake. The staff of the hotel could have it for an early, sugary breakfast when they came in tomorrow morning.

She breezed through the hall and out the front doors, into

the damp, salty air. It had been a cool day, but now, with the sun dipping down below the horizon, the air coming in off of the bay was downright chilly. Which was good, because now, if anyone saw her lip tremble a little bit, she could blame the cold.

She didn't want to be emotional, not over something that wasn't even intentional, and with Zack, she knew it wasn't. Zack wasn't mean, more than that; he simply wasn't all that emotional, so he never assumed that anyone else was.

Everything was so surface to Zack. Nothing seemed to get under his skin. Nothing seemed to throw him off, even for a moment. Not even a canceled wedding.

Anyway, she'd had enough intentional digs taken at her in her life to know that things could get far too dramatic if she didn't make people have to work at hurting her feelings.

But since her feelings for Zack were a constant jumble, her reactions to anything involving him were always strong. Most of the time, though, she managed to keep that fact hidden from Zack. A lot of the time, she kept the extent of her feelings hidden from herself.

"Clara."

She turned and saw him standing just behind her. She didn't say anything. She crossed her arms beneath her breasts and fixed him with her best glare.

"You're the second woman to abandon me today."

Her face flooded with prickly heat. "See, that comparison is not very flattering, considering you've already used the word replacement in regards to me."

"That's not what I meant."

"Then what did you mean?"

"That I need someone to come with me, and actually, under the circumstances you're a better fit than my ex-fiancée."

For a full second she could only think of one thing his statement could possibly mean. Images clicked through her mind like close-up still-shots. Tan hands on a pale, bare hip

Masculine lips on a feminine throat. Blood roared through her body, into her cheeks, making her face burn. She was sure they were the color of ripe strawberries, broadcasting her thoughts to anyone who looked at her.

"What?" she asked.

"Hannah's smart, don't get me wrong, but she doesn't know this market quite like you do. Prices on stocks, maybe, but it will be nice to have you on hand to offer an opinion about marketing and flavor."

Business. He was talking about business. And somehow, to Zack, business was more important than romance and making love on his honeymoon?

At least he was pretending it was. There was something different about his expression, a dark light behind his gray eyes. She'd seen Zack nearly every day for the past seven years. She knew his moods, his expressions as well as she knew her own.

And this was a different Zack. Well, she thought it was. For some reason, the hardness, the intensity, seemed more true than what she thought she knew of him.

Strange. But then, the whole day had been strange. Starting with the interminably long silence after the strains of the Bridal March had faded from the air and the aisle remained vacant.

All right, he'd made her mad. It wasn't the first time. He was bullheaded and a general pain in the butt sometimes. He was also the smartest man she knew, with a cutting wit that always kept her amused. He was one of the few people who'd never doubted that her ideas were good.

If she didn't go with him, she would spend her evenings hanging out by herself, reading and experimenting with cupcake recipes and licking the batter off the spatula. Fun, sure, but not the kind of fun she could have in Thailand.

Again, those images, erotic and explicit, assaulted her. No, that wasn't the kind of fun she would be having in Thailand.

Zack had never looked twice at her in that way and for the most part, she was fine with that. She'd had a crush on him at first, but even then she hadn't expected anything to come of it.

And, yes, Hannah had come in and stirred up some strange feelings. Because as long as Zack had simply been there, at work every day, and available for dinner meetings and a lot of other things, it had been comfortable. Zack was in every space in her life, at work and home.

But then along came Hannah, and she took up his time, and, Clara had assumed, that he loved her. And having to share Zack's emotion with someone else had felt... It had felt awful. And it had made her jealous, which didn't make sense because she'd never even tried to cross the boundaries of friendship with Zack. So it wasn't like Hannah had been encroaching on her territory or anything. But she'd been so jealous looking at Zack and Hannah she'd felt like her stomach was turning inside out, and she knew, that even if she could never have Zack, she didn't want anyone else to have him, either.

Which was just stupid and childish. About as stupid as going with a man on his honeymoon, platonically, in place of his bride, to conduct business with him. Platonically.

She needed her head checked. She needed some sanity. Maybe the problem was that Zack did take up all the spaces in her life. Maybe it would have to change.

Just the thought of that, of pushing him away, sent a sharp dose of pain through her system. She was addicted to him.

"All right. I'll go. Because I would rather have a paid vacation in Thailand than spend the week hanging out in the office and orchestrating the return of all your wedding presents."

"I'm not returning my wedding presents."

"You can't keep them, Zack."

"Of course I can. I might need a food processor someday. What does a food processor do?"

"I'll teach you sometime. Anyway, yes, I'll go with you."

The corner of his lip curved up into a wicked smile that

made her stomach tighten in a way that wasn't entirely un-pleasant. "Excellent. Looks like I won't be spending my wedding night alone, after all."

It probably wasn't nice of him to tease Clara. But he liked the way her cheeks turned pink when he slipped an innuendo into the conversation. And frankly, he was in need of amusement after the day he'd had.

But amusement hadn't been his primary goal when he'd given her the wedding-night line out in front of the hotel. He'd been trying to atone for his ill-spoken remark about her being a replacement. In truth, he had more fun with Clara than he did with Hannah. It wasn't as though he disliked Hannah; quite the opposite. But he hadn't been marrying Hannah for the company.

She'd needed a husband to help her climb the corporate ladder, a little testosterone to help her out in a male-dominated field. And a wife…well, a wife like her was a convenience for a lot of reasons.

But Clara was not his wife. In a lot of ways, she was better. And he hadn't intended to hurt her feelings. She'd been quiet on the ride from the hotel back to her town house by the bay, and once they'd gotten inside to her place she'd dashed into her bedroom to pack a few things "real quick" which, in his experience with women meant…not quick at all.

He sat in her white leather chair, the one that faced her tiny television. Not state of the art at all, nothing like his place. The home theater had been one of his first major purchases when Roasted had become solvent. Clara's had been an industrial-grade mixer for her kitchen. That was where all *her* high-tech gear was. She had a stove with more settings than his stereo system.

"Ready." He looked up and his stomach clenched.

Clara was standing at the end of the hallway, large, pink leather bag draped over her shoulder, dark jeans conforming to the curve of her hips, and a black knit top outlining the contours of her very generous breasts. He hadn't gotten married today, so he was going to allow himself a longer look than he ever did. He'd noticed her body before, but he'd never allowed himself to really look at her as a man looked at a woman. He didn't know why he was letting himself do it now. A treat in exchange for the day, maybe. Or exhaustion making him sloppy with his rules.

Clara was an employee. Clara was a friend. Clara was not a possible lover, and normally that meant no looking at her like she could be.

But tonight wasn't normal. Not by a long stretch.

"Good." He stood up and tried to keep his interest in her body sublimated. But he was just a man. A man who had been celibate for a very long time. A man who had been expecting a reprieve on that and had been sadly disappointed.

"Are we taking the company jet?" She smiled, her perfectly shaped brow raised.

She really was beautiful, and not just her curves. He didn't stop to notice her looks very often. She was like…not furniture, but a fixture for sure. Someone who was always there, every day, no matter what. And when someone was always there, you didn't stop and look at them very often.

But he was looking at her now. Her face was a little bit round, her skin pale and soft. Her eyes, dark brown and wide, were fringed with dark lashes, surprising given her auburn hair color. And her lips…full and soft looking, a very delicate shade of pink.

Looking at her features was a nice distraction, especially since he was about to make her very, very angry. Normally he didn't care for other people's feelings. Not enough to lose any sleep over. He was in command of his world, and he didn't question his decisions.

But Clara was different. She'd always been different.

"There's something I didn't tell you yet." And it might have been wise to save it until she was safely on the plane. And had had a glass or two of champagne.

"What's that?" she asked, eyes narrowing.

"I was supposed to get married today."

Her eyes became glittering, deadly slits. "Right."

"I was meant to be going on my honeymoon with my wife. And now, here I find myself jilted. No bride. Barely any pride to speak of."

She arched her brow, her mouth twisted into a sour expression. "What, Zack?"

"I need you to come with me. As more than my friend. Not really more than my friend, but more as far as Amudee is concerned."

She shook her head and let her pink bag slip off of her shoulder and onto the hardwood floor. "That's…that's insane! Who would believe you'd hooked up with someone else already?"

"Everyone, Clara. I'm a man who, as far as the public is concerned, is in the throes of heartbreak. Everyone knows about our business relationship. About our friendship. Is it so insane to think that, after suffering heartbreak, I looked to my closest friend and found so much more?"

Oh, it was sick. It really was. To hear him saying something that was…that was so close to her real-life fantasies it was painful to listen to the words fall from his lips. "No. No, I am not playing this game. That's ridiculous, Zack. Go on your own."

"I can't."

"Why?"

"Look, my pride will survive. But if I show up alone, and without my wife, looking the part of lonely loser who couldn't hold on to his woman…well, who wants to cut a business deal with that guy?"

"So offer him more money," she hissed.

"That's the thing with Amudee. Money isn't the main objective. If I could throw a bigger check at him, I would. But it's not only about that. It's about people, the kind of people he wants to do business with, and for the most part, I am that man. I care deeply about fair trade, about the work he has going on there in Thailand. I have to look like I call the shots in my own life, and I will not let an inconsequential hiccup like Hannah's cold feet affect that."

She shook her head. "No. Zack just…"

"If I lose the deal because of this…"

"I'm fired? I doubt it. And I can't imagine him passing this up just because you aren't getting married now."

"This growing project is a huge thing for him, his life's work. He's poured his entire fortune into this. He has high principles, and, yes, a lot of it does have to do with bringing money into Northern Thailand, for the people that live there, but he won't go into something if he doesn't feel one hundred percent about it. I can't afford to let it slip to ninety-nine percent. And if you tip the deal over, then I need you."

"So buy your beans from someone else," she said. "Someone who doesn't care what your personal life looks like."

"There is no one else. Not with a product like this. He understands the foundation I've built Roasted on. That it's always been my goal to find small, family run farms to support. He's a philanthropist and what he's done is give different families in the north of Thailand their own plots to cultivate their own crops. Tea and coffee is being grown there, of the highest quality. And I want the best—I don't want to settle for second."

Clara bent and picked her bag up from the floor. She really hated what Zack was proposing. Not just because she didn't exactly relish the idea of lying to someone for a week; there was that, but also because the idea of playing the part of his lover for a week made her feel sick.

She'd done a good job, a damn good job, of pretending that all she felt for Zack was friendship, with a very successful working relationship thrown into the mix. She'd pretended not just for him, but for herself.

Because she didn't want to desire a man who was so out

of her league. A man who dated women who were her polar opposites in looks and personality. Women who were tall and thin, blonde and as cool and in control at all times as he was.

Wanting Zack was a pipe dream of the highest order.

Yes, it had been harder to ignore those sneaky, forbidden feelings when his engagement was announced, but she'd still done it. She'd baked his wedding cake, for heaven's sake.

But this, this was one ask too many. Even for him. To go to a romantic setting, pretend she was experiencing her deepest fantasy, all for show, just seemed too masochistic.

And yet, it was hard to say no to him, too. Not when, as much as it galled to be asked to do this, it would give her this sort of strange, out of time, experience with him.

And definitely not when the whole thing was such a big deal to the future of Roasted. Her wagon was well and truly hitched to the company, and in order for her to succeed, the company had to succeed.

Her wagon was hitched to more than the company, if she was honest. It was Zack. Zack and his wicked smiles, Zack and that indefinable thing he possessed that made her want to care for him, even though he never let her.

Zack was the reason she didn't date. Not because, as a boss he kept her so busy with work, though she'd pretended that was it for a long, long time. It was Zack the man. Because her feelings for him were more than just complicated. And she was… she was a doormat.

She'd baked the man's wedding cake. And then what had she thought would happen? She was going to stay at Roasted, after Zack married? Play Aunt Clara to his kids? Watch while he had this whole life while she died a virgin with nothing but her convection oven for company?

Sick. It was sick.

And now she was really going with him to Chiang Mai to play the part she knew he'd never really consider her for?

She needed to get a life.

She was right. What she'd thought earlier at the hotel had been right. A moment of clarity. It wasn't healthy to have him in everything. He was her boss, her best friend. He filled her work and personal hours, and even when he wasn't around, he was in her thoughts. Zack had dates, he had a life that didn't include her and she…didn't. She couldn't do it anymore.

"If I do this… If I do this, then it's going to be the last thing I do at Roasted." She thought about the bakery, the one she'd been dreaming of for the past few months. The one she'd drawn up plans for. It had been in her mind ever since Zack and Hannah got engaged. Just a mere fantasy of escaping that painful reality at first, but now…now she thought she needed to make it happen.

She needed to make some boundaries. Have something that was hers. Just hers.

"What?" he asked, his dark brows locking together.

"If I go with you and play arm candy then I'm done. It's not…it's not the first time I've thought of this." It wasn't. When he'd come into the office with Hannah and announced that the whole thing was official, well, she'd just about handed in her resignation then and there.

But of course his smile and his innate Zack-ness had stopped her. Because in her mind, it was better to have crumbs from him than everything from someone else. Because he was so enmeshed in her life, so a part of her routine. Her first thought in the morning, her constant companion throughout the day. And it was his face she saw when she drifted off to sleep.

He was everything.

And the real truth of the situation was that while Zack cared for her, and even loved her, possibly like some sort of younger sister figure, she wasn't everything to him. And he didn't want her the way she wanted him.

"What the hell?" he asked.

"I'm…I'm having a revelation, hold on."

"Could you not?"

"No. I'm sorry. I'm...I'm sorry, Zack. This really has been... It's been brewing for a while and I know it wasn't the best day or the best way to say it, but...it does have to be said."

"Why?"

"Because... Because it's eating my life!" The words exploded from her. "And if that isn't made completely obvious by the fact that I'm agreeing to drop everything at the spur-of-the-moment to fly to Asia to go on your honeymoon in place of your fiancée and pretend to be your *new* girlfriend...well...I can't help you."

"No. No, I don't agree."

"And what, Zack? You can't force me to stay at my job."

He looked like he was searching for some loophole that would in fact give him that authority.

"I need a good severance, too. I want to open my own bakery."

"The hell you will!" he said, his voice hard, harsher than she'd ever heard.

"The hell I won't," she returned, keeping her own voice steady, though, how she managed, she wasn't sure.

"Non-compete."

"What?"

"You signed a non-compete."

"A bakery would not compete with Roasted, not really," she said, planting her hands on her hips.

"It could, on a technicality, especially as we'd likely share a very similar desserts menu, seeing as you planned all of mine."

"I'm not talking about a worldwide bakery chain, I'm talking... I want to open one up that I run myself. Here in San Francisco. Something personal, something me. Something that would give me a chance to have a life."

"No."

It was shocking, Zack's transformation from unaffected, jilted groom, to this. She would have expected this kind of reaction from Hannah not showing up to the wedding, not to her asking to quit the business. Where was his control? Zack always had control. Always.

Except now.

"Then I won't go with you. And I get the feeling that a female companion is a bit more important than you let on. I know you too well for you to hide it from me."

His gray eyes glittered in the dim light of her apartment. "There is some competition. Sand Dollar Coffee is competing for the chance to get these same roasts, and Mr. Amudee, traditionalist he is, is very likely to give preference to their CEO. They were just there for a week in the villa, Martin Cole, his wife and their four children. Mr. Amudee was charmed."

"So you do need me. You need me to give you an edge. To make sure Amudee knows you're a macho man who can have his way with whomever, whenever. We're friends, Zack. I don't know why it has to be like this…."

"You were the one leveraging," he bit out.

"Because I can't do this anymore. The beck-and-call thing. I need more. *You* were getting married, you should get that."

"You want to get married?"

Her stomach tightened. "Not necessarily. But I don't even have a hope of it as long as I'm working sixty-hour weeks. And since I don't believe in practical arrangements, like the one you and Hannah have, that will keep me from having a successful relationship."

"Fine," he said, the word stiff. "But you stay on until the deal with Amudee is done. Got it? I'll need you to be around, at the business, my assumed lover, until the ink is dry on the contract."

It was cold and mercenary. And it was tempting. Tempting to play the part. To immerse herself in it for a while. Just thinking about it made her stomach tighten, made her shiver.

No. You can't forget. This is just a game to him. More business. "Yes. I won't let you down. If I say I'm going to do something, I'll do it."

"I know."

"And when it's over?"

"You can open your bakery. I'll make sure you're compensated for your time here."

Clara stuck out her hand, her heart cracking in her chest. "Then I think we have a deal."

CHAPTER THREE

ZACK was in a fouler mood than he'd been when the double doors of the hotel's wedding hall had opened to reveal, not his bride, but a very panicked wedding coordinator who was hissing into her headset.

He leaned back in his seat on his private plane and stared at the amber liquid in the tumbler on his tray. Turbulence was bouncing the alcohol around, sending the strong aroma into the air. He wasn't tempted to take a drink. He didn't drink, it was just that his flight attendant had heard about the disaster and assumed he might be in need.

He looked across the wide aisle at Clara, who was, sitting on a leather love seat in the living-room-style plane cabin, staring fixedly at her touch-screen phone.

"Good book?" he asked.

Her head snapped up. "How did you know I was reading?"

"Because you always read."

"Books make better company than surly bosses."

"Do they make better company than bitchy employees? If so, perhaps I should read more."

She looked at him, her expression bland. "I wouldn't know."

"No. You wouldn't. Look, I gave you what you asked for."

"After a big ugly fight."

"Because I don't want to lose you."

A strange expression flashed in her brown eyes. "Right."

"You've been here since the very early days of Roasted, and you've been key to the success of the company, of course I don't want to lose you."

She looked back down at her phone. "Well, I can't live my entire life to make you happy."

He frowned. "That's not how it's been, is it?"

"No," she said, her tone grudging. She put her phone down and stretched her legs out in front of her and her arms straight over her head, back arching, thrusting her breasts forward. His body hardened, his blood rushing through his veins hotter and faster.

That was a direct result of the fact that he was supposed to break his long bout with celibacy tonight, on this very plane, and it wasn't happening now. Still, his body hadn't caught up with his mind yet. Damned inconvenient considering he was now fixating on his friend's breasts. Breasts that he was not supposed to fixate on. Basically two of the only breasts on earth that were off-limits to him.

More inconvenient, considering they were about to spend the week in Chiang Mai in a very secluded and gorgeous honeymoon villa. Even more when you considered that she was leaving the company soon after.

Well, that wasn't happening. He would make sure of that. He would offer her whatever he had to offer to get her to stay, and until then he would simply nod whenever she brought it up.

He wasn't sure how he would convince her, only that he would. He'd successfully stolen her away from her bakery job back when he'd only had a handful of coffee shops to his name. He had no doubt he could do an even better job of keeping her now that he had so many resources at his disposal. He could give her whatever she wanted, more freedom, more time off. And she was his friend. She wouldn't leave him.

She was just mad about the whole fake fiancée thing. But she would get over it. She always did. It wasn't the first time he'd made her mad. Likely it wouldn't be the last. But that was just how it was. She wouldn't really leave him.

He was a master negotiator. And he didn't lose. He was good at keeping control, of his life and of his business.

"The property we're staying on is supposed to be amazing. It borders a Chiang Mai, and there's a spa right on site. It's more of a resort than anything else, but you have to be invited to stay there by the owner. Very exclusive." He got nothing but silence in response.

"They have unicorns, I hear," he continued, "with golden hooves. You'll love it."

He heard her try to stifle a very reluctant snicker.

He leaned in and looked at her face, at the faint shadows marring the pale skin beneath her eyes. "Are you tired?" he asked.

She leaned back in the chair. "You have no idea."

"There's a bedroom." His blood jumped in his veins again, like the kick-start on a motorcycle. "You could lay down for a while if you want."

"How long have we got?"

"Ten more hours."

"Oh, yeah, I need sleep." She stood up and did another little stretch move that accentuated her breasts.

Clara needed more than sleep. She needed to get out of the tiny, enclosed space with Zack and all of his hot, male phero-mones that were wreaking havoc on her good sense. If she had any at all to wreak havoc on. Well, she did have some. She'd used it to ask for her out.

For a little bit of a chance to move on and forward with her life. Because Zack hadn't married Hannah today, which was fine and good, but he would marry someone. He'd decided to, and when Zack put his mind to something, he did it. That meant it would happen, sometime in the very near future, she imag-ined, now that she knew love wasn't necessarily on the docket. Heck, if he smiled just right at the flight attendant they would probably be engaged by the time they landed in Thailand. And then she could sleep in the guest room in the villa.

She snorted.

"What?" he asked.

"Nothing."

"The scariest word known to man when issued from the lips of a woman."

Her lip curled voluntarily at his statement. "Sexist."

"I prefer realist, but you're free to call it as you see it."

"So tell me this, Zack."

"What?" he asked, one dark eyebrow arched.

"I assume you'll attempt marriage again."

"If I find the right woman."

"And by that, you don't mean the woman you love?"

Something in Zack's posture changed, subtle but obvious to her, his shoulders straightening, his muscles tensing beneath his expertly tailored shirt. His eyes changed, too. There was something dark there, haunted, something she'd never seen before, not this clearly. She'd felt it before, an intensity lurking beneath his cool exterior, but she'd never seen it so plainly.

It was almost frightening in its intensity, transforming a man she'd seen every day for seven years into a cold stranger.

"I don't do love, Clara. Ever." He turned his focus to the newspaper that was folded on his lap. "Good night."

Clara turned toward the bedroom, exhaustion burrowing beneath her skin, down into her bones. Yesterday, everything had been the way it had always been. It had sucked; it had been heading in a direction she hadn't liked, but for the most part, it had been the same.

Today everything felt different. Most of it was her fault. And even though she wouldn't change it, she hated it.

"We just landed."

Clara sat up and pushed the wild mass of auburn curls out of her eyes. She blinked a few times and Zack's face came into focus. For a moment, she didn't do anything. She didn't move, she didn't breathe, she just concentrated on his face being the first thing she saw.

She'd never woken up next to a man before. And, yeah, this wasn't really waking up next to a man in the traditional sense. And he was more leaning over than next to her. But it was a really nice thought, and it was a very nice sight first thing in the morning. If it was even morning. She had no idea.

"What time is it?" she asked.

"It's 10:00 p.m. local time."

She flopped backward. "Oh, no. Why did you let me sleep?"

"I tried to wake you."

"No, you didn't."

"I did, you were out."

She felt a strange sort of disappointment curling in her stomach. She wished, well, part of her did, that he had woken her up. She swallowed hard. Her throat felt like it was lined with cotton. It was far too easy to think of a lot of very interesting ways he might have woken her up.

No. Bad.

"I'm going to be a wreck."

"Sorry."

"I take it you didn't sleep?" She looked down and realized she was still wearing her jeans.

"No. But then, I don't sleep all that much."

That didn't surprise her. She'd never really quizzed him on his sleeping habits, but honestly, he just didn't seem like the kind of man who could sleep at all. He had too much energy and drive to stop even for a moment. Whenever she'd thought of him in bed…well, it hadn't been images of him sleeping plaguing her.

"We're at the airport?" she asked, peering out one of the windows, confused by how dark it was outside.

"Don't know if I'd say airport so much as landing strip.

We're on Mr. Amudee's property. It backs the city, but there's a lot of forest in between his land and civilization."

"Oh."

"There's a car waiting for us, and your luggage, such as it was, is already loaded in it."

She stood and her breasts nearly brushed his chest. She'd misjudged the distance. Her breath caught in her throat and nearly choked her.

Zack didn't seem affected at all. He just smiled at her, one of his wicked smiles, all of the ghosts she'd glimpsed in his gray eyes before she'd gone to sleep were banished now, leaving behind nothing but the glint that was so familiar to her.

"I didn't have—" she had to take in another breath because being so close to him had kind of sucked the other one out of her "—that much time to pack. Otherwise I could have had just as many bags as your high-maintenance ladies."

"You aren't like the women I date. You aren't high maintenance. I like that about you." He turned and headed out the bedroom and she followed him, her chest suddenly feeling tight.

What he meant was, she wasn't beautiful. Not like the women he dated. The women who were all high-fashion planes and angles. And cheekbones.

Her mother was like that. Her sister, too. Tall and leggy with hip bones that were more prominent than their breasts. And that was the look that walked runways. The look that was fashionable, especially in southern California.

And she just didn't have the look. She had curves. An abundance of them. If any of the chi-chi boutiques had bras with her cup size, they were very often too small around, meant for women who'd gone under the knife to give them what nature had bestowed upon her so liberally. And her stomach was a little bit round, not concave or rippling. She wasn't sure if she'd ever seen her ribs.

Standing next to the women in her family just made her

feel...inadequate. And wide. And short. She'd tried to subsist
on cabbage and water like her mother and sister, but frankly,
she'd felt like garbage and had decided a long time ago that
feeling healthy beat being fifteen pounds lighter.

Of course, that decision didn't erase a lifetime of insecurity.
And that insecurity wasn't all down to weight, either.

"Great. Glad to be so...easy."

The door to the plane was standing open, and a staircase
had been lowered to the tarmac. Zack stood and waited for her
to go in front of him. She passed him without looking, trying
not to show the knockout effect the slight scent of his cologne
had on her as she moved by him.

"I wouldn't call you easy," he said.

She stopped, third stair from the top, and whipped around
to look at him. "That's not what I meant."

"Not what I meant, either," he said, his expression overly
innocent.

"Yeah. Right. Are you determined to drive me absolutely
insane for this whole trip?" She continued down the steps and
hopped onto the tarmac, the night air balmy and thick with
mist, blowing across her cheeks and leaving its moist hand-
print behind.

"We are supposed to be a couple."

"Fair enough."

She was reluctant to get into the glossy black town car that
was parked right by the plane. Because she'd only just gotten
Zack-free air, and she didn't really relish the thought of getting right back into a tight, enclosed space with him.

She needed to be able to breathe. To think. And she couldn't
do it when he was around.

That realization alone reinforced her crazy, spur-of-the-
moment decision to move on with her life, and away from
Roasted.

The idea made her slightly sick and more than a little bit
sad. Roasted had been her life since Zack had hired her on. The

day-to-day of it, the constant push to invent more and more goodies, to push the flavor profiles, to push her creativity... there would never be anything else like it.

But she needed to stand on her own feet. To move on with life. She'd gone from her parents to Zack, and while she didn't feel familial about Zack in any way, he represented comfort and safety. And other stuff that wasn't comforting or safe. But being with him, like she was, wasn't pushing her to move forward.

So she was pushing herself. It was uncomfortable, but that was the way it worked. She hoped it would work.

He opened the door to the town car for her and she slid inside, and he came in just behind her. "So, do you and your boyfriends have fights?"

He must know she never had boyfriends. The odd disastrous date that never went past the front door. Emphasis on the odd, since half the men picked her up while she happened to be in the flagship store. And, in her experience, men who picked you up at ten in the morning in coffeehouses were a bit strange.

"How many long-term relationships have I had, Zack?"

"Well, Pete was around a lot until he moved for work."

"Pete? He was a friend from high school. And I was not his type, if you catch my drift."

"You weren't blonde?"

"Or male."

"Oh."

"Point being, I haven't done a lot of long-term." Any, but whatever. "And if I'm ever going to...move on, go into that phase of life then I need to be less consumed with work."

A muscled in his jaw ticked. "But you won't make this kind of money running your own bakery."

"I know. But I have a decent amount of money. How much do I need? How much do you need?"

There was a pause. Zack's hand curled into a fist on the leather seat, then relaxed. "More. Just...a bit more."

"And then you're never done."

"But if not for that then what am I working for?"

She swallowed. "A good question. Good and scary. Though I suppose adding a wife will add…something. When you find a new prospect, that is. Did Hannah have an equally efficient and driven sister, by chance?"

"Not that I'm aware of."

She snapped her fingers. "Darn."

"Don't lose sleep over it."

"I won't be sleeping tonight, anyway. Because you didn't wake me up on the plane." She couldn't resist the jab.

"Because you sleep like a rock and snore like a walrus."

"Might be why my relationships aren't long-term," she said drily. Not that any man had ever heard her snore but she was so not admitting to that.

"I doubt that."

"Do you?"

His eyes locked with hers and something changed in the air. It seemed to crackle. Like a spark on dry leaves. It was strange. It was breathtaking, and electrifying, and she never wanted it to end.

"Why?" she asked, pressing. Desperate to hear more. A little bit afraid of hearing more, too.

"Because a little bit of snoring wouldn't deter a man who'd had the pleasure of sharing your bed."

She sucked in a sharp breath and looked out the window, and into the inky-black jungle. She felt dizzy. She felt…hot.

"Well, thanks," she said.

He chuckled, low and rich like the best chocolate ganache. Just as bad for her to indulge in as the naughty treat, too. "You seem uncomfortable with the compliment."

"You and I don't talk about things like that."

"Only because it hadn't come up."

"Do you snore?" she asked.

"Not that I'm aware of."

"Then your lack of long-term relationships doesn't really make sense at all."

He arched one dark brow. "Was that a compliment?"

"More a commentary on the transient nature of your love life."

"I'm wounded."

She winced. "Well, maybe in light of all that happened today it wasn't the best thing to say."

"You've never pulled punches before, don't start now."

"I don't know any other way to be."

"Now that may account for your own short-term relationships."

She whipped around to face him and her heart stalled. He was looking at her like she was a particularly interesting treat. One he might like to taste.

The car stopped and she nearly breathed a prayer of thanks out loud. She needed distance. She needed it desperately.

"Well," Zack said, opening the door. "Time to go and have a look at our honeymoon suite."

CHAPTER FOUR

THE honeymoon villa was the epitome of romance. The anterior wall of the courtyard was surrounded by dense, green trees, clinging vines and flowers covering most of the stone wall, adding color, a sense that nature ruled here, not man. There was a keypad on the gate and Zack entered a code in; a reminder that the man very much had his fingerprints all over the property.

"Nice," she said, as the gates swung open and revealed an open courtyard area. The villa itself was white and clean. Intricate spires, carved from wood and capped in gold, adorned the roof of the house, rising up to meet the thick canopy of teak trees.

"Mr. Amudee had planned on giving Hannah and I a few days of wedded bliss prior to meeting with me, so he made sure I had the code, and that everything in the home would be stocked and ready."

Clara tried not to think about Zack and Hannah, using the love nest for its intended purpose. More than that, she tried not to think of her and Zack using it for its intended purpose.

She really did try. There was no point in allowing those fantasies. Those fantasies had led to nothing more than dateless Friday nights and lack of sleep.

"Well, that was…thoughtful of him."

"It was. I believe he has some activities planned for us, too."

Oh, great. She was going to be trapped in happy-couple-honeymoon-activity hell.

She followed Zack through the vast courtyard and to the wide, ornately carved double doors at the front of the villa. She touched one of the flower blossoms etched into the hard surface. "These are gorgeous. I wonder if I could mimic the design with frosting."

"I will happily be a part of that experiment." He pushed open the doors and stood, waiting for her to go in before him.

"You do seem to hang around a lot more when I'm practicing my baking skills."

"I don't know how."

"I could teach you," she said. "Maybe sometimes after I can teach you how to use a food processor."

"I think I'll pass. Anyway, I'm a bachelor. Have pity on me. I wasn't supposed to be a bachelor after today, but I am, and now I still need my best friend to cook for me."

"And probably do your laundry."

"I wouldn't mind."

Basically he wanted her to be his wife with none of the perks. She nearly said so, but that would sound too much like she wanted the perks, and even if a part of her did, she'd rather parade naked through the Castro District than confess it.

"I'm not doing your laundry."

Zack closed the door behind them and a shock of awareness hit her, low and strong in her stomach. She felt so very alone with Zack all of a sudden that she could hardly breathe. And it wasn't as though she'd never been alone with him. She had been. Hundreds of times. Late nights in the office, at her apartment cooking, at his luxury penthouse watching a movie.

But this wasn't San Francisco. It wasn't their offices; it wasn't one of their apartments. It felt like another world entirely and that was…dangerous.

She looked up at the tall, peaked ceilings, at the intricately carved vines and flowers that cascaded from wooden rafters.

Swaths of fabric were the only dividers between rooms, gauzy
and sexy, providing the illusion of privacy without actually
giving any at all.

And in the middle of it all was Zack. He filled the space, not
just with his breadth and height, but with his presence. With
the unique scent that was so utterly Zack mingling with the
heavy perfume of plumeria. Familiar and exotic all at once.

This was like one of her late-night fantasies. Like a scene
she'd only ever allowed herself to indulge in when she was
shrouded in the darkness of her room. And now, those fantasies were coming back to bite her.

Because they were mingling with reality. This was real.
And in reality, Zack didn't want her like she wanted him. But
in her fantasies he did. There, he touched her like a lover, his
eyes locked with hers, his lips…

She needed her head checked.

"I have a housekeeper, anyway. I was teasing," he said.

"I know." She hoped she didn't look as flushed as she felt.

"I don't think you did. I think you were about to bite my
head off." He looked…amused. Damn him.

"Is there food?"

His lips curved into a half smile. "I can check."

He wandered out of the main living area, in search of the
kitchen, she imagined, and she took the opportunity to breathe
in air that didn't smell of Zack. Air that didn't make her stomach twist.

She walked the opposite direction of Zack, through one of
the fabric-covered doorways and stopped. It was the bedroom.
The bed was up on a raised platform, a duvet in deep red spread
over it. Cream colored fabric with delicate gold vines woven
throughout hung from the ceiling, shielding the bed. It was
obvious that it wasn't a bed made for one, or for sleeping.

She swallowed heavily, her eyes glued to the center of the
room.

She heard footsteps behind her and turned. "I found food."

"Good," she said, trying to ignore the fast-paced beating of her heart. Zack and the bed in one room was enough to make her feel like her head might explode. "There is… I mean, this isn't the only bedroom is it?"

"I'm not sure."

"Oh," she said.

"I set dinner out on the balcony, if you want to join me."

"Don't you want to go to bed?" she asked, then immediately regretted the way the words had come out. Heat flooded her face, and she was certain there was a very blatant blush staining her cheeks. "I mean…well, you know what I mean. That wasn't… I meant you. By yourself. Because I slept and I know you didn't."

"At least let me buy you dinner first, Clara," he said, his mouth curved in amusement, his eyes glittering with the same heat she'd noticed earlier. It made her uncomfortable. And jittery. And a little bit excited.

She laughed, a kind of nervous, fake sound. "Of course."

Zack ignored the jolt of arousal that shot through his veins. For a moment at least, he and Clara had both been thinking the same thing. And it had involved that bed. That bed that was far too tempting, even for a man who prided himself on having absolute control at all times.

Things with Clara had always been easy. No, he'd never been blind to her beauty, but their relationship had never been marked by moments of heavy sexual tension. Not until today.

And knowing that, even for a moment, she'd shared in the temptation, well, that made it all worse. Or better. No, definitely worse, because in his life, he valued boundaries. Everything and everyone had a place and a purpose. Clara had a place. It was not in his bed.

Or this bed.

It was important that his life stay focused like that. Controlled. That nothing crossed over. He'd been rigid in that, uncompromising, for the past fourteen years.

"This way, beautiful," he said, clenching his hand into a fist to keep from putting it on Clara's lower back. He would have done it before. But suddenly it seemed like far too risky of a maneuver.

Clara shot him a look that was pure Clara, his friend, and it made the knot in his chest ease slightly. Though it didn't do much for the heat coursing through his veins.

He was questioning why he'd thought bringing her was a good idea. And he never questioned his decisions. Not anymore. Because he thought everything through before he acted. Not thinking, letting anything go before reason, was a recipe for disaster.

And bringing Clara had been the logical choice. At least until thirty seconds ago.

He moved in front of her, under the guise of leading her to the deck, but really just so he wouldn't let himself look at her butt while she walked. Occasionally he allowed himself the indulgence of looking at her curves. Harmless enough. He was human, a man, and she was a beautiful woman. But it seemed less harmless after a moment like that.

"This is really nice," she said when they were outside.

Her words were true, banal and safe. He'd set the table and turned on the string of lanterns that were hung above the table. A moderate effort, but he had wanted it to be nice. Now it felt strangely intimate.

He couldn't remember the last time a dinner date had seemed intimate. He couldn't even remember the last time that word had seemed applicable to something in his life. Very often, sex didn't even seem all that intimate to him.

Of course, it had been so long since he'd had sex maybe that wasn't true. That was likely half of his problem now.

Clara wandered to the railing and leaned over the edge, tossing her glossy copper curls over her shoulder and sniffing the air. Or maybe the sex wasn't the problem. Because being alone with Hannah hadn't made him feel this way. And there were days when the scent of Clara's perfume hitting him when she walked past made his stomach tighten...

But he ignored that. He was good at ignoring it.

"What are you doing?"

"It smells amazing out here. Like when you bake bread and the air is heavy with it. Only it's flowers instead of flour." She turned to him and smiled, the familiar glitter back in her eyes.

The knot inside him eased even more.

"I would never have thought of it that way." He pulled her chair out and nodded toward it and she walked over to the table and took her seat.

He sat across from her, ladling reheated *Tom Yum Ka* into her bowl and then into his. She smiled at him, the slight dimple in her rounded cheeks deepening as she did.

Things seemed to have stabilized, even if her sweet grin did have an impact on his stomach.

"So, tell me more about this deal with Mr. Amudee."

He put his forearm on the table and leaned forward. "I think we covered most of it. Although, another reason it's nice to have you here is your palate. I'd like you to taste the different roasts and come up with pairings for them. It would be particularly nice to have in our boutique locations."

"Pairings!" Her eyes glittered. "I love it."

"Good coffee or tea really is just as complex as good wine. There are just as many flavor variations."

"I know, Zack," she said.

"Of course you do. You appreciate good coffee. It's one reason we get along so well."

Clara took another bite of her soup and let the ginger sit on her tongue, enjoying the zip of spice that hurt just enough to take her mind off the weird reaction she was having to Zack. Yes, being attracted to him was nothing new.

But this was different. The attraction she felt at home was like a sleeper agent. It attacked her when she least expected it. In dreams. When she was looking at other men and contemplating accepting a date. It wasn't usually this shaky, limb-weakening thing that made her feel tongue-tied and exposed in his presence. Maybe it was the feeling of utter seclusion. Or maybe it was because she knew just what that big bed was here for, what he'd been planning on doing with it.

"That and I bake you cupcakes," she said, swallowing the tart and spicy soup.

"There is that." Zack looked toward the railing of the deck, off into trees, the look in his eyes distant, cold suddenly. "Tell me about your bakery."

"The one I hope to have?"

"Yes. And the life you're going to put with it."

Her chest constricted. "It will be small. I'll have regular menu items and daily specials. I'll have more time to make fancy little treats with a lot of decorations. I'll have a hand in everything instead of just conceptualizing and farming the instructions out to hordes of employees."

"And that's important to you?"

"It's how we started. Me in the flagship store, you going back and forth between your— What did you have when I met you? Fifteen stores up and down the West Coast? It was fun."

"Yes, but now we have money."

She nodded. "We do. And it's great. You've done this incredible thing, Zack. The growth has been…amazing. Way beyond what I imagined."

"Not beyond what I imagined."

"No?"

He shook his head. "It was always the plan. Planning is key. It's when you don't plan, when you drift, that's when things are a surprise. Good or bad."

"You didn't plan for Hannah to opt out of the wedding."

"I didn't plan for you to leave Roasted, either. Sometimes other people come in and mess with your plans," he said, his dark eyebrows locked together.

"This doesn't mean I won't see you anymore," she said.

Though she probably shouldn't. But the thought of that made her chest feel like there was a hole in it. Still, she'd baked the man's wedding cake. She was such a pushover, such a hopeless case, it was obscene. It had to end.

She didn't want it to. But if she didn't see him at work every day…it would be a start.

"I know you'll still see me," he said, his mouth curving. "You'd have withdrawals otherwise."

If only that weren't true. "Right. Can't live without you, Zack." She felt her throat get tight. *Stupid.* So stupid. But Zack really did mean the world to her, and she had a very strong suspicion that her statement was nothing but the truth. He had offered her support when no one else in her life had. He still did.

She regretted saying she wanted to leave Roasted. Regretted it with everything in her. But she couldn't change her mind. The reasoning behind the decision was still sound. And she really would still see him. He just wouldn't fill up her whole world anymore. She couldn't let feelings for him, feelings that would never be returned, hold her back for the rest of her life.

Zack's arm twitched and he reached into his pocket. "Phone vibrated," he said. He pulled out his smart phone and unlocked the screen, a strange expression on his face. "Hannah texted me."

"Really?"

"She's really sorry about the wedding."

"Oh, good," Clara snorted. The weird jealousy and protectiveness were back together again. She was still righteously angry at Hannah for what she'd done, even while she was relieved.

"She met someone else."

"What?"

"Yes." He looked up, his expression neutral. "She's in love apparently."

"And she's texting this to you?"

He shrugged. "It fits our relationship."

"No, it doesn't. Love or not, you still had a relationship."

"We weren't sleeping together."

Clara felt her stomach free fall down into her toes. "What?" That didn't even make sense. Hannah was a goddess. A sex bomb that had been detonated in the middle of her life, making her feel inadequate and inexperienced.

And he hadn't slept with her? She'd assumed—imagined even, in sadly graphic detail—that half of the meetings in his office had been rousing desk-sex sessions. And…they hadn't been? So much angst. So much stomach curling angst exerted over…nothing, it turned out.

"Why?" she asked, her voice several notches higher than usual.

"Hannah's kind of traditional. Because we weren't in love… well, she needed love or marriage. We were going to have marriage."

"Hmm. Well, then maybe texting is appropriate. I don't understand how you were going to marry this woman."

"Marriage is a business agreement, like anything else, Clara. You decide if you can fulfill the obligations and if they'll be advantageous to you. Then you sign or you don't."

"Cynical."

"True."

"Then why bother to get married? I don't understand."

He shrugged. "Because it's the thing to do. Marriage offers stability, companionship. It's logical."

"Good grief, Spock. Logical. That's not why people get married." She snorted again. "Did your parents have a horrible divorce or something?"

Zack shook his head. "No."

"You never talk about your family."

He looked down at his soup. "Not on accident."

"Well, I figured. That's why I never ask."

"This isn't never asking."

She looked at him, at the side of his head. He wouldn't look at her. "We've known each other for seven years, Zack."

"And I'm sure I don't know everything about you, either. But I know what counts. I know that you lick the mixer. Even if it's got batter with raw eggs on it."

She laughed. "Tell anyone that and I'll ruin you."

"I have no doubt. I also know that you like stupid comedies."

"And I know that you put on football games and never end up watching them. You're just in it for the snacks."

He smiled, his gray eyes meeting hers. "See? You know the real truth."

Except there was something in the way he said it, a strange undertone, that told her she didn't. She wasn't sure how she'd missed it before. But she had. Now it seemed blatant, obvious. Zack had a way of presenting such a calm, easy front. In business, she knew it was to disarm, that no matter how easygoing he appeared, he was the man in charge. No question.

Now she wondered how much of the easy act in his personal life was just that. An act.

His eyes lingered on her face for a moment, and she suddenly became acutely conscious of her lips. And how dry they were. She stuck out the tip of her tongue and moistened them, the action taking an undertone she hadn't intended when she'd begun.

This week was going to kill her. Eventually the tension would get too heavy and she would be crushed beneath the weight of it. There was no possible way she could endure any more.

"I'm really tired," she said, the lie so blatant and obvious it was embarrassing.

To Zack's credit, he didn't call her on it. "The inner sanctum is all yours. I'll make do with the couch."

She wasn't going to feel bad about that for a second. "All right, I'll see you in the morning."

Maybe by morning some of the surrealism of the whole day

would have worn off. Maybe by morning she wouldn't feel choked by the attraction she felt to Zack.

Maybe, but not likely.

CHAPTER FIVE

"Mr. Amudee has extended an invitation for you and me to have a private tour of the forest land."

Zack strode into the kitchen area and Clara sucked coffee down into her lungs. He was wearing jeans, only jeans, low on his lean hips, his chest bare and muscular and far too tempting. She could lean right in and...

"Coffee for me?" he asked.

"Oh, yes. Sure." She picked up the carafe and poured some coffee into a bright blue mug. "It's the shade-grown Chiang Mai Morning Blend. Really good. Strong but bright, a bit of citrus."

"I love it when you talk coffee to me," he said, lifting the mug to his lips, a wicked grin curving his mouth.

There was something borderline domestic about the scene. Although, nothing truly domestic could have such a dangerous, arousing edge to it, she was certain. And Zack, shirtless, had all of those things.

"All right, tell me about the tour," she said, looking very hard into her coffee mug.

"Very romantic. For the newly engaged."

Her stomach tightened. "Great."

"I hope you brought a swimsuit."

Oh, good. Zack in a swimsuit. With her in a swimsuit. That was going to help things get back on comfortable footing. She looked at Zack, at the easy expression on his handsome face. The ridiculous thing was, the footing was perfectly comfortable for him. Her little hell of sexual frustration was one hundred percent private. All her own. Zack wasn't remotely ruffled.

Typical.

"Yes, I brought a swimsuit."

"Good. I'll meet you back here in twenty minutes."

"Right." Unfortunately it would take longer than twenty minutes to plot an escape. So that meant Zack and swimsuits.

She tried to ignore the small, eternally optimistic part of her that whispered it might be a good thing.

Clara tugged at her brilliant pink sarong and made sure the knot was secure at her breasts before stepping out into the courtyard, where Zack was standing already.

"Ready. What's the deal? Give."

"You have to wait and see," he said, moving behind her, placing his hand low on her back as he led her to the gate and out onto a narrow path that wound through a thick canopy of trees and opened on an expansive green lawn.

"Are you kidding me?" she asked, stopping, her eyes widening.

There were two elephants in the field, one equipped with a harness that had small, cushioned seats on top. He was large enough he looked like he could comfortably seat at least four.

"Elephant rides are a big tourist draw in Chiang Mai," Zack said, the corner of his mouth lifting. "And I've never done it before, so I thought I would take advantage of the offer."

"First time for you?" she asked. She'd intended it as a joke, but it hit a bit to close to that sexual undercurrent they'd been dealing with since they left San Francisco.

A slow smile spread across his face. "Just for the elephant ride."

"Right. Got it." She was sure she was turning pink.

"You?"

She just about choked. "The elephant?"

"What else would I have been asking about?"

Her virginity. Except, no he wouldn't have been asking about that. It wasn't like she had a neon sign on her forehead that blinked red and said Virgin on it. Unless she did. Maybe he could tell.

She really hoped he couldn't tell.

"Yes, first time on an elephant," she said drily, aiming for cool humor. She wasn't sure she made her mark, but it was a valiant effort.

"Mr. Parsons." There was a man in white linen pants and a loose white shirt approaching them, his hand raised in greeting. "Ms. Davis, I believe," he said, stopping in front of her, his dark eyes glittering with warmth.

"Yes," Clara said, extending her hand. He bent his head and dropped a kiss on it, smiling, the skin around his eyes wrinkling with the motion.

"Isra Amudee. Pleasure." He straightened and shook Zack's hand. "Very glad you could make it. Especially after what happened."

Zack put his arm around Clara's waist and Clara tried to ignore the jolt of heat that raced through her. "Really, it didn't take me long to discover it wasn't a problem. Clara…well, I've known her for a long time. I don't really know how I missed what was right in front of me."

Mr. Amudee's smile widened. "A new wedding in your future, then?"

Zack stiffened. "Naturally. Actually I've already asked."

"And she's accepted?" Amudee looked at her and Clara felt her stomach bottom out.

Zack tightened his hold on her. "Yes," she said, her throat sandpaper dry. "Of course."

"And you, I bet, will have the good sense to show up. Now, I'll leave you to the elephants. I have to go and take a walk around the grounds. But I'll see you later on."

Clara watched Amudee walk away and tried to ignore the buzzing in her head as the man who was with the elephants introduced himself in English as Joe. He explained how the ride would work, that the elephant knew the route through the forrest and up to a waterfall, and she wouldn't deviate from that.

"They're trained. Very well. Safe. You'll be riding Anong." Joe indicated the elephant who was harnessed up. "And I'll follow on Mali. Just as a precaution."

He tapped Anong on her back leg and she bent low, making it easy for them to climb up onto the seat. Zack went first, then leaned forward and extended his hand, helping her up onto the bench.

"Seat belts," he said, raising one eyebrow as he fastened the long leather strap over both of their laps.

"Comforting," she said, a tingle of nerves and excitement running through her.

"Ready?" their guide called to them.

"I have no idea," she whispered to Zack.

"Ready," Zack said.

The elephant rose up, the sharp pitch forward and to the left a shock. She lurched to the side and took hold of Zack's arm while Anong finished getting to her feet, each movement throwing them in a different direction.

"I think I'm good now," she whispered, her fingers still wrapped, clawlike around Zack's arm.

"Just relax, he said this is a path she takes all the time. New for us, but not new for her."

She didn't actually want to know the answer to the question, but she asked it anyway. "Accustomed to calming the nerves of the inexperienced?"

"No. I don't mess around with women who need comforting in the bedroom. That's not what I'm there for."

She felt a heavy blush spread over her cheeks. "I guess not."

She was alternately relieved and disappointed by that bit

of news. Relieved, because she didn't really like to think of her friend as some crass seducer of innocents, and she really couldn't picture him in that role, anyway.

If he was the big bad wolf, it would be because the woman he was with wanted to play Little Red Riding Hood.

But it was disappointing, too, because that pushed her even farther outside the box that Zack's "ideal woman" resided in.

Ideal bedmate.

Sure, maybe it was more that than any sort of romantic ideal, but she would like to just fit the requirements for that. Well, really, being the woman he was sleeping with was very far away from what she actually wanted, but it would be a start.

A wonderful, sexual, amazing start…

She jerked her thoughts back to the present, not hard to do with the pitch-and-roll gait of the elephant rivaling a storm-tossed boat. It was a smooth, fluid sort of motion, but it was a very big motion, to match the size of the animal.

It also wasn't hard to do when she remembered that, as far as their host was concerned, she and Zack were now engaged.

"A tangled web, isn't it, Parsons?" she asked.

"What was I supposed to say?" he countered. "Ah, no, this is just my best friend that I brought along for a roll in the hay."

"The truth might have worked. He seems like a nice man."

"Look, it's done. I'm sure his assumption works even more in my favor, in favor of the deal, and that's all that really matters, right? We know where we stand. It's not like it changes anything between us."

She felt like the air had been knocked out of her. "No. Of course not."

They moved through the meadow and down into the trees, onto a well-worn path that took them along a slow-moving river, the banks covered in greenery, bright pink flowers glowing from the dark, lush foliage.

She tried to keep her focus on the view, but her mind kept wandering back to Zack, to his solid, steady heat, so close to her. It would be easy to just melt into him, to stop fighting so hard for a moment and give in to the need to touch him.

But she wouldn't. She couldn't. Nothing had changed between them, after all. His words.

There was a reason she'd never made any sort of attempt to change their relationship from friends to more-than-friends. The biggest one being that she didn't want to jeopardize the most stable relationship she had, the one closest to it being unable to stomach the thought of being rejected by him.

Of having him confirm that everything her mother said about her was true. Of having her know, for certain, that a man really wouldn't want her because she just wasn't all that pretty. Her mother had made sure she'd known men would still sleep with her, because of course, men would sleep with anyone. But she wasn't the sort of woman a man would want for a wife. Not the type of woman a man could be proud to take to events.

Not like her sister. Gorgeous, perfect Lucy who was, in all unfairness, smart and actually quite sweet along with being slender, blonde and generally elegant.

Lucy actually would have looked more like Hannah's sister than like *her* sister.

A sobering thought, indeed.

She should make sure Zack never met her sister.

The sound of running water grew louder and they rounded a curve in the path and came into a clearing that curved around a still, jade pool. At least twenty fine steams were trickling down moss-covered rocks, meeting at the center and falling into the pool as one heavy rush of water.

Anong the elephant stopped at the edge of the pool, dropping slowly down to her knees, the ground rising up a bit faster than Clara would have like. She leaned into Zack, clinging to the sleeve of his T-shirt as Anong settled.

"All right?" he asked.

She looked at where her hand was, and slowly uncurled her fingers, releasing her hold on him. "Sorry," she said.

He smiled, that simple expression enough to melt her insides. He was so sexy. Time and exposure, familiarity, didn't change it. Didn't lessen it.

Just another reason for her to leave Roasted. If exposure didn't do it, distance might.

Zack moved away from her, dismounting their ride first and waited for her at the side of their living chariot, his hand outstretched. She leaned forward and took it, letting his muscles propel her gently to the ground. Her feet hit just in front of his, her breasts close to touching his chest, the heat from him enticing her, taunting her.

"Do you want me to wait for you?" their guide asked.

Zack shook his head. "We'll walk back. Thank you for the ride. It was an experience."

He nodded and whistled a signal to Anong, who rose slowly and turned, going back with her owner and friend. She watched them round the corner, a smile on her lips. Yesterday, she was at a beachside hotel in San Francisco, expecting to lose half of her heart as Zack married another woman.

Today she was with him on his honeymoon. Riding elephants.

"An experience," Zack said, turning to face the water.

"It was fun," she said.

"Not relaxing exactly."

"No," she said, laughing. "Not in the least."

"Mr. Amudee informed me by phone this morning that this is a safe place to swim. Clean. They don't let the elephants up here and the waterfall keeps it all moving."

She made a face. "Good to know. I liked the elephants, don't really want to share a swimming hole with them. It looks pristine," she said, moving to the edge, looking down into the clear pool. She could see rocks covered in moss along the bottom, small fish darting around, only leaving the cover of their hiding places for a few moments before swimming behind something else. "Perfect."

Zack tugged his black shirt over his head, leaving him in nothing more than a pair of very low-cut white board shorts that, when wet, she had no doubt would cling to some very interesting places.

Her mind was a filthy place lately. And the sad thing was, it was hard to regret. Because it was so enjoyable.

"Swimming?"

"No." She shook her head and gripped her sarong.

"Why?"

"It looks cold."

He put his hands on his lean hips and sighed, the motion making his ab muscles ripple in a very enticing fashion. "It's so hot and muggy out here it could be snowmelt and it would feel good. And I guarantee you it's not snowmelt."

"It just looks…cold." Lame. So lame. But she didn't really want to strip down to her swimsuit in front of him, not when he looked so amazing in his. She was… There was too much of her for a start. She was so very conscious of that. Of the fact that she had hips and breasts, and that she could pinch fat on her stomach.

Zack's girlfriends had hip bones and abs that were just as cut as his.

"Ridiculous." He walked over to her and scooped her up in his arms, her heart climbing up into her throat as he did. His arms were tight and strong around her, masculine. Lifting her seemed effortless. His large hands cupped her thigh and her shoulder, his heat spreading through her like warm, sticky honey, thick and sweet.

She realized what was happening a little bit too late, because sexual attraction had short-circuited her brain. She put her hand flat on his chest, another bolt of awareness shocking her even as Zack took two big steps off the bank and down into the water.

The hot and cold burst through her, her body still warm from his touch on the inside, the water freezing her skin.

"Zack!"

He looked down at her, smiling. She sputtered and clung to his shoulders, his arms still wrapped tightly around her. His skin was slick now, so sexy, and it took everything in her arsenal of willpower to keep from sliding her palms down from their perch on his shoulders and flattening them against his amazing, perfect pecs.

She wanted to. She wanted to press her lips to the hollow of his throat, lick the water drops that were clinging to his neck.

She wiggled against him and managed to extricate herself from his grasp. Fleeing temptation.

She walked up to the shallow part of the pool, her pink sarong limp and heavy now, clinging to her curves like a second skin. She untied it and looped it over a tree branch. There was no point in it now.

She felt exposed in her black one-piece. It was pretty modest by some suit standards, but anything that tight tended to make her feel a bit exposed.

"Well, that's one way to get me in the water. Brute force," she sniffed, walking back to the water and sinking into the depths quickly, desperate for the covering it would provide.

"Brute?" Zack swam to where she was, treading water, his eyes glinting with amusement.

"Uh…yeah. You took advantage of me."

He paddled closer, his face a whisper from hers. "I didn't take advantage of you. If I had, you'd have known it, that's for sure."

Strangely, with her body half submerged in water, her throat suddenly felt bone-dry. "I feel um…taken advantage… You… picked me up and threw me in and I'm…wet."

His expression changed, his eyes darkening. "Interesting."

"Oh, *pffft*." She dunked her head, letting the cold water envelop her, pull the stinging heat from her cheeks. She paddled toward the waterfall, away from Zack. Away from certain mortification and temptation.

She surfaced again and looked back at Zack, still treading water where she'd left him.

Nice, Clara. Next time just tell him straight up that you're hot for him and would like to jump him, if that's all right with him.

She pulled a face for her own benefit and climbed up one of the mossy rocks that sat beneath the slow flowing falls, water trickling down, mist hovering above the surface of the cool, plant-covered stones.

She pulled her knees to her chest and looked up, squinting at the sunlight pouring through the thick canopy of trees.

"You're like a jungle fairy."

She looked down into the water and saw Zack, his hair wet and glistening.

"You're startling me," she said. More with his statement than with his presence, but she didn't intend to elaborate.

He planted his palms flat on the rocks and hoisted himself up, the muscles in his shoulders rolling and shifting with the motion. He sat next to her, the heat from his body a welcome respite from the cold. But that was about all it was a respite from. Because mostly he just made her feel edgy.

And happy. He made her so happy that it hurt. Just being with him made everything seem right. Like a missing part of herself was finally in place. Like some of her insecurities and inadequacies didn't matter so much.

And that was just stupid. Not to mention scary. Because it was an illusion. He would never be with her in the way she wanted, and watching him marry another woman, give someone else everything she longed for, *that* would turn her happiness into the bitterest pain.

The kind she wasn't sure she could withstand.

"You're beautiful," he said.

She turned sharply to look at him, her heart in her throat. "What?"

"Just stating a fact."

"It's not one you typically state. About me, I mean."

He put his hand out and brushed a water drop from her cheek with his thumb, the motion sending an electric shock through her body, heat pooling in her stomach and radiating from there to her limbs.

"Well, I thought it needed to be said."

It was so tantalizingly close to what she wanted. But to him it was simply an empty compliment, or maybe he even meant it. But not in the way she would. He didn't mean she was beautiful in the same way she found him beautiful. The way that made her body warm and her heart flutter.

"Thanks for that. You aren't so bad, either." She tried to sound casual. Light. Like a friend. Like she was supposed to sound.

He smiled and lifted his arm, curling his fist in, showing off his very, very impressive biceps.

"You're shameless," she said, somehow managing to laugh around her stubborn heart, still lodged firmly in her throat.

"Sorry."

"About as sorry as you are for dumping me in the water?"

"Yeah. About." He leaned in, his arm curving around her waist and everything slowed down for a moment. He tightened his hold on her, his face so close…

And then they were falling.

She shrieked just before they hit the water. And surfaced with a loud curse, unreasonable anger mingling with disappointment. "Zack! You jackass!"

She moved to him and planted her hands on his shoulders, attempting to dunk him beneath the water. He put his hands on her waist and held her still in front of him, her movements impotent against his strength.

"You can touch bottom here, can't you?" she asked, her feet

hovering above the sandy floor of the pool while Zack seemed
firmly rooted.

"Maybe."

His hands slipped down, resting on her hips, the heat from
his touch cutting through the icy chill in the water. He kept
one hand there, the other sliding around to her back, his fingers drifting upward, skimming the line of her spine.

She shivered, but she wasn't cold. And he didn't let go.

His eyes were locked with hers, the head there matching the
heat he was spreading over her skin. Her hands were still on his
shoulders. And since he'd just moved his hands, it seemed...
somehow it seemed right to move hers.

Her heart thundered in her chest as she slid her hands down,
palms skimming his chest hair, the firm muscles beneath, as
she rested them against his chest. She could hardly breathe. He
chest, her stomach, every last muscle, was too tightly wound

His fingers flexed, the blunt tips digging into her flesh. His
hands were rough, strong, everything she'd ever imagined and
so much more.

Zack loosened his hold, a muscle in his jaw jerking. She
pulled away from him, the water freezing where his hands had
been.

"We should go," Zack said, his words abrupt.

"I... We haven't been here very long." She felt muddled, as
though the mist from the waterfall had wrapped itself around
her, making everything seem fuzzy.

And she was glad. Because she had a feeling that when the
reality of what had just happened, of how stupid she'd been,
hit, it was going to hit hard.

"Yes, but I have some things to take care of before tonight.
We have dinner reservations at the restaurant down in the main
part of the resort."

He reversed direction and swam to shore, walking out of the
pool, his muscular legs fighting against the water pressure, his
swim trunks conforming to his body. A hard pang hit her in

he stomach when she looked and saw the outline of his erec-
ion. Had she really gotten him hot? Was that about her?

He turned away from her and pulled his shirt on.

And was the arousal why they were leaving now?

So he felt something. Even if he was running from it.
Something that was at least physical.

Her hart hammered, echoing in her head, making her tem-
ples pulse.

Maybe she did matter to him, like that, at least a little bit?
Maybe... Yes, she knew men were excited by women but this
had to be personal. It had to be about her, at least a little bit.
Did he think she was sexy?

She followed him to shore, scrambling onto the sandy
ground, her feet picking up grains of dirt, clinging to her toes.
She shook her foot out, grateful to have something else to concentrate on for a moment.

She looked back up and saw Zack, his eyes on her, his jaw
locked tight.

She swallowed hard and grabbed her sarong. "So we're having dinner out tonight?"

"Yes," he bit out. "I have to go and pick up a package down
in town and then I'll meet you back up at the villa. The car
will be by around seven."

"Okay." She wished she could come up with something better than the bland, one-word answer, but she just couldn't.

Something had changed. The air around them seemed tight,
the way Zack looked at her new and strange. And for the first
time, she felt power in her beauty, in her body.

And she wondered if maybe he could want her. If she could
be the sort of woman he wanted.

Maybe tonight she would actually try.

It was criminal. The dress that Clara was wearing should be
illegal. She certainly shouldn't be allowed out in public. It
was tight, like that black, second-skin swimsuit, accentuat-

ing curves that, until this afternoon, he hadn't realized were quite so...lush.

Breasts that were round and perfect, firm looking. They would overflow in his hands. And her hips were incredible nothing like the androgynous, straight up-and-down supermodels that were so in style. Not even like Hannah, whose image he was having trouble conjuring up.

Today, at the river, with her body pressed against his, wet and slick, soft and feminine, he'd had a reaction he really hadn' counted on. He hadn't counted on touching her like he had either. Exploring the elegant line of her back. Holding her to him. It had been a big mistake.

Getting out of the water, in front of his best friend, sporting an erection inspired by her, hadn't really been his idea o a good time.

He put his hand in his pocket, let his fingers close around the velvet box that was nestled there. The one that Hannah had had rush delivered to the resort. Because it was the right thing to do, or so she'd said. He hadn't really cared whether he go the engagement ring back or not. But he could use it.

The thing with Amudee, his assumption, had been unex pected. But Zack was good at reading people and the older man's delight at the thought had been so obvious, there had been no way he would disappoint him. Not with so much rid ing on things going well this week.

His other plans had all gone to hell. He wasn't sending thi one there with the rest of them.

"What exactly is that?" he asked. They were in the car being driven up to the main area of the resort, and being closed in with her when she looked like that and smelled, well, she smelled sweet enough to taste, was a bit of torture.

"What?" she asked.

"What you're wearing."

Her cheeks colored. "A dress."

"But do you...call it something?"

"A dress," she said again, her voice low now, dangerous.

"It's a nice dress."

She looked straight ahead. "Thank you."

The car stopped in front of an open, wooden building that had all the lights on despite the late hour. There were people sitting at a bar, musicians set down in the center of the seating area, and dancers out on the grass, candles balanced on their hands as they moved in time with the music.

He opened his door and Clara just sat, her posture stiff. "What?"

"Now I'm not sure if I should go back and change."

"I don't even want to understand women," he said.

"Why?"

"You just changed into that dress, so clearly you thought it was a good choice, and now you want to change back?"

"Because there must be something wrong with what I'm wearing. Although, you didn't seem to have a problem with my bathing suit, and it showed a lot more than this." She put a hand on her stomach. "It's too tight."

His body hardened. "Trust me, it's not. Every man in the bar is going to give himself whiplash when you walk by."

She frowned. "Really?"

She looked…mystified. Doubtful.

"Did you not look at yourself in the mirror?" he asked, completely incredulous that she somehow didn't see what he did. That she didn't realize how appealing a dress that was basically a second skin was to a man. It showed every bit of her shape, while still concealing the details. Made him feel desperate to see everything, the tease nearly unbearable.

She looked away from him. "That's the trouble, I did, and chose to wear it anyway."

"What makes you think it doesn't look good?"

"You reacted…funny."

"Because I'm not used to seeing so much of you. But what can see is certainly good."

"Really?"

He took a lock of her silky hair between his thumb and fore finger. A mistake. It was so soft. Like he imagined the rest o her would be. "Didn't I tell you any man would put up with your snoring for the pleasure of having you sleep with him?"

His eyes dropped to her mouth and he felt an uncomfort able shock of sensation when, for the second time in the pas hour, she stuck her pink tongue out and slicked it across he lips, leaving them looking glossy and oddly kissable.

Clara felt like there was someone sitting on her chest, keep ing her from breathing. The knot of insecurity that had tie up her stomach was changing into something else, somethin dangerous. A strand of hope she had no business feeling. A kind of feminine pride that didn't make sense.

Zack was a charmer. He could charm the white gloves of a spinster, and what he was saying to her was no different Empty charm that had no real weight behind it. It was easy t say that some other man would like to share her bed. It didn' mean he did. Or that anyone he even knew would.

All right, in reality, she knew how men were about sex If she was willing to put out they wouldn't care if she had pinch of extra flesh around her middle, but that wasn't reall the issue. She didn't want to be a second choice. Second bes

She was even second-guessing the physical reaction Zac had had to her down at the river. Because that could simply b a man overdue for sex. Nothing more. She'd made it persona because she'd been desperate for it. But in reality, he was sup posed to be here, with his wife, having lots and lots of sex, an he wasn't. But she doubted he'd forgotten.

She was tired of being in the shadow of someone else. Eve tonight, she was the consolation prize for Zack. Rather tha spending the night with Hannah, he was with her, watching tra ditional dancing instead of having hot, sweaty, wedding nigh sex. Ah, yes, all fine and good for him to say those things t her, but he wasn't really backing it up.

She forced a smile. "You did. All right, let's go…drink or something."

He chuckled. "Sounds like a good idea to me."

They both got out of the car and walked over to an alcove, shrouded in misty fabric, like everything in the whole resort property. It was designed for people to take advantage of the perceived privacy. It was an invitation to some sort of heady, fantastic sin. Traditional values her fanny.

She sat down on one of the cushions, positioned in front of a low table. Zack sat next to her, so close she could feel the heat radiating off his body.

"So what about my comment spawned the dress edition of twenty questions?" he asked.

"I don't usually wear things that are this tight, so you…your reaction made me think it looked… You've met my mother, right?" She changed tactics.

"Yes."

"She's like a model. And my sister…well, she takes after my mom. I take after my dad."

"Something wrong with that?"

"Well, I'm just not…not everything Lucy is. And my mother let me know that. Let me know that I was second best in nearly every way. She didn't just get beauty, she had a perfect grade-point average without even trying. I was just average. I liked school, but I didn't excel at it. The only thing I've ever excelled at is baking, which in my mother's estimation contributes to my weight issues."

Zack swore and Clara jumped. "Weight issues? You don't have weight issues."

"I did. More than I do now, I mean. It was a whole…thing in high school. Remember, I mentioned the time my date stood me up?"

He nodded and she continued on, hating to dredge up the memory. "Asking me was a joke in the first place, not that I had any idea, of course. And I was supposed to meet him by the stage in the gym, which is where the dance was, and he walked up with his real date, and the guys doing the lights knew to put a spotlight on me right then. And I was all chubby and wrapped up in this silly, tight pink dress that was just so... shiny. That stays with you. Sometimes, for no reason, I still feel like the girl under the spotlight, with everyone looking at all my flaws."

He swore sharply. "That's bull. That's...kids are stupid and that's high school." He swallowed. "It's not real life. None of us stay the same as we were back then." His words ended sounding rough, hard.

"Maybe not. Still, even though I've sort of...slimmed out as I've grown up, as far as my mom is concerned, since I'm not six feet tall and runway ready, I'm not perfect. I have her genes, too, after all," she said, echoing a sentiment she'd heard so many times. "And that means I could be much thinner if I *tried*."

"Let me tell you something about women's bodies, Clara, and I know you are a woman, but I'm still going to claim the greater expertise. Men like women's bodies, and there isn't only one kind to like, that's part of the fun. Beauty isn't just one thing."

She tried to ignore the warm, glowy feeling that was spreading through her. "I know that. I mean, part of me knows that. But it's hard to let go of the second-best thing."

"Better than feeling like you're above everyone else," he said slowly. "Like nothing can touch you because you're just so damn perfect life wouldn't dare."

"I don't know if Lucy feels that way, my mother might but..." She trailed off when she noticed the look on his face. There was something, just for a moment, etched there that was so cold, so utterly filled with despair that it reached inside her and twisted her heart.

"Zack..."

He shook his head. "Nothing, Clara. Just leave it." The danc

rs had cleared the area out on the lawn and there were couples
moving out into the lit circles, holding each other close, looking at each other with a kind of longing that made Clara ache
with jealousy. "Care to dance before dinner is served?"

Yes and no. She felt a bit too fragile to be so close to him,
and yet a part of her wanted it more than she wanted air. Just
like in the water today, she'd wanted to run and cling at the
same time. She was never sure which desire would win out.

He offered his hand and she took it, his fingers curling
around hers, warm and masculine. He helped her up from her
seat and drew her to him, his expression still strange, foreign
more than familiar. He looked leaner, more dangerous. Which
was strange, because even though Zack was her friend, she always felt an edge of danger around him, a little bit of unrest.
Probably because she was so attracted to him that just looking
at him made her shiver with longing.

"Just a warning," he said, as they made their way out onto
the grass. "People will probably stare. But that's because you
look good, amazing even. And you certainly aren't second to
any woman here."

"Flatterer."

"No, I'm not, and I think we both know that."

"Okay, I suppose that's true," she said, kicking her shoes off
and enjoying the feeling of the grass under her feet. Although,
losing the little lift her shoes provided put her eyes level with
Zack's chest.

He pulled her to him, his hand on her waist. She fought the
urge to melt into him, to rest her head on his chest. This wasn't
that kind of dance; theirs wasn't that kind of relationship. That
didn't mean she didn't want to pretend. It was easy, with the
heat of his body so close to hers, to imagine that tonight might
end differently. To imagine that he saw her as a woman.

Not just in the way that he'd referenced, that vague, sweet,
but generic talk about women and their figures. But that he
would desire her body specifically. She kept her eyes open,

fixed on his throat. She knew him so well, that even looking there she knew just who she was with. And she didn't want to shut that reality out by closing her eyes. She wanted to watch, relish.

For a moment reality seemed suspended. There wasn't time, there wasn't a fiancée, one more suited to Zack than she was looming in the background. There was only her and Zack, the heat of the night air, the strains from the stringed instrument weaving around them, creating a sensual, exotic rhythm that she wanted to embrace completely.

She loved him so much.

That hit her hard in the chest. The final, concrete acknowledgment of what she'd probably always known. A moment that was completely lacking in denial for once. She loved Zack. With her entire heart, with everything in her. And she was in his arms now.

But not in the way she wanted to be. She breathed in deeply, smelling flowers, rain and Zack. Her lungs burned, her stomach aching. She wished it was real. So much that it hurt, down to her bones.

Maybe, just for a moment, she could pretend that it was real. That this was romance. That he held her because he wanted her. Because after this, after the fake engagement, after the ink was dry on the contracts, there would be no more chance to pretend.

She would go her way, and she would leave Zack behind. Why couldn't she ignore it now? Just for now.

She didn't want the song to end, wished the notes would linger in the air forever, an excuse to stay in his arms. But it ended. And that was why she shouldn't have said yes to the dance in the first place. Playing games wouldn't come close to giving her what she wanted with Zack. It just made her aware of how far she was from having what she really wanted.

He took her hand and pulled her away from the other dancing couples, and for one heart-stopping moment, she though

e might lean in and kiss her. His lips were close to hers, his
reath hot, fanning across her cheek. Her body felt too tight,
er skin too hot. She needed something. Needed him.

"I have something for you," he said. "For tomorrow."

"I like presents," she said, trying to keep her voice from
ounding too shaky. Too needy. Too honest. "It's not a food
rocessor, is it?"

He chuckled, a low, sexy sound that reverberated through
er. "I told you, I'm keeping my food processor."

She tried to breathe. "All right then, I can't guess."

He reached into his jacket pocket and pulled out a small
elvet box. Everything slowed down for a moment, but unlike
efore, when the gauzy, frothy film of fantasy had covered it
ll, this was stark reality. She shook her head even before he
pened it, but he didn't seem to notice.

He popped the top on it and revealed a huge ring, glittering
old and diamonds. She sucked in a sharp breath. Such a per-
ct ring. Gorgeous. Extravagant. Familiar. The ring he'd given
Hannah. The exact same ring. The ring for the woman who
as supposed to be here. The ring for the woman he should
ave danced with, the woman he would have kissed, made love
.

A well of pain, deep, unreasonable and no less intense for
, opened up in her, threatened to consume her. What a joke.
cheap trick. And the worst part was that she'd played it on
erself. Letting herself pretend that he'd wanted *her* at the river,
aying like he wanted her in his arms tonight.

Letting hope exist in her, along with the futile, ridiculous
ve she felt for him. Ridiculous, because for half a second,
r breath had caught when she'd seen the ring, and she'd for-
otten it was fake.

"No," she said.

"Clara…"

"I don't…" She was horrified to feel wetness on her cheeks,
ars falling she hadn't even realized were building. She backed

away from him, hitting her shoulder against one of the bar ar
ea's supporting pillars. But she didn't stop. "I'm sorry."

She wasn't sorry. She was angry. She was hurt. Ravage
to her soul. Maybe it had been ignorant of her not to think a
the way to the ring. To think that the farce wouldn't includ
that. Of course it would. Zack didn't cut corners and he didn
forget details. So of course he wouldn't forget something a
essential to an engagement as a ring.

But it hurt. To see him, impossibly gorgeous and, in so man
ways, everything she'd always dreamed of, offering her a ring
a ring he'd already given to another woman, as part of a lie,
killed something inside her.

Maybe it was just the fact that it pulled her deepest, mo
secret fantasy out of her and laid it bare. And made it into
joke. Designed to show her that there was no way he woul
ever consider her. Not with any real seriousness. That she wa
nothing more than a replacement for the woman he'd intende
to have here with him.

That she was interchangeable.

She was hopeless. She needed a friend to tell her what
head case she was. To tell her to get over him. To take her ot
to pie and tell her she could do better, have better.

But Zack should have been that person. *He* was her bes
friend. He was the one she talked to. The one she confided in
And she couldn't confide this, couldn't tell him that he'd ju
shredded her heart. Couldn't tell him she was hopelessly i
love with a man she couldn't have, because he was the man

The crushing loneliness that thought brought on, the pai
was overwhelming.

Her stomach twisted. "I have to… I'm sorry."

She turned away from him, walking quickly across the law
back to into the lobby area to find a car, an elephant, whatev
would get her back to the villa the fastest.

She was running and she knew it. From him. From her hu
And from the moment she knew would come, the one whe

she'd have to explain to him just why looking at the ring had made her cry.

It was an explanation she never wanted to give. Because the only man she could ever confide her pain in, was also the one man she could never tell. Because he was the man who'd caused it.

CHAPTER SIX

Zack's heart pounded as he scanned the villa's courtyard. It was too dark to see anything, but he was sure this was where she was. Unless she'd called the car service and asked them to come and get her, which, if Clara was really upset, he wouldn't put past her. She could be on the next plane back to the States.

His plane.

Which, he had a suspicion he might deserve.

There was a narrow path that led from the main area of the courtyard into an alcove surrounded by flowering plants and trees. And he was willing to bet that, if she was still in the villa, she'd gone there.

He was right. She was sitting on the stone bench, her knees pulled up to her chest. She was simply staring, her cheeks glistening in the moonlight. The sight made him ache.

He was all about control, all about living life with as few entanglements and attachments as possible. But Clara was his exception. She had been from the moment he'd met her.

She was the one person who could alter his emotions without his say so. Make him happy if he really wanted to be angry. Make his gut feel wrenched with her tears.

"Are you okay?"

She dropped her knees and put her feet on the ground, straightening. "I'm sorry. That was stupid. I overreacted."

He moved to the bench and crouched down in front of it, in front of her. "What did I do?"

"I was just...I told you, it was an overreaction. It was nothing, really." She sucked in a breath that ended on a hiccup and his heart twisted. "I can't really...explain it."

The confusion he felt was nearly as frustrating as the pain he felt over hurting her. He didn't really understand exactly what he'd done, but not understanding it didn't make it go away.

Without thinking, he lifted his hand and curved it around her neck, stroking her tender skin with his thumb. It was a gesture meant to comfort her, because he'd upset her somehow, for the second time in forty-eight hours, and he hated to upset her. She meant too much to him.

But something in the touch changed. He wasn't sure exactly when it tipped over from being comfort to being a caress, he wasn't sure how her skin beneath his fingers transformed from something everyday to something silky, tempting.

She looked at him, her eyes glistening, the expression in them angry. Angry and hot. And that heat licked through him, reached down into his gut and squeezed him tight.

It was close to what he'd felt down at the river, but magnified, her anger feeding the flame that burned between them. And he couldn't walk away from it. Not this time.

Without thought, without reason or planning, without stopping to think of possible consequences, he leaned in and closed the space between them, his lips meeting hers. First kisses were for tasting, testing. They were a question.

At least historically for him they had been. This kiss wasn't.

Something roared through him, filling him, a kind of desperation he'd never felt before. He didn't ask, he took. He didn't taste, he devoured. The hunger in him was too ravenous to do anything else, so sudden he had no chance to sublimate it. He wrapped his arms around her, and she clung to his shoulders, her lips parting beneath his.

He growled and thrust his tongue against hers, his body

shuddering as his world reduced to the slick friction, to the warmth of her lips on his.

Clara was powerless to do anything but cling to Zack. Powerless to give anything less than every bit of passion and desire that was pouring through her. To do anything but devour him, giving in to the hunger that had lived in her, gnawed at her for the past seven years.

This was heaven. And it was hell. Everything she'd longed for, still off-limits to her for the same reasons it always had been. Except for right now, for some reason, it was as though a ban had been lifted. For this one moment, a moment out of time. A moment that she needed more than she needed air.

His lips, firm and sure, were everything she'd ever dreamed they might be, his hands, heavy and hot on her back even more arousing than she'd thought possible.

This was why there had been no one else. Because the idea of Zack had always been more enticing than the reality of any other man. And the reality of Zack far surpassed any fantasy she'd ever had. Maybe any fantasy *any* woman had ever had.

She slid from the bench and onto the stone-covered ground, gripping the front of his shirt, their knees touching. He pulled her closer, bringing her breasts against his hard, muscular chest. She arched into him, craving more. Craving everything. All of him.

When they parted, he rested his forehead against hers, his breathing shallow, unsteady, loud in the otherwise silent night.

She didn't know what to say. She was afraid that he would try to say something first. Something that would ruin it. A joke. Or maybe he'd even be angry. Or he'd say it was a mistake. All valid reactions, but she didn't want any of them. She didn't want to deal with anything. She simply wanted to focus on the pounding of her heart, the swollen, tingly feeling in her lips. On all the really good, fizzy little sensations that were popping in her veins like champagne.

Zack let out a gust of air. "Damn."

She laughed. She couldn't help it. Of all the reactions she'd expected, and dreaded, that hadn't been it. That he would allow an honest reaction, and that his reaction would match hers, hadn't seemed likely.

"Yeah," she said.

He braced his hand on the bench behind her and pulled himself up, then extended his hand to her. She gripped it and let him help her to her feet. She brushed some dried leaves from her knees, ignoring the slight prickle of pain and indents of small twigs left behind on her skin.

Her eyes caught his and held, and all of the good exciting feelings that had been swirling through her dissolved. The cushion of fantasy yanked from under her, there was nothing but cold, hard reality. She'd kissed Zack. More than kissed, she'd attacked him.

And there was nowhere for it to go from that point. If she leaned in again, if she kissed him again, then what? They might go to bed together. And where would that leave her after? Where would it leave them?

No, he hadn't slept with Hannah, but he'd slept with other beautiful women. Lots of them. She'd met a good number of them. And she was…she was inexperienced, unglamorous. And she was here as a replacement. If something happened between them now, on a night that was meant to be his wedding night with another woman, she would always feel like she'd been second.

He was a man, and the pump was well and truly primed. He'd been promised sex after what had been a lengthy bout of not having sex, so of course he was hot for it. But he was hot for it. Not for her.

He'd never kissed her before tonight. That, if nothing else, cemented the point.

She wasn't going to cry again. She wasn't going to let him know how vulnerable she was to him. Wasn't going to let him know how bad it hurt to pull away now.

"This has been a bit of a crazy day," she said.

"I can't argue with that."

"Sorry. About this." She gestured to the bench. "All of it… I don't…I don't really know what that was about."

The flash of relief she saw in Zack's eyes made her heart twist. She would finish now. Make sure he'd never want to talk about it again.

"I mean…how do you feel?" She'd said the magic feel word. Zack didn't like to talk about how he felt. Not in a way that went any deeper than happy, or angry, or hungry.

"Fine. Good, in fact. Kissing a beautiful woman is never a bad thing."

She felt heat creep into her cheeks. She shouldn't respond to the compliment. It was empty, an attempt to smooth things over. But it affected her, and she couldn't stop it from making her stomach curl in traitorous satisfaction.

"I might say the same. Not the woman part but the… You get it."

"I did something wrong. With the ring. I'm sorry. I'm not hitting them out of the park with you today, am I?"

"I don't think either of us is at our best right now," she said. That at least was true. Of course, she hadn't been her best since the engagement announcement. Her safe little world had been chucked off-kilter in that moment and she'd felt out of balance ever since.

"Probably need sleep."

She forced a laugh. "You probably do. I got that extra sleep on the plane, remember?"

"But you should sleep again. Otherwise you'll be off for even longer."

She did feel tired suddenly. And not a normal tired, an all-consuming sort of tired that went all the way down into her bones. "Yeah. You're right. I can sleep on the couch tonight."

"I'll sleep on the couch again. After being left at the altar, sleeping alone in the honeymoon bed is just a bit depressing, don't you think?"

For a moment, she thought about inviting him to join her. To play the vixen for once. To say to hell with all of her insecurities and just be the woman she wished she could be.

But she didn't.

"Yeah, maybe a little." She swallowed and stuck her hand out. "I'll take that ring though."

"You sure?"

"I told you, I was being stupid. Emotional girl moment. The kind specifically designed to boggle the minds of men. Actually, a little secret for you, they occasionally boggle our minds, too. So, ring, give."

She held her hand out and he took it in his, turning it over so her palm was facing down. He took the ring box out of his pocket and took the ring out of its pink silk nest, holding it up for a moment before sliding it on to her ring finger.

She looked down at it, then curled her fingers into a fist, trying to force a smile.

"Looks good," he said.

"It's a diamond, it can't look anything else," she said, trying to sound breezy and unaffected. Both things she wasn't.

"Perfect. And now we're ready for tomorrow. I hope you brought shoes you can walk in."

"Of course I did."

"That's right. I forgot."

"Forgot what?" she asked.

"That you're different. Come on, let's go try to get some sleep."

She followed him out of the courtyard, trying to leave everything behind them, all the needs, desires, pain, back in the alcove. But his words kept repeating in her head, and she could still feel his kiss on her lips.

And she felt different. Like a completely different woman

than the one who had walked into the garden with tears streaming down her face.

One kiss shouldn't have that kind of power. But that kiss had. She felt changed. She felt a a tiny bit destroyed, and a little bit stronger. And she wasn't sure she would take it back. Even if she could.

Sleep had been a joke. An elusive thing that had never even come close to happening. Zack looked at the tie he'd brought with him for meetings with Mr. Amudee, and decided against putting it on. Not twice in one week.

He left two buttons undone on his crisp white shirt and pushed the sleeves halfway up his forearms. That should be good enough. They were spending the day looking at where the coffee and tea plants were grown.

Maybe spending the day outdoors would clear his head. Would lift the heavy fog of arousal that had plagued him since the kiss. Not just the kiss, since that strange, tense moment at the lake before the kiss.

But the kiss… A few more minutes and he would have had her flat on her back on the stone bench with more than half of her clothes stripped from her gorgeous curves.

He bit down hard, his teeth grinding together. He shouldn't be thinking of her curves. But he was.

"Zack?"

The sound of her voice hit him like a kick in the gut.

"Here," he said, sliding his belt through the loops on his pants and fastening the buckle as she walked around the corner, into the bedroom. Her pale cheeks colored slightly when she saw him.

"How did you sleep?" she asked.

"Great," he lied. "Thanks for letting me use the room to get ready."

"Yeah, no problem. I got up pretty early. Wandered around in the garden. There are so many flowers here."

And she'd put a few different varieties in her hair. It was silly. And it was cute. She had a way of making that work for her.

"I didn't know you liked flowers so much."

She shrugged. "I always have some on my kitchen table."

She did, now that he thought about it. He wondered if anyone ever bought them for her. He wondered why he'd never really stopped to notice before. Why he'd never bought her any.

Because, bosses don't buy employees flowers. And friends don't buy friends flowers.

Friends also didn't kiss each other like he and Clara had done last night. His pulse jump-started at the thought, his blood rushing south. He tightened his hands into fists and tried to will his body back under control.

"Ready to go?" he asked, his voice curt because it was taking every last bit of his willpower to keep his desire for her leashed.

She frowned slightly. "Yeah. Ready."

"Good. Remember, you're my fiancée, and we've been very suddenly overcome by love that can no longer be denied."

One side of her mouth quirked up. "Is that the story?"

"Yes. That's the story. As Amudee created it, so he'll believe it. He's the one who assumed."

"A romantic, I suppose. Either that or he just thinks you move fast."

"I'm decisive. And we've known each other for years." He studied her face for a moment, dark almost almond-shaped eyes, pale skin, clear and smooth. Perfection. Her lips were pink and full and, now he knew, made for kissing. And he had to wonder how he'd known her for so long and never really looked at her.

Because if he had he would have realized. He would have had to realize, that she was the most gorgeous woman. Exquisite. Curved, just as a woman should be, in all the right places. Beautiful without fuss or pretension.

"Yes, we have," she said slowly, those liquid brown eyes locked with his.

"So it stands to reason that after Hannah decided not to go through with things…"

"Right."

The air between them seemed thicker now, that dangerous edge sharpening. Now that he knew what it was like to touch her, to feel her soft lips beneath his, well, now it was a lot harder to ignore.

"So let's go, then," he said.

"Right," she said again.

He moved to her and slid his arm around her waist. It was more slender than he'd imagined it might be. "We have to do things like this," he said, his voice getting rougher as her hips brushed against his.

She nodded, her eyes on his face. On his lips. She would be the death of him.

"Lovely to see you again, Ms. Davis," Mr. Amudee said, inclining his head. "And with a ring, I see."

Her heart rate kicked up several notches.

"Oh. Yes. Zack…made it official last night. It's lovely to see you, too." She touched the ring on her finger and Zack tightened his hold around her waist. She nearly stopped breathing, her accelerated heart rate lurching to a halt with it. From the moment they'd arrived at Mr. Amudee's house, he had put his arm around her and kept it there. She'd assumed she would get used to it, to the warm weight of his touch. But she wasn't getting used to it. If anything, she was getting more jittery, more aroused with each passing second.

The sun was hot on the wide, open veranda that overlooked rows of coffee trees with flat glossy leaves and bright red coffee cherries. But Zack's touch was the thing that was making her melt.

"I had not met the other woman you intended to marry,

Zack, but I must say that comparing the photos of the first one, to Ms. Davis, I find I prefer Ms. Davis."

Clara's heart bumped against her chest. "That's kind of you to say." She knew her face had to be beet-red, it was hot, that was for sure. Because it was nice of him to say, but there was no way it could be true.

There was no comparison between her and Hannah. Hannah was...well, sex bomb came to mind yet again.

"Not kind," Isra said. "Just the truth. I was married, a long time ago, to the most wonderful woman. I have a good judge of character. Unfortunately I was too busy to see just how wonderful she was. Don't make that mistake."

Zack cleared his throat. "Clara is also very knowledgable about our product. I know we'll both enjoy getting a look at the growing process today. And we're both excited about the tasting."

Back to business. Zack was good at that. Thank God one of them was.

"I'm excited to share it with you. Come this way." They followed him down the stairs that led to the lush, green garden filled with fragrant foliage. He moved quickly for a man his age, his movements sharp and precise as he explained where each plant was in the growing stage, and which family was leasing which segment of the farmland, and how the soil and amount of shade would affect the flavor of each type of coffee, even before it was roasted.

The tea was grown in a more remote segment of the farm and required walking up into the rolling hills, where the leaves were in the process of being harvested.

"A lot depends on when you pick them," Mr. Amudee said, bending and plucking a small, tender-looking cluster of leaves. "Smell. Very delicate."

He handed the leaves to Zack and he did as instructed. Then he held them out for Clara. She bent and took in the light fragrance. She looked up and her eyes clashed with Zack's and her heart beat double time.

"And this will be…what sort of tea will it be?" she asked, anything to get her mind off Zack and his eyes.

"White tea," Zack said. "Am I right?"

Mr. Amudee inclined his head. "Right. Ready to go and taste?"

Her eyes met Zack's again, the word tasting bringing to mind something new and different entirely. Something heady and sexual.

She swallowed hard.

"Yes, I think we are," Zack said slowly, his eyes never leaving hers.

And she wondered if he'd been thinking the exact same thing she was. And if he was thinking the same thing, if he wanted to kiss her again, she wasn't sure what she would do.

No, that was a lie. She was sure. She would kiss him again. Like nothing else mattered. Like there was no future and no consequences. Because she'd had enough of not getting what she wanted out of life. Quite enough.

She looked at Zack again and she wondered if she'd only imagined that momentary flash of heat. Because his eyes were cool again, his expression neutral.

She tried to convince herself that it was better that way.

Clara spent the next few days carefully avoiding Zack. It was easier than expected, given the cozy living situation. But during the day he had meetings with Mr. Amudee and when she wasn't needed, she took advantage of all the vacation-type things that were available in the resort.

There was a spa down in the hotel, and also some incredible restaurants. Her favorite retreat was up on the roof of the villa that gave her a view of the mountains, and the small town that was only a short walk away, the golden rooftops reflecting the sunlight like fire in the late afternoon. It was the perect view for yoga, which kept her mind focused and relaxed at the same time.

She even managed to forget about the kiss. Mostly. As long as she made a concerted effort not to think of it. And as long as she didn't get into bed before she was ready to fall asleep instantly. Lying awake for any length of time was a recipe for disaster. And for replaying that moment. Over and over again.

Clara took a deep breath and tried to focus on the scenery, on the sky as it lightened. Orange fading into a pale pink, then to purple as the sun rose from behind the sloping hills. She would focus on that. Not Zack. Because that door was clearly closed. He hadn't touched her again, unless it was absolutely necessary, since the night in the garden. Since the kiss that had scorched her inside and out.

The kiss that didn't even seem to be a vague memory to him.

"Got plans for today?"

She turned and her heart lodged itself in her throat. Zack strode onto the roof in nothing more than a pair of low-slung jeans, his chest, broad and muscular, sprinkled with the perfect amount of chest hair, was streaked with dirt and glistening with sweat.

She had to remind herself to breathe when he came closer. And she had to remind herself not to stare at his abs, bunching and shifting as he moved.

"Do I…" She blinked and looked up at his face. "What?"

"Do you have plans? You've been busy. Remarkably so for someone on vacation."

"Well, down in the village they have these neat classes for tourists. Weaving and things like that. And one of the restaurants in the hotel has a culinary school."

"I thought you wanted to relax."

"Cooking is relaxing for me." And it had been conducive to avoiding him. "Anyway, now I can make you some killer Pad Thai when we get back home."

"Well, I support that."

"What are you doing up so early?"

"Working. Before the sun had a chance to get over the moun‐
tains and scorch me. Part of the deal. I need to understand
where it all comes from. How important the work is to the
families. I'm really pleased we're going to be part of this pro‐
cess."

"Me, too," she said. Although, she wouldn't be. Not once
everything was in place. This was it for her.

"I'm going up to Doi Suthep, to see the temple. I thought
you might want to come with me."

She did. Not just to see the temple, although that was of
major interest to her, but to spend some time with him. It was
that whole inconvenient paradox of being in love with her best
friend again. She wanted to avoid him, because she felt con‐
flicted over the kiss. She wanted to be with him, confide in
him, because she felt conflicted, too.

"I..."

"Are you avoiding me?" he asked, hands on his lean hips.
"Well, I know you're avoiding me, but I guess I don't know
why. Does this have to do with you leaving Roasted?"

"No!"

"Then what the hell is your problem?"

Hot, reckless anger flooded her. "My problem? Are you
serious? You asked me to come here, and play fiancée, and
have. I don't have a problem."

"When you aren't avoiding me."

"I have done exactly what you asked me to do," she said.
"I have played the part of charming, simpering fiancée, I've
worn this ring on my finger, and you can't, for one second see
why that might not be...something I want to do. And then you
kiss me. Kiss me like...like you really are on your honeymoon
and you want to know what my problem is?"

He looped his arm around her waist and drew her to him,
his eyes blazing. She braced herself against him, her palms fla‐

on his bare chest. "I think I do know what your problem is. I think you're avoiding me because of the kiss. Because you're afraid it will happen again. Or because you want it to happen again."

She shook her head slightly. "N-no. I haven't even thought about it again."

"Liar." He dipped his head so that his lips hovered just above hers. "You want this."

She did. She really did. She wanted his lips on hers. His hands on her body. She wanted everything. "You arrogant bastard," she said, her voice trembling. "How dare you?"

"How dare I what? Say that you want it again? We both know you do."

His lips were so close to hers and it was tempting, so tempting, to angle her head so that they met. So that she could taste him again. Have a moment of stolen pleasure again.

"You do want it," he said again, his voice rough, strained.

"So?" she whispered.

"What?"

"So what if I do?" she said, finding strength in her voice. "What then, Zack? We'll kiss? Sleep together? And then what? Nothing. You and I both know there won't be anything after that. We'll just ruin what we do have."

He released his hold on her and took a step back, letting his hands fall to his sides. "Sorry."

"You've been apologizing to me a lot lately," she said, her voice trembling. "You don't need to do that."

He nodded. "I'm going to take a quick shower."

"Not going to the temple?"

He smiled ruefully. "Still am. And you can come if you want. Provided you've worked the tantrum out of your system."

"That was your tantrum, Parsons, not mine."

"Maybe." He tightened his jaw, his hands curling into fists. "Just tense I suppose. Coming with me or not?"

She hesitated. Because she did want to go, but things

weren't…easy with him at the moment. And the scariest thing was she wasn't sure she wanted them to be easy again. She was sort of liking this new, scary dynamic between them. The one that made him touch her like she did something to him. Like he was losing control.

"I'll be good. I promise," he added.

She laughed, a fake, tremulous sound. "I wasn't worried."

Zack wasn't the one who worried her. She hesitated because she wasn't sure she trusted *herself* to behave.

"I was," he said, turning away from her and walking back into the house. She watched him the whole way, the muscles on his back, the dent just above the waistline of his jeans, and his perfect, tight butt.

She let out a slow, shaky breath. Yeah, it was definitely herself she didn't trust.

The temple at Doi Suthep was crowded with tourists, spiritual pilgrims and locals. Clara and Zack walked up the redbrick staircase, the handrails fashioned into guardian dragons with slithering bodies and fierce faces.

They were silent for the three-hundred-step trek up to the temple, Clara keeping a safe distance between them, in spite of the crush of people all around them. She was mad at him.

And fair enough, he'd been a jerk earlier. That was sexual frustration. Sexual frustration combined with the desire to give in to the need to kiss her again. To do more than kiss her.

Damn.

He could still remember the first time he'd seen Clara. She was working behind the counter at a bakery, flour on her cheeks. She was cute. Not the kind of woman he was normally attracted to. But she'd fascinated him. Utterly and completely. It had turned out she'd made great cupcakes, too. And that she was smart and funny. That it felt good to be with her.

The emotional connection to her, when he'd been lacking a connection with anyone for years, had been shocking, in-

tant, and had immediately found him shoving his attraction
to her away.

A friendship with her was fine. Anything else…he didn't
have room for it. Anything else would go beyond the boundaries he'd set for himself. And he needed his boundaries. His
control. He valued it above everything else.

Just another reason he'd intended to marry Hannah.
Marriage brought stability, a sort of controlled existence that
attracted him. One woman in his bed, in his life.

And now that that had gone to hell, it seemed his feelings
for Clara were headed in the same direction. He'd done with
her, for seven years now, what he did with everything in his
life. She had a place. She was his friend. She didn't move out
of that place in his mind.

His body was suddenly thinking differently. He'd made a
mistake. He'd allowed himself too much freedom. He'd indulged his desire to look at her body. To touch her soft skin
when they'd gone swimming. And that night, he'd given in to
the temptation to allow her to feature in his fantasies. To find
release with her image in his mind.

He'd allowed himself to cross the line in his mind, and that
was where control started. He knew better. Yet it was hard to
regret. Because wanting her was such a tantalizing experience.
Just feeling desire for her was a pleasure on its own.

Her sweet, short, sundress was not helping matters. Though,
thankfully she'd had to purchase a pair of silk pants to wear
beneath it before they could head up toward the temple.

Still, even with her legs covered, there was that bright, gorgeous smile that had been plastered on her face since they'd
arrived. She was all breathy sighs and sounds of pleasure over
the sights and sounds. It was the sweetest torture.

"Incredible," she breathed, her voice soft, sensual in a way.
Enough to make his body ache.

"Yes," he agreed. Mostly, he was looking at her, and not the
immense, gold-laden temple.

He forced himself to look away from Clara. To keep hi focus on the gilded statues, the bright, fragrant offerings o flowers, fresh fruit and cakes left in front of the different al ters that were placed throughout the courtyard. A large, dome shaped building covered entirely in gold reflected the sun, th air bright, thick with smoke from burning incense.

Monks in bright orange robes wove through the crowds talking, laughing, offering blessing.

It *was* incredible. And still nowhere near as interesting a the woman next to him.

"Have you been enjoying yourself here?" he asked.

"More or less," she said, looking at him from the corner o her eye, color creeping into her cheeks. Probably not the smart est question to ask. Why was he struggling with his words an actions? That never happened to him. Not anymore.

"The less would be me being a jerk and planting my lips o you, right?" Might as well go for honesty. Clara was the onl person in his life who rated that. He didn't want to violate it.

She blew out a breath. "Um…mostly the being a jerk. You'r a pretty good kisser, it turns out."

"So you didn't mind that?"

"Not as much as I should have." Her words escaped in rush.

"Glad to know I'm not the only one," he said, forcing th words out.

"Not sure it helps anything." She walked ahead of him straying beneath the overhang of a curled roof, her eyes on th murals painted on the walls of the temple.

"Maybe not." He leaned in, pretending to examine the sam image she was.

"So…is there a solution?" She put her hand on the wall tracing the painting of a white elephant with her finger.

He covered her hands with his, his heart pounding, his han shaking like he was a teenage virgin. "Let me see."

He leaned in, his mouth brushing hers. He went slow thi

time, asking the question, as he should have done the first time
he'd kissed her. She didn't move, not into him or away from
him. He angled his head and deepened the kiss and he felt her
soften beneath him, her lips parting beneath his, her breath
catching, sharp and sweet when the tip of his tongue met hers.

He pulled away, his eyes on hers.

She released a breath. "How do you feel?"

"I was going to ask you the same thing."

She looked up. "The roof didn't fall in."

"No," he said, following her gaze. "It didn't."

She leaned into him, her elbow jabbing his side, a shy smile
on her face. "Good to know anyway."

"Glad it comforts you."

She laughed, her cheeks turning pink, betraying the fact that
she wasn't unaffected. "Comfort may not be the right word."

He looked around the teeming common area, at the completely unfamiliar surroundings. And he found he wanted to
pretend that the feelings he was having for Clara were unfamiliar, too.

But he couldn't. Because they had been there, for a long
time, lurking beneath the surface. Ignored. Unwanted. But
there.

"No. Comfort is definitely not the right word."

They'd spent most of the day at the temple, then taken a car
back to Chiang Mai where they'd wandered the streets buying
food from vendors, and watching decorations go up on every
market stall for a festival that was happening in the evening.

Now, with the event coming close, the streets were packed
tight with people, carrying street food, flower arrangements
with candles in the center, talking, laughing. It was dark out,
the sun long gone behind the mountains, but the air was still
thick, warm and fragrant. There was music, noise and movement everywhere. The smell of frying food mixed with the

perfume of flowers and the dry, stale scent of dust clung to the air, filled her senses.

It almost helped block out Zack. But not quite. No matter just how much it filled up her senses, it couldn't erase Zack. The imprint of his kiss. It had been different than the first one. Tender. Achingly sexy.

It had made her want more. Not simply in a sexual way, but in an emotional way. It didn't bear thinking about. Still, she knew she would.

She kept an eye on the food stalls, passing more exotic fare, like anything with six legs or more, for something a bit more vanilla. Maybe food would help keep her mind off things. At least temporarily.

"I definitely don't need this," she said, stopping to buy battered, fried bananas from the nearest food stall.

"But you bought it," he said, breaking a piece off the banana and putting it in his mouth.

"Well, that's because sweets are my area of expertise. You're here for the beans and tea leaves, I'm here for the pairing, right? This is research. It's for work. I need to capture the new and exotic flavor profiles Chiang Mai has to offer," she said, trying to sound official. "Maybe I can write off the calories?"

They dodged a bicycle deliveryman and crossed the busy, bustling street, moving away from the stalls and toward the river that ran through the city. "You don't need to worry about it. You're perfect like you are."

She looked down at the bag of sweets. "You're just saying that."

"I'm not."

She sucked in a sharp breath and looked at the lanterns that were strung from tree to tree, glowing overhead. "We should do this more. At home."

"Eat?"

"No. Go do things. Mostly we work, and sometimes I feed

you at my house, or we watch a movie at yours. Well, we do go
out to lunch sometimes, but on workdays, so it doesn't count."

"We're busy."

"We're workaholics."

Zack frowned and stopped walking. He extended his hand
and took a lock of her hair between his thumb and forefinger,
rubbing it idly. "Is that why you're leaving me?"

She looked up at him. "I'm not leaving you. I'm leaving the
company." And she was counting on that to put some natural
and healthy distance between them. Roasted had brought them
together, and because they got along so well, after spending the
day at work together, half of the time it felt natural to simply
go and have dinner together. Watch bad reality TV together.
Once they weren't involved in the same business it would only
be natural they would drift apart. And with any luck, it would
only feel like she was missing her right arm for a couple of
years.

"What do you need? I'll give it to you."

"You're missing the point, Zack. It's about having something of my own."

"Roasted isn't enough for you? You've been there from the
beginning, more or less. You've helped me make it what it is."

"No. I just bake cupcakes. And there are a lot of people who
can do my job."

"But they aren't you."

She closed her eyes and let the compliment wash over her.
She'd say this for Zack; he gave her more than most anyone
else in her life ever had, including her family. But it was still
just a crumb of what she wanted.

"No," she said, "some of them are even better."

She wove through the crowd to the edge of the waterfront.
People were kneeling down and putting the flower arrangements with their lit candles into the stream. The crowd standing on the other side of the waterfront was lighting candles

inside tall, rice paper lanterns, the orange spreading to the inky night, casting color and light all around.

Zack was behind her, she could sense it without even turning around. "I'm glad we came tonight," she said.

Zack swept his fingers through Clara's hair, moving it over her shoulder, exposing her neck. He didn't normally touch her like that, but tonight, he found he couldn't help himself. Things were tense between them. The kiss at the temple certainly hadn't helped diffuse it.

He wondered if most of the tension had started in the bedroom back in the villa. That moment when they'd both looked at the bed and had that same, illicit thought.

If it had started there, they might be able to finish it there.

Temptation, pure and strong, lit him on fire from the inside out. She turned, and his heart slammed hard against his rib cage, blood rushing south of his belt, every muscle tensing. He could feel the energy change between them, like a wire that had been connecting them, unseen and unfelt for years had suddenly come alive with high-voltage electricity. He knew she felt it, too.

"We broke things, didn't we?" she whispered.

It was like she read his thoughts, which, truly, was nothing new. But inconvenient now, since his thoughts had a lot to do with what it might be like to see her naked.

"Because of the kisses?"

She nodded once. "I can't forget them."

"I can't, either. I'm not sure if I want to."

She took a deep breath. "That's just what I was thinking earlier."

"Was it?"

"Yes. I should want to forget it, we both should. So we can get things back to where they're supposed to be but…"

He leaned down and pressed his lips to hers, soft again. "Do you think we could break it worse than we already have? Or is the damage done?"

"I have no idea."

Everything in him screamed to step back. Because this was an unknown. A move that would affect his life, his daily life, and he couldn't see the way it would end. And that just wasn't how he did things. Not since that night when he'd been sixteen and he'd acted unthinkingly, impulsively, and ruined everything.

He wasn't that person anymore. He'd made sure of it. If he didn't walk away from Clara now, from the temptation she presented, if he didn't plan it out and look at all the angles, he was opening them both up to potential fallout.

He stepped forward and kissed her again. Deepening the kiss this time, letting the blood that was roaring in his ears drown out conscious thought.

Clara knew she should stop this. Stop the madness before it went too far. It already had gone too far. It had gone too far the moment she agreed to come. Because the desire for this, for the week to turn into this, had been there. Of course, she'd never imagined that Zack would—could—want her.

The breaking of things wasn't just down to the kiss. It was the day at the river, the intense moment on the balcony. The fact that she'd realized she was deeply, madly, irrevocably in love with a man who was just supposed to be her friend.

He kissed the tip of her nose, then her cheeks. "Zack," she whispered.

"Clara."

"Are we trying to see if we can break things worse?"

"Actually, I'm not thinking at all. Not about anything beyond what I feel right now."

"What is it you feel?" she asked, echoing what she'd said after they'd kissed.

"I want you."

She hesitated, her heart squeezing tight. "Do you want me? Or do you want to have sex?"

He looked at her for a long time, the glow of flames across

the river reflected in his eyes. "I want you, Clara Davis. I have never slept with one woman when I wanted another one, and I would never start the practice with you. When I have you, I won't be thinking of anyone else. I'll only have room for you."

His words trickled through her, balm on her soul. Exactly the right words.

The real question was, did she want to accept a physical relationship when it was only part of what she wanted?

You only have part of what you want now. A very small part

"Just for tonight," she said, hating that she had to say it but knowing she did. Because she knew for certain that there could be no romantic future for them. She loved him, she was certain of it now. She had for a long time, possibly for most of the seven years she'd known him. It had been a slow thing working its way into her system bit by bit. With every smile, every touch.

And he didn't love her. Looking at him now, the light in his eyes, that wasn't anything deeper than lust. But if that was all she could have, she would take that. Right now, she would take it, and she wouldn't think about the wisdom of it, or the consequences.

Because she was staring hard into a Zack-free future, and she would rather have all of him tonight, and carry the memory with her, than be nothing more than his trusty sidekick forever, standing by watching while he married another woman. Watching him make a life with someone else, someone he didn't even love, while her heart splintered into tiny pieces with every beat.

"One night," she repeated. "Here. Away from reality. Away from work and home. Because… We can't keep going on like this. It can't be healthy."

The people around them started cheering and she looked around them, saw the paper lanterns start to rise up above them, filling the air with thousands of floating, ethereal lights.

"Just one night," he said, his voice rough. "One night to explore this." He touched her cheek. "To satisfy us both. Is that really what you want?"

"I want you. So much."

He kissed her without preliminaries this time, her body pressed against hers, his erection thick and hard against her stomach as his mouth teased and tormented her in the most delicious way. She wrapped her arms around his neck and gave herself up to the heat coursing between them. When they parted she felt like she was floating up with the lanterns.

One night. The proposition made her heart ache, and pound faster. It excited her and terrified her. She didn't know what she was thinking. But one thing she did know: he wanted her. He wasn't faking the physical reaction she'd felt pressed against her.

The very thought of Zack, perfect, sexy Zack wanting her, was intoxicating. Empowering. She wanted to revel in the feeling. One night. To find out if her fantasies were all she'd built them up to be. One night to have the man of her dreams.

One night to make a memory that she would carry with her for the rest of her life.

CHAPTER SEVEN

BACK at the villa, Clara started to question some of the bravado she'd felt down in the city. It was one thing to know, for a moment, in public, fully dressed, that Zack was attracted to her. It was another to suddenly forget a lifetime's insecurity. To wonder if it would be Hannah on his mind.

They were in the bedroom. And her eyes were fixed on the bed, that invitation to decadence, to passion unlike anything she'd ever known. With the man she loved.

She sucked in a breath. She wasn't going to worry about how attracted he was to her, where she ranked with his other lovers. This night was for her. It was the culmination of every fantasy, every longing she'd had since Zack had walked into the bakery she worked at seven years ago and offered her a job.

He pulled her to him and kissed her. Hungry. Wild. She felt it, too, an uncontrollable, uncivilized need that had no place anywhere else in her life. No one had ever made her feel like this. No one had ever made her want to forget every convention, every rule, and just follow her body's most untamed needs.

But Zack did.

"I want you," she said, her voice breaking as they parted. She had to say it. Because it had been building in her for so long and now she felt like she was going to burst with it.

"I want you, too. I've thought of this before," Zack said, unbuttoning his shirt as he spoke, revealing that gorgeous, toned chest. "Of what it might be like to see you."

"To…to see me?"

"Naked," he said.

"You have?" she asked, her voice trembling now, because she'd hoped, maybe naively, that he would want the lights off. She didn't want him to see her. Touch, yes. Taste, sure. But see?

"Of course I have. I've tried not to think about it too hard. Because you work for me. Because you're my friend. And it's not good to picture friends or employees naked. In my life, everything has a place, and yours was never supposed to be in my bed. And I was never supposed to imagine you naked. But I have anyway sometimes."

"I have a hard time believing that."

"Why?" He shrugged his shirt off and let it fall to the floor, then his hands went to his belt and her breath stuck in her throat.

"Because I'm…average."

He chuckled, his hands freezing on the belt buckle. "Damn your mother for making you believe that garbage." He took a step toward her and put his hand on her cheek, his thumb sliding gently across her face. "You are exquisite. You have such perfect skin. Smooth. Soft. And your body." He put his other hand on her waist. "I thought of you last night. Of this. Of how beautiful you would look."

Reflexively she pulled back slightly.

"What?" he asked.

"I'm not… What was Hannah? A size two? I'm…I'm not a size two."

"Beauty isn't a size. I don't care what the number on the tag of your dresses says. I don't care what your sister looked like, or what your mother thought you should look like. I know what I see. You have the kind of curves other women envy."

He reached around and caught the tab on her summer dress with his thumb and forefinger and tugged it down partway.

Her hands shook, her body trembling inside and out. She felt like she was back beneath the spotlight again. Just waiting to have all of her flaws put out there for everyone to ridicule.

"Wait," she said.

His hands stilled. "I don't know if I can."

"Please. Can were turn the lights off?"

There was only one lamp on. It wasn't terribly bright in the room, but she still felt exposed already, with the zipper barely open across the top part of her back. She felt awkward. Unexceptional. Especially faced with all of Zack's perfection. He didn't have an ounce of spare flesh, every muscle perfectly defined as though he were carved from granite.

He put his hands on her hips and pulled her to him. She could feel his erection again, hard and hot against her. "You are perfect." He moved his hands around to her back, to her bottom, cupping her. She gasped. She'd never been this intimate with a man. She wondered if she should be more or less nervous that it was Zack she was finally taking the step with.

No one had seen her naked, not since she was in diapers. She didn't even change in public locker rooms. She would hide in bathroom stalls, needing the coverage of four walls and a door. And Zack wanted...

"Please."

"Let me see you first." Her eyes met his and she drew in an unsteady breath. "It's me, Clara."

"I know," she said.

"When you're ready."

She took a breath and turned away from him, catching the zipper and tugging it down the rest of the way, letting her dress fall to the floor. Zack moved behind her, his arm curving around her, his palm pressed flat against her stomach.

He swept her hair to the side and pressed a kiss to her neck. "As I said. Perfection."

He turned her slowly, keeping his arms around her, holding her against him, his hard body acting as a shield. Cocooned in his arms, she didn't feel quite so naked.

She looked at his eyes, so familiar, yet different at the same time. Zack's eyes, filled with a kind of raw lust she'd never had directed at her before. Not by him, not by any man. The enormity of the moment hit her then. She was about to be with Zack. About to make love to him.

She started shaking then, her hands, her entire body, from the inside out. He wrapped his arms around her and held her against him. "Are you okay?"

"Yes," she said, her voice shaking. "I'm okay."

"Why are you shaking?" She couldn't answer. "Be honest," he said.

"Because it's you."

He tilted his head to the side and kissed her. She closed her eyes determined to do nothing more than luxuriate in the moment. The heat of his mouth, the slide of his tongue. She was going to believe, in this moment, that she could be the woman he wanted.

He reached around and unhooked her bra. He pulled back from her for a moment so he could remove it the rest of the way, leaving her exposed to his hungry gaze. "I said you were perfection, but I didn't know just how true that was."

A hot flush spread over her entire body, heating her. Embarrassment battling with desire.

He cupped her breasts, sliding his thumbs over her nipples. And that was when desire won. She shook with pleasure, her stomach tightening, her internal muscles pulsing, her body ready, demanding, more of him. Demanding climax. She was close to finding it, with just the touch of his hands. Maybe it was because in her mind she had found pleasure with him so many times, in reality, it was effortless to get close to the peak.

A hoarse sound caught in her throat and she felt herself go over the edge. She gripped his forearms, her fingernails digging into his flesh. As soon as the numbing pleasure washed away, embarrassment crashed in on her. She couldn't believe she'd come so quickly. Telling in so many ways. She hadn't realized just how impossible it would be to keep secrets when they were like this, hadn't realized just how intimate it would be.

"I…" She looked at his face, and his expression stole the words from her lips. A look of pure masculine satisfaction, combined with total arousal. The embarrassment dissolved. She reached forward and put her hands on his belt buckle, undoing it and pulling his belt from the loops.

He pulled her to him again, kissing her like a starving man. She reached between them and undid the closure on his pants, pushing them down his hips, along with his underwear. She felt his bare flesh against her for the first time, so impossibly hot and hard.

She wrapped her fingers around him and squeezed. She wasn't sure why, only that she wanted to. That she wanted to touch him, taste him, everywhere. To make him feel half of what he'd made her feel.

So this would be about him, a little bit. But mostly, she was just going to enjoy having the man she'd dreamed of having for so long, completely available to her. For tonight, he was hers.

He put his hand on her thigh and pulled her leg up over his hip. She held on to his shoulders and he curled his fingers around her other thigh, lifting her off the ground and walking her to the bed, up the step, laying her down on the soft mattress, his body over hers, making her feel small. Feminine. Beautiful.

He dipped his head and slid the tip of his tongue around the edge of one of her nipples. She arched into him and he sucked the tip into his mouth, his eyes never leaving hers.

"You're so sensitive there," he said, his voice sounding different, strained. "I love it."

"I like it, too," she said. It was the first time she'd ever really liked her body.

He tugged her panties down her thighs and she helped kick them off of the bed. "I stand by what I said earlier. Perfection." He kissed her ribs, just beneath her breasts, down to her belly button. "Designed to take pleasure. For me to give you pleasure. Exquisite." He moved lower, his lips teasing the tender skin. He parted her thighs and slid his tongue over her clitoris. White heat shot through her body, a deep, intense pleasure tightening her muscles. She gripped the sheets, trying to hold herself to the bed.

He slid one finger inside her and she thought she might explode. Then another finger joined the first and a slight stinging sensation cut through the pleasure. She held her breath for a moment and waited for it to fade. It would. She knew it would. And all the better if he took care of it this way.

He worked his fingers in and out of her body, each time, the discomfort lessened. And he didn't seem to notice. Which was fine by her.

"I can't wait anymore," he said, his voice rough, broken.

"I don't think I can wait, either."

He moved up so that the head of his erection was testing the entrance to her body, his arms bracketing hers, his biceps trembling slightly. He was as undone as she was. It was such a wonderful, incredible feeling. It made her truly believe that she was beautiful.

He pushed into her partway then pulled out completely, swearing sharply.

"What?" she asked, hoping it had nothing to do with her virginity. Because she couldn't stop. Not now.

"Condoms," he said, his hands unsteady as he opened the drawer to the bedside table. He opened the box and pulled out a packet, getting the condom out and rolling it on to his length quickly.

"Oh. Good." She didn't know why she hadn't thought of

it. She should have. But there were so many things filling her head. So many emotions. She'd almost forgotten the most important thing.

Then he was back, poised over her, ready to enter her.

He slid back in as far as he'd already been, then pressed in the rest of the way. It was tight, but it wasn't painful, the evidence of her virginity likely dealt with earlier.

He flexed his hips, his pelvis pressing against her clitoris at exactly the right angle, the sensation of him being inside her as her muscles clenched tight around him so incredible she couldn't stop the moan of pleasure from escaping her lips.

She gripped his tight, muscular butt, so much more perfect than she'd even imagined. Everything so much more perfect than she'd imagined.

She wrapped her legs around his calves and held him to her, moving in rhythm with his thrusts, the pleasure building low in her stomach, emotion swelling in her chest, threatening to overflow. It came to a head, pushing her until she was certain that unless she found release, she would break apart into tiny little pieces beneath the weight of the pressure inside of her.

Then she was falling apart, splintering, release, pleasure, love, pouring through the cracks, filling her, washing through her. She dug her fingernails into his back, squeezing her eyes closed tight. She didn't even try to stop the sharp cry that was climbing her throat, couldn't feel embarrassed that she was arching and moving against him with no control at all.

Because he was right with her, his entire body trembling, his fist gripping the comforter by her head, a low, intense growl rumbling in his chest as he found his own release.

He lay above her, his breathing harsh, his heart pounding so hard she could hear it. And she was pretty sure he could hear hers, too.

"Wow," she said.

He moved to the side, withdrawing from her body, one arm resting on her body. He was watching her closely, like he wanted to ask her something. Or like he thought he should but didn't want to.

"You've never been careful about what you said to me before," she said. "Don't start now."

He huffed a laugh. "Clara..."

"Actually I changed my mind," she said. "We have one night. Why talk about anything?"

Something in his expression changed, hardened. "I think that's a good idea." He rolled to his side and stood up. "I'll be back in a minute."

He went into the bathroom and came back out a moment later.

"What do you propose we do, if we aren't going to talk?"

She got up on her knees and went to the edge of the bed, wrapping her arms around his neck, uncharacteristic boldness surging through her. "I'm sure we can think of a few things."

This was her night to have all of the man she loved. And she wasn't going to miss out on a single experience.

Morning came too quickly, light breaking through the gauzy curtain that surrounded the bed, bringing reality in with the sunbeams.

She didn't want the night to end. She didn't want to face reality. She'd felt like a princess last night; beautiful, desired. She'd felt like her dream was in her grasp. And this morning she felt like she'd turned back into a pumpkin. Reality sucked.

She looked at the man sleeping next to her, the only man she'd ever really wanted. The only man she'd ever loved.

And today, she would have to get up and forget that last night had happened. She would have to consign it to the "perfect memories" bin along with other things she pulled out when she was feeling lonely, or when things weren't going well.

The thought made her whole body hurt.

"I arranged to have the plane leave in an hour or so," he said, his eyes still closed.

"Okay," she said, swallowing thickly and sliding out of the bed, clutching the sheet tightly to her breasts, desperate to cover herself now, in the light of day. It was one thing to feel sexy, to be all right with her nudity when he was looking at her like he was starving and she was a delicacy. A lot less easy when he seemed…uninterested.

"I'm going to take a shower real quick."

He made a noise that might have been a form of consent, but she didn't ask for confirmation before beating a hasty retreat to the bathroom. She turned the water on and sat on the closed toilet lid, letting the tears fall down her cheeks, hoping the sound of the water hitting the tile would drown out the sound of her sobs.

Zack sat up, a curse on his lips. Last night…last night had been an aberration. A hot, amazing aberration, maybe, but it could never happen again. He had been careless. He'd nearly forgotten to use a condom. And she'd been a virgin.

If he'd thought about it, if he'd thought at all, he would have guessed that. He knew her well enough to have picked up on how nervous she was, to understand what that meant. He also knew her well enough to know she wasn't really a one-night-stand woman. She was sensitive, emotional. Sweet.

His stomach twisted, nausea overtaking him, spreading through his limbs. She probably wasn't on birth control, and there was a possibility that in that moment, when he'd been inside of her without protection, that he'd made a very big mistake.

No, he knew he'd made a mistake. He hit his fist on the top of the nightstand and stood, stalking through the room collecting his clothes. Had he learned nothing? Was he as stupid now as he'd been fourteen years ago?

His heart froze for a moment, the events of what sometimes felt like a past life, playing through his head from start to finish. Like a horror film he couldn't pause.

No. He'd worked way too hard to leave that person behind. That boy, who had been so irresponsible. Who had caused so much damage.

Last night he'd lost control. With Clara, of all people. She shouldn't have tempted him like that. But she had. She'd made him shake like *he* was the virgin.

It couldn't happen again. It wouldn't. He might have lost his control for a moment, but he wouldn't do it again.

Clara appeared a few moments later, her face scrubbed fresh and pink, her hair wet and wavy. She was dressed, a fitted T-shirt and jeans meaningless now since he'd already seen her naked and his mind was doing a very good job of envisioning her as she'd been last night.

All pale skin and soft curves. Pure perfection. Better than he'd ever imagined.

"Hey," she said, trying to smile and not quite managing it.

"Are you all right?" he asked. He'd never slept with a virgin before, but that was only part of the foreign, first-time feeling he was dealing with. The other part of that was because it was Clara. And the rest was because of his carelessness.

Carelessness that had to be addressed.

"I'm fine," she said.

"Are you on birth control?" he asked.

She narrowed her eyes. "No."

He tried to get a handle on the gnawing panic in his gut. Condoms were reliable. He knew that. But there was the matter of his impatience, of his entering her, even briefly, without protection. He swore. "Why not?"

"What?" She crossed her arms beneath her breasts. "I'm sorry, was I supposed to start taking the pill just in case you invited me on your honeymoon and we hooked up? I was a virgin, you jackass."

"I know," he shouted, not sure why he was shouting, only that his blood was pumping too fast through his veins and his heart was threatening to thunder out of his chest. "I know," he said again, softer this time.

"You used a condom," she said, her cheeks flushing pink.

"Yes, I did, eventually. There's a chance that kind of care-lessness could have gotten you pregnant. It's not a big chance, but there is a chance."

"I…I seriously doubt that I'm pregnant. Well, obviously I'm not pregnant yet since things take a while to travel and…well, that's high-school health, you know all that."

"But there's a chance. I'm usually more careful."

"Zack, I think you're overreacting."

"Is that what you think, Clara?" he asked, his voice deadly calm. "You think I'm overreacting because you think it can't happen. But then, you've never been pregnant, obviously. And I have gotten a woman pregnant, so I think I might be a bit more in touch with that reality than you are. Do you know what it's like? To know that everything in your life is going to have to change because for one moment you were so utterly selfish and consumed with one moment of pleasure that you didn't think about anything else?"

Clara's heart was in her throat. She felt like she couldn't breathe. It was like a shield had been torn away from Zack, like his armor had dissolved, crumbled around his feet, leaving nothing but the man he was beneath his facade. A facade she hadn't realized was there.

This was the man she'd seen glimpses of. The reason for the darkness that she saw in his eyes sometimes. And she was afraid to hear the rest. But she had to.

His chest rose and fell sharply. "I was sixteen. And I was more interested in getting some than thinking about using a condom. Turns out you can get someone pregnant after just one time, regardless of the idiot rumors floating around the high school saying otherwise."

She didn't ask him what happened. She didn't interrupt the break. She just let his silence fill the room, and she felt his ain. Felt it in her, through her. She didn't have to know what happened to know that it was bad. Devastating. To know that knowing it was going to change her. The way it had changed Zack.

"I didn't want a baby, but we were having one. She wanted it. I didn't want him," he said. "But I got a job so that I could pay for the doctor bills. So I could help her raise him. Because at least I knew that I should do the right thing." A muscle in his jaw jerked. "He came too early. And by the time I realized how badly I did want him, it was too late. By the time I realized that a baby can very quickly mean everything in the world to you, he was gone."

She tried to hold back the sob that was rising inside her. His face was blank now, void of emotion, flat. Like he was reading a story in a newspaper, not telling her about his life.

"Another reason Hannah was so perfect for me," he said. "She didn't want kids."

"You don't... You don't want kids?"

"I had one, Clara. I would never...I will never put myself through something like that again. I nearly died with him. I don't make the same mistakes twice. I'm always careful now."

Except last night, he wasn't as careful as he usually was, obviously. And she wasn't sure how she felt about that. Or what it might mean. And right now, she wished they had never slept together. Because she wanted to comfort him as a friend. To tell him how much her heart ached for him. But she wasn't sure if it was her place now. She wasn't sure what she was supposed to do. What he expected. What he would allow.

Because now she saw just how much he had always hidden from her. She saw a stranger. She wondered if it was even possible that this man, hard and angry, was the same man she'd seen every day for the past seven years.

"How did you...how did you cope with it?"

"I don't need to talk about it, Clara. I don't talk about it, ever. This isn't an invitation for you to psychoanalyze me. But now you know why I insist on being careful. That's the importan part of the story. And you'll tell me, if you're pregnant."

"I'll let you know," she said. "But I'm sure everything wil be fine."

He turned away from her and shrugged his shirt on.

"Everything will be fine," she repeated. That assurance wa just for her. And she wasn't certain she believed it.

CHAPTER EIGHT

THE plane ride back to San Francisco was a study in torture. Zack was hardly speaking to her and she felt battered from the inside out. Her body was a little bit sore from her first time, and her heart felt like it had been wrung out and left to dry.

Zack was acting overly composed. His focus on work, not on her. Not on the revelation that had passed between them, both in bed and out.

She didn't feel like the same person. She felt changed. She wasn't sure if Zack was the same person, either. Or maybe he was; maybe it was just that she saw him better now.

"I think I'll probably take a couple days off," she said, looking over at Zack who was engrossed in his laptop screen. "Recover. From the jet lag."

"Fine."

The chill in his response made her shiver. "And I'm thinking of buying a pony."

"You don't have anywhere to keep one," he said drily, still not looking up.

"Just a small one. For the rooftop garden."

He did look up this time. "Your neighbors would complain."

"I don't like my neighbors." That earned her a slight smile. "So, what's the plan when we get back to civilization?"

"With any luck, things can go back to normal."

Two questions flitted through her mind. Luck for who? And what's normal? She didn't voice either of them. "Okay."

"I still need you there, at Roasted, until Amudee signs off on the deal."

"Right." She looked down at her hand. The ring was still there. "You'll want this back, I assume." She pulled the ring off and got up, walking over to his seat and depositing it on the desk in front of him. "Since we won't need it."

A relief. Wearing another woman's ring made her feel weighted down.

"No. We won't." His eyes met hers and held. She felt heat prickle down her arms, her nipples tightening as a flash of arousal hit her.

"Great. I'll um…I'm going to try to sleep."

As she drifted off in the plane's bedroom, she tried not to be disappointed that Zack didn't join her.

"Amudee is coming here."

Clara looked up and saw Zack. For the first time since they'd landed in San Francisco three days earlier. She'd taken a couple of days to get over her jet lag, and had sneaked around the office yesterday like a cat burglar, trying to get work done without encountering him.

Because ultimately, avoiding him was simply easier than trying to juggle all the emotions she felt when she saw him. Cowardly? Yes, yes, it was. But she felt a bit yellow-bellied after all that had happened between them, and she was wallowing in it.

"What?"

"He's coming here to see how we run our operation. He wants to talk to employees, to see where we work. If we truly do conduct business in an ethical manner."

Zack reached into his pocket and took out an overly familiar velvet box. He set it on the edge of her desk, his expression

grim. "And now it continues. And every single person work-
ng in the this office has to believe it, too."

"Zack this can't... It has to end."

"It will. After. And you can take as much money as you
need for a start-up. You can have my blessing, hell, you can
have free Roasted coffee for the first five years. But I want
his deal to go through."

"Ironic that you're trying to convince him of your business
ethics by using a lie," she said, annoyance spiking inside her.

"Odd that it's necessary, too, don't you think?"

"He's a nice man."

"And a romantic, it seems. He loves you. He wants to make
sure he sees us together as a couple again while he's here."

"Tangled web," she snapped, putting her pencil down on
the desk.

"Isn't it?"

The air between them seemed to crackle, everything slowing for a moment, the silence so tense and brittle she was certain she could splinter it into tiny pieces if she spoke.

"Put it on," he said, looking at the ring.

"I gave it back," she said tightly.

"Clara, I need you to do this for me."

She fought the urge to make a rude gesture with a different finger than the one meant for a ring and grabbed the box,
opened the lid and slid the ring on. "There."

"Come on."

"What?"

"We have to make an announcement."

"Zack..."

"We're going to see this through, right? Then you can leave.
Whatever you need to do, you can go do it, but finish this with
me."

"Fine." She stood up and rounded the desk, he wrapped his
arm around her waist and drew her to him. Heat exploded in

her, stronger than she remembered, more arousing than any thing had a right to be.

Instantly she was assaulted by images of their night together His mouth, his hands, the way it had felt when he was over her in her. It was torture. She clenched her hands into fists and the heavy ring band bit into her fingers.

There was a small group of employees who worked on he floor, their desks clustered in the center of the room. Roasted' office had a social atmosphere, which Zack had always believe made for optimum creativity. Because Zack was a great boss the kind who made everyone feel appreciated, all the time.

And he never, ever showed the dark, tortured side of him self she'd seen in Chiang Mai. He never showed the intense sexual side of himself, either. But she'd seen it. She'd felt it.

"Clara and I have an announcement to make."

Ten heads instantly popped up, eyes trained on her and Zack. Her heart started pounding, her palms sweating. It wa one thing to lie to a man she'd never met before. A thing sh hated. But it was really quite another to lie to people she worke with every day. People who she considered her friends.

"We're getting married," he said.

"Pay up." Cynthia, a woman with gray hair and pronounce smile lines turned to Jess, a twenty-something computer whi who did their online marketing.

Jess swore and took his wallet out.

"What is this?" Clara asked.

"Congratulations," Cynthia said, beaming. "We had bet placed on this. I bet you would get married. Most everyon changed sides when Mr. Parsons got engaged to someone else But I held out. And now I'm collecting."

"Unbelievable," Clara muttered. She wasn't sure how sh felt about this revelation, either. A little bit flattered that peo ple believed it was possible.

"Clearly I'm not giving people enough work to do," Zack sai

"Kiss her!" This from Jess, who undoubtedly considered it a consolation prize.

Everything inside Clara seized up, her muscles locking tight. Zack looked down at her, his fingers brushing her jaw. He dipped his head and kissed her. A perfectly appropriate kiss to give her in front of his employees. Nothing scandalous or overly sexual. But it grabbed hold of her world and shook it completely. Shook her.

When he lifted his head there was a smattering of applause. "Feel free to spread the news," Zack said, lacing his fingers through hers and leading her toward his office.

He closed the door tightly behind him, taking long strides to the far window that overlooked the bay, his back turned to her.

"Good show," she said icily.

He looked over his shoulder. "You could have been a little less stiff," he said.

"You…" She strode across the room, embracing the anger, unrest and desire that was rioting through her. "You…" She grabbed the lapels of his jacket and stretched up onto her toes, kissing him with every last ounce of passion and frustration that she felt.

He locked his arm around her waist and drew her up tight against his body, his erection hard and hot against her. He spun them around and backed her against the wall, pressing her against the hard surface, his lips hungry as he tasted her, feasted on her.

She wrapped her arms around him, sifted her fingers through his thick brown hair, holding him to her as she returned each stroke and thrust of his tongue. The days of not touching him, thinking of him and denying herself the pleasure of even seeing in him, crashed in on her, fueled her desperation.

She growled in frustration, needing more, faster. Now. She pushed his jacket down his arms and onto the floor, grabbing the knot on his tie and tugging it down as he put his hands on her thighs and pushed the hem of her skirt up. She wrapped one leg around his calf and arched against him.

He tore his mouth away from hers and put his palm flat on the wall behind them, a short, sharp curse punctuated by heavy breaths escaped his lips.

The full horror of what she'd done hit her all at once, like getting a bucket of freezing water dumped in her face. She echoed his choice of swear word and ducked beneath his arm, leaning forward and bracing herself on his desk.

"That shouldn't have happened," she said.

"For more than one reason."

"Why don't you list them?" she said sharply.

"Fine. I'll list them. We said one night. And that kind of kiss doesn't stop at just a kiss. The second reason is that you mean more to me than this," he said.

"Than what?"

"Than an angry make out session against a wall. Than you sneaking around, avoiding me, because we slept together. You mean more to me than sex."

That cut. And maybe it shouldn't have, but she couldn't separate having sex with Zack from the emotions she felt for him. She loved him; sex had been an expression of that. Being joined to him, intimate with him, it had been everything.

But not to him. To him, the sex was separate from the feeling.

"Great. But I apparently don't mean so much to you that you won't use me as a pretend fiancée." Her argument was thin, because frankly, if her feelings for him were platonic, the engagement thing would be nothing big at all.

But her feelings weren't platonic. Not even close.

"Then leave, Clara. If you don't want to do it, don't do it. I'm not holding you hostage. But understand this. I will likely lose the deal with Amudee, and then I won't be able to get the product I need to start the boutique stores. And my search for

an acceptable product will continue. It will cost everyone time
and money, lots of it. That's just stating a fact—it's not emotional blackmail or anything else you might be tempted to accuse me of."

Clara looked at his face, at the familiar planes and angles.
The mouth she'd seen smile so many times, the lips she'd kissed
just now. She knew him differently now than she had a week
ago. She knew his body, she knew his loss. And as hard as it
would have been for her to walk away then, it was impossible
now. Impossible to leave him when she'd promised she would
see this through.

"I'll do it. I'll play the part, I'll keep playing the part, I mean.
But I didn't expect for it to go this far."

"I know. But we had a deal." He probably thought she meant
the farce, but she was thinking of the sex. Or maybe he knew
what she was really talking about and he was content to leave
it ambiguous, just like she was.

"When the ink is dry on the agreement, it can be finished.
You gave me your word," he said.

"That's low, Zack," she said, sucking in a deep breath, trying to make her lungs expand.

"It's true. I've been there for you when you needed me. I
held your hair while you…"

"I know. Food poisoning. Please don't bring that up." It was
right up there with her high-school humiliation. Zack watching her vomit. But he had taken care of her. There hadn't been
anyone else. Truly, they were the key players in each other's
lives. They were there for each other, at work and at home.

"My point is, I've helped you. Help me. I'm asking you as
a friend, not your boss. Your friend."

She gritted her teeth, raw emotion, so intense she couldn't
identify it, flooded her. She swung her arms back and forth,
trying to ease the nervous energy surging through her limbs.
"So when does Mr. Amudee get here?"

"Soon. He'll be in the office tomorrow morning, so it would be good if we came in together."

If they spent the night with each other, it would be even easier for them to commute to Roasted together, but she didn't say that. And she wouldn't. One night, that was all it was supposed to be and that was all it would be. Make-out sessions against the wall would be immediately stricken from record and forgotten. Completely.

"Then I'll see you tomorrow."

"We should probably leave together, too," he said.

"Probably." That would mean an evening waiting around for him to leave. "I'm going to go down to the kitchens and fiddle around with some recipes."

"I'll see you down there."

"See you then." Hopefully a little baking therapy would clear her mind. Because if not, they were both in trouble.

By the time Zack made it down to the kitchen he didn't have a handle on his libido or his temper. He'd figured a couple of hours separation for him and Clara would be a good idea, but it hadn't accomplished anything on his end.

No, he wouldn't feel satisfied until he was in bed with her again. Or just against the wall. That was why he had stopped kissing her, though. He didn't have a condom.

As an adult he hadn't had all that many lovers, mostly because he believed in taking things slowly, and making sure everything was completely safe. He liked for the woman to be on the pill, and he still used condoms, every time.

Already with Clara he'd been lax, skipping steps he hadn't since high school, and then he'd been ready to forgo any sort of protection in his office so that he could be with her again. In her. Because the truth of the matter was, he hadn't stopped thinking about how amazing that night had been since they'd arrived back in California. Not even close.

He'd dreamed of it, or rather, fantasized about it since sleep had eluded him. And when he hadn't been thinking about making love with her, he'd been replaying the moment he'd told her about his son. Over and over again.

He never talked about Jake. Ever. Not since he'd died, still in the hospital he'd never had a chance to leave, only a couple of days old. Sarah had never wanted to talk about it, and they hadn't had a romantic relationship at that point, anyway.

His parents...they had been horrified that their star football-playing son was going to give it all up to raise a child. If anything, they'd been relieved.

That day had changed everything. He'd been nothing more than a spoiled brat. An only child, destined to skate through college on a football scholarship. He'd taken everything, the adoration of the girls at his school, the free passes the teachers had given him, as his due.

But when Jake was born, he'd felt the weight of purpose. And when he died, it hadn't gone away. He hadn't fit anymore. In one blinding, clear moment he saw everything he'd done that was wrong, selfish, careless. He saw how his stupidity had cost everyone so much.

And he'd left. Left who he was. Left everyone he knew. And every day that passed was one day farther away from that awful day in the hospital. That day that had felt like someone reaching into his chest and yanking his emotions out, twisting them, distorting them.

He had never wanted to feel that way again. Ever. Even more importantly, he'd never wanted to have anything unplanned happen ever again. He wanted control. To plan, to consider the cost of his actions. To be in charge of his life.

He wasn't sure why he'd told Clara about it. Although she had asked why the birth-control lapse was such a big deal to him. But then, a few of his girlfriends had wanted to know why he used every method he could think of to prevent pregnancy. It had cost him relationships since the women involved had taken it as a sign of just how much he didn't want to be with them.

And while it was true he hadn't been looking for forever, his reasoning hadn't quite been what they'd assumed. Still, he hadn't felt compelled to tell them the story. Maybe it was because Clara was...Clara. She was the one person who had been in his life with any regularity for the past decade.

And now he'd likely screwed it up by sleeping with her. Or by kissing her. Or maybe he'd screwed it up the moment he'd asked her to play fiancée and go on his honeymoon.

He pushed open the stainless-steel double doors that led to the baking facility and saw Clara, bending down and looking in one of the ovens.

He took the opportunity to enjoy the view, the way her skirt hugged the round curve of her butt. It was a crime that she'd been made to feel insecure about those curves. He flashed back to the heady moments in his office, when he'd had her skirt pushed up around her hips, when he'd been ready to...

She straightened and turned, her brown eyes widening. "Oh! I didn't know you were here."

"Just walked in. What did you make me?"

"I think you'll like them. I have some cooling. I'm going to pass them out at lunch hour tomorrow."

"No walnuts?"

"None. They're Orange Cream. Don't look at me like that, they'll be good." She handed him a vaguely orange cupcake with white frosting, coated in bright orange sugar crystals.

"It has orange zest in the cake, and there's a Bavarian cream in the center. And the frosting is buttercream."

"All things I like." He took a bite, relishing the burst of sweet citrus and cream. She really was a genius. She'd hooked him with her cupcake-making skills the first time he'd met her, and he'd known then he had to have her for his company. That with her, his line of baked goods would be a massive success. And they had been.

And now she was leaving him.

"Good," he said, even though now he was having a hard time swallowing the bite.

"See? I told you."

"And I told you you wouldn't be easily replaced. You're the best at what you do."

She smiled, a sort of funny smile that almost made her look sad. "I do bake a mean cupcake. I'm glad you like them."

He wasn't going to ask her what was wrong. Because he wasn't sure if he could fix it, and he was afraid he might be the cause of it. "Ready to go?"

"Yes, ready. Oh, wait." She stopped and moved toward him, her eyes fixed on his mouth. His entire body was hot and hard instantly. Ready for her touch, her kiss. She extended her hand and put her thumb on the corner of his mouth. "You had some frosting there," she said, her tone as sweet as her cupcakes, her eyes filled with a knowing, sexual expression that told him she was tormenting him, and she knew it. It was going to be an interesting few weeks.

CHAPTER NINE

"I'm not going to bite you."

Clara glared at Zack from her position in the passenger side of his sporty little two-seater. She was clinging to the door handle, her shoulder smashed against the window. As much space between them as was humanly possible in the tiny metal cage.

The first words that bubbled up were *well that's a shame*. But she held them back, because she was not going to flirt with him. Was not. And she was going to forget about that lapse in the kitchen when she'd wiped the frosting from his mouth. She hadn't licked it off and that had been her first inclination, so really, her self-control was pretty rock solid.

"I know," she said. Much more innocuous than an invitation to bite her, that was for sure.

"Then stop clinging to the door handle like you're planning on jumping out when there's a lull in traffic."

She laughed, somehow, even though most of her felt anything but amused by the entire situation. "I'm not, I promise." She relaxed her hold on the door.

"Good." They pulled down into the underground parking lot of Roasted and into the spot that was second closest to the elevator. He'd given her the closest spot years ago. Some sort of chivalrous gesture, silly, but at the time she'd loved it.

He put the car in Park and killed the engine, getting out

and closing the door behind him. She watched him straighten his shirt collar through the window. He hated ties. He didn't wear them unless he had to. It was sexier when he didn't, in her opinion. It showed a little bit of his sculpted chest, a bit of dark hair. Of course, it was sexier when he didn't wear a shirt at all.

She felt the door give behind her and she squeaked, tightening her hold on the handle. Zack had opened it, just a bit, and was looking down at her, the expression on his face wicked.

"Are you going to sit in there all day? Because we have a meeting," he said.

"Creep," she said, no venom in her tone.

He winked and darn it all, it made her stomach turn over. "Only during business hours."

She released her hold on the door and he opened it the rest of the way, waiting for her to get out before pushing the up button on the lift. When they got in and the door closed, the easy moment evaporated.

The tension was back, and so thick she could hardly breathe. Judging by the sharp pitch of his chest when he drew in a breath, he felt the same. It made her feel better. Slightly.

"So, when is he coming in?"

"Soon," Zack said, his eyes fixed on the doors.

"Oh."

The elevator stopped and the doors slid open. Clara nearly sagged with relief as she scurried out of the elevator, eager to get back into non-shared air space.

When she and Zack walked into the main reception area the employees milling around, scavenging on last night's baking efforts stopped and clapped for them. She ducked her head and offered a smile and finger wave. She didn't know if Zack made a reciprocal gesture or not. She was far too busy not dying of humiliation.

The gleaming, golden elevator doors that would take them

up to their offices were just up ahead. She made a dash for it, and Zack got in behind her, the doors sliding closed.

"So many elevators," she said.

"Is that a problem?"

"Not at all," she said.

Two interminable minutes later they were on the floor that housed both of their offices. "I have work to do," she said, heading toward her own office. A little sanctuary would not go amiss.

"No time, Amudee is in the building. My office."

He put his hand on the small of her back and directed her into his office, closing the door behind them. A horrible, hot, tantalizing sense of déjà vu hit her. Their eyes clashed and held, his all steel heat and temptation. He took a step toward her just as the intercom on his desk phone went on.

"Mr. Parsons? Mr. Amudee is here to see you."

Zack leaned back and punched a button on the phone. "Send him in."

She wished she were relieved. She wasn't. She was just disappointed that she hadn't gotten to experience the conclusion of Zack's step forward. Of what he might have intended to do.

Zack's office door opened and the reason for their charade walked in, looking as personable and cheerful as ever, the lines by his dark eyes deepening as he smiled. "Good to see you again. Zack, I stopped by one of your locations here in the city on my way in, I was very impressed."

"Thank you, Mr. Amudee," Zack said, his charm turned on and dialed up several notches.

She watched Zack work, a sense of awe overtaking her. He was good, and she knew that, but seeing him in action was always incredible. He was smart and he was savvy. And the best part was, he really was a man of ethical business practices.

That, she knew, was the thing that made working with Amudee so important to him. Because he didn't just want to import coffee and tea from any farm. He didn't want to get involved in a share-cropping situation. He didn't want anyone being taken advantage of so that he could turn a profit.

Unfortunately Amudee seemed just as picky about who he did business with. And when money wasn't the be all and end all...you couldn't just throw dollars at it to solve everything. Dollars Zack had. It was the fiancée he'd found himself short of.

She toyed with the ring on her finger, her secondhand ring. The one that had belonged to Hannah. She would be a happy woman the moment she could get it off her finger and keep it off, that was for sure.

"So, dinner tonight, then?" Zack said. "Clara?" he prompted.

"Oh, yes. Tonight. Dinner."

"And as for today, I'd be happy to give you a tour of the corporate office. You can see how we run things here."

Mr. Amudee nodded in approval and started to head out the office door with Zack. "So," she said, "I think I'll go to my office and get some work done then."

"Great." He leaned in and kissed her cheek before walking out of the room.

She knew it was an empty gesture, all part of the show. But it still made her feel like she was floating to her office instead of walking. And no matter how much she tried to tell herself not to think about it, her cheek burned for the rest of the morning.

"What is this?"

When Zack had seen Clara's number flash onto his cellphone screen, he'd heard her sweet hello before he'd even answered. So being greeted by a venomous hiss was an unexpected, unpleasant surprise.

"What is what, Clara? I'm currently battling traffic on North Point so I have no idea what you're talking about."

"This dress. This... Do you even call it a dress? I mean it's short and slinky and I think the neckline is designed to show skin all the way down to a woman's belly button."

"I saw it, and I liked it, so I had my PA send it over."

"I agreed to a lot when I agreed to play fiancée, but I did not," she growled and paused for a moment before continuing, "agree to stuff myself into a gown that has all the give of saran wrap like a Vienna sausage!"

"I like the visual, but your attitude needs work."

"Your head needs work," she shot back.

"Wear the dress." He hung up the phone and tossed it onto the passenger seat before maneuvering his car against the curb in front of Clara's apartment.

He didn't bother to wait for the elevator. He took the stairs two at a time and knocked on her door, beneath the pretty, pink flowery wreath thing she had hung there. A clever ruse to make people think the owner of the apartment was sweetness and light when, at the moment, she was spitting flame and sulfur.

The door jerked open and he met Clara's glittering brown eyes. And then he looked down and all of the blood in his body roared south.

She was right about the dress. A deep scarlet, it would draw the eye of everyone in the restaurant. And while it didn't show her belly button, it did put her amazing cleavage on display. The soft, rounded curves of her breasts were accentuated by the sweetheart neckline, the pleating in the waist showing off just how tiny she was, before her hips flared out, the fabric conforming to that gorgeous, hourglass shape of hers.

"I am not going out in this."

"It's too late for you to change," he said, barely able to force himself to raise his eyes to her face. He had to admit, the dress was counterproductive as when it came to trying to put Clara back into the proper compartment she was meant to be in in his life, he didn't want her to change.

He wanted to look at her in that dress for as long as he could

And then, he wanted to lower the zipper on the back of it and watch it slither down her body. He wanted to see her again, soft, naked and begging him to take her.

"Zack…"

"Do you have something against looking sexy?"

"What? No."

"Then what's the problem? If it honestly offends your modesty in some way, fine, change. But otherwise, you look…"

"Like I'm trying too hard?"

He took a step and she backed away from the door, letting him into the apartment. He shouldn't touch her. Not even an innocent gesture. Because with the thoughts that were running through his brain, nothing could be innocent.

He did anyway, and he ignored the voice in his head telling him to stay in control. He was in control. He could touch her without doing more. He was the master of his body, of his emotions.

He put his finger on her jaw, traced the line of it down her neck, to her exposed collarbone.

"You look effortless. As though bringing men to their knees is something you do every day of the week without breaking a sweat. You look like the kind of woman who can have anyone or anything she wants."

"I…I…well, I don't appreciate you dressing me," she said. "It's demeaning."

"I don't know if it was demeaning, but selfish, perhaps."

"Selfish?"

"Because I'm enjoying looking at you so much."

She bent down and picked up a black shawl from the couch, looping it over her arms before grabbing a black clutch purse from the little side table. "You shouldn't say things like that."

She breezed out the door ahead of him, clearly resigned to wearing the dress.

"Probably not," he said, his tone light.

"But you did anyway," she said, turning to face him.

"I did. There are a lot of things I shouldn't have said or done over the past couple of weeks, and yet, it seems I've said and done them all."

"I haven't," she said, turning away from him again and heading down the stairs, eager to avoid being in an elevator with him, he imagined.

"Oh, really?"

"Mmm. I have been virtuous. I've wanted to say and do many things in the past week that I haven't."

"Why do I feel disappointed by that news?"

"I don't know. You shouldn't be," she said, her stilettos clicking and echoing in the stairwell. "You should be thankful." She pushed open the exterior door and they both walked out into the cool evening air.

"I find I'm not."

"I can't help you there."

Something hot and reckless sparked in him. She must have noticed because she backed away from him until she bumped against his car. That was a picture, Clara, in scarlet silk, leaning against his black sports car. The fantasies that were rolling through his mind should be illegal.

"I wish you could," he said, taking a step toward her.

She shook her head. "There's no help for either of us."

"I'm starting to think that might be true."

He wanted to kiss the red off her lips. He wanted to take her back upstairs and do something about the unbearable ache that had settled in his body more than a week ago and hadn't released him since.

"Let's go. We have a dinner date," he said, his voice curt, harsher than he'd intended.

She nodded and went around to the passenger side and he let out a long, slow breath, trying to ease the tension in his body.

Being with her once hadn't helped at all. One night hadn't been enough.

But there wouldn't be another night. There would be no point to it.

CHAPTER TEN

"THANK you for doing that," Zack said, once they were back in the car and away from the presence of the man they were putting on the show for.

Dinner had gone well, and it looked like everything was on track for Mr. Amudee to sign the exclusive deal with Roasted. It turned out he was thrilled that Zack was marrying a woman he worked with, a woman who understood and shared his passion for the business. It was one of the things, they'd found out over dessert, that had placed Zack slightly ahead of his rival at Sand Dollar. Because Amudee felt Zack and Clara were working together, and the owner of the other coffee-shop chain would be spending more time away from his family.

So, just another way their farce had helped. She still didn't feel good about it.

"You're welcome."

"I'm serious. I should have thanked you before."

"Gourmet dinner after a week in Thailand? I'm not all that put out by it." A big lie, and they both knew it.

"I'm sorry about earlier," she said. "About freaking out about the dress."

"Not a big deal."

Tension hung thick in the air between them. She just felt… restless and needy. The kiss, the one they'd shared in his office, still burning her lips.

It was only supposed to be the one time. Just once. In Chiang Mai, not here.

"I really liked my...salmon," she said. It was lame but she didn't want to leave Zack yet. Didn't want to get into her cold, empty bed and slowly die, crushed beneath the weight of her sexual frustration.

A dramatic interpretation of what would actually happen, but she felt dramatic.

"You didn't have salmon."

"I didn't?" she asked.

"No. You had...I think you had chicken."

"Oh."

The only thing she could remember about dinner was trying not to melt every time Zack looked in her direction.

"So...I guess I'll see you tomorrow, then," she said slowly, reaching for the door handle.

"Wait." She froze. "I have a nice vintage wine at my house. I've been meaning to have you come and try it," he said.

She moved away from the car door, letting her back rest against the seat again. "Really?"

"Yes. Do you want... You could come over and have some?"

Zack could have cut his own tongue out. As pickup lines went, it was a clumsy one. He shouldn't be handing her pickup lines at all, clumsy or otherwise. They'd committed to only sleeping together one time, and the fact that he was so turned on his entire body had broken out into a cold sweat shouldn't change that. Once should have been enough. But it wasn't.

He watched her face, watched her eyes get round, her mouth dropping open. As if she'd just realized what the hidden question was.

It was hidden. If she said no, they could both pretend that it wasn't another night he was after. They could brush it under the rug. Simple.

"Now?" she asked.

He nodded once.

"I don't…" She looked at her apartment building for a moment, her hands folded in her lap, toying with the fabric of her skirt, twisting it. "I'd love some wine."

"Good."

He turned the key over and the engine purred as he pulled away from the curb and headed out of the city, toward the waterfront.

Zack's house was a marvel, grand and pristine, massive windows with views the bay and the Golden Gate Bridge. It was a physical testament to the wealth he'd accumulated since he started his business. How much he had done. How far he had come on his own.

Every time she came over, she stopped and looked at the gorgeous, stained-glass skylight in the entryway. Not this time, though. This time, she didn't have energy to focus on anything beyond Zack and the desire that was roaring through her body. Desire that was finally going to be satisfied tonight.

A week without him, without him inside of her body, had been far too long of a wait.

He closed the door behind them and stood still, poised near the door. He looked like a predator lying in wait. The thought of it, of being the object of his desire, heated her from the inside out.

When he moved, it was quick and fluid. He wrapped his arms around her, kissing her deep and long, his tongue stroking against hers, the evidence of his arousal hard and tempting against her body.

"You're sure?"

"No," she said.

"I'm not, either."

"But I want to."

"Me, too. You know where the bedroom is," he said.

"I do. But I haven't spent that much time in it."

"You'll be lucky if I let you out of it tonight," he said, his

oice a low growl. Feral and uncontrolled. It sent a shiver of
ure need all the way down to her toes.

It was crazy. Stupid crazy and not at all what they'd agreed
o.

Just one more time. One more night.

"I don't mind."

She walked ahead of him, to the winding staircase that led
up to his room. She heard him following behind her as she
walked up the stairs, and she knew the action was making her
dress ride up, made it hug the curve of her bottom, and barely
covered it at all.

He grabbed her arm and turned her to him. He was on the
step below her, which, with her heels, made them close to the
same height. He put his hand on her lower back and pressed
her to him, kissing her again, his mouth hot and hungry on
hers.

She cupped his face, his stubble rough on her fingertips, a
potent, sexy reminder of his masculinity. He reached up and
took her hands, lacing his fingers through hers and backing
her against the wall as he stepped up onto the stair she was on.

He pressed his body against hers, hard and long, perfectly
muscular. She started working the buttons on his shirt, pop-
ing a few of them off in her haste to get him undressed. He
elped with the sleeve cuffs and tossed the shirt down to the
ottom of the stairs.

"Oh, yes," she breathed, running her hands over his bare
hest, the crisp hair tickling her palms. "You're so hot."

He chuckled. "I could say the same." He gripped the zip-
er tab of her dress and tugged it down, letting her dress fall
ff her body. She hardly had time to think about it, to worry
bout how she looked to him.

She kicked the dress down to the next stair, still wearing
er heels, a strapless bra and a pair of underwear that may as
ell not exist for all that they covered.

But tonight, she really did feel sexy. She didn't feel the need to cover herself, to hide anything. And she really didn't want him hiding anything. She made quick work of his slacks, pushing them down his muscular thighs, her body heating when she looked at him, dressed in nothing more than a pair of tight black boxer briefs that revealed the outline of his erection in tantalizing detail.

She put her hand on him, sliding her palm over his cloth covered length, reveling in his harsh, indrawn breath.

"Do you know how many times I thought of you?" she asked, the question requiring a whole lot of boldness she hadn't realized she possessed. "Of touching you. Having my way with you. You've kept me up a lot of nights, Zack. Imagining what it would be like if you kissed me."

"You thought of me?" he asked, his words rough.

"I did."

He didn't have to ask why she hadn't acted on it. Because what would the point have been? They didn't want the same things. He wanted a loveless marriage, no family. She wanted more. There was still no point to this. No point beyond trying to satisfy the sexual hunger that was burning between them.

And the burning hope in her that she couldn't quite snuff out that wondered if he could change his mind…

"Do you know what *I've* thought about?" She pushed his underwear down and he kicked them down with the growing pile of clothes on the staircase. She started to kneel down in front of him and he forked his fingers through her hair, halting her for a moment, the sting from the tug on her hair sending a sharp sensation of pleasure through her.

"Careful," he said. "I'm close."

"We have all night. I'm not worried. And I've had a lot of fantasies about this. You wouldn't deny me a little fantasy fulfillment, would you?" She leaned forward and flicked the tip of her tongue over the head of his shaft. He sucked in a breath, his hold on her hair tightening again.

She took him into her mouth, loving the taste of him, the

ower she felt. That she could make his thigh muscles shake,
nake his hands tremble. He kept one hand in her hair, one on
he staircase railing, bracing himself as she continued to ex-
·lore him.

"Clara...I need...not like this."

She raised her head, her heart nearly stopping when she saw
is face. He had sweat beads on his forehead, the tendons in
is neck standing out. He looked like a man who'd been tor-
ured with pleasure.

And she'd been the one doing the torturing.

"I don't mind."

"I do. I need to have all of you."

"Maybe we can make it the rest of the way up the stairs?"

"If we hurry," he growled.

So she did, walking in front of him, knowing her thong and
igh heels were making a provocative visual for him. The feel-
ng of confidence she felt, the absolute certainty that he en-
»yed looking at her, that, for now at least, she was the woman
e desired, was amazing. New.

His bedroom door was open, and she walked inside and sat
own on the bed, waiting for him. He stood in the doorway,
is eyes hot on her. The lights were off, moonlight filtering
hrough the window. The darkness felt like a cover, made her
eel more confident.

"Take everything off," he bit out.

She undid the front clasp on her bra and was gratified by
1e sharp rise and fall of his chest as she revealed her breasts
o him. She stood and tugged her underwear down her legs,
aving the high heels for last.

"Want to help with these?" she asked, sitting again, holding
er foot out.

He smiled and walked over to the bed and knelt in front of
er, putting his hands on the curve of her knees, sliding them
own her calf, he bent his head down and kissed her ankle as
e took one of her shoes off and dropped it onto the carpet.

He did the same with the other one, slow, erotic movement making her shiver all over. And when he leaned in and presse his mouth between her thighs she nearly came apart with th first stroke of his tongue.

"I'll confess, I didn't think about this very much until re cently," he said. "But I haven't stopped thinking about it sinc last week. Every night, I dream of you," he said, his voice roug as he continued to pleasure her with his hands.

"Me, too," she said, panting, her body on the brink of cl max, so close she felt it all through her, tension drawing all c her muscles tight.

Zack stood up, his smile wicked as he looked at her. H leaned over and took a condom from the nightstand. He tor the packet open and rolled a condom onto his length befor joining her on the bed.

He put his hands on her thigh and pulled her over him s that her legs were bracketing his and his erection poised at th entranced to her body. Her eyes locked with his, she lowere herself onto him, a low moan climbing in her throat as he fille her.

She gripped his shoulders, enjoying the feeling. Enjoyin the moment of being joined with him completely.

She moved slowly at first, trying to find the right rhythm her confidence increasing as his grip on her hips tightened, a she started to move closer to the edge of climax.

She was saying things, words, about how good it felt, ho much she cared about him, but she wasn't sure what she wa saying exactly. She didn't care. She couldn't think, she coul only feel.

Could only hold on to Zack as her orgasm pushed her ove the edge and into an abyss of light and feeling, where there wa nothing, no one, except for her and Zack. There was no pas and there was no future. There was only the two of them.

In that world, in that moment, everything could work Everything was perfect.

The ascent back to reality was slow and fuzzy, and she almost regretted it when it happened. But even reality, his skin hot and sweaty beneath her cheek, his chest hair a little bit scratchy, was pretty near perfect.

She didn't have the assurance of a future. But for now she had Zack. And she would take him. She felt tears sting her eyes and she squeezed them shut, trying to hold them at bay.

She had him tonight. And it would be perfect. She wouldn't ruin it by crying.

"I'll go and take care of things," he said.

Clara sat up and let Zack get out of bed and go into the bathroom. He came back a couple of moments later and slid back into bed. She looked at his profile. Strong, set. So handsome, so special to her. For so long she'd imagined that she knew everything about Zack. Now she found out there was a huge piece missing.

"Zack…" She knew she probably shouldn't say what was on her mind, but they were naked and in bed together. If they couldn't be honest now, when could you be honest with anyone? "What happened?"

"I told you," he said, his voice stilted. He knew what she meant. No need to clarify.

"Sort of."

"You want to hear more?"

"I want to know what happened. Have you ever told anyone?"

There was a long pause, Zack shifted next to her. "I don't talk about this, Clara. Not ever. Not with anyone."

She put her hand on his shoulder. "And I don't let men see me naked. Not ever. But I let you. So tell me."

He paused and she thought, for a moment, he wasn't going to say anything. "We named him Jake. He lived for forty-eight hours. No one at the hospital thought, even for a moment, that he had a chance. But I did." Silence hung between them, heavy and oppressive. She didn't interrupt it.

Zack breathed in deeply. Faintly, in the dim light filtering in through the windows, she could see a single track of moisture shining on his cheek. "I was wrong. There was no miracle. No beating the odds. I'd thought…I was sure he'd have to be okay. I'd changed all my plans, in my head, my whole future was different. And then it was back to being the same, except it wasn't. It never would be again. And my parents…I think they were relieved. They'd been so angry that I was throwing my future away. I think they were relieved when my son died, Clara."

"Zack…" She started to offer something. Comfort maybe. But she wasn't sure if there was any comfort for that kind of pain. She wasn't sure if it was a wound that could heal.

"Sarah didn't want to talk to me again and I don't blame her. Every time I looked at her I just remembered. I think it was the same for her. So I just left. I couldn't stay there." He paused for a moment. "He would be fourteen now. Just two years younger than I was when he was born. Maybe he'd play football, like I did. He'd be close to the age where I would be teaching him how to drive and telling him about girls. I think about it still. About him. I didn't understand how one person could, even for such a short amount of time, became my whole world. For those two days, I breathed for him. And when he stopped, I almost forgot why I was still trying. Rock bottom is…something else. There's a lot of alcohol there, let me tell you. But not even that fixes it. It just makes you pathetic. But I got hired on at a coffeehouse here, even though I was an aimless wreck. Once I had that job, I had a new focus. I got my GED, I found out I loved coffee. I worked my way up in the company, and I bought it from my boss when he retired. I think that's the beginning of what you, and everyone else, already knew."

She wiped at a tear that was sliding down her cheek, her heart aching, her entire body aching, real, physical pain tearing at her. She turned to the side and rested her head on his shoulder, her hand on his face. He wrapped an arm around her and held her to him.

"But that changed me," he said, his voice strong. "It made me grow up. Made me move forward. It taught me to value control. Responsibility and planning. It's why I'm here. Why I'm so successful and not some burned out, ex-college football star has-been."

He believed it. She could tell he did. But the road to success had been hard. It had hurt. And along with conviction, she heard the pain in his voice, too.

"Arrogance, impulsiveness. That leads to disaster. It creates grief. Needless grief," he said.

She wished she could tell him how much she loved him, but she knew that it was the last thing he wanted to hear. So she just held him, and let him hold her. Let him offer her comfort, so that he didn't realize she sas offering him everything.

"So," she said after a while, "do you want me to go?"

"I want you here," he said. "Spend the night with me."

"Sure, Zack," she said, breathing a sigh of relief.

He tightened his hold on her and neither of them spoke.

Tonight they were together. She hoped she didn't fall asleep. She didn't want to miss a moment.

Clara rolled over and stretched in the morning, her eyes opening to a familiar sight. Zack's room. Though, it wasn't familiar at all to wake up in Zack's room. Even less familiar to wake up in Zack's room after making love with him all night.

A slow smile spread across her lips, followed by a pang of sadness when she remembered their conversation. When she remembered his story about his son.

She looked at Zack, his eyes still closed. She wished, more than anything, that she could take his pain from him. His grief was something she couldn't begin to understand, the kind of cut it would leave so deep she wasn't sure if it could heal. She knew it couldn't, not really. It would never disappear. He'd said himself it had changed him. Had changed the course of his entire life.

His eyes opened and he smiled. "Good morning."

"Morning."

"So, I guess we should get ready to go to work," she said.

"You think so?"

"Well, it's almost time."

"True," he said, wrapping his arms around her and rolling her beneath him. "But you might be able to go in late today. I know the boss."

"So do I," she said, wiggling underneath him. "He's kind of intense about people being at work on time. A bit anal, even."

His eyebrows shot up. "Really? Well, I have a feeling that he'll look the other way today."

CHAPTER ELEVEN

"I got an invitation in the mail. For me and my wife." Zack walked into her office and tossed a cream-colored envelope onto her desk.

She grimaced. "Don't people read the news?"

"Well, I called the charity putting the event on and I explained to them what happened. Of course, they would still like me to come and buy two dinners at four hundred dollars a plate, so my new fiancée is more than welcome."

"Well, hopefully the deal will be finalized by then," she said, looking down at the spiteful ring. "And I'll be off the hook."

"Good for both of us, but even if you are, you still might like to come. As my friend."

"Right." Yes. They were friends. First and foremost, before the sex stuff. At least in his mind. She was his friend, and he was hers, her very best friend. But he was so much more to her than that.

"It's for charity. Something I've been planning on for a while, though, thanks to everything that's been happening the timing slipped my mind. And I can't take anyone else until all of this is finished."

She noticed he didn't say that he didn't want to take anyone else. Only that he *couldn't*.

Being a bit oversensitive, aren't we? Maybe. Or maybe not.

"When is it?" she asked.

"Thursday. How are things going today? Have you come up with anything to go with the white tea from Amudee's? I'm thinking of a gourmet tea cake. Wondering if we could start making our own preserves. That has definite mass-market appeal. Are you closer to reaching a deal?"

"It looks that way. I'm optimistic. He's a hard man to read but he seems reasonably satisfied that Roasted is run to the sort of standards he likes to see."

"Good." She fought the urge to reach out and touch him, to forge a connection. That would just come across as needy and she didn't want to seem needy. Even if she did feel a little bit needy.

"What's this?" He took a sheet of paper off her desk and she cringed.

"Uh…a list I was making. For my bakery."

Her bakery. The dream that wasn't really her dream. She loved her job at Roasted, but if things didn't work out with Zack she was going to need her escape more than ever.

"Oh. Right." He set it back down. "Working on it during business hours?"

"Or during lunch. Or maybe during business hours, but you know I put my time in," she said stiffly.

"I'm not going to give you special treatment just because we slept together."

His words hung in the air, too loud in the small office, and far too harsh for her already-tender insides.

"Of course not. That would be ridiculous," she said, picking up a stack of unidentified papers from her desk and walking over to the industrial stapler. She punched it down in three places and hoped that they were at least documents that went together. "Why would you do that?"

The truth was, he had always treated her like she was special, and having him say something like that made her feel demoted.

"You know what I meant."

"I guess I don't."

He rounded her desk and cupped her chin with his thumb and forefinger, tilting her face up so that she had to meet his eyes. He leaned in and pressed a light kiss to her lips. He didn't apologize. He didn't say anything. Even so, all of the fight drained out of her.

"I'm going to be busy tonight," he said.

That was probably for the best. Distance was probably a really, really good idea. Because she desperately didn't want it, and that meant she very likely needed it. Because last night was proof neither of them were thinking clearly where the other was concerned.

They'd done it again. And there could be no more sex. None. It was too dangerous for her, too stupid. Too little. It was physical only for Zack, and she wanted more. She needed more.

"All right. Me, too, actually." She'd find something to be busy with. She would. Except, the only people she ever hung out with, besides Zack, were the people she worked with. And it would be hard hanging out with them now when she was lying to them.

Maybe she'd work on some of the tea pastries she'd been thinking of.

"See you tomorrow, then. At work," she said, feeling very accomplished that she was managing to seem cool and aloof about the whole thing.

"See you then," he said, nodding and walking out of the room.

When he left she blew out a breath. The affair, fling, whatever, was supposed to ease some of the tension between them. But if anything, it seemed more intense than it had before.

She looked back down at her list. The items she was choosing for if she opened her own bakery. For if she had to leave Roasted so she could get away from Zack.

She was starting to hope she wouldn't need it.

* * *

Clara put a pan of twelve cupcakes into the oven and closed the rack with her foot. They were pineapple cupcakes which she was intending to pair light, whipped frosting and candied mango on top. They might very well taste like a Caribbean vacation gone wrong, but she was feeling risky.

She was also feeling restless and sad.

It was Monday and normally Zack would come over for a football game neither of them would pay attention to. He would bring takeout, she would provide all things baked and sinful.

She missed that. And she wondered if the status quo hadn't been so bad after all.

Right. Because you were such a sopping, sad mess you made his wedding cake even though it destroyed you to do it. And you've barely had a date since you met the man.

All true.

She growled into the empty room and turned her focus to whipping her frosting. That, at least, was physically satisfying. She dipped an unused spoon into the mix and tasted it. She hit Play on her kitchen stereo system and turned to the pantry, humming while she rummaged for a can of pineapple juice.

She heard a sharp knock over the sound of her acoustic guitar music and she stopped rummaging. She frowned and walked over to the door, peeking through the security window at the top.

Zack was there, looking back down the hall, like he was thinking about leaving. He had a brown paper bag in his hand, his work clothes long discarded in favor of a gray T-shirt and a pair of dark fitted jeans.

Her heart crumpled. Seeing him was almost painful. A reminder of how close they'd been physically. How far apart they were emotionally.

She braced herself for the full impact of his presence and opened the door.

He turned to her, smiling. "Hi."

"I thought you were busy."

That wasn't what she'd intended to lead with, but it had sort of slipped out. Things just seemed to be "happening" around him without her permission a lot lately.

"It turns out it could wait." He slipped past her and stepped into her apartment, depositing his bags of food on the counter and pulling white boxes from it without even asking for permission.

"Why are you…here?"

"It's Monday."

"And?"

"Football." He shrugged as he opened the first container, revealing her favorite, Sweet and Sour Pork. Like nothing had changed.

It was comforting in a very bizarre way. And a tiny bit upsetting, too. She wasn't sure which emotion she was going to let win. She'd give it until after dinner to decide.

"Right." She turned and made her way around the counter, taking plates and utensils out of the cupboard and drawers. Zack dished up the food and neither of them spoke as they took their first few bites.

"You could turn the game on," she said.

Zack walked across the open room and took her remote off the couch, aiming it at the TV and putting it on the local channel broadcasting the event.

"Who's playing?" she asked.

"No idea." He tossed the remote back where it had been and crossed back into the kitchen, taking a seat at one of the bar stools that lined the counter.

"Important enough to come over for, though," she said, looking down at her plate and stabbing a piece of meat with her fork.

"I missed you," he said, his voice rough.

"What…me? You missed me?"

"Yes. We always get together Monday. And I found myself wandering around my house. Thought about turning the game on. But you're right. I don't really care about football, probably a side effect of coming down from the high of being the world's most entitled high-school jock. I didn't really want to watch sports, but I did want to eat dinner. With you."

"I missed you, too, Zack," she said.

His smile. His presence. His arms around her while she slept. But she wasn't allowed to miss that last part. That had to be done. Over.

As for their friendship...she didn't know what she would do without him. But she didn't know if she would ever get over him if he was always around, either.

But she had to be with him, at least until she left Roasted. She would worry about the rest then.

"Making cupcakes?" he asked.

"They're going to be very tropical." She took a bite of fried rice and stood up, walking back into the kitchen to grab the can of pineapple juice she'd been after when he came to the door. "Not sure about them yet."

She punched the top of the tin and drizzled some juice into her frosting, stirring it in slowly.

Zack leaned over the counter and stuck his finger in the bowl. She smacked the top of his hand. "I will frost your butt, Parsons. Keep your fingers out of my mixing bowl."

He held his finger near his lips and gave her a roguish smile. "Is that what the kids are calling it these days?" He licked his frosting-covered finger and her internal muscles clenched in response.

She snorted. "No. I don't know. You know what I meant."

"Yeah."

Her heart fluttered, but it was a manageable amount. "Behave."

He arched one eyebrow. "Can't make any promises."

She rolled her eyes and sat back down to her dinner.

"Heard anymore about the store in Japan?" she asked.

That got Zack rolling on statistics and sales figures and al sorts of things he found endlessly fascinating. She liked that about him. Liked that his job sometimes gave him a glint in his eye that made him look like an enthusiastic kid.

Then he launched into a story about the street performers that had been out in front of the restaurant tonight when he'd picked the food up, which reminded her of the time they'd been all but accosted by a street mime on their way to lunch one day.

She really had missed this. Sharing. Laughing. She loved that he knew her, that he knew all of her best stories, her most embarrassing moments.

The timer pinged for the cupcakes and she got up to check them.

"Finished?" he asked.

"Yes," she said, pulling them out with an oven mitt and setting them on the counter. "But hot." She nearly laughed at his pained expression. "I have some cool ones, though. I know you don't bake, but if you want to frost them you're welcome to."

"I think I can handle that."

"Bear in mind they are highly experimental."

He smiled. "Sounds exciting, anyway."

"Or a potential disaster of epic proportions, but we won't know until we taste them."

She loaded up a frosting bag and handed it to Zack while she set her own up and got started on leaving little stars all over the surface of one of the cupcakes.

Zack sneaked his hand past her and dipped it into the bowl again. She grabbed the spatula and smacked the back of his hand, leaving a streak of white frosting behind. "I said stop!" she said, laughing as he examined the mess she'd left behind.

"But the frosting is the best part."

"You didn't try the cake yet."

He shrugged and raised his hand to his lips cleaning off the frosting she'd left behind, then he moved his finger near her mouth. "Taste?" he asked.

In that moment, it felt like her vision tunneled, reduced to nothing but Zack. The game, the sounds of the whistle, the crowd, the announcers, faded, blood roaring in her ears.

It was innocent. Or it should have been. She tried to tell herself that for about ten seconds. Because there was no female friend on earth, no matter how close, who would have offered what Zack was at the moment.

So it wasn't innocent. She looked up, her eyes clashing with his.

They were dark, intense. Aroused. The air between them seemed to thicken, the only sound her breath. Too loud. Too obvious.

It wasn't innocent at all.

She'd promised herself it wouldn't happen again. That their last night together had been exactly that: their last night together.

It won't happen again. I just need a taste.

She leaned in and slid her tongue along the line of his finger and her entire body tightened when a rough groan escaped his lips. The salt of his skin gave bite to the super-sweet frosting. If her cupcakes were a bust maybe she could just spread it all over Zack…

No.

She pulled back sharply, shaking her head. "Sorry. Just… sorry, I…"

He wrapped his arm around her waist and kissed her, deep and long, his tongue still coated in icing. When he released her, she felt dazed in the very best way.

She licked her lips. "You taste like a pineapple," she said, her breath erratic, her heart pounding.

"Is that a good thing?" His voice sounded strained, like each word was an effort.

"I might have to…test it out again."

He smiled and her stomach curled in on itself. "I'm more than willing to aid you in the testing."

He dipped his head and she closed the distance between them, sliding her tongue over his bottom lip, reveling in the rough groan that rumbled in his chest.

He dipped his fingers back in the bowl and tugged at the hem of her shirt, drawing it over her head. "I feel at a disadvantage," he said, sliding his fingers over her stomach. "Because you got a chance to taste me this way, and I haven't gotten to do the same."

He bent down and slid his tongue over her stomach. She shivered, gripping his shoulders, knowing they were going too far, not sure if she wanted to stop.

He stood and reached behind her, unhooking her bra with one hand. "You're better at that than I am," she said, her voice shaking.

"Good. That's kind of the idea. I'd hate to think you'd be better off doing this for yourself." He cupped her breast and slid his thumb off her nipple, leaving a faint dusting of icing covering her there. He bent his head and circled the tightened bud with his tongue before drawing it into his mouth.

She forked her fingers through his hair, holding his head to her as he continued to lavish attention on her breast.

"Oh, no…I could not do this by myself," she breathed.

He lifted his head and captured her lips, sweetness clinging to his tongue, his grip tight on her hips as he tugged her body against his. "You're beautiful," he said, abandoning her mouth to skim kisses down her neck, across her collarbone.

"You make me believe it."

He raised his head, his expression serious. "You should never doubt it, not for a moment. You make me lose control."

The words hung between them, an admission that held power. Because she knew Zack, and she knew what he prized. His control. Above everything. She knew why now, too. She even understood it. And he was saying that her beauty, her body, took it from him.

"Me?" she asked.

"You," he repeated, his voice hard. "Everything about you." He moved his palm over her breast and she shuddered. "Now that I'm allowing myself to look…I can't stop myself. I can't stop at just looking, I have to touch you, then I have to taste you. And it's still not enough."

Zack's heart raged out of control. It was more than just arousal. His chest burned, the need going so much deeper than sex. It was pleasure and pain, heaven and hell. But he couldn't turn away from any of it. He didn't want to.

This wasn't what was supposed to happen tonight. He'd missed Clara, Clara his friend. The companionship she provided, the safety. She was the one person he ever let his guard down with. The one person he laughed with. Relaxed with.

It wasn't supposed to turn into this. But his desire for her was like a storm, devastating everything in its path. Devastating his control.

And he'd admitted it to her. Because what else could he do? She'd brought him to his knees.

"It's a nice apartment," he said, trying to lighten the moment, to bring himself back to earth. "I bet the bedrooms are really nice."

She snorted a laugh and buried her face in his neck. "You've been in my bedroom."

He sifted her hair through his fingers. "I've never slept in your bed."

"Do you want to?" She posed the question as though she was asking if he wanted something purely innocent.

"After we get some other business taken care of."

"I'm in complete agreement with that."

He swung her up into his arms and she squeaked, looping her arms around his neck and laughing as he dashed to her bedroom.

Zack set Clara down when they got inside her room. A room he'd been in more times than he could count. But never like this. She kissed him, her mouth hungry, pulled his shirt off him in one swift motion. Trading piece of clothing for piece of clothing until they were both naked, limbs entwined, her full breasts pressed against his chest.

It was almost enough for a while, to simply lay on the bed with her, moving his hands over her bare curves, kissing her. Doing nothing more than kissing.

It was almost enough, but not quite.

He swore sharply. "I don't have anything. I didn't plan this."

"It's okay," she said, wrapping her hand around his length, squeezing him. He groaned, her soft flesh against his almost making up for the fact that he couldn't be inside her. Almost.

He put his hand between her thighs and drew his fingers over her clitoris, then repeated the motion.

She gasped and arched against him, tightening her hold on his arms, fingernails digging into his skin. "Oh, Zack," she breathed, his name on her lips like balm to his soul.

Everything after that was lost in a frenzy of movement, sighs and graphic words that he'd never heard come from Clara's mouth before. But it was only more exciting, because it was her. Because he knew that he was able to do that to her, to make her say things, feel things no other man ever had.

They reached the peak together, his body shaking down to his bones as he found his release.

He held her soft body against his afterward, a sort of strange contentedness spreading through him that he'd never felt before.

"You're beautiful, you know?" he asked, pushing her hair to one side and kissing her neck.

She turned to look at him, rolling to her side, making the curve of her hip rounder, her waist smaller. And her breasts…

"You keep saying that."

"So that you can't doubt it."

"I'm starting to believe you, actually," she said, a smile curving her lips. She reached out and put her finger on his biceps, tracing a long line up to his shoulder. "You're not so bad yourself."

"I'm flattered." He leaned forward and kissed her nose, the contentedness morphing into something else. Something that felt light and…happy.

He wrapped his arms more tightly around her and rolled onto his back. She planted her palms on his chest, her body half on his.

"Hi," she said, smiling.

"I just want you to know that you're not second to anyone," he said, cupping her cheek. "There's no other woman on earth I would rather be with."

Her brown eyes glistened. "You really are good for my ego."

"I'm glad. Someone has to be."

He wanted to say something. Something bigger than he should, than he could. He just wanted more. In that moment, with her body, so soft and bare and perfect, pressed against his, with her smiling at him like he could solve all of the world's problems, he wanted to offer her the world. He wanted more than temporary, more than distant for the first time in his memory.

She rested her head on his chest, her fingertips moving lightly over his skin until her breathing deepened and her eyes fluttered closed.

It wasn't until she was asleep that panic slammed into him. The full enormity of what had happened. He'd lost control. More than that, he'd been letting go of it, inch by inch, with Clara for the past seven years.

With everyone else he was guarded. He never dropped his defenses. He never talked about his past.

He'd cried in front of her. He had allowed real, raw weakness and emotion to escape in her presence when he never even let himself give in like that in private. She was under his skin. So much so she felt like she was a part of him.

A necessary part.

What if he lost her? No, it wasn't even a matter of if, it was when.

The terror that thought evoked, the absolute, gut-wrenching horror was a sobering as a punch to the jaw. He was playing a game he had no business playing, flirting with things he shouldn't be. Tempting feelings he couldn't risk having.

He slid out of her hold and she stirred briefly, stretching, arching her back. His mouth dried. He shook his head and bent to collect his clothes, dressing and walking out of her bedroom, closing the door quietly behind him, ignoring the continual stab of pain in his chest.

He paused in her living room for a moment, the weight of the familiarity of his surroundings crushing him, a feeling of claustrophobia overtaking him.

He had to leave. He had to think. He had to find his control.

He walked out her front door, closing it behind him and making sure everything was locked so that she would be safe. He walked out into the cold night, sucking in a deep breath and blaming the cold for the pain that came with it.

"Where were you this morning? When did you leave?" Clara whispered the words when she went into Zack's office in the early afternoon. He'd been out of the office all morning, and he had been very noticeably not at her apartment before that.

"I had some things to do," he said, his voice flat. "Could you bring me a coffee?" His phone rang and he picked it up. She stomped out of the room and picked up the freshly brewed pot that was sitting in the main area of the office. She poured a half a cup and dumped powdered creamer in, no sugar, and stirred it halfheartedly with one of the little wooden sticks that was on the coffee station.

There were still little lumps of powder floating on the top.

She went back into his office and plunked it onto his desk, letting some of it slosh over the side. He didn't flick her or the coffee a glance as he continued his phone call. He picked it up and took a sip then grimaced and set it back down, shooting her an evil look. She responded with a wide, saccharine smile.

"I'll call you back," he said into the phone, hanging up. "Do you have something on your mind?"

"Yes. Where were you this morning, and do not give me another half-assed answer."

"Clara, there's a way I conduct physical relationships. I don't always stay for the whole night."

She felt like he'd slapped her. Like she was just the same as every other physical relationship he had. But she wasn't. She knew she wasn't.

Anger made her scalp feel prickly. "Don't give me that. Don't even try. I made you shake last night. Made you lose control." Boldness came from anger, and she could't regret it.

His eyes glittered and he looked like he might pounce on her. But he didn't. "I just went home, so that I could get a good night's sleep. I have to go over some legalese in the contract I'm having drawn up for the deal with Amudee. That's all."

That wasn't all. She knew it wasn't all. But she didn't know what the rest of it was, either, so that didn't help.

"And that looks like it's going to go through?" she asked, looking down at the ring again, the ring she was starting to hate, willing to let the subject drop, for now.

"Looks like, but nothing is finalized. So we're still in this until the ink is dry."

She nodded. "I know."

It was all about the contract to Zack. Last night…she could have sworn that last night something had changed. There had been more in their lovemaking. There had been fun. Their friendship had been in it.

It had been special.

Well, today things felt different. It just wasn't the sort of different she'd been hoping for.

"I'll be down in the kitchen," she said, eager to get away.

It was going to take a whole lot of cupcakes to make this day feel okay.

The next few days Zack really did manage to be busy and stay busy. He didn't stop by her apartment late at night, or any time of day. Her head hurt and her bed felt empty. Which was silly, since her bed had been empty of anyone other than her for twenty-five years.

It was just the past couple weeks she'd had Zack sometimes. And she found she really liked it, and it wasn't just because of the orgasms. It was just listening to him breathe. Feeling his body heat so close to hers. Just being with him, finally, finally able to express how much she wanted him. To not have to hold such a huge part of herself back from him anymore.

She loved the way he made her feel about herself. That he wanted her in a sexy red dress, or yoga pants, or nothing. That he made her feel beautiful. That he made her see things in herself she hadn't seen before.

And if she told him that he'd undoubtedly run away screaming.

Tonight, the contracts remained unsigned and that meant they still had plans to go to the big charity event. Something to do with a children's hospital. She wondered if that was by design. If it would bother him. Make him think of his son.

Her heart hurt every time she thought of Zack's past. Of what that false front of his was created to hide. To hide what he'd been through, who he really was. He had perfected a persona, controlled, light, charming, and even she had bought into it. Not even *she* had seen everything.

But she was starting to.

Tonight was going to feel more like a real date. A public event with just the two of them, not with Mr. Amudee sitting by, watching their performance as a couple. She was dressing up in a dress she'd selected this time. Something between her usual fare and that screaming, sex-on-a-hanger number Zack had picked out for her.

It was a full-length gown with a mermaid-style skirt that conformed to her body before flaring out around her knees. It swished when she walked, and a halter-top neckline showed her cleavage. And she felt sexy in it. She felt like a woman who was ready to conquer the world. One who could outshine other women, at least for the man she was with. And that was what mattered, anyway.

She heard a knock on her door and she tried to shove her feet into stilettos, while standing, and fastening dangly diamond earrings. "Coming!"

She opened the door and all the air rushed out of her body. Zack was a wearing a suit, black jacket, crisp white shirt and a perfectly straight black tie. He was the epitome of gorgeous. He always was, half dressed, all dressed or completely naked. But there was something about a man in a suit…

It sort of reminded her of his wedding. The wedding that wasn't.

"You look…you look great," she said.

"So do you. I brought you something," he said.

There was something strange about his tone, something formal and distant. It matched his clothing. Cool, well-tailored, nothing out of place. And yet, that in and of itself felt out of place. Zack wasn't formal with her. Why should he be? They'd known each other for years. They had slept together for heaven's sake.

She held her hand out and smiled, trying to make him smile. It didn't work.

He took a flat, black box from his jacket and opened it.

"Oh, my…Zack this is…it must have cost…" None of her words would gel into a complete sentence, everything jumbling and stalling half thought through.

It was a necklace, a truly spectacular necklace, not the sort you saw under the display case of just any department store.

Not even the sort of thing you saw at Saks. It was too unique, too extravagant.

She reached out and touched the center stone, a deep green emerald, cut into the shape of a teardrop and surrounded by glittering diamonds.

"I don't think I can accept this."

"Of course you can," he said, his voice still tinged with that unfamiliar distance. "Turn around."

She did, slowly, craning her neck to look at him. He swept her hair to the side and took the necklace from the box, draping it over her, the stone falling between her breasts, the chill making her shiver. He clasped the necklace, his fingers brushing the back of her neck as we worked the tiny clasp.

"This isn't…this isn't a friendships gift," she said, her voice trembling.

That did earn her a short chuckle. "Maybe tonight friendship isn't what I want."

His words made her shiver, the sensual promise in them turning her on. The underlying, darker meaning she couldn't quite grasp making goose bumps break out on her arms. "It really is too much," she said, turning to face him, her nose nearly touching his.

He straightened putting some distance between them. "It's a perfectly fitting gift for a lover. Are you ready?"

"Yes," she said, turning his choice of word over in her head. Yes, she was his lover, in the sense that they'd slept together. But there was something in the way he said it, something that seemed cold, when a lover should be something warm. Something personal.

She touched the necklace, the gems cold beneath her fingertips.

CHAPTER TWELVE

THE charity ball was crowded already when they arrived, a sea of beautiful people dressed in black positioned around the ballroom, chatting and eating the very expensive canapes.

Heads turned when she and Zack walked down the marble staircase and down into the room. Everyone was looking at Zack, because it was impossible not to. She was fully appreciating just how he was viewed in the community now. A man of power and wealth, a man of unsurpassed beauty. If you could call what he possessed beauty. It was too masculine for that, and yet she wasn't sure there was another word for it, either.

Pride flared in her stomach, low and warm. All the women in the room were looking at Zack with undisguised sexual hunger. And Zack was with her. Touching her, his hand low on her back, possessive.

She turned and pressed a kiss to his cheek. He looked at her. "What was that for?"

"Because," she said.

He looked at her for a moment, a strange light in his eyes. "Let's go find our table."

"Okay," she said, trying to ignore the tightening in her throat.

There was a table, for two, with place cards set on each empty plate. Zack held her chair out for her and she sat, her heart slamming against her ribs as she read the name that had been written in calligraphy on her place card.

Hannah Parsons.

With Zack's name tacked on to hers, even. Clara felt dizzy. She looked down at the ring. Hannah's ring. Hannah's seat. Hannah's man. She had to wonder if the necklace had been meant for Hannah, too.

She wrapped her fingers around the card and curled them into a fist, crumpling it and tossing it onto the marble floor.

"What the hell?" Zack asked.

"It had the wrong name on it," she said stiffly.

"Does it matter?"

That hit even harder than seeing the name. "I suppose not." She put her foot over the crumpled paper and squished it beneath the platform of her stiletto.

"You're the one who's here with me." He stretched his hand toward hers, covering it, stroking her wrist. "No one else."

She knew it. And in some ways she knew his words were sincere. But there was also something generic in them. There was something strangely generic to the whole evening and she couldn't quite place what it was or why.

"Of course." She looked into his eyes, tried to find something familiar now. Something of her friend. But she didn't see it. She only saw the man as he presented himself to the world. Aloof, put together, charming. But there was no depth there. No feeling or warmth.

It was frightening.

Dinner was lovely, tiny bits of sculpted beauty made to be admired before being eaten. Of course it was marked up extravagantly, because the whole point of the evening was that the charity received donations.

A woman in a long, flowing dress walked up onto the stage, her air of authority making it obvious that she was the coordinator of the event, and a hushed silence fell over the crowd.

"Thank you all for coming tonight," she said. "And for the

very generous donation of your time and money to the Bay Area Children's Hospital."

She turned and looked toward their table, a smile on her face. "And tonight, we would also like to give special acknowledgment to Mr. Zack Parsons, who has donated enough money to revamp the entire Neo-Natal Intensive Care Unit. Everything in the unit will be state of the art. It will be the best equipped facility in the state of California. There have been major advances in the field of Neo-Natal medicine over the past few years. We're able to offer hope to babies, to families, who wouldn't have had any as little as five years ago. And now, we're able to offer even more. So, thank you, Mr. Parsons."

The room erupted into applause and everyone stood. Except for Zack. Except for her. Her eyes stung, her entire body feeling numb.

Zack lifted his hand and nodded once, his acknowledgment. Her heart broke for him. What a wonderful gift he was giving to so many families. A gift he hadn't been able to give to himself, to his own son.

She wanted to howl at the universe for the unfairness of it all. And yet there was no point. And Zack was there, broken, and probably in pain. She could be there for him. It was all she could do. And she would. Because she was his friend. His lover.

The speaker went on to talk about some more donations and then invited everyone to stay for dancing and an open bar.

After the applause died away, people started to wander around the room, talking and laughing, some people came to talk to Zack. She wanted to tell them to go away. Because she could feel the dark energy, the grief, radiating from him like a physical force. How was everyone else missing it?

She didn't understand how they could miss what was so clear to her.

"Let's go." She put her hand on his, felt his pulse, pounding hard in his wrist. She ran her fingers along his forearm.

She didn't think he would accept loving words, but she could offer him comfort in another way. A way he could accept.

There was no question where things would end up tonight. No fighting it. They both knew it.

He nodded once and stood, she stood, too, and went to him, putting her hand on his back. He wrapped his arm around her waist as they headed out of the ballroom.

Zack's chest felt too full. Everything felt like too much. The whole day. He shouldn't have brought Clara with him tonight. It was one thing to sit in a room full of strangers and have them talk about his contribution to the NICU, but it was another to have someone sitting there, knowing why he'd done it. Someone else thinking of Jake. It was hard enough to be alone in it. Sharing it made it seem more real. It made him feel exposed.

It made him feel like everything, his failures, his pain, was written on him. Something he couldn't hide, or scrub off no matter how many layers of control he tried to conceal it with.

Clara saw him.

When he'd picked her up tonight, he'd fully intended on keeping her at a distance, putting her in her place. A new place. Because he had mistresses, women who were with him for the sole purpose of warming his bed and accompanying him to events.

He wasn't friends with those women. He didn't eat their baked goods, he didn't know that they wore yoga pants to bed when there wasn't a man around. He didn't know that they were insecure about their bodies, or that their favorite band was still that group of long-haired teenage boys that had been so popular in the nineties.

He didn't know anything about them beyond what they looked like naked.

He knew the other stuff about Clara. And he knew the naked stuff. And tonight he'd been determined to focus only on the latter. If he couldn't keep her as only a friend, and he'd proven he wasn't doing a very good job of that, then he would have her as a mistress. Because what had happened at her apartment, the way they'd shared dinner, jokes, then made love, him holding her while she'd slept…he couldn't do that. It was too reckless. To out of his control.

He had to move her into the compartment he could deal with. And she seemed determined to push her way back out.

The expression on her face when she saw the wrong card in her spot had been so sad, stricken, as though someone had slapped her.

And he'd felt it in him. As though her emotion was his. He'd always felt connected to Clara, but this was different. Sharper. Impossible to deny. Beyond his control.

He should have taken her home. Yet he'd still taken her back to his house. Because he had planned on having her tonight, had been obsessed with it all week. If only to prove that he could sleep with her without having his insides flayed. Sex was only sex. It didn't have to be personal, it didn't have to mean anything. It didn't have to be related to the awful, tight feeling in his chest.

She was beautiful tonight, incredible in that form-fitting black dress and the gem, enticing in the valley of her cleavage, drawing his eye, tormenting him.

She was standing by the massive living-room windows, the bay in the background, city lights glittering on the inky surface of the waves. He wanted her. Here and now. A good thing he'd planned for it. It wasn't spur-of-the-moment, it wasn't beyond his control.

He had condoms and everything else he needed. He was in control. He desperately needed the control. He tightened his hand into a fist, steadied it, ignored the tremor that ran through his fingers and skated up his arm, jolting his heart.

Ignoring the strange tenderness he felt when he looked at

her. This wasn't about feeling, not in an emotional sense. This was physical. It was sex.

"Take off your dress," he said.

She reached behind herself and unzipped the gown, letting it fall to the floor. She wasn't wearing a bra, only a small triangle of lace keeping her from being completely bare. That and the necklace, the emerald heavy and glittering between her breasts.

She reached around to remove it, her breasts rising with the action, pink tipped and perfect.

"No," he ground out. "Leave it on." A reminder. A reminder that she was the same as every other woman he'd ever been with. The exchange of gifts, jewelry, that was how it worked. It was invariable, it was safe. It was unchallenging.

She dropped her hands to her sides and he walked closer to her, loving the way the moonlight spilled silver over her pale curves. The way the deep shadows accentuated the dip of her small waist, the round fullness of her hips and breasts.

She was a woman. There was no denying it. And he was starving for her.

But he would wait. He would draw it out. Because he was the master of this game. He was always in charge. He had forgotten that sometimes over the past few weeks, had allowed her inexperience, the nature of their friendship, to change the way he approached it.

Not now.

She's a woman. Only a woman. The same as any other.

No. Not the same. His mind rebelled against that thought immediately. There had never been a more exquisite woman, that much he knew for certain. There had never been a figure, not since Eve, better designed to tempt a man.

She was the epitome of sensual beauty, more seductive simply standing there than any other woman could have been if she'd been trying.

Clara.

Her name flashed through his mind, loud, a reminder.

No. He didn't need it. He wasn't thinking of her. Only of his own need and how she might fulfill it. He would pleasure her, too, as he did all of his lovers. But it wasn't different. It couldn't be different. Not again. Not after that night in her apartment.

"Turn around for me," he said. "Face the window."

She obeyed again. She was like a perfect hourglass, the elegant line of her back enticing. He walked over to her, extending his hand and tracing the dip of her spine. She shivered beneath his touch.

"Do you like that?" he asked.

"I've liked everything you've ever done to me." Her voice, so sweet, a bit vulnerable. Not a temptress.

Clara.

He put his hands on her hips and tugged her back against him, let her feel the hard ridge of his arousal, the blatant, purely sexual evidence of what he wanted from her. Her indrawn breath, the short, sweet sound of pleasure that escaped her lips, let him know that she was tracking with him. Important.

He would never do anything she didn't want.

He put his hand on her stomach, soft, slightly rounded. He liked that about her, too, that she was so feminine, curved everywhere. Absolute perfection.

He cupped her butt with his other hand, her flesh silken beneath his palm. "You're beautiful," he said. She leaned back against him, her head against his chest. Her slid his hand up to palm her breast, teasing her nipples as he continued to stroke her backside.

He gripped the side of her panties and drew them down her legs.

He move his hand back behind her, moving it forward, teasing her slick folds before parting them and sliding his fingers deep inside of her. She gasped, spreading her thighs a bit wider to accommodate him.

The line of her neck was so elegant, irresistible. He bent his head and kissed her there, tasting the salt of her skin, so familiar now, as he slid his free hand up to her breast and squeezed her nipple tightly between his thumb and forefinger. She arched against him, her breathing growing harsher, more shallow.

He had her pleasure in his hands, how he touched her and where, dictating everything she did. Everything she felt. This was like everything else. Every other sexual encounter he'd had as an adult. He was in charge of their pleasure, both of them. He decided when things happened and how.

This thing with Clara hadn't been right from the beginning, because he hadn't managed to put her in her place for their affair. He hadn't separated their friendship from it. That was why he'd shared with her, held her while she slept. That was why he'd started feeling things.

But he knew it now. He knew what he had to do. He could still have her. He could get a handle on everything, and then he could have her. He touched the necklace between her breasts, fingers sliding over the gem. A reminder of exactly what they had between them.

She tried to turn and he held her so she was facing the window, away from him. He reached over and picked up a condom sheathing himself and turning her to the side so that she was standing in front of the couch.

"Hold on to the back of it," he said. She obeyed, bending at the waist, gripping the back of the couch. She looked back at him, her eyes round, questioning. Familiar.

He chose not to focus on her face. He gripped her hips, looked at the curve of her hips, how her body dipped in beautifully, perfectly, at her waist.

He positioned himself at the entrance to her body.

She made a short, low sound that vibrated through her. "Okay?" he asked, his teeth gritted tight, every ounce of control spent on moving slowly, on not thrusting in to her the rest of the way and satisfying the need that was roaring inside of him.

"Yes," she said.

He pushed into her the rest of the way, her body so hot and tight it took every ounce of his willpower to keep from coming the moment he was inside.

"Oh, Zack," she breathed. "Zack."

His name on her lips, her voice, so utterly Clara. So familiar and still so exciting.

Clara. Her name was in his head on his lips, with each and every thrust, with each sweet pulse of her internal muscles around his shaft.

And suddenly there was no denying it. It didn't matter that he couldn't see her face. Her smell, the feel of her skin beneath his fingertips, the way it felt to be in her body, all of it was pure, undeniable Clara Davis.

The woman who baked orange cupcakes and had a pink wreath on the door. The woman knew about his past, about the darkest moments of his life. The woman who smiled at him every morning. Who could always make him smile, no matter what. Who put powdered creamer in his coffee when he made her angry.

The woman who lit him on fire, body and soul.

He couldn't pretend she was someone else, or that it didn't matter who she was. There was no way. No one had ever been like her before, no one ever would be.

He had no control. He had nothing. He was at her mercy. If he'd had to get on his knees and beg her for a kiss tonight he would have done it, because he needed her.

Not just in a purely sexual sense. He needed *her.*

His climax built, hard and fast, the pitch too steep, too unexpected for him to control. He put his hand between her thighs and stroked her, trying to bring her with him. Her body tightened around him, her orgasm hitting hard and fast. When she cried out her pleasure, then he let go.

"Clara," he whispered, resting his forehead on her back as he gave in. As he let the release crash through him, devastating everything in its path.

He released his hold on her hips, his body shaking, spent as though he'd just battled his way through a storm. Sweat made his skin slick all over. His hands were trembling, his breathing sharp and jagged.

He looked at her. At Clara. There were red marks on her hips where his fingers had pressed into her flesh. Where he had lost all control. He brushed his fingers along the part where he'd marked her, his chest tightening, regret forming, a knot he couldn't breathe around.

She turned to look at him, a smile on her lips. She straightened, naked and completely unconcerned about it. Nothing like she'd been at first. Her confidence, the fact that she felt beautiful, shone from her face.

Her beautiful face. Unique. Essential. So damn important.

"I'm sorry," he said.

She blushed, looking away from him. "Didn't I tell you not to apologize to me all the time?"

"What about when I need to?" he asked, moving toward where she was standing, brushing his fingertips over her hips. "I was holding on to you too tightly," he whispered.

She met his eyes and they held. He saw deep, intense emotion there. A connection, affection. Something real. It wasn't part of a facade, or a game. It was the way she always looked at him, whether they were in his office, in her living room or in bed. She was the same woman. She cared for him. She looked at him like he mattered to her.

The realization rocked him, filled him. Every piece and fiber of his being absorbing it. It made it easier to breathe, as though he hadn't truly been drawing in breath for years and now he was again.

For the first time in fourteen years. Since he'd lost his reason for breath, his desire to give any sort of emotion, to give of himself. He felt like he'd found it again. In Clara's eyes.

"I didn't mind," she said.

The moment, the tiny sliver of freedom he felt evaporated, chased away by a biting, clawing panic that was working from his stomach up through his chest. He had felt this way before and it had ended in utter destruction.

He knew what this was. And he knew he couldn't have it. Wouldn't allow himself to have it. Not ever. Not ever again.

He took a step away from her and bent down, picking her dress up from the floor, rubbing his fingers over the sequins. He felt choked, like his throat was closing in on itself, like his chest was too full for his lungs to expand.

He could do it. He could have her still, keep her where she belonged in his life. In his bed.

He had been careless again. He had lost control. He could find it again. He had to.

"Get dressed," he said, handing her the gown.

"What?"

"I'll drive you home."

"What?" she said again.

He didn't look at her face. He couldn't.

"You and I are having an affair, Clara, I made that clear the other day. I don't cuddle up with the women I'm having sex with at night, and I damn sure don't have their toothbrush on my sink. That's just how it works."

"And I think I told you, I am not just one of your mistresses."

"When you're in my bed…or my couch, you are."

"I am your friend," she said, her voice ringing in the room.

"Not when we're here, like this. Now, you're just the woman I'm sleeping with. We aren't going to curl up and watch a chick flick after what just happened."

She jerked back, pulling her dress over her breasts. "I'm going to go get dressed. Send the car. I'm not riding back with you, and I'm not staying, not now so I think the decent thing to do, if you still remember decency, would be to arrange me a ride."

"Clara…"

"We'll talk tomorrow. I can't now."

She turned and walked away, her steps clumsy. She ducked into his downstairs bathroom and closed the door. He heard the click of the lock.

And he didn't blame her. But he had to define the relationship, as much for her benefit as for his. Yes, he had lied. She was different. But she couldn't be. It couldn't happen.

He would fix it. He'd gotten it wrong tonight, by denying the one thing that had been there from the beginning. His feelings. The sex…he would pretend it hadn't happened. Whatever he had to do to fix it, to have her never look at him like that again. As if he was a cold stranger, as if he'd physically hurt her.

It would have to go back to how it was. Because he could live without sex. He wasn't sure he could live without Clara.

It was the longest car ride in the world. No one was on the streets, and it technically took half the time it normally did to get from Zack's place to hers, but it seemed like the longest ever.

Because everything hurt. And she was wearing a really fabulous gown that had already been torn from her body once, during the most intense, emotion-filled sexual encounter they'd ever had. There had been something dark in Zack tonight. A battle. She wasn't stupid. She knew something had changed, she knew, at least she hoped, that he wasn't as horrible as he'd seemed when he'd sent her away.

She bunched up the flaring skirt of her gown when the car stopped and she slid out, letting the dress fan out around her. She gave the driver a halfhearted, awkward wave. He knew her. She'd used his services quite a few times with Zack. Having him be a part of this, the most awful, embarrassing, heart-wrenching moment of her life wasn't so great.

Because it was two in the morning and it was completely obvious what had just happened. That Zack had had sex with her, sex, at its most base, and had her go home rather than have her spend the night in his bed.

She curled her hands into fists and let her nails cut into her palms, tears stinging her eyes. She almost hated him right now. It almost rivaled how much she loved him.

Almost.

If she didn't love him, it wouldn't hurt so bad.

You're my mistress.

Like hell she was. He might be the only man who'd seen her naked, but she was certain, beyond a shadow of a doubt, that she was the only woman who'd ever seen him cry.

CHAPTER THIRTEEN

She really hoped everyone wanted cupcakes for lunch. Because there were cupcakes. Nine varieties of them, and someone had to eat them.

She didn't think she could eat and she was *not* sharing them with Zack, which meant they would be going straight into the break room. On the bright side, she'd found a few new varieties that had worked out nicely.

The sea-salt caramel one was her favorite. She just couldn't force down more than two bites at a time. Anything beyond that stuck in her throat and joined the ever-present lump that made her feel like she was perpetually on the edge of tears.

She was just too full of angst to eat anything. She hadn't been able to eat anything since she'd been dropped at the front of her building by Zack's driver.

Zack.

She put her head on the pristine counter of the office kitchen and tried to hold back the sob that was building in her chest.

Something had broken in him last night. It had started after their time together at her place, the night he'd left. And last night it had snapped completely. But she didn't know what it was. She didn't know how to pull him out of it. If she could, or if she even should.

"Clara."

Clara looked up and saw Jess standing in the doorway of the kitchen. "Zack is looking for you."

"Oh," Clara straightened and wiped her eyes. Normally Zack would come and find her himself. Because there was a time when he'd wanted to be with her simply to be with her. Now she wondered if she had any value when she wasn't naked. "I'll be there in a second. Take…" She gestured to the platters of cupcakes. "Take some of these with you. I can't eat them by myself. If Zack comes near them, tell him they have walnuts."

Jess's eye widened. "They all have walnuts?"

"No. But tell him they do. All of them."

Jess gave her a strange look and picked two of the platters up, heading back out the door.

She had no choice now. She had to go face the man himself. And figure out exactly what she was going to say. As long as it didn't involve melting into a heap, she supposed almost anything would do.

"You sent Jess after me?" She looked inside of Zack's office, waiting to be invited in. Silly maybe, since she hadn't knocked on his office door in the seven years since she'd started working at Roasted. But she felt like she needed to now.

"Yes. Come in." His tone was formal, like it had been the night before when he'd given her the necklace. Distance. Divorced from emotion.

That was the strange thing. He'd been aloof the night of the charity, until they'd made love. Then he'd been commanding, all dark intensity and so much emotion it had filled the room. It had filled her. It hadn't been good emotion. It had been raw and painful. Almost more than she could bear.

It had caused the break. That much she knew.

But he was back to his calm and controlled self now, not a trace of last night's fracture in composure anywhere. She almost couldn't believe he was the same man whose hands had trembled after they'd made love.

She almost couldn't believe he was the same man she'd known for seven years. The same man she'd watched movies with, shared dinners with.

But he was. He was both of those men.

He was also the cold man standing before her, and she wasn't sure how all of those facets of himself wove together. And she really wasn't sure where she fit in. If she did at all.

She stepped into the office, watching his face for some sort of reaction. He had that sort of distant, implacable calm he'd had on his wedding day, standing and looking out the window as though nothing mattered to him. As though he had no deeper emotion at all.

She knew differently now. She saw it for what it was now. A facade. But she wasn't certain there was a way through it, unless he wanted her to break through.

"I'm about to sign the final paperwork for the deal with Amudee. I wanted to thank you for your help."

For her help. "Of course."

They were talking like strangers now. They'd never been like strangers, not from the moment she'd met him. They'd had a connection from the first moment he'd walked into the bakery.

Now she couldn't feel anything from him. Now that they'd been so intimate, she felt totally shut off from him.

"Once everything is finalized we can let everyone know that our engagement has been called off," he said.

"Right," she said, clenching her left hand into a fist.

"That's all." He looked back at his computer screen for a moment, then looked back up. "Are you busy tonight?"

Her heart stopped. Did he want sex? Again? After what he'd done last night?

"Um…why?"

"Because I thought I might come over and watch a movie."

His words were so unexpected it took her brain a moment

to digest them, as though she was translating them from a foreign language. "And?"

He shrugged. "Nothing."

He was behaving as if…as if nothing had changed. As if they'd gone back in time a few weeks.

He was pretending, she was certain of it, because he certainly wasn't acting normal, whatever he might think, but she was insulted that he was trying. After what he'd said to her last night. After the way he'd objectified her.

She wanted to yell at him. Maybe even hit him, and she'd never hit anyone in her life. But she wanted a reaction. She didn't want his control.

"Are you going to pretend last night didn't happen?" she asked, her voice low, unsteady.

Zack remained calm, his control, that control he claimed to have lost, the control she witnessed in tatters last night, firmly in place. "I think we both know that's not working out. But you're right. You're my friend, and I didn't treat you like a friend last night."

"An understatement," she spat. "You treated me like your whore."

She saw something, an emotion, faint and brief, flicker in his eyes before being replaced by that maddening calm again. That same sort of dead expression he'd worn when he'd been jilted on his wedding day.

"I apologize," he said. "I wasn't myself."

She curled her hands into fists, her fingernails digging into the tender skin on her palm, the pain the only thing keeping her from exploding. "Do you know what I think, Zack? I think you were yourself. This? This is the lie. This isn't you. It's you being a coward. You can't face whatever it is that happened between us last night and now you're hiding from it."

"It isn't working. That element of our relationship." The only thing that betrayed his tension was the shifting of a muscle in his jaw. "But we've been friends for seven years. That works for us. We need to go back to that."

"Are you…are you crazy?" she asked, the words exploding from her. "We can't go back. I've been naked with you. You've been… We've made love. You can't just go back from that like it never happened. I don't care what we thought, we were wrong. That one night, that one night that's turned into four, it changed everything. You can't just experience something like that with someone and feel nothing."

"I can."

"Do you really think this is nothing? That we're nothing?"

"We're friends, Clara. You mean a lot to me. But it doesn't mean I want to keep sleeping with you. It doesn't mean I want this kind of drama. We need things back like they were so that the business can stay on track…."

"I'm leaving Roasted. You know that."

He tightened his jaw. "I didn't think you would really leave."

"What? Now that we've slept together? You can't have it both ways. Either it changed things or it didn't."

"I care about you," he said, his tone intensifying.

"Not enough." She shook her head, fighting tears. They weren't sad tears. She was too angry for that. That would come later. "I am your sidekick, and that's how you like it. As long as I give you company when you want it, eat dinner with you when you're lonely, bake your wedding cake when you decide it's time to have a cold, emotionless marriage, well then, you care about me. As long as I'm willing to pretend to be your fiancée so you can get your precious business deal. But it's on your terms. And the minute it isn't, when I start having power, that's when you can't handle it."

He only looked at her, his expression neutral.

"I'm done with it, Zack," she said, pulling the ring, the ring that wasn't hers, from her finger. "All of it."

She put the ring on his desk and backed away, her heart thundering, each beat causing it to splinter.

"We have a deal," he bit out.

"You'll figure it out. If that's the only reason you don't want me to go…if that's all that's supposed to keep me here… I can't."

Zack stood, his gray eyes suddenly fierce. "So, you're just going to walk out, throw away our friendship over a meaningless fling?"

"No. It's not the fling, Zack, it's the fact that you think it's meaningless. The fact that I've realized exactly where I rate as far as you're concerned."

"What do you want?" he exploded. "Why is what we have suddenly not good enough for you?"

"Because I realized how little I was accepting. That everything was about you. I'm just willing to take whatever you give me, whether it's a spot in your bed or a job baking your wedding cake and it's…sick. I can't keep doing this to myself." She turned to go and he rounded the desk, gripping her arm tightly.

"I'll ask you again," he said, his voice rough. "What do you want? I'll give it to you. Don't leave."

"So I can wait around for you to decide you want to try a loveless marriage again? So I can bake you another cake? Maybe I'll help the bride pick out her dress this time, because, hey, I'm always here to do whatever you need done, right?"

"Does it bother you? The thought of another woman marrying me? Then you marry me." He reached behind him and took the ring off the desk, holding it out to her, his hand shaking. "Marry me. And stay."

She recoiled, her stomach tight, like she'd just been punched. "For what purpose, Zack? So I can be the wife you don't love? Your stand-in for Hannah, different woman, same ring. Doesn't matter, right? You're still doing it. You're trying to keep me from leaving, trying to keep control. You'll even marry me to keep it. That's not what I want."

He took her hand in his, opened it, tried to hand her the ring.

She pulled back. "Don't," she said, her voice breaking. "Don't. I'm going to clean my desk out now."

"Clara."

Zack watched as she turned away from him and walked out his office door, closing it sharply behind her. Everything was deathly silent without her there, his breath too loud in the enclosed space. The ring too heavy.

Had he truly done that? Offered her Hannah's ring? Begged her to marry him just so she would stay?

He had. She had gone anyway and there had been nothing he could do to make her stay. All of his control, all of his planning, hadn't fixed it. He had lost the one person in his life who had given things meaning.

He'd been pretending, from the moment he'd met Clara, that she was only his friend. Only one thing. Because he'd known she could very easily become everything. How had he not realized that she'd been everything from day one?

Pain crashed through him, a sense of loss so great it stole the breath from his lungs.

His chest pitched sharply, his body unable to take in air.

He dropped the ring and it fell to the floor, rolling underneath his desk. He left it. It didn't matter.

He'd just broken the only thing in his life that did matter.

Control. She spoke of his control, how he tried to control her, keep her in his life on his terms. And she was right. Because he'd known instinctively that if he ever let go of that control she would take over.

She had. His control was shattered now, laying around his feet in a million broken pieces he would never be able to reclaim.

And if finding it again meant losing Clara, he didn't want it, anyway.

He hadn't chosen to lose his son, it had been a tragedy, one that had painted his life from that moment forward. He'd let

Clara leave, because he'd been too afraid to give. Too afraid to let his barriers down.

Because he'd been certain he couldn't live with the kind of pain love would bring, not again. But now he was certain he couldn't live without it. Without Clara. He loved her so much his entire being ached with it.

And if he had to lay down every bit of pride, every last vestige of control and protection to have her back, he would.

CHAPTER FOURTEEN

Clara had looked at nine buildings in the space of four hours. She'd hated them all. The idea of having her own bakery… it had been so great before. But she realized now that when she pictured it, when she saw the image of a shop filled with people enjoying her cupcakes, Zack was there. At a table that she knew, in her imagination, anyway, was the one he sat at every day.

And she would come and sit with him when she took a break. And ask him what his favorite confection was. How his day had been. If he'd run in to any mimes. Because in her mind, in her heart, she'd never truly thought he would be gone from her life altogether.

The truth was, a life without him had been impossible to imagine.

In the three days since she'd walked out of Zack's office, it had changed. She didn't have a vision when she viewed the potential bakery locations. She saw nothing more than brick and wood. There were no visions. No warmth.

There was no Zack.

When he'd handed her the ring…the temptation to say yes had been there, and it had sickened her. That she would continue to be the void filler in Zack's life, while she let him be her everything. It was wrong. And she knew it.

Still, a part of her wished she could go back and say yes. She despised that part of herself.

She sighed and walked up the narrow staircase that led to her apartment. She hadn't taken the elevator in three days, either. Because it reminded her of the elevator rides with Zack, the ones rife with sexual tension. It was almost funny now.

Almost. She'd discovered a broken heart made it mostly impossible to find things funny.

When she reached her floor she walked slowly down the hall. She was exhausted, but going back to her apartment wasn't a restful thought. Because he was everywhere there. Memories of him. On her couch, in the kitchen, most recently, in her bed.

She stopped midway down the hall, her eyes locking on the small pink and brown box placed in front of her door. She eyed it for a moment before making her way to it, kneeling down and lifting the lid.

Her breath caught in her throat when she saw the contents. Cupcakes.

The ugliest cupcakes she'd ever seen. The frosting was a garish orange, the cake a sort of sickly pale gray. There was a note tucked into the side and she took it out and unfolded it.

I know I said I don't bake. I did, though. For you. Because it means something to you and I wanted to try it. It made me feel close to you to do it. Please don't eat them, they're terrible. I miss you.
Zack

She traced the letters with her fingertips, his handwriting so familiar. So dear to her. The note was scattered, funny. Sweet. She could hear him reading it to her.

A tear slipped down her cheek. "I miss you, too," she said. "But I couldn't let things stay the same."

"Don't cry. I know they're awful, but they aren't that bad are they?"

Clara looked up and saw Zack standing in the doorway of the elevator. He looked tired, the lines around his mouth deeper.

She wiped her cheeks. "They're pretty bad."

"Almost as bad as their creator." He took a step toward her. "I'm sorry. About the other day. About the past few weeks."

"Zack can we not do this? I don't think…I don't think I can."

"Well, I can't walk away. I won't. So if you don't mind me camping out here in front of your door until you're ready, then I can wait."

Clara crossed her arms beneath her breasts, curling her hands into fists, trying to disguise that she was shaking, trembling from head to toe. "What is it?"

"I told Amudee that I lied."

"And?"

"We still have a deal, but not based on how he feels about me as a human being. More about my corporate track record."

"Why did you do that?"

"Because I had to clean this up. I used you. I didn't want to gain anything from that."

Clara tried to smile. "I appreciate that, Zack, but…"

"I'm not finished."

She blinked and tried not to cry. She wasn't ready for this. Wasn't ready for him to try to repair their friendship, not when she needed more.

"You were right. About me," he continued. "I have been trying to control everything in my life, including you. Because I felt like there was safety in control. I felt like it was responsible, and I never wanted to deal with the consequences of a lack of control again."

He took a step toward her, put his hand on her cheek, and her heart stopped. "Clara, from the moment I met you I felt a connection with you. And I had to make a very quick decision about where to put you in my life. It was conscious. It was controlled. So I decided you would be my friend, my employee, but never anything more. Because I think part of me knew that if I let you, you could mean everything to me. If I didn't keep you in your place you would fill my life, every part of me. That I would love you. But then in Chiang Mai, being near you like that, I couldn't deny it anymore. I couldn't pretend I didn't want you. And we gave in. I lost control. So then, I thought maybe if I put you in that same place in my head I put my lovers, I could have you in my bed, without risking anything more. Without things getting deeper."

Clara's entire body trembled as she looked up at Zack, as she watched his face, so tired and sad. Mirroring her own, she knew.

"But they got deeper," he said, his voice rough. "And I couldn't stop it. Then I tried to reset things, and that didn't work, either. Not just because you told me where to stick it, which I absolutely deserved, but because things changed too much. Because knowing what it is to be skin to skin with you, has changed me. And it terrified me to admit that, even to myself."

"Zack…"

"You have every right to be angry at me. To hate me."

"I don't hate you."

"That's good, because it makes this next part easier. Because as terrified as I was the first time we kissed, I'm even more afraid now." He took a deep breath, his nerves visible, his control absent. "You're right, Clara Davis, you do make me tremble. You have been my friend, my partner, my lover. I want you to be all of those things to me for the rest of my life. I'll understand if you don't want the same from me. But no matter what, you have to know that I love you."

Clara felt dizzy, her fingertips numb. "You…you love me?"

"With everything. After we made love at my house, the last time, I felt like I could breathe again for the first time in fourteen years. For the first time since I lost Jake, I felt something real, something bigger than myself. Do you have any idea how much that scared me? But I realized something, the other day as I was reaching for a bottle of alcohol, to drink away the pain for the first time in fourteen years. That love can make you strong. I've always thought of it going hand in hand with loss, with weakness. But being with you…it makes me better. That's just one reason I love you so much. One of the reasons I had to tell you. Because all of my control, all of my pride, was just to cover up how scared I was. How weak I was. You've made me stronger. You've made me stop hiding."

A sob worked its way up her throat. "Zack, I thought I knew you. For seven years I thought I knew you. I thought you were this suave, together guy who had an unshakable calm that I really, really envied. And then I found out how broken you were, how messed up. I loved you before. I loved that guy I thought I knew. His jokes, his company, everything."

She pressed on, her voice cracking. "But do you want to know something? I love this man more." She stepped forward and put her palm flat on his chest, her hand unsteady. "Because this is you, and this is real. And I know you've been hurt. I know you've hurt in ways I can't imagine. And I know you aren't perfect. But you're perfect for me."

And then he was kissing her, his lips hot and hungry on hers. Her chest expanded, love, hope, filling every fiber of her body. When they parted, they were both breathing hard.

"Do you really love me?" he asked, wiping away tears she hadn't realized were on her cheeks.

"From the moment I met you."

"What a fool I was."

"I wouldn't trade the time, Zack. I wouldn't give back those years of friendship, not for anything. They made us who we are. They made us right for each other."

"I don't know if you can ever know how much your friendship has meant to me, how much your love means to me now. You're the only person I've shared myself with in so long, the only person I've wanted to share with. Without you…there would have been nothing in my life but work. You brought color, flavor."

"Cupcakes."

"That, too. And as you can see, I need someone to provide them for me because I'm useless at doing it myself. You make my life worth living, Clara. You make me better."

"I can say the same for you. I never felt beautiful, never felt special, until you."

"You're all those things. Never doubt it."

"I never will again."

"I have something for you," he said.

She smiled through a sheen of tears. "I love presents."

"I know." He reached into his pocket and pulled out a box. This one wasn't black and velvet. It was pink silk with orange blossoms. "Because you like flowers. And pink." This was for her. Only for Clara.

"I do," she said, opening the lid with shaking fingers. The ring inside was an antique style, a round diamond in the center and smaller diamonds encircling the band.

"It reminded me of you," he said. "Mostly just because it's beautiful. And so are you."

She laughed through new tears and held her hand out. "That's so lame, Zack."

"I know. It is. It's really lame. I make bad jokes sometimes, but you know that. You know everything there is to know about me, and if you can do that and love me anyway, I consider myself the luckiest man on earth."

"I do," she whispered. "Put it on me."

He took the ring out of the box and got on his knee in front of her. "Will you marry me? Clara Davis, will you be my wife, in every way. Will you understand that you are first for me, in every way. Will you love me, and let me love you?"

She wiped a tear away that was sliding down her cheek. "I will."

"And will you bake me cupcakes for as long as we both shall live?"

A watery laugh escaped her lips. "Without a walnut in sight."

He stood and kissed her on the lips. "I love you. As my friend, my future wife, my everything."

"I love you, too." She kissed him again.

"Would you mind if I stayed the night with you?" he asked, his lips hovering near hers.

"One night only?" she said, turning to him.

"No. It would never be enough. I want you every night for the rest of our lives, does that work for you?"

"Yes, Zack. I think a lifetime sounds about right."

EPILOGUE

Clara Parsons looked at the mostly uneaten cake. Three tiers of blue frosting that had been perfectly smooth just a few hours earlier, before two, chubby hands had taken some fistfuls out of the side.

"That was the most extravagant cake I've ever seen at a one-year-old's birthday party," Zack said, looking down at the crumbs all over the kitchen floor. "And I don't think Colton ate half of it. He mostly just spread it around."

"That's what kids do, Zack."

"He's asleep. I think we put him in a sugar coma. Anyway, you only get one first birthday, I suppose. You might as well live it up."

Clara looked at the cake again. "This reminds me of another cake I made that didn't really get eaten. A wedding cake."

"I'm still very thankful that one didn't end up being used for its intended purpose."

"Oh, so am I. Because then we wouldn't have had our wedding cake, or our wedding."

"Or our son," Zack said.

"So, all things considered, it was a pretty important uneaten cake."

Zack advanced on her and pulled her up against his body, resting his forehead against hers. Her heart stopped for a moment, like it always did when she looked at him. Like it had from the moment she'd first met him.

"A lot has changed since that day," he said, dropping a kiss on her lips.

"A whole lot," she agreed.

"Do you know what's stayed the same?"

"What's that?"

"You're still my best friend."

She kissed him, deeper this time, love expanding her chest. "You're my best friend, too."

* * * * *

LET'S TALK
Romance

For exclusive extracts, competitions
and special offers, find us online:

f facebook.com/millsandboon

𝕏 @MillsandBoon

⊡ @MillsandBoonUK

Get in touch on 01413 063232

For all the latest titles coming soon, visit
millsandboon.co.uk/nextmonth

MILLS & BOON
A ROMANCE FOR EVERY READER

- **FREE** delivery direct to your door

- **EXCLUSIVE** offers every month

- **SAVE** up to 25% on pre-paid subscriptions

SUBSCRIBE AND SAVE

millsandboon.co.uk/Subscribe

WANT EVEN MORE
ROMANCE?
SUBSCRIBE AND SAVE TODAY!

'Mills & Boon books, the perfect way to escape for an hour or so.'

MISS W. DYER

'Excellent service, promptly delivered and very good subscription choices.'

MISS A. PEARSON

'You get fantastic special offers and the chance to get books before they hit the shops.'

MRS V. HALL

Visit millsandboon.co.uk/Subscribe and save on brand new books.

JOIN US ON SOCIAL MEDIA!

Stay up to date with our latest releases, author news and gossip, special offers and discounts, and all the behind-the-scenes action from Mills & Boon...

 @millsandboon

 @millsandbooonuk

 facebook.com/millsandboon

 @millsandboonuk

It might just be true love...

MILLS & BOON

MODERN

Power and Passion

Prepare to be swept off your feet by
sophisticated, sexy and seductive heroes, in
some of the world's most glamourous and
romantic locations, where power and
passion collide.

Eight Modern stories published every month, find them all at:

millsandboon.co.uk/Modern